A WILLI

AUTHOR'S NOTE

This book is a work of fiction and names, places and incidents resembling real-life are coincidental.

Published in the
United States of America
1997

ISBN 0-944 514-20-0

DEDICATION

This book is dedicated to my family who has been my greatest support. They never stopped encouraging me to write and fulfill a long time dream.

To my parents
E.W. and Ruby Dix

To my sisters, brothers
and their children

Jerry, Doritha and Stephanie Lynn Dix, Janie and David Linton Elgin Jamel "Masta Killa," Sharon, Shirell, Jamel and Randall Turner, Moses, Francine, Renae and Courtney Dix, Evelyn, William, Chris and Devin McKnight, Robert, Lillie, Rodrick and Donnie Dix, George, E.W., Jr., Myra, Tosh and Tara.

ACKNOWLEDGMENTS

To Christopher L. Scott,

Thanks for listening in the middle of the night as I told this story to you. Your patience, understanding and support will always be remembered.

I am grateful to many co-workers, relatives and friends, especially those who read the manuscript during its early stages and encouraged me not to give up on this project. Thank you Linda, Edna, JoAn, Sandra, Martha, Nancy and Timmie.

Thanks to Mrs. Kissie Jacobs, Earnestine S. Fairey, Mary K. Frederick, Danny Collins, Carl Owens, Debra McClinton, Rose Dublin, Patti Henry, Brandolyn Pinkston, Coretta Simmons, Sandra English, Sharon Jones and Robin Taylor for their help, inspiration and encouragement.

A very special thanks to Marie Dutton Brown, a New York agent, D. M. Michaels, Editor, Magnolia House, Columbia, SC and Cecil Williams, my publisher, who provided helpful information and encouraged me to go forth with my manuscript. Thanks to Reginald Bennett, my nephew who helped rescue this manuscript from a computer failure even though he was in his finals at Clemson. Thanks to Sheila Morant for her help in typing and retyping this manuscript when it began years ago. And, I thank God for keeping me healthy and focused while completing this six year long task.

MINNIE DIX
FROM MY FRONT PORCH

Minnie Dix has always enjoyed writing but she developed a real love for writing while living in New York and working at *Readers Digest*. Miss Dix returned to South Carolina where she continues to write. She recently had a short story published entitled, *The Storm Within*, and she is currently working on several pieces with one very near completion entitled, *Secrets, Secrets. Everybody's Got Secrets*.

CHAPTER 1

"God, when did it all happen? When did my life change so much?" Rayanne said one day, as she sat in a rocking chair on her front porch with her brown legs spread apart. It was strange how things turned out, she thought, running her long thin fingers through a mass of long, dark brown hair that was smooth only by the relaxer it received every six weeks. One day she was living in New York, one of the fastest moving, most fascinating cities in the world, enjoying her life as a glamorous, successful playwright, and the next, she was residing in a small city in South Carolina, where the majority of its residents were in bed by midnight. "When did it all happen?" she whispered. One thing was certain, it didn't happen in just one day. The changes were gradual, but they were profound, and Rayanne Wilson's life would never be the same.

Rayanne experienced a gamut of emotions during the eight years after returning to South Carolina. She'd become many things for many people. She witnessed the death of her parents, one after the other, she became a nurse, without having had a license to practice, for her brother, Josh, who until this day denies that he's an alcoholic, although he'd been in and out of substance abuse centers more times than she cared to remember. Rayanne became the mother to her nephew, Jeremy, and his daughter, Little Charlotte, who was later given the nickname, Swan, because of her gracefulness as a child, and although it seemed, without foresight or purposeful intentions, Rayanne had become the victim of a conspiracy

1

of events that proved to be devastating to the point that she was spending an hour on a therapist's couch once, sometimes twice a month, because of a guilt complex she'd developed. Rayanne had found though that in comparison to the rat race of living in larger cities, some of the changes now were refreshing. She'd become a home girl again. She'd developed a greater appreciation for the simpler things in life, but in the course of that appreciation, there was baggage that she definitely could live without. Rayanne had learned early in life that it doesn't matter who you are, that no one was immune from the victimizing efforts of others. She didn't realized when she moved back into the family home that she'd be taking on the responsibilities of everyone who happened to take up residence in that home. Rayanne didn't have a clue as to why she felt responsible for things that happened of which she had absolutely no control. For some time, she'd felt guilty when Josh was committed to a drug rehabilitation center. Her mother had blamed her and the guilt, coupled with the fact that her mother had died without having forgiven her, wore on her like a tight suit.

At 6:15 that Friday morning, her main goal that day was to rid herself of the guilt and the feeling of being caught within the suffocating walls of the house that would always be known as the family house, even though her parents had deeded the house to her many years before their death. It was time to access her own life, to scrape off the miserable residue of her former life from the soles of her shoes. It was time to move forward.

As she thought of returning some order to her own life, Rayanne's thoughts drifted back into the yesteryears. She remembered her excitement the Spring she graduated from college, earning a Degree in Drama and a minor in computer science. She'd worked diligently in preparations to leave the South. Although she loved her home, she'd grown up with the thought that she'd, one day, move away, putting her home town behind her, and build a new and exciting life for herself, in some glamorous city. Rayanne knew when she boarded the plane for New York that Sumter would never be home for her again. At least that was what she'd thought at the time. She was in pursuit of a career that would provide an opportunity to travel, explore other challenges, experience other cultures, and that was exactly what had happened, because the ten years that Rayanne resided in New York, she'd done those things and more. She went to parties, museums, the theater, art shows, she had season tickets at Lincoln Center, where she enjoyed wonderful operas, she took in countless plays that came to Broadway and Off Broadway, and which she, herself, had become a participant. She frequented Radio City Music Hall, enjoyed numerous elegant restaurants and rode in horse drawn carriages along Central Park. Rayanne went to basketball games every chance she got, she'd become a New York Knicks fan and she cheered her team on to many victories. The earlier years, she and her friends went to the Apollo Theater and it became their second home, especially on Wednesday nights, which was talent night for any amateurs who opted to showcase their talents in the hope of becoming a star. The Apollo offered that opportunity to amateurs, many of whom went on to become successful stars. As the years evolved, Rayanne met and socialized with a variety of people, some of whom were wealthy, powerful and famous and where she was also thought of as a young wealthy socialite. But, all of that had changed, her life was uprooted, she was back at square one and was walking to the beat of a different drummer. But, how did it come to this, Rayanne thought, and she began to reflect.

CHAPTER 2

Rayanne moved to New York, at the age of 20, where she shared a loft with two girls, one black and one white. She'd joined a small theater group, and after countless auditions, she'd landed a bit part in an Off Broadway play, and even though she got the lead in a play, Rayanne didn't feel the satisfaction that one should feel by playing the lead in a play. And as a result, she couldn't really identify with the characters she portrayed, she didn't feel she did her best work.

When Rayanne was a child, she made up stories to tell her family and friends and she was encouraged to pursue that avenue because of her wonderfully imaginary and creative abilities. The idea worked for her, and as it turned out, she wrote and directed skits, she played the piano in church and for many of the local talent shows. Rayanne aspired to become an actress, a writer, a director, or a producer in the theater, she was prepared to work hard to attain her goal, and she'd do whatever it took to get there.

***

Rayanne arrived at LaGuardia Airport. She was among the first to exit the plane, but Ivory was no where in sight. She eyed the crowd as she made her way toward the main terminal where she saw people of all nationalities, but still no Ivory. She couldn't

4

have gotten the time mixed up because Rayanne was certain that when they spoke nearly four hours ago, that she had told Ivory the exact time of arrival. Ivory had come to New York a year earlier to pursue a career in modeling and had done okay, between waitressing jobs, and although her dream of becoming a top model in this country as well as abroad was uppermost in her mind, her long range goal was geared towards becoming an interior decorator, perhaps owning her own business one day.

Although Rayanne was excited and was experiencing a different sense of independence, still the feeling of being alone in this strange city was a little intimidating. But relief poured through her when she caught sight of Ivory. Both girls squealed with delight as they ran and embraced. Ivory's appearance totally contradicted her name. Her complexion was radiant and flawless and coal black. Her hair was dark brown and long which she wore straight most of the time. Her nose was small and keen, she had a set of pouting lips that covered even white teeth, and her large hazel eyes, surrounded by thick black lashes, stood out in a face that was exquisitely beautiful.

"Hey, girlfriend," Rayanne said as they released one another.

"Hey yourself. How the hell are you?" Ivory responded, flashing her pearly whites.

"I'm fine, what about you? You look great." Rayanne had seen Ivory only two weeks ago when she came home for Rayanne's graduation. Ivory was beautiful then and as Rayanne faced her now, she was even more so.

"Of course, "Ivory replied. "So do you."

"Where is Dorian?" Rayanne asked looking around. "I thought she'd be with you."

"She would've come but something came up. She'll be at the loft when we get there. You're gonna love her. Dorian is the greatest," Ivory said. People were buzzing around like bees and Rayanne's body shivered with excitement. The atmosphere was different, New York was different, and Ivory was amused at the look on Rayanne's face as she was completely caught up in that atmosphere.

On the way to collect Rayanne's luggage, she asked Ivory, squinting, "You told me Dorian got a job working as a waitress just because you do?"

"That's right," Ivory answered, "she said if I was going to have to work between modeling assignments to make ends meet, than she would too. She's better than I am because I don't think I

5

would've done anything like that," Ivory said and laughed that deep throaty laugh that was so infectious and Rayanne couldn't help but think how that laugh affected her. Ivory could say something that was borderline funny, but it was the way she laughed that brought people to their knees with laughter. When Ivory and Rayanne recovered from laughing, Ivory said, looking Rayanne up and down, "So you're finally here."

"Yeah, and not a minute too soon," Rayanne said, her eyes shining.

"Good flight?"

Although the trip to New York was only an hour and fifteen minutes, to Rayanne it seemed an eternity, but she answered, "it was okay." By the time the girls reached the Baggage Claims Section, the luggage was already coming in.

"Which pieces are yours," Ivory asked, taking the claim checks from Rayanne's hand. "You don't still have that yucky orange set, do you? If you do, I can tell you right now that Dorian's gonna laugh at it, then she'll probably go right out and buy you a new set."

"My luggage is brown and new, thank you very much," Rayanne said and was glad that she'd accepted her mother offer of a new set of luggage.

Ivory compared ticket numbers and pulled off two pieces of luggage, she looked at Rayanne and gave her a thumb's up as Rayanne laughed. When they'd collected all five pieces, Ivory said, "Come on. let's get out of here. I wanna introduce you to the third side of this triangle and our little mascot."

"Mascot," Rayanne echoed as a crease appeared in her forehead. Ivory didn't answer. She smiled and rolled her eyes up to the sky and Rayanne thought, don't ask. The bags were put into the cab, and they chatted all the way to the loft.

As they passed through some parts of the City and again a crease formed on Rayanne's brow, Ivory said, "Don't worry, it gets better." Rayanne's face relaxed a little as they continued on their journey.

Rayanne and Ivory had been best friends since elementary school. They attended high school and college together, and although Ivory was a year older and a grade ahead of Rayanne, they did everything together, and because they were two of the prettiest girls in their school, they dated often, and they'd had some hellacious times. Rayanne and Ivory shared everything. Well, almost everything, because Ivory also had a secretive side. There were times when that sly smile would snake its way across her face, and Rayanne, knowing Ivory as she did, often pressed to learn the secret, only to be kept waiting at least a day because Ivory knew it drove Rayanne up the wall. One secret was that Ivory was having an affair with an older man. That was all Rayanne knew and she remembered being shocked when she learned that the man was a widowed deacon in their church. Ivory never kept any secret more than a day, she liked keeping people guessing, she liked games, and she was definitely a player. There was a time when everyone in school suspected that one of the girls was dating Mr. Roberts, the English teacher, but no one except Rayanne, Ivory and Mr. Roberts knew which one it was. It was Ivory. When she thought back to when Ivory had first shared that little secret, Rayanne believed that Mr. Roberts had fallen in love with Ivory the day she entered high school. He always got a different look in his eyes whenever he looked at her. It was easy to see any man falling in love with Ivory. How could they not, Rayanne thought. Ivory was far more mature than most of the girls her own age. She was popular and smart, she had a great sense of humor, and her tall, slender body was graceful. Ivory was beautiful, but, above all else, she was quite the little prankster, a quality which carried over into her adult life. And, although Mr. Roberts didn't pursue Ivory until she was in her senior year in high school, two weeks prior to graduation, he asked her to marry him. Ivory refused, of course, and although Mr. Roberts was left feeling hurt and rejected, Ivory couldn't concern herself too much about it because she, too, had set her own goals. She wanted to live a little, enjoy life, cultivate a career, and marriage would have to wait until later, much later.

Rayanne and Ivory entered the loft. "Well, here we are," Ivory said.

"Wow," Rayanne said, her mouth dropped opened, as she stepped across the threshold of the loft for the first time. The view was breathtaking. A small chandelier hung from the ceiling, a coat and umbrella rack stood on one side and a table with a telephone was placed on the other, just under a mirror. The entry door led to a large room that looked like a picture taken from one of those home magazines. Rayanne could hardly believe that she, a little girl from the South, would be living in a place like that, sharing such elegance.

When Dorian heard the front door open and close again, the carefree, spirited nineteen year old, green eyed beauty, jumped up from the couch with a cat in her arms. She quickly put the cat down on the floor and rushed over to meet Rayanne. Dorian, an inch taller than Ivory, who stood 6 feet in stocking feet, was also pursuing a career in modeling. Her face with its exquisite features, was framed with nearly white blond hair that hung below her waist. "You must be Rayanne," Dorian said excitedly as she approached the girls. "I'm so glad to finally meet you." She opened her arms and embraced Rayanne. "Ivory has told me so much about you."

"All good things, I hope." Rayanne laughed, wondering just how much did Ivory share with Dorian. She thought of some of the things she and Ivory had gotten themselves into. She wasn't sure she wanted to share all those things with anyone else. Once was when she was in her early teens and took on baby sitting jobs, she'd feed the babies all the jarred vegetables but she'd eat the good stuff like the applesauce and apricots, herself.

"Of course," Ivory said, interrupting Rayanne's thoughts and chuckling, knowing Rayanne would faint if she knew some of the things that she'd shared with Dorian. Especially the time when Rayanne attempted to pass gas in class and had an accident in her clothes. There were other episodes, many of them funny and embarrassing, some of which Rayanne would not have wanted to share with anyone else. But would Ivory keep all of her secrets.

Probably not, Rayanne thought, smiling and said, "And you must be Dorian."

"Yes," Dorian answered. "How was your flight?"

"It was fine, but I thought I'd never get here."

"Well, you're here now, and you're going to love it." Dorian's mind already at work on how they were going to spend some of their time together.

"I suppose that takes care of the introductions, except Sapphire," Ivory said.

"Sapphire?" Rayanne asked, a bit puzzled.

"That's Sapphire over there," Ivory said, pointing to the white Longhair, blue-eyed cat that had been observing the girls from the time they entered the loft. "She's our little mascot and she thinks she owns the place. She needs to start paying rent," Ivory declared, and explained that one of Dorian's boyfriends had searched all over the city to find that cat as a gift for Dorian's 19th birthday, simply because she'd wanted it.

"She's precious," Rayanne said.

"Yeah, Precious Sapphire," Ivory snickered and pulled out a pack of cigarettes. Sapphire's eyes sparkled like huge blue diamonds, and it was obvious why Dorian had named the cat, Sapphire. Rayanne turned her attention to Ivory and saw her light up a Salem.

"When did you start smoking?" Rayanne asked, knowing that good health was always paramount to each of them. Ivory had written Rayanne and told her that she wasn't the same little girl that left South Carolina, but how much had she changed, Rayanne wondered.

"A couple of months ago," Ivory answered Rayanne, then to Dorian, "didn't I tell you she can be an old mother hen?" Remembering back to when she wanted to sneak out of the house after her parents' were asleep, when she'd already been grounded because of something she'd done but shouldn't have, and Rayanne insisting on obeying their parents and doing what they were told.

"Why?" Rayanne asked.

"Why what," Ivory asked, lifting her eyebrows.

"Why did you start smoking?' Rayanne asked.

"Get over it, will you?" Ivory laughed. "It's no big deal. Besides, I only do it occasionally."

"But those things will kill you. Do you want cancer or something?"

"If this doesn't kill me, something else will," Ivory threw back in good humor.

"Since when did we become so cavalier about life or should I say death?" Rayanne asked, and added with a frown, "besides, smoking is a nasty habit."

"True, so what else is new?" Ivory chuckled.

"If you don't care about your own health, you know what they say about secondary smoke."

"Yeah, yeah, yeah," Ivory said, and noticing the frown that appeared on Rayanne's forehead, said, "and get that buckle out of your brow."

"You sound just like mama," Rayanne laughed.

"I know," Ivory said, and she turned to Dorian and explained, "whenever Rayanne had something heavy on her mind," Ivory snickered, "she always wrinkled up her forehead and her mother would say," and Rayanne and Ivory said in unison, "honey, get that buckle out of your brow." Dorian joined them in laughter. "Girl, I'm so glad you're here. We're going to have some big time fun," Ivory said.

"And, you can take that to the bank," Dorian said.

Ivory had written and told Rayanne about the loft, but when

they showed her around, Ivory's description didn't come close to what Rayanne encountered. The loft was a spacious, beautiful symphony of pink and white, with French doors that stood open to the terrace. There were three bedrooms, each coupled with a private bath. There was a guest bathroom, living and dining rooms, a den and a full kitchen. The square glass-topped table, set for six, sat in the middle of the dining room. A large arrangement of pink silk flowers, adorned its center and two candles with holders sat on either side of the arrangement, a large crystal chandelier, in all its splendor, hung over the center of the table, and there was no way that Rayanne could have known that she and the girls would have many formal dinner parties at the very table.

The pieces of artwork that accentuated the walls of the loft blended perfectly with the other decor, and Rayanne remembered thinking whomever had made the selections, really knew their art. The many plants that punctuated the loft, added lush to the surroundings. The walls and drapes were white, the windows were large and deep, and while some of the hardwood floors were polished and buffed until they shined, others were adorned with good fake oriental rugs that looked real. The skylight, coupled with the windows brought in a lot of light and the terrace held a white wrought iron table with matching chairs, and the white flower boxes housed real geraniums. A promenade was built a couple of floors down and when you peer down over the balcony, the flowers, benches, people strolling around, while others sat engrossed in conversations or just relaxing in the sun, were visible. A lawn, resembling a green carpet, ran almost the full length of the promenade. It was a place of beauty and although Rayanne was in complete awe of her new home, the terrace and the view were the main attractions for her, not to mention the fish tank that held an assortment of fish that stood behind the couch in the den. As they took in the view of the city, a record was playing on the stereo and the sound filtered out through the French doors onto the terrace. The tune was the song Diana Ross had said adios to The Supremes, and even though years had passed since the song was recorded, 'Someday We'll Be Together,' still sounded good.

As the girls peered over the balcony, Rayanne said, "Ivory told me the two of you met at a modeling agency." Ivory had written her that each of them had answered a call for a possible modeling assignment. Ivory was sitting, looking confident, but without thinking, she was gripping the sides of the chair so tightly that she accidentally broke a nail. When Ivory realized what she'd done, she began rummaging through her bag. When she was unable to locate the nail repair kit she normally kept with her, she panicked. As she looked up, clicking her teeth in exasperation, Dorian was standing there smiling and holding a nail repair kit. She assisted Ivory in repairing the nail, and, although neither girl got the job, "but," Ivory had said, "we became great friends."

"And, we've been friends since that time," Dorian now said.

"That's right. I've never been bought so cheaply. She bought my friendship for the price of a nail," Ivory giggled.

"It turned out to be one of the cheapest and best friendships I've ever had," Dorian said.

"I'll say. Ivory talked about you all the time," Rayanne said.

"Okay, okay, that's enough. Let's not give old big head here the big head," Ivory said, ushering the girls back inside, and they giggled some more.

"Are you hungry?" Dorian asked, as they returned to the living room.

"Of course she is," Ivory said. "I'm sure they only fed her that rabbit food." Actually, Rayanne was on a lunch flight and even though what they served didn't look too bad, she was too excited to eat. The only thing she could think about was getting to New York to be with her best friend, meeting Dorian, and embarking on a career.

"Ivory and I thought we'd take you out for dinner, but we've got lots of snacks around. I can make up a sandwich or something for you now," Dorian offered.

"Thanks, but I'm fine," Rayanne said standing in the center of the living room. She slowly turned around and marveled at the beauty, the sheer elegance of the loft's wonderful decor. Talk about atmosphere, this certainly is wonderful atmosphere to soak up. This is magnificent."

"Of course. What'd you expect?" Ivory said.

"I don't know, but I don't think I expected this," Rayanne answered, lifting her arms in a sweeping gesture.

"Come see your room," Dorian said slipping her arm under Rayanne's and leading her off to the middle bedroom.

"Dorian fixed it up for you all by herself," Ivory commented, following the two girls. Sapphire tagged along as Dorian reached down and gathered her up into her arms and gently stroked her silky coat. "She wouldn't let me do a thing. I just told her that your favorite color was yellow, and this young lady took matters into her own hands," Ivory explained. The bedroom and its accompanying bath were done in yellow and white. The bed was almost covered with pillows, the area rugs were thick and fluffy and yellow, and the vanity was well stocked with various toiletries. Rayanne's bedroom was always neat, clean and quite comfortable, but this was a far cry from her old bedroom back home. Dorian's bedroom was pink and white and Ivory's, wouldn't you know, was almost entirely in white, except for a mint green dust ruffle and matching trim along the edge of her vanity.

Dorian and Ivory helped Rayanne put away her things. Rayanne brought Ivory up-to-date on what was happening back home, and Dorian and Ivory filled her in on some of their activities. Rayanne could tell that both girls were far more adventurous and sexually advanced than she, and although she wasn't without carnal knowledge of men, listening to them made her wonder where had she been all this time.

The following morning, Rayanne searched the kitchen for something for breakfast. Ivory and Dorian had gone out jogging and hadn't returned when Rayanne got up. She opened the cabinets to find a jar of instant Maxwell House coffee, a can of pink salmon, a can of tuna and a large bag of potato chips. In the refrigerator, was a container of strawberries, a couple of packages of cold cuts, a loaf of whole wheat bread, cantaloupes, a half quart of skimmed milk and one shelf completely filled with 8 oz. bottles of spring water. Is this really the way models eat, Rayanne wondered. Both, Ivory and Dorian were as thin as rails, and if that was the way they wanted to look, that was fine, she thought, but she wasn't a model and had no desire to be one or to look like one. Rayanne prepared a bowl of fresh fruit, toast and coffee, and that would be fine for today, she thought, but tomorrow is another day, and she'd have a nice southern style breakfast.

Rayanne had liked Dorian immediately, and as time passed, she learned that Dorian was a wonderfully caring person, generous to a fault, and she was real down to earth, for a white girl. Dorian was dating Henry Farnsworth, an older man, who was the owner of a magazine company and other real estate including the building where they lived. Rayanne had learned that it was Dorian who'd bought food for the loft when Ivory's funds ran short and it was she who was responsible for the loft's present mode. Henry adored Dorian and her every wish was his command. Rayanne thought if she were ever to become a kept woman, she'd do it Dorian's way. The girl had it made. She was livin' large, as the saying goes. And, although New York was exciting and there was always something to do, Rayanne missed home and her family terribly. She wrote to her parents, her sister Maxine, Aunt Bessie, her father's sister, and to Ms. Abigail, one of their neighbors who was one of her mother's oldest and dearest friends.

One day, shortly after her arrival in New York, Rayanne wandered out onto the terrace, she looked around, observing the city and thought of something Ivory had said to her the day she arrived in New York. She'd said they were two proud black women, strong beyond all definition and they were going to affect change in the world, make their mark. They were going to make something happen, and it was going to start right here. Rayanne believed her then and she believed her now, although the largest portion of Ivory's salary came from waiting tables. Rayanne looked out over the city as far as her eyes could see. "So this is New York, this is where it all happens," she said, placing her hands on the railing of the terrace. It was everything Ivory told her it would be, and more. The city was large, it was filthy and if one wasn't careful, it could be dangerous, but the career opportunities were endless and you couldn't find a better hot dog anywhere. "New York, New York. Yes, this is New York, the Big Apple," Rayanne said, and tilting her chin towards the sky, she added, her voice trailing off into a whisper, "and, it is ready to be eaten to the core."

CHAPTER 3

Ivory and Dorian arranged their schedules to spend time with Rayanne and familiarize her with the city. Rayanne had brought her life's savings with her which included money she received as graduation gifts and which came to just over $6,000, but at the rate things were going, it wouldn't be long before she'd be out of funds. The first couple of weeks, the girls went to parties, movies and plays, danced until they were soaked to the skin, bowled, skated on ice, and they enjoyed numerous other social functions, some of which required fancy evening dresses that they couldn't afford. Rayanne chuckled when she thought of the times when they were invited to formal functions and didn't have the proper attire. It was Ivory who'd talked the girls into charging extravagant, drop dead gorgeous gowns, only to wear them, dry clean them, if necessary, and return them. Rayanne chuckled even louder when once they went out and she'd danced, to Ivory's thinking, a little too much, and Ivory tapped her on the shoulder, told her to sit her behind down before she soiled that dress and they'd have it for dinner the next two weeks. Rayanne had liked a lot about New York, even the church they had chosen in which she soon became involved just as Ivory and Dorian had.

The weeks quickly changed into months, and as the season changed from spring to summer then, fall and Rayanne's savings were rapidly being depleted, it was time she begin to focus on her future, establish some goals and work towards them. She examined the Classified Section of the newspaper on a daily basis for acting jobs, and she read the Variety for whatever information that was available that might assist in her endeavors. Unfortunately, the months that followed didn't even bring a phone call, and since Christmas was approaching and Rayanne's savings, at that time, was down to less than $1,000, she considered other possibilities to support herself. She spent days placing applications with temporary agencies, and almost immediately she was contacted for her first assignment as a computer programmer at a bank. Working through a temporary agency would allow her to free herself up with a simple phone call if she was called for an audition. Although, working in a bank wasn't Rayanne's life long dream, the salary was decent, it allowed her to have some of the things she wanted, and it was a job. It wasn't long before Rayanne found she had a real affection for the city and an infinity for both, Ivory and Dorian, and Lionel, the new man who'd come into her life, wasn't half bad either.

***

The movie the girls were watching ended at 9 o'clock. Rayanne got up and turned off the TV set. "Good movie," Ivory said and sighed.

Dorian sniffled and removed several tissues from its box. She wiped her eyes and blew her nose. "Great movie. I always cry when I watch sad movies," Dorian said and smiled when she thought of something Ivory had said. She had said Dorian cry at the sad movies, the happy movies, and the not so happy ones, that Dorian just loves to cry, and it was true, but she especially loves old movies and she always cried while watching them.

"Dorian, have you seen Imitation of Life, the one that Lana Turner starred in where Mahalia Jackson sang *Trouble Will Be Over?*" Rayanne asked, clutching her chest, remembering the emotions evoked by the movie.

"Oh God, yes. What a tear jerker? I was so weak when that movie ended that I thought I was going to be sick." Dorian sucked in her breath just thinking about the movie. Rayanne explained that when her older brother, Sam, had taken them to see the movie, they cried so much that they had to sit through it twice in order to catch the entire movie, forcing Sam to stay with them.

"I know Dorian didn't pee for a whole week after she saw it," Ivory said, and they laughed.

15

"It was a great movie, but it wore me out," Rayanne said. They saw that movie the summer the two girls had run away from home, which of course was Ivory's idea, but it was without much difficulty talking Rayanne into going along with her. Ivory, at 13, became interested in a boy who was 18. She asked to go to a movie with the young man, but when her parents learned his age and forbade Ivory's seeing him, she became angry and decided to run away. She urged Rayanne to come with her, and being the level headed girl she was, Rayanne tried to discourage it, but Ivory told Rayanne if she didn't go, she'd go alone and that Rayanne would never see her again. After some tears, Rayanne was persuaded, and they ran away together. Ivory had an extraordinary ability to talk Rayanne into doing just about anything, although that episode lasted only three hours. They were on their way to the bus station, changed their minds and Rayanne called Sam, who drove over, picked them up and the three of them went to a movie and saw 'Imitation of Life,' twice. Some time after the movie, Sam had a talk with the 18 year old, and although Ivory and Rayanne never knew why the young man quit speaking to them, Sam did.

"Are we still going to the show at Radio City tomorrow night?" Dorian asked, interrupting Rayanne's thoughts.

"Is that tomorrow night?" Rayanne asked.

"I think so," Dorian said, looking up from the mirror she had sitting on her knees, tweezing her eyebrows.

"Yeah, it's tomorrow night, but I'm not sure I can make it," Ivory said, resting her head against the back of the couch and smiling, she laid a finger against her lips.

"You've got other plans?" Rayanne asked, seeing that mischievous grin on Ivory's face.

"I don't know yet, but I'm working on it."

Rayanne groaned. "When will you know?"

"I don't know that either," Ivory stated, and there was that secretive smile again, one that she'd reacquainted herself with recently. Ivory still got a kick out of keeping people guessing. She was usually very straight forward, but there were times when she could be just as mysterious.

Dorian said, "All right, out with it."

"It's no biggie. I'm just trying to decide whether I wanna go with y'all or do something else. Know what I mean?" Ivory replied, raising her eyebrows up and down in a comical gesture. That heffa's got something up her sleeve, Rayanne thought, and it ain't her arm. "So what's up for tonight?" Ivory asked.

16

"I'm gonna call mama, then return these books to the library. After that, I'm gonna stop by to see Lionel," Rayanne said, gathering several books from the desk and stacked them on the coffee table.

"Tell mama Ruth I said Hi, and I love her," Dorian said, and she meant it. She hadn't met the girls' families yet, but they'd talked so much about Rayanne's mother, that Dorian looked forward to meeting her, especially.

"Mama Ruth is wonderful and she's so darn cool," Dorian remembered Ivory saying long before Rayanne had moved to New York. "You're gonna love her. We all talk to Mama Ruth about everything," Ivory had said.

"Say hey for me, too," Ivory said, lighting up a joint that she took a hit from before passing it to Rayanne.

"Y'all know mama's gonna talk to each of you before she lets me hang up," Rayanne said, took a hit, inhaled and dialed the number, "and I don't want you two staying on the phone all night either, because I want to get out of here in a little bit." Rayanne took another hit and wondered what her mother would do if she knew her baby was in the big city smoking grass. She didn't really have to wonder, because if her mother knew, Rayanne was certain she'd walk all the way to New York and kick her butt all the way back to South Carolina. Well, her mother didn't know and what she didn't know surely wouldn't hurt her. Dorian leaned over, took the joint from Rayanne's hand, and plopping down on the couch, took a hit. "Hey Mama," Rayanne said, already feeling the affect of the marijuana when her mother came on the line. "Yes, we're fine. How are things at home. That's great. What's daddy doing. Yeah, I figured he'd be busy, he's always busy. "What about Aunt Bessie?" She asked and when her mother replied that Aunt Bessie was as feisty as ever, Rayanne chuckled. "Give Daddy and the others my love." When Rayanne was finished, each girl had a turn talking with Ruth. Rayanne went into her bathroom to freshen up. She returned with her purse hanging on her shoulder and was surprised to see Dorian still on the phone. "What are you doing? Hang up that phone," Rayanne mouthed to Dorian, making sure her mother didn't hear her.

After another moment, Dorian hung up. "Rayanne, I swear your mom is so cool," she said.

"She's something else. Mamas are so wise. I wonder whether we'll ever be as wise and together when we get married and become mothers," Rayanne said.

"Speak for yourself," Dorian said.

"Don't you want to get married and have children one day?" Rayanne asked.

"Sure. I want to get married, but children are kind of far into the future for me."

"If you intend to marry Henry and have his children, you'd better not put it off too far," Ivory said. "You're good to go for a few decades, but Henry, now that boy is another story. He's just about ready for the old folks home now." Sapphire made an entrance, stretched and yawned and walked over to Dorian, who picked her up and stroked her.

"There you go with the age thing again," Dorian replied, then to Sapphire, "isn't that right, baby. Talking about daddy like that." She held Sapphire up and looked at her.

"I'm only speaking the truth," Ivory said.

"You guys decide what you're gonna do tonight," Rayanne said, returning to their earlier conversation.

"I'm going to do interesting things like my nails, shampoo my hair and a little studying," Dorian answered.

"You finished that paper?" Rayanne asked, knowing Dorian had a paper that was due soon.

"I did my research today, and I'm going to write the paper tomorrow," Dorian said.

"When is it due?" Rayanne asked, walking over to Dorian.

"End of the week."

It was Monday night and Rayanne wondered why wait. "Do you want to do it tonight?" Rayanne asked, "I'll be glad to help."

"I'll do it tomorrow. I've got all the information, but I'll need help organizing it."

"Ok, leave it on the table. I'll take a look at it when I get in tonight and we'll work on it tomorrow," Rayanne said, then she looked at Ivory, "and you?"

"I'm gonna do some laundry" Ivory said. She'd put off doing the laundry for a week already and if she didn't do it soon, she wouldn't have a thing clean to wear. "Anything you two want washed?"

"Yeah, that white blouse," Rayanne said remembering the soup stain she got on her favorite white blouse when she wore it two days ago, the blouse that she intended to wear day after tomorrow. "I'll go get it." She dashed off to get the blouse. The girls didn't have any scheduled chores, whomever was available did what was necessary and it worked out fine.

"What about you?" Ivory asked Dorian.

"Nope," Dorian replied, flipping through a pile of magazines.

Rayanne returned to the room, "here." She stuffed the item into the bag of soiled laundry. "So, who's coming over? Sean?"

"Sean?" Ivory said. "Get outta here."

"I thought Sean was history," Dorian said, got up, went into her room and returned with an assortment of nail care products and plopped back down on the couch.

"Sean is history," Ivory said, crinkling her nose. "I quit seeing him weeks ago. You guys know how I love to kiss. Well, it takes some doing to get past Sean's breath. I swear, he must've never heard of mouth wash."

Rayanne laughed and asked, "Then who?"

"Cal," Ivory said and poking out her tongue in a childish gesture said, "Any objections?"

"Isn't he that joker you just met?" Rayanne asked, her eyebrows jerked upward.

"So what? What's wrong with Cal?" Ivory asked.

What's right with Cal, Rayanne thought, he was the son of a New York police captain, but he was the slickest, most unscrupulous person she'd met. She also knew that he'd been hitting Ivory up for money, always under the guise of it being a loan, only Rayanne knew he never paid Ivory back. Ivory wasn't rolling in cash, she made good money, but after she met Cal, she was almost always broke. "Why would you want to waste your time with him?" Rayanne asked.

"Yeah Ivory, why?" Dorian asked. Cal wasn't one of her favorite people.

"Why, why, why? Why don't you two ask me something that is your business?" Ivory grinned.

"Cal's a jerk, and he has a colossal gall," Dorian said, filing away at a nail.

"You can say that again," Rayanne agreed. Cal wasn't one of her favorite people either.

"Cal has got a lot going for him," Ivory defended.

"Like what?" Dorian asked, lifting her hands to satisfy herself with the way the nails looked before applying the base coat of polish.

"He's wonderful. He is..." Ivory began, but Rayanne interrupted.

"Ivory, Cal's a jerk, he has no scruples, so don't try to turn him into something he's not."

"I'm not and don't give me a hard time about Cal," Ivory said.

"I just think you can do a heck of a lot better," Rayanne said, tilted her head to the side, a meditative expression on her face, remembering better times, times when they dated guys who weren't nearly as self centered, who were considerate, fun to be with, unlike Cal, guys who had a real working brain in their heads.

"I agree," Dorian said, "a heck of a lot better."

"Is there an echo in here," Ivory said, looking up at the ceiling. "Of course I can do better. I'm just testing the waters right now. I'm not planning to marry the guy or anything like that, but Cal's a sweet man."

"Just don't let that supposedly sweetness cloud your judgment. I for one don't know where he's coming from most of the time," Rayanne said.

"I know, but don't worry about it. I'm a big girl, and I can take care of myself," Ivory said confidently and Rayanne, had to give it to her. Ivory went into relationships that were doomed from the beginning, but she always managed to land on her feet. And, although Rayanne had to admit that Ivory never got caught in the same type situation twice, she wished Ivory would use better judgment in her relationships, but she said, "I don't doubt that, but I think maybe you'd better take it slow and easy until you get to know this Cal better."

"I agree with Rayanne. Cal's a smooth operator, so I'd pursue that with extreme caution, if I were you," Dorian said.

Ivory looked shocked and said, "Look who's talking. Dorian, you go out with a different man every other night."

"Don't be sarcastic. We're just trying to help," Dorian replied, alternately shaking and blowing her nails so that they could dry quicker.

"Save it girls. I appreciate your concern, but I'm gonna go for it. I wanna see just where it leads."

"Why would you want to do that?" Dorian asked

"Because she likes living on the edge," Rayanne said and grimaced at the thought of some of the situations Ivory had gotten, not only herself into, but Rayanne as well, and the thought made her shudder. "She's that kind of woman. She likes a good game."

"You got that right," Ivory said.

"Whatever," Rayanne hunched her shoulders and looked at her watch. "Dorian, we'll work on that paper tomorrow. I'll see you guys later." Rayanne walked towards the door, turned and looked over her shoulder, "goodnight, Sapphire."

"We won't wait up for you," Ivory teased.

"I'm crushed."

"Yeah, sure I bet," Ivory said.

"Don't keep Lionel waiting," Dorian giggled.

"Go soak you head," Rayanne laughed as the phone rang.

"If that's for me, I'm not here."

"Hello?" Dorian blew her nails again and answered, she looked at Rayanne and nodded no. Rayanne waved to the girls and left.

Dorian got an A on her paper. She'd worked hard in gathering her facts and with a little help in arranging the information, she'd done a good job. And, as time passed, the girls became closer, they dated frequently, but they always made time for one another, at times referring to themselves as the Manhattan Trio. They had dreams and goals, and they felt that between the three of them, they could do anything. If there was something they wanted and it was possible to obtain, they'd have it.

***

It was Rayanne first winter in New York. She exited the building and walked towards the corner to catch the 42nd Street bus up to Lexington and 59th Street to her job at the bank. When she reached the corner, she stood with her eyes closed and allowed the wind to hit her face. The air was cold, frigid in fact, but she was dressed for it. That was another thing her mother had made sure of before she left South Carolina, and that was that she had plenty of warm clothes "to bare a New York winter," was how she'd put it. There standing in the freezing temperatures, Rayanne realized once again that her mother was right and she agreed, there was nothing as cold as New York in winter.

The three girls spent weeks tracking down the perfect gift for each other, their families and friends. They watched as the tree was lit at Rockefeller Center, and three days before Christmas and after arranging with a neighbor downstairs to take care of Sapphire and the fish, they flew to South Carolina for the holidays. They alternated, spending nights at either Ivory or Rayanne parents' home. Dorian met everyone, relatives and friends of both girls, and she was welcomed by all. On Christmas Eve, they attended evening services at church and assisted Ruth in handing out Christmas presents to the children. They spent a couple of hundred dollars, purchasing a variety of items for children of all ages, but the most enjoyable part was seeing the look on the faces of the children, the joy in their eyes, at receiving the gifts.

On Christmas morning, Rayanne got up early and went to her

21

parents' room. She gently knocked on the door. "Come in," her mother responded to the knock.

"Good morning," Rayanne said and kissed each parent before sitting on the side of the bed, her mother sliding her feet over to make room for her.

"How you doing," Ruth said. "You look good. Doesn't she Raymond? New York agrees with you."

"It's big," Rayanne said.

"Is that all," her father teased.

"No daddy, it's a lot more than that. It has so much to offer. I really like it a lot."

"I'm glad, honey. You still auditioning," Ruth asked.

"Every chance I get. Nothing's happened yet though," Rayanne said.

"Give it some time and trust in the Lord, honey. It'll happen for you," her mother said. "Apart from the Lord, you can't do anything." Rayanne's mother was a woman of deep faith and was always quoting the Bible.

"Always remember girl that Rome wasn't built in a day you know," her father said.

"I'll remember that daddy," Rayanne said, thinking how lucky and blessed she was to have the love and support from this incredible family.

The house quickly filled up with children that morning, mostly her nieces and nephews, who'd also come to visit for the holidays, but the others were neighborhood kids, and they all sat on the floor and listened as Dorian sat with her legs tucked under her body and read to them. She read with such expressions that the children hung on her every word and when she finished the fourth book, they begged for more, which she gladly obliged. Dorian enjoyed the stories as much as the children, who listened intensely, but when Ivory arrived, it was only minutes before the place was turned into complete turmoil. They played games, they played with their toys and the house was filled with sounds of laughter, talking, children squealing, and wonderful odors of food being prepared in the kitchen. Dorian loved the closeness of the families and although Rayanne thought she saw a brief touch of sadness in her eyes, by the end of the day, Dorian had been a hit with the children, had become an honorary family member and Rayanne couldn't remember ever seeing her happier.

Rayanne received several phone calls, she placed others and that evening, they joined friends, and from the time they entered the club, their table was frequented by all kinds of men, skinny ones, fat ones, short ones, tall ones, some were handsome, some not so handsome, but they all seemed to know how to party.

Jimmy Robinson, an old friend of Rayanne and Ivory's, sat at the table and the one thing they remembered about Jimmy was that he was one of the greediest and stingiest boys at their school, and Ivory had hoped that he was still attached to that reputation. He'd sat and talked with them, but he never once offered them a drink, or anything, for that matter.

Ivory removed a box of Chicklets from her purse, toss a tablet into her mouth and dropped the box onto the table. For something as insignificant as a box of Chicklets, Jimmy's eyes lit up and became glued to the box. Rayanne took two white squares from the box, popped them into her mouth and placed the box back on· the table. Jimmy picked up the box and after he shook four pieces into his hand, he looked at Ivory and asked, "Do you mind?"

"Of course not," she replied. "Help yourself."

Jimmy tossed the four pieces of gum into his mouth and as the evening aged, he shook out three additional pieces, put them into his pocket and said, holding several additional pieces in his hand, "I'll hold onto these for later."

"Jimmy Robinson, you haven't changed a bit," Ivory said. "You still look good, man. You were fine in high school, and you're fine now." A part of what Ivory said was true. Jimmy was tall, dark and handsome, but what Ivory really meant was that he'd not grown out of his parsimonious and gluttonous ways, and the man still didn't know how to treat women. He always acted as though women owed him....everything.

"You think so, huh?" Jimmy said. "You are finer than ever yourself, sister."

"So what are you doing now, Jimmy?" Ivory asked, but knowing him as she did, she knew it wasn't anything that would cause him to get dirt under his nails or work up a sweat.

"I'm an insurance salesman," he answered, looking really pleased.

"Really? What type of insurance do you sell?" Dorian asked.

"Life insurance. Are you ladies well covered?" he asked, eyeing each girl.

"Does one ever have enough insurance? " Rayanne asked.

"Good question, Rayanne, and the answer is no," Jimmy said over the music.

"I think I have as much as I need for the time being," Ivory said, and asked, "where are you? Did someone say you're in Philly?"

"Yeah. Almost two years now."

"How do you like selling insurance?" Rayanne asked.

"It's not bad. It gets me out of the office several days a week." He grinned.

"Bet you get a lot of personal stuff done on office time. I know you, Jimmy," Ivory teased, but she was also remembering how Jimmy always got over any way that he could.

"Don't get me wrong," he began, "I sell a lot of policies. I made salesman of the month three months consecutively this year," he boasted.

"That's wonderful," Dorian commented.

"Yeah, congratulations," Rayanne said.

If Jimmy was anything like he was, Rayanne and Ivory knew that he used his charm on vulnerable women and sold the majority of his policies to them, whether they could afford them or not. Some of them probably could barely feed themselves and their children. As long as Jimmy took home the almighty dollar, he didn't care much about what happened to the rest of the world. Jimmy picked up the pack of cigarettes that Ivory had laid on the table, took out one and then asked, "May I?"

"Of course," Ivory consented.

"That guy's a freaking moocher," Dorian whispered to Rayanne.

"No joke," Rayanne said. "He's always been that way."

"It's a good living," Jimmy was saying. "I make good money, and I like what I'm doing."

"It doesn't get much better than that," Ivory said.

"You got that right," he said. He took the gum out of his mouth, looked at it with a scowl on his face and stuck it to the ash tray. Ivory had a particular aversion to gum plastered in ashtrays and the fact that Jimmy had put it there, put out his cigarette on it and took another from her pack, was particularly annoying to her.

"So what are you girls into?" Jimmy asked, looking from one girl to the other.

"I pick up a modeling assignment every now and again, but my main source of support is waiting tables. Eventually, I plan to go back for my Master's," Ivory said.

"Sounds good to me," Jimmy said.

"Rayanne's a computers programmer at a bank, but she wants to act. She writes a little too."

"You still writing, girl," Jimmy said to Rayanne.

"Just a little, Rayanne replied"

"That's great. I remember those plays you wrote while in high school. Some of them were pretty good, too."

"Yeah, she's still at it, and Dorian's a Junior at New York University, business major. She wants to own a modeling agency or a boutique shop. She also models a little and waits tables." It was Rayanne who shared with Jimmy the story about Dorian's waiting on tables because Ivory did.

They chuckled and Jimmy said, "you can't beat that kind of friendship, and in the meantime, you're waiting for that big break, huh. I hear ya. You girls are doing it."

Rayanne and Ivory were thinking that Dorian certainly wasn't waiting for her big break. She'd found it when she found Henry, but Ivory said, "We're making ends meet."

Dorian put out the cigarette she'd lit up and took two draws from. She'd been trying to quit smoking, and she reached for the box of Chicklets but Rayanne nudged her gently in the ribs. Dorian looked at Rayanne and the eye contact alone told her that the Chicklets were forbidden. A small snicker escaped Dorian's lips. She looked at Ivory, who simply returned the look with raised eyebrows and a slight lifting of the shoulders, but the gesture was confirmation. Jimmy didn't seem to notice the unspoken exchange between the girls. As the night wore on, the girls prepared to leave, but Jimmy, prior to departing, noticed the Chicklets box on the table, he dumped several more tablets into his hand and tossed them into his mouth. He handed the box to Ivory. "You keep them," she said, "but save some for tomorrow." He emptied the box, tossed the last two pieces into his mouth, and they left the club.

"I certainly hope Jimmy hasn't planned a busy day tomorrow," Ivory laughed as she drove them home.

"I know because when that Feenamint kicks in, he'll be out of it for sometime," Rayanne said and more laughter followed.

"But Rayanne, didn't you have some of the tablets?" Dorian asked and turned to look at Rayanne who was sitting in the back seat.

"Yes, but only two pieces. I needed it," Rayanne replied.

"Oooh, I see," Dorian laughed and turned back around in the front seat, "Jimmy is going to have one hell of a day tomorrow." They laughed some more.

"That'll teach him to use up all of my shit," Ivory said, not laughing, pretending to be angry, but the squeals from the others made her laugh so hard that her head touched the steering wheel.

"You'd better look where we are going," Rayanne said, still laughing. They didn't see or hear anymore from Jimmy that trip. On December 27, after a brief visit with Aunt Bessie, Ms Abigil and a few other friends, they returned to New York, and on December 28, the girls boarded a flight for four fun filled days in sunny California. They checked into a Four Star hotel, basking in elegance which included a crown room which provided a view of San Francisco. They rented a car and took in sites, such as the wine country, the Golden Gate bridge, the rugged coast. They swam in the ocean, played volleyball on the beach, snorkeled and shopped by day and partied at night. When they boarded the plane for New York, Rayanne was quiet. She'd over spent and was wondering how was she going to make ends meet until she got her next pay check. She'd allowed Ivory to talk her into taking the trip to California, which she couldn't really afford and although they had a great time, that trip had darn near left her in dire straits. She'd not paid her share of the expenses for the month and was wondering what could she do without over the next couple of weeks to free up enough money to be able to meet her share of the responsibilities. She looked over at Ivory who was in the same financial situation, but appeared to not have a care in the world, except when the next party was going to be. Ivory lived by the rule, live for today and tomorrow will take care of itself. Rayanne was sitting in an isle seat, with Dorian in the center, and Ivory at the window. Rayanne shifted her position and looked out through the window on the other side of the plane. Sure hope I get an acting job soon, she thought. It would mean being involved in the kind of work she loved and in addition to that, it would put extra money into her pocket.

"You're quiet," Ivory said, interrupting her thoughts, "what's up?"

"Oh nothing really. I was just thinking," she said, but what she meant was that she was worrying. The rent was one thing because Henry wasn't a problem, but food, and utilities, now that was another story.

"I know that, silly," Ivory said, "thinking about what. You had a good time, didn't you?"

"Yeah, I had a great time."

"Then what are you worrying about?"

"I didn't say I was worrying."

"You didn't have to say it, Rayanne, but I know you, and I can tell you're worrying and chances are, you're worrying about the money you spent. Look, six months ago you graduated college, you came to New York and shortly afterwards, you went to work. You took a little time for yourself, you got away, had a chance to relax a little and you had a good time, so don't worry about it. Anyway, what are your creditors gonna do. It's not like you have a car that they can come and repossess. Don't worry, they'll get their money. Besides," Ivory smiled, "tomorrow will take care of itself."

Rayanne thought about what Ivory had said and agreeing that tomorrow is another day, changed the subject. "Wouldn't it be great if I got that part, but any part would be fine by me."

"Yeah. You could play any part in that play. You have seen it every day for two weeks. You know all the lines." Rayanne and Ivory laughed. Rayanne had expressed interest in a play that was currently running. The original play was going on the road and they were recasting the play and would keep it running in New York as long as possible.

Dorian who'd been asleep from the time they boarded the plane, asked, putting her seat in the upright position and tossing the pillow in the overhead compartment, "What going on?"

"We were talking about Rayanne's acting career," Ivory informed.

"What acting career?" Rayanne asked. She knew she'd make it as an actress, at least she hoped she would, but the real question was when, just how long would it take to get there.

"I know I'm not hearing doubt in your voice, Rayanne Wilson," Dorian said, using both hands to wipe the sleep out of her eyes.

"Oh no, I know it's gonna happen, but it hasn't yet and sometimes I get a little anxious."

"There's nothing wrong with feeling that way and I know we have to pay our dues, but shoot, I know what I want to do and I don't want to wait a hundred years to get there. I want it all just like that," Ivory said snapping her fingers. "I've had a good assignment here and there but that's nothing compared to what I really want. I want to tour the world, strut my stuff up and down those long runways, looking gorgeous in those fabulous clothes. I want all that glamour and glitter. I can see it all now," Ivory said, sitting up in her seat, making gestures with her hands and adding, "not to mention this face on the cover of every major magazine in this country and Abroad. Yes, I can see it now. That's what I want and I can't wait to have it."

"Neither can I," Rayanne said, reaching across Dorian to give Ivory five.

"I'm being realistic though, y'all," Ivory said, looking thoughtful for a moment. "I'm not gonna be in the modeling business forever. I want to do it now, but later on, I want to decorate big beautiful homes."

"We know that, Ivory," Dorian said.

"Good, 'cause I don't want y'all to forget," Ivory said, they laughed, and settling back in her seat, she added, "When I get my portfolio finished, I'm going on some serious interviews, gon' get this show on the road."

"How is that coming?" Rayanne asked.

"I'm putting a little money aside for my next photo shoot which should be soon."

"Ivory, you know you don't have to wait," Dorian, who already had an impressive portfolio, said. "I'll be glad to let you have the money."

"Haven't I told you I don't want you giving me Henry's money for my portfolio. I appreciate the offer, but I'm saving a little and before you know it, I'll have enough."

"Henry is not loaning you the money, I am," Dorian said.

"Yeah right. The money would be coming right out of Henry's pocket into yours then mine."

"What difference does it make," Rayanne said, "you'd be paying it back."

"I'm doing okay," Ivory said.

"That's very generous of you though," Rayanne said to Dorian. But it's Henry's money she's being generous with, Ivory thought. "Henry has been generous, as well," Rayanne said as if she'd read Ivory's mind.

"Of course he is. Why do you think blondie is still with him," Ivory said.

Dorian turned to Ivory and said, "It's more than that," then she said to Rayanne, "She doesn't know what she's talking about."

"Do to," Ivory said grinning.

"Not so," Dorian came back.

"Children, children," Rayanne teased.

Ivory lifted her hands into the air, settled back in her seat and looked at her watch. "We should be getting there soon."

The plane landed within an hour, they exited, collected their bags and took a taxi home. Upon arriving, they checked messages and the mail, reading only the pieces that looked important, while casting the bills and junk mail aside. Suddenly, Rayanne was heard screaming from her room. Ivory and Dorain rushed in to see what was wrong. Rayanne had gotten a call to audition for a play. Was her dream about to come true, she wondered? Well, she'd know soon enough because she'd return that call first thing in the morning. Another surprise came shortly afterward when the door bell rang. Ivory, finishing up one long braid at the back of her head, bounced to the door and answered it. "Ricky," she said, after swinging the door open. It was the grocery boy from one of the neighborhood grocery stores who had delivered groceries for them previously. The only thing was that they hadn't placed the order this time. "What are you doing here?"

"I have a delivery for you all," he said and proceeded to cart in at least 10 bags of groceries. Henry was good about doing things like that, especially when the girls had done something that required them to spend heavily. And anytime they went on a trip, they usually threw caution to the wind and returned almost penniless.

"Well," Ivory said with a wave of her hand, "bring it on in."

When the packages were brought in, Rayanne said, "Wait, let me get you something."

"Thanks, but that's been taken care of," Ricky said.

Rayanne didn't care at that time what Henry's reason was for coming through once again for them, she just knew that his generosity could not've come at a better time and she was thankful. She looked up at the ceiling and whispered, "Thank you, Lord, and you too, Henry."

Neither of the girls went out that night. They unpacked, returned phone calls, and made others, with Rayanne and Ivory telling Dorian to be sure to thank Henry for the groceries. Then, Dorian and Ivory began teasing Rayanne about becoming an actress. "Now girls, let's not get carried away. I'm just being asked to audition for a part. I haven't been guaranteed the part." There's a big difference in auditioning for a part and actually landing it, Rayanne thought as she sorted clothes to do laundry, but she was hoping and praying that she would get that part or any part.

"If you read for it, you're gonna get it, Rayanne. Do you realize that you haven't failed at anything you ever tried," Ivory said.

"Those things were insignificant. This is the real world, and things don't happen that way."

"It's gonna be fine, Rayanne. Just you wait and see," Dorian said.

"Sounds exciting," Ivory said. "When do you go for the reading?"

"I'm gonna call then in the morning but the audition is day after tomorrow."

"Well, good luck," Dorian said.

"Thanks," Rayanne said.

Luck, Ivory thought, shit this girl's gonna be fine. She's gonna knock them dead. Rayanne's got luck built right in. The girl's a walking four leaf clover, a freaking rabbit's foot.

On Tuesday, after ending one assignment and a promise to call for another in a day or so, Rayanne went for the audition. The part she read for was small, but two days later after waiting on pins and needles, she was called back for a second reading, and she got the part. One play led to another and eventually, she got the lead in a play. It wasn't until she'd acted in several plays that it occurred to her that she'd rather create the characters. It was then that she purchased a memory typewriter. She enjoyed writing so much that her career as an actress was short lived. She became so focused on writing that it became her main goal while everything else became secondary. Writing was easy. The hard part was shopping the finished product. Although perseverance was one of her strong points, after many meetings and luncheons and rejections and disappointments, Rayanne decided that before long she'd heed to the suggestion of her roommates and others. She'd get an agent. When Rayanne first arrived in New York, she came stocked with the idea that she was going to do it herself, make it on her own. How naive she was, because little did she know that for the type of career that she was interested, agents were necessary, managers, lawyers, and others.

CHAPTER 4

"Sure you won't change your mind and come with us?" Ivory asked one evening, throwing her cape around her shoulders, as she and Dorian were preparing to go out to dinner.

"I'm sure," Rayanne responded from the typewriter, her fingers racing over the keyboard. "I want to get this script finished so I can deliver it tomorrow."

"You never go out with us anymore," Dorian said pretending to pout.

"That's not true," Rayanne said, continuing to type, "I just can't go tonight." But, Dorian was right, she thought, she didn't go out with the girls or anyone else. She'd decided that she wanted a career, therefore, romance and good times would have to wait. She had goals in mind and she never lost sight of them.

"You're always so in control," Dorian began, "so pulled together, you bang it out constantly and never get discouraged. How do you do it? I get so depressed when I go for an interview and I don't get the job, especially one that I would simply die for, but not you. You seem to be fine either way. What is it that always keeps you so up?"

"Dorian, all I can say is I grew up in a house where I was taught that I can do anything, that I should not be afraid to step out into the unknown and take risks on things that are important to me.

We were taught to always keep faith. Dorian, when you have faith in God, anything is possible."

"Do you really believe all that?" Dorian asked.

"Of course I do, don't you?" Rayanne asked.

"I'm just not sure," Dorian said with a puzzled look on her face.

Rayanne explained further. "Let me put it this way. I approach everything with the attitude that if I work hard, really apply myself and keep faith with me, then I can do anything that I want to do."

Dorian, still looking a little puzzled, asked, "aren't there times when a person does all of that and they still don't get the breaks that they strive so hard for?"

"Of course," Rayanne said.

"Then what?" Dorian asked.

"Dorian, when you've put everything you've got into something that's important to you and it still doesn't work out, then you'll know that it wasn't meant to be," Rayanne answered.

"And you can accept it as that?" Dorian frowned and rubbed the side of her head.

"Sure I can," Rayanne said and she stopped typing, "but I don't give up. I keep trying. If something's gonna happen, it'll happen. We have to pay dues. That's what it's all about. That's what living is to me. You live your life, have experiences, learn and grow as a result of them, and you keep on going. The thing to remember is that we have to keep trying. We'd never get anywhere in life if we didn't try, motivation and commitment."

Dorian moved her head up and down, understanding, and said, "You are so centered, so focused."

"You could be also. If you want something badly enough, you'd be 100% committed. I want to be a successful writer so I'm willing to work hard."

"Brilliant, isn't she," Ivory said.

"You ain't joking," Dorian, who rarely used slangs, said.

"She wants to be black so bad," Ivory said and they laughed as Rayanne resumed typing. Then the telephone rang, and Dorian answered it. When she hung up, Ivory asked, "what was that about? Are we still on for dinner?" She knew from past experience when she and Dorian had made plans that a phone call could alter whatever earlier plans that had been made.

"That was Henry. I'll run over and see him after dinner," Dorian said.

"The Senior Citizen strikes again," Ivory said and laughed.

"Go on and laugh, make fun of my man. Henry may be a little older than I, but..." Dorian began, but Ivory interrupted.

"A little older? A little older. Please, Henry is as old as dirt," Ivory laughed.

Dorian ignored Ivory and said, "As I was saying before I was so rudely interrupted, Henry may be a little older than I, but he's got everything else going for him. He is kind, gentle, understanding, compassionate, everything you could want in a man."

"I didn't hear the word generous," Ivory said, making quotation marks with her fingers to the word generous.

"You didn't let me finish," Dorian said and continued, "generous, caring and above all, he's honest. And, that's a lot more than I can say for some of those bull shitting, womanizing younger guys out there."

"The girl's got a point," Ivory agreed.

"If you don't need us to do anything for you," Dorian said, checking her watch, "then I suppose we should be getting out of here."

"No, you guys run along. I'll be finished in a little while," Rayanne said, her fingers continuing to race over the keyboard, her creative juices continuing to flow.

"Well we'll see you later," Dorian said.

"Dorian, say hello to Henry for me," Rayanne said, "and Ivory, will you be seeing Cal?"

"No, and I don't think we'll be seeing much of him around here anymore either," Ivory answered. Another one bites the dust, Rayanne thought, continuing to type. "See you later," Ivory said going towards the door and looking over her shoulder, said, "and, we won't tell you what you missed."

"You got that right," Dorian agreed.

And in response, Ivory said to Rayanne, "This girl wants to be black so bad."

"It works for you two," Dorian spat out, and they laughed. "Sure you don't want to come?"

"I'm sure. Now you two get outta here. I've got work to do," Rayanne said and Ivory and Dorian went out and got a taxi to the restaurant. Rayanne didn't stop typing until she had finished the script. "It's done," she said, eyes closed, her back against the chair, cheerfully sighing with relief, although her shoulders sagged with fatigue. The script took longer than she thought but she was glad it was finished. She thought of Lionel, she'd promised to call him when she was done. She looked at her watch, reached over for the phone and dialed his number. Although the hour was late and he still wanted to see her, Rayanne begged off, promising to see him tomorrow. He argued, but Rayanne prevailed and felt a sense of succor at the thought of going to bed one night before midnight. One hour later, Rayanne emerged from the Madison Avenue Copy Shop, armed with five copies of her script, and before returning home, she stopped at Nathan's for a hot dog and orange juice. In the morning she'd take a copy of the script to The Writers Guild, one copy to each of the three major production companies, and she'd file her copy and wait. As it turned out, the call she waited for, hoped for, would've done anything for, didn't come, and of course, she was disappointed because although she'd written many plays, that was the one that she really felt good about.

CHAPTER 5

It was Friday evening. Ivory and Dorian went to a football game with Cal. Rayanne, deciding to spend a quiet evening at home, lit some candles, put on some classical music and settled on the couch with a book. After several hours of reading, she put the book away and the evening dragged on interminably. As it did, her mind conjured up many thoughts. She'd learned a lot about New York. She could travel anywhere in the city alone with directions, she'd met a lot of people and she'd dated some wonderful men. Well, almost all of them were wonderful because there were always exceptions, and in this case, the exception was Ronnie Freeman. The thought of Ronnie Freeman being romantic made her want to laugh out loud. Ronnie had appeared less experienced than Billy Peterson, the boy she'd made out with in the back seat of his father's old Chevy, when they were both seniors in high school. Rayanne remembered one of her dates with Ronnie as being anything but exciting. In fact, it had been so boring that she mentally drafted an outline for a play, while sitting in his car at a drive-in movie. He'd taken her to one of those plotless, senseless, X-rated movies that they'd driven forever to get to, when all the time she would've preferred a nice quiet evening at home or at one of the clubs with some of their friends. When Rayanne kissed Ronnie good-bye at the end of that date, that's exactly what it was, because she never went out with him after that.

Rayanne got up from the couch and went to bed, only to stare up at the ceiling before finally drifting into something resembling sleep. What she encountered was a horrible monster that ran wild in her mind, and the horrible nightmare it created made sleep a mockery at best. She'd dreamed that her father had died. The dream seemed so real that it left her more than shaken. Rayanne turned over in bed, finding the sheets wrapped tightly around her body. She peeled them away and looked at the clock. It was four forty-five and had it not been so early, she would've called her parents to make sure everything was all right. She got out of bed and was on her way to the kitchen for a cold drink, when she saw Ivory letting Cal out. Not only had Ivory started seeing Cal again, he'd been staying overnight regularly. But what was more amazing was the frequency in which Henry had stayed all night with Dorian. How did he ever manage to explain his absences to his wife?

Rayanne's typewriter was set up at the far end of the den. There were nights when she'd go off into that room, close the door in order not to disturb Ivory and Dorian, put on some music and escape from the rest of the world, where she became emerged in her characters, characters which she breathed energy, humor, and compassion into their lives. She felt a connection with her characters. They were like a part of her own family. Rayanne had found, through her writing, that she could visit places where she'd never been, places she'd only read about, toured only in her mind, and where for hours at a time, she could leave the problems of the real world, such as hunger, abuse, violence and the like, behind. At 6:15 that morning, Rayanne, knowing her parents were early risers, picked up the phone, dialed their number and shortly afterwards, she was being assured that all was well with her family. She returned to bed and she lay still, happy that it was Saturday, and she didn't have to go off to work. She was very tired.

On Tuesday afternoon, Dorian opened the door and stormed into the loft wearing a pair of designer jeans and a white blouse with the sleeves rolled up, her hair, loosely pinned up in a ponytail that trailed down her back. She threw her portfolio onto the couch and plopped down beside it. "Hey guys," she said, removing her shoes.

"Hey yourself," Rayanne responded looking up from her typewriter.

"You're at it again, I see," Dorian said.

"What can I say," Rayanne said. "How did the interview go?"

"I didn't get the assignment, but I wanted it so badly," Dorian said, folding her arms across her chest.

"I know," Rayanne, seeing Dorian's disappointment, switched off the typewriter and went over and sat beside her, "but there'll be other jobs, better ones even."

"That's right, Dorian," Ivory said from the floor where she was counting her money. "How about this. Why don't we get some of that great Chinese food that you love so much, and a bottle of wine and celebrate." Ivory took out two $20 bills, placed it to the side, and she put the other bills back into the small square box and rushed off to her room.

"What are we celebrating?" Dorian called out after her.

"Anything, life, us being together. What difference does it make," Ivory said returning to the room. "So don't worry about it. Just hang in there." Dorian smiled half heartedly. She'd been so accustomed to getting what she wanted, but now she was visibly affected by the rejection, or was it something else that had Dorian troubled. Ivory looked at her, seeing the perplexed look on her face. "Something else is bothering you? You graduate college in a couple semesters, and you got a man who is richer than God. Gee, those things alone should make you happy."

"I won't graduate if I don't get a handle on that Math," Dorian said, wrinkling up her face.

"Math? Is that what's bothering you?" Ivory said. "Get your book and let's have a look."

"Are you good at Math?" Dorian asked, a little surprised. She knew Ivory was smart but had no idea that Math was one of her better subjects.

"Ivory is a mathematical genius," Rayanne put in as Dorian jumped up from the couch and rushed off to get her book. When she returned, she sat on the floor beside Ivory, and they began working on some of the problems. Rayanne got up and returned to her typewriter.

After a while, Dorian slapped the book shut. "By George, I think I've got it," she said, her eyes dancing in her head.

"I think so too. See, it wasn't all that bad, was it?" Ivory said.

"I had no idea you were so good at this stuff."

"And, I had no idea you were having problems with it. You should've said something."

"I was thinking of getting with a study group. I had no idea you knew this stuff."

37

"Well, now you do, so anytime I can help, let me know," Ivory offered.

"Thanks, I appreciate that," Dorian said, removing the clip from her hair and running her fingers through the silky blond strands. She gathered her things and headed for her room. When she returned, she asked, "How's that portfolio coming?"

"It's getting there. I just need to upgrade a few shots, than it's gonna be smooth sailing," Ivory said. She knew that in order to get a good agent to represent her, she'd need a decent portfolio.

"Ivory, it's going to take a while to put together enough money to get the kind of portfolio that you need. You really should let us help. I'd be more than happy to loan you the money," Dorian said and she meant it because money wasn't a problem for her since she met Henry. She'd been able to update her portfolio every six months or so.

"And I can help a little," Rayanne said because of late, since she'd not been going out spending like money was going out of style, she'd managed to put a little aside.

"Nope, I'm gonna do this on my own." Ivory was one of the nicest persons anyone could meet, but she was just as stubborn. She was saving a little money out of each pay check, and she knew that the portfolio would be completed soon. "But, I appreciate what you guys are trying to do." She walked over to the telephone and dialed the number for the Chinese restaurant.

"But, you'll pay us back. It's not like we're giving you the money," Rayanne said.

"I hear ya, but guess what," Ivory said, "I've got a new job, the pay is better so a lot more money will be coming in, so there."

"Oh yeah. Where," Dorian said rushing off to the kitchen for a bottle of mineral water and returned to the den.

"Yeah, where?" Rayanne asked excitedly.

Ivory held up a finger to silence the girls, she placed the order and after hanging up, she said, "Over at Jacko's."

"Really? I hear the tips are good there, too," Dorian said.

"But better than that, I get to wear one of those cute, sexy little outfits."

"When do you start?" Rayanne asked.

"Tomorrow."

"Tomorrow?" Rayanne looked at Ivory, a wrinkle in her brow.

"Did you give notice at your old job?"

"No, but I think they'll notice that I'm gone," Ivory answered, giggling.

"Girl, you're too much," Rayanne said, giggling as well.

"Of course," Ivory answered, then to Dorian, "so what's cooking?"

"I thought we'd go over to LaVoice's tonight," Dorian replied in a matter of fact tone.

"What's happening over there?" Ivory's ears stood up with interest. LaVoice's was one of those posh clubs that she'd wanted to go to from the time she'd heard about it. She got up, walked over to the record cabinet, and took out a stack of albums. She sat on the floor near Rayanne and began flipping through them.

"They're having a birthday party," Dorian said, "and we're invited."

"Whose chain did you pull?" Ivory asked, looking at Dorian with a sly smile.

"Honey child, I've got connections," Dorian joked.

"No lie," Ivory agreed. Rayanne looked at Ivory, cocked her head to the side and asked, "what is LaVoice's? I don't think I've ever been there? If I have, I don't remember." It wouldn't be the first time she'd been somewhere and didn't remember where she was, when she'd gotten there or when she left, she thought because for a while there, she drank pretty heavily and some of their activities were just a blur. "You girls have really been a bad influence on me. Got me smoking and drinking and partying all night," Rayanne teased.

"And, you love every minute of it, too," Ivory said.

"What kind of place is this LaVoice's?" Rayanne asked.

"It's one of those exclusive, private clubs," Ivory explained and emphasized the word private by making quotation marks with her fingers. "It's up on the West side, and only the rich and famous gain entry."

"Whoa, I don't think I've ever been to any place like that," Rayanne said, "and," she said to Dorian, "you said we were invited?"

"Yes."

"Well, like Ivory said. Whose chain did you pull?"

"Leave it to Dorian to make things happen. The girl's got it going on," Ivory said getting up to put a Marvin Gaye album on the stereo and returned to the floor.

"Look who's talking," Dorian said, flopping down to the floor, "besides, we are not chopped liver, you know."

"Girl, I've seen you operate and for you," Ivory said, "life is a bowl of pitted cherries."

"Oh gee," Dorian said, making a face, then asked, "so are we on?"

"Sounds good to me," Rayanne said jubilantly.

"What about you, Ivory?" Dorian asked.

"Why not? It's something to do," she answered, and of course she was joking because Ivory would've given her eye tooth to go to that club.

"Then it's settled." Dorian lay back on the floor, folded her arms under her head and stared up dreamily at the ceiling. "That guy is really kicking," she said, and she sang a few bars of Marvin Gaye's 'I Want You'. Dorian freed one hand, snapped her fingers and rolled her head from side to side, listening to the music.

When the record ended, Ivory noticed Dorian as she continued to stare at the ceiling, and Ivory asked, "what's that look all about?"

"Oh nothing," Dorian said.

"Don't lie to me. Something's going on in that head of yours, so out with it," Ivory said.

"I talked with Henry today."

"Forgive me if I don't applause, but don't you talk with him everyday? What else is new?" Ivory asked.

Rayanne said, "Ivory, hush up please and let her finish."

"What did I say?" Ivory asked.

"Just shut up, will ya," Rayanne said to one girl, then to the other, "go on, Dorian. What did you and Henry talk about?"

"He's asking Olympia for a divorce," Dorian announced. She'd met Henry one Saturday morning shortly after her arrival in New York. She was having breakfast at a coffee shop when Henry approached her table and asked if he could join her. She said yes. Henry was so taken by Dorian's beauty that after they'd had lunch, they walked in Central Park, talked and time led them into dinner and before they parted that evening, she'd learned that Henry was a business tycoon. In addition to the magazine company he owned, there was also a house on Long Island, a summer place on Martha's Vineyard as well as other real estate. Henry learned that Dorian arrived in New York several months earlier, alone, she was attending a community college, taking some courses, not sure what she wanted to do with her life, no direction. She'd not shared much more than that. Nothing about where she'd come from or her family.

"No shit," Ivory said.

"That's what he said."

"This is what you want, isn't it?" Rayanne asked.

"Yes. I love Henry," Dorian replied. "I want to be with him."

"And he said he's giving the old biddie up, huh?" Ivory asked.

"Yes," Dorian responded.

"Well, it's about time," Ivory said.

"Ivory," Rayanne said.

"What did I say?" Ivory asked.

"Are you sure this is what you want?" Rayanne asked.

"Yes," Dorian considered, "I think so." She knew she loved Henry, but there were times when she questioned whether she was in love with him.

"You think so?" Ivory said looking intently at her. "Is that what you said?"

"Yes, this is what I want," Dorian answered.

"You do love him, don't you?" Rayanne asked.

"Yes."

"You do not," Ivory said. "You know you don't love that old ass man."

"Of course, I love Henry," Dorian said, then added, "and, he's not that old."

Ivory said, "he is too."

"What difference does it make how old he is as long as he loves you, respects you, treats you good and makes you happy," Rayanne said.

"Hell, Rayanne, don't get so serious on us," Ivory said.

"Divorce and marriage are serious matters, Ivory," Rayanne said.

"I know that, but if I thought Dorian was serious about Henry, I'm sure I would have a different attitude about all of this. But our friend here only wants to get control of old Henry's wallet."

Rayanne laughed and said, "you're kidding."

"No, square business," Ivory said.

"Ivory, that's a terrible thing to say," Dorian said, pretending to pout.

"But true," Ivory said.

"Are you going to marry him when the divorce is final?" Rayanne asked, interrupting Ivory.

"He hasn't officially asked me yet."

"You know he will. He loves you so much," Rayanne said.

"I suppose he does," Dorian responded, wistfully, and Rayanne wondered why a girl as young, as beautiful and had as much going for her as Dorian, would depend so much on Henry. He was a

41

much older man, and he wasn't all that attractive, and although Henry was very wealthy, Dorian had the potential to make a lot of money on her own. There was nothing wrong with a girl looking out for her future, but Dorian's dependency on Henry appeared to be more, much more.

"Henry does love you. We all know that. The problem is that you can't control him. You've finally met a man you can't control. I never thought I'd see the day," Ivory said, remembering some of the men Dorian dated, how she had them wrapped around her little finger.

"Don't tell me you're one of those control freaks," Rayanne laughed. "I didn't know that."

"That man would walk through hell with gasoline drawers on for her, but he ain't giving up control of the purse string. You'd think that the old dude would just lay down and die just to be able to screw her, right? Huh uh, not Mr. Henry. That old bastard maintains a high level of control," Ivory said.

"Don't talk about my old man that way," Dorian teased.

"Old is the operative word, and another thing, you don't care how I talk about Henry," Ivory joked.

"Yes I do," Dorian said, as the door bell rang. Ivory answered it. Minutes later, they were seated at the table, enjoying chicken fried rice, egg foo yong, sweet and sour chicken and egg rolls. Ivory and Dorian probably wouldn't eat for a week after that meal.

"So, when he proposes," Rayanne interrupted, "are you going to accept and marry him?"

"Can we just get through with one situation before we pounce on another?" Ivory asked.

"Dorian, the important thing is that you're happy. That's what matters," Rayanne said.

"What do you want out of life, Rayanne? What would make you happy," Dorian asked.

Rayanne sat and studied Dorian's face, then she answered, "When I get a buyer for one of my plays. That would make me happy."

"You heard the way she phrased that, didn't you?" Ivory said, wiping her mouth and getting up from the table. She cleared it, dumping the scraps into the garbage disposal and tossing the paper plates into the trash. "She said 'when' not 'if' but 'when.' That's what she said."

"And, I'm sure she'll get to where she wants to be," Dorian said.

"That's right and I swear to God, when she gets a buyer for one play, it's gonna be so good that they are gonna want everything the girl writes. Just wait and see. It's gonna be the start of something big," Ivory said. Sounds good to me, Rayanne thought and smiled, hoping everything would turn out just the way Ivory had described. "I believe it," Ivory said, as they returned to the den. "It's true. There are people out there who have been writing for years and then, just like that," she snapped her fingers, "one will hit. Then, they sell everything they've written. Sometimes these industry power suits will buy a story before the book is written." Ivory smiled. "Look at us, Dorian will soon graduate and when I get the break I'm looking for, we're gonna be cooking with gas."

"I know that's right," Dorian said and reached over to give Ivory five.

"She wants to be black so bad," Ivory said, and they laughed. The phone rang. Rayanne jumped up and answered it.

"Hello?" She listened for a moment, rolled her eyes towards the sky and hung up.

"Who was that?" Ivory asked.

"That obscene caller again, I'll bet," Dorian said, remembering they'd received a number of calls from him before. He was someone whom they didn't know or wanted to know.

"That stupid ass hole has nothing better to do," Ivory said. The phone rang again.

"Hello?" Rayanne answered, laughing. It was the obscene caller again, he went through his usual spill about how fine she was and all the things he was going to do to her. Rayanne said, "do those things to your mama," and she hung up.

"Way to go, Rayanne. You little devil, you," Ivory said. Rayanne sat back down, and they rolled on the floor, squealing with laughter. Ivory got up from the floor and when she managed to stop laughing, she said, "that oughta put him on ice for a little while." She stacked the albums back into the record cabinet and just as she finished, the phone rang again. Rayanne looked at it, lifted both hands into the air and was about to get up to answer it. "Wait," Ivory said holding up a hand, "let me get it." She walked over to the telephone, placed one hand on her hip and lifted the phone from its cradle. Rayanne was the sensible, most serious one of the girls, but Ivory, the fun loving, wise cracking prankster that she was gave as good as she got. "Hello?" she answered.

"Hello there, sweet cakes," the caller said.

"Who is this?" Ivory asked.

"That's not important," he said.

"I agree, so why are you calling?"

"Because I've got something to tell you, baby. I've got something good for you."

"You do? What is it?"

"I want to stick my dick in you," the Caucasian caller said.

"You want to do that to me?"

"Yes, you. I want to put my tongue between your legs."

"But, I thought you were interested in my friend." Dorian jumped up and rushed over to put her ear to the phone.

"I'm interested in both of you. I'll do you first, then your girlfriend. How's that? Would you like that? huh?"

"Well I don't know. My girlfriend isn't into the group thing," Ivory cooed.

"Oh yeah, baby. I could change her mind, and I know that I could have a lot of fun with you. I could give you a lot of pleasure."

"You think you could?"

"I know I could. Call it a man's intuition. I can tell from the sound of your voice that you're hungry for it, baby. You're the kind of girl who's really got it together. Like I said, baby, I want to do you, then your girlfriend. I could make both of you feel so good."

"That might be nice if you had something to do it with, but I'm afraid Kemosabe that you'd just be a waste of time," she said, as Dorian held a hand over her mouth to suppress a snicker.

"Baby, I could have you talking out of both sides of your mouth," he said.

"Let's get down to the brass here, my friend. What are you going to make me feel good with. Tell me, sweetheart, with what?" Ivory asked.

"My dick, baby, what else?" he asked sounding proud.

"And you think you've got one?" Ivory asked, "a dick, I mean."

"Oh yes," he said, "and I want to feed it to you, inch by inch."

"Well, that shouldn't take long," she said, a snicker almost emerged, as she pushed Dorian, who was silently laughing, away. Ivory was trying so hard not to laugh that her stomach ached.

"Oh, you're that hot, huh?" he asked.

"Yes, you freak, I'm just that hot, but that's something you wouldn't know a damn thing about. The point I'm trying to make is that you don't have enough dick to do anything with, and if you feed it to me inch by inch, why your time would be very limited," Ivory said, running the nail of her thumb under the other nails and reaching the end of her patience level with the caller. She'd had her fun and she didn't want to play his little game anymore.

"You wait one minute, bitch," he began, but Ivory cut him off.

"No mother fucker, you wait a minute." Ivory had really become annoyed with him by that time. "I've allowed you to have your fun, but I don't want to play anymore."

"Bitch..." he began and again Ivory interrupted.

"Do you think I am stupid," she continued. "You aren't equipped with enough manhood to even think about any of the things you're suggesting. Frankly, I wish you were, perhaps, I'd think about inviting you over. If you had something to fuck with, do you think you'd be on the phone wasting this kind of time? Hell no." Ivory knew if the man had more than a peanut between his legs, he'd be out somewhere screwing somebody's head off, so who was he kidding, she was about to ask when she heard the sound of him hanging up. Ivory looked into the ear piece of the phone. "The nerve of that guy hanging up on me." She placed the phone back into its cradle and slapping her hands together, said, "well so long to you too, ass hole." They all laughed.

"Sure bet he won't be calling here again," Dorian said.

"I wouldn't if I were he," Rayanne said, and they laughed out loud.

"So what are you whores wearing tonight?" Ivory asked.

"Whores? I beg your pardon," Rayanne said.

"Well, we'll probably all be before we decide to settle down with one man," Ivory said.

"Speak for yourself," Dorian said.

"Hell no, I'm speaking for all of us," Ivory said.

"That we all will be whores before we get married, Ivory please," Rayanne said, "you can't be serious." She looked at Ivory whose face was as serious as she'd ever seen it, then asked with raised eyebrows. "Ivory, do you really believe that?" Rayanne laughed a little.

"No," Ivory said. Rayanne sighed and wondered why Ivory taxed herself, conjuring up statements like that, but she didn't ask. She didn't have to because she knew what her answer would be. She'd say 'because it made her feel good'.

"Speaking of marriage," Dorian said, "we've got to plan for that. We're going to be in each other's wedding, right?"

"Of course we are, but why are we talking about marriage

now," Rayanne asked, wondering why was Dorian suddenly so preoccupied with getting married. There was plenty of time for that.

"Unless someone here's pregnant. No one here is pregnant, are we?" Ivory asked, looking around and rolling her eyes.

Dorian hesitated a moment, looking from Ivory to Rayanne. "I'm not, but I think we should at least think about it."

"We've got plenty of time for that," Ivory said.

"Are we going to wait until we're old to start planning?" Dorian asked.

"Good question," Rayanne said, "I sure would like to catch a good man before I'm too old and ugly to attract one."

"You gals have the kind of skin that looks really great for a long time," Dorian said.

"What the hell is she talking about now?" Ivory said to Rayanne, then to Dorian, "you're so damn gorgeous that you'll probably look good after you've been dead and buried a hundred years."

"Ain't that the truth," Rayanne said.

Dorian said, "we aren't getting any younger."

"Okay," Rayanne said, "let's talk about it. When would you like to get married?"

"In a couple of years," Dorian said.

"In a couple of years? Why?" Ivory asked.

"Why not?" Dorian responded.

"Okay, okay. What about you, Ivory?" Rayanne asked.

"When I'm thirty."

"You sound as though you've given this some thought," Rayanne said.

"And you, Rayanne," Dorian asked."

"I don't think I wanna wait until I'm thirty," she answered.

"Neither do I," Dorian agreed.

"Let me tell you guys about the positive side to this," Ivory said.

"Is there a positive side to getting married at thirty?" Dorian asked.

"Sure there is," Ivory answered.

Rayanne got up from the floor, walked over to the fish tank, dropped several pieces of fish food into the water, went back to the couch and picked up an apple from the bowl that sat on the coffee table. She wiped it off on her shirt and said, "let's hear it." Ivory and Dorian looked at Rayanne with raised eyebrows.

Rayanne had just polished off a good serving of Chinese food, now an apple. Rayanne, reading each girl's thought said, "no, I'm not pregnant. I just want this apple." Then they returned to the discussion. "What is the advantage of being thirty when we get married?"

Ivory explained that they all want to be artists, they plan to travel, hopefully a lot and that each of them was as selfish as hell in their own way; therefore, by the time they were thirty, they'd already have embarked on fabulous careers, travel all over the globe and done everything else they wanted. "We'd be ready to become domesticated by that time, but for now, we need to get on with the important things," Ivory snickered, "like what are we going to be wearing tonight."

"Ivory, be serious, will you," Dorian said.

"All right already. I was just kidding," Ivory retorted. Love and marriage and children were important to each of them, but it seemed much more so, at that time, to Dorian.

"I don't think that's anything to joke about. And," Dorian said lifting an index finger, "there isn't anything that is more important than family and friends." Both, Ivory and Rayanne agreed, they were friends, more like family and obviously they loved each other, but what was Dorian getting at.

"Dorian," Ivory began, "we feel the same as you do."

"But," Dorian began.

"No buts, we're not gonna get into all that shit again. We'll always be there for each other, but we won't always have the fun, carefree, throw caution to the wind times like we're having right now. For me, I want to hold on to this a while longer before giving it up for a husband and children," Ivory said.

"Don't minimize their importance, Ivory," Dorian said.

"I'm not. All I'm saying is that when I do take that step, I don't want any interference. I want to devote myself totally to being a good wife and mother."

"I can see that," Rayanne said bowing her head back and forth in agreement.

"Yeah. Just consider what I've said, Dorian, and you'll agree that it would be better if we waited a while. Come on gals, there's lots to do out there and we're gonna be so busy that we'll be thirty before we know it," Ivory said.

"If this comes to past, you'll be the first to marry, then Rayanne, then me."

"Dorian, please, forget about it, will you?" Ivory said with a wave of a hand.

"I just don't want to be the one left alone," Dorian said, her beautiful eyes sad. Rayanne wondered why were they having that conversation now as she took a large bite out of the apple. They were getting all bogged down in something that they didn't have to think about for years.

"We're family, right," Dorian asked and Rayanne and Ivory looked briefly at each other.

"Yes we are and that's not going to change," Rayanne assured her, "we love you, silly." Dorian didn't answer, she just smiled at both girls and that smile touched her eyes and a twinkle replaced the sadness that was there before.

"Do you want us to carve that in stone?" Ivory smiled.

"No, that won't be necessary. I love you guys too, I trust you implicitly," Dorian said, "and I just want it to always be this way for us."

Rayanne and Ivory exchanged another brief look, and Rayanne said, "it will be, you know that."

"I hope so," Dorian said and there was a lull in the conversation.

"Hey, hey," Ivory said, "my question is back on the table." Dorian and Rayanne looked questioningly at Ivory, who looked from one girl to the other with a straight face and said, "What are you bitches wearing this evening?"

"Oh Jesus," Dorian said laughing.

"She's incorrigible, what can I say," Rayanne said and she and Ivory joined in the laughter.

CHAPTER 6

They arrived at the party, each wearing a tight, knit mini dress. Each girl had dashed to and from one another's vanity, selecting matching accessories, nail polish, nylons, whatever was necessary to complete her outfit that evening. Rayanne took Dorian's berry berry red nail polish and did her nails to match the lipstick that she'd be wearing. Those colors would be a perfect match for the blood red dress she had selected. Dorian borrowed a pair of midnight blue nylons to wear with her navy blue dress, and Ivory rummaged through Rayanne and Dorian's trays until she found just the right pair of earrings and hair clip to accessorize her white outfit. They'd gone to numerous parties, discos and other functions and had danced their nights away, getting by with not more than a couple of hours of sleep a night, but, they'd loved it. Each girl was different, each had her own agenda, but they meshed and got along like a well oiled machine. They'd formed a bond, they were like family. Wherever they went, they caused a stir. They were poised and elegant and they were beautiful.

The next hours at the party were interesting, and although they ran into several acquaintances, they met a multitude of new peoples, mostly enterprising business people. Rayanne had danced until she was dizzy before returning to the table. She sat and sipped thirstily on her drink, and watched as Ivory and Dorian continued to dance. Those girls have stamina, Rayanne thought and laughed. Then she noticed a man who'd been pestering Ivory most of the evening, tapping her on the shoulder again, asking for a dance. Ivory was dancing and smiling until she saw who it was, then her smile faded. She continued to dance with the partner with whom she'd gone out onto the dance floor, ignoring the pest. Rayanne turned her attention elsewhere, everyone was having a good time and she thought how perfect her life was. She couldn't ever remember being happier. She was sharing a wonderful home with two very dear friends, she had a decent job, and she was living in one of the most glamorous, exciting cities in all the world. This was a perfect picture, she was young, life was free and great, and she would have it forever.

Rayanne was first joined at the table by Ivory, who was perspiring and touching her forehead lightly with her hand. She grabbed her purse and rushed off to the ladies room. Dorian, however, returned to the table looking as fresh as a daisy, took one sip from her frosty drink, and was immediately back on the dance floor where she disappeared into the crowd. Ivory returned to the table shortly after having freshened up. "This is a nice party," she said.

"I'll say," Rayanne agreed, thinking it was the nicest party she'd ever attended, and there was something to be said about the caliber of people in attendance. This was a group of affluent people and from snatches of conversations, Rayanne knew that these were powerful people in big businesses and she definitely wanted to be a part of that.

"That must be the birthday girl," Ivory said as a young pretty blond entered with an escort and was greeted at the door by several people yelling happy birthday.

Rayanne looked around and asked, "where?" as the lights of several cameras went off and took pictures of the couple.

"Where are your glasses, grandma?" Ivory asked.

"I don't wear glasses," Rayanne said.

"Well, you must need them because they're right over there," Ivory said, nodding her head in the direction of the couple and the flashing lights.

She's either the birthday girl or some celebrity, Rayanne thought and said after observing the couple, "I think they make a good looking couple, don't you?"

"No, I think they're all wrong for each other," Ivory said, thinking the guy could do a lot better. Rayanne was at a loss, she didn't see anything wrong. She looked at Ivory who lifted her shoulders and said, "She looks fake and cheap, that's what's wrong, but as they say, there's no accounting for taste."

"Ivory," Rayanne said, "don't worry about it. We're here to have a good time, that's all, all right."

"I'm having a wonderful time. I just said the chick looks cheap and fake."

"And I disagree."

"Rayanne, I'm glad we agreed long ago that it was okay to disagree."

Dorian returned to the table. They chatted, observed couples dancing, as well as the arrival of some late comers. After a while, Ivory became quiet and Rayanne knew she was thinking about Cal, but why. They were at a wonderful party with wall to wall men, and all she could think about was Cal. And, when they were together, they treated each other like crap. Go figure. "You may as well call him," Rayanne said.

"What are you talking about," Ivory asked, blinking.

"You broke up with the man and now you're missing him. If you're this miserable, you may as well get back with him. You know what they say," Dorian said, smiling wickedly, "you don't miss your well until your water runs dry."

"You don't miss your water until your well runs dry," Rayanne and Ivory corrected in unison and Rayanne said, "and you, Dorian, could never get an adage right." They laughed. Ivory's pest returned and tapped her on her shoulder. She turned to see who it was, and she let her head drop to the table. The girls ignored him. When Ivory lifted her head, the man was still there. She paused to draw in a deep breath, she closed her eyes, hard pressed to know whether she should scream in frustration or be happy at the thought that this may just be the man who would be at the receiving end of one of her cruel pranks at the end of the evening. Although, she began to figure the pest into her plans for later, Ivory realized she still had to keep up her little charade, pretending to not want to be bothered with him. She opened her eyes and through clenched teeth with eyes rolled towards the ceiling, said, "I can't believe this is happening to me. How can this be happening to me? Why is this happening to me?" The man wasn't a bad looking guy. As a matter of fact, he was very attractive but he acted like he wrote the book on stupidity. Ivory loved men, all men, but she didn't have much use for stupid ones. "What do you want now?" A sound of irritation caught in her throat.

"The American flag, I see," he said, "red, white, and blue." The girls looked up at him. "The way you're dressed, I mean," he said. The girls looked at each other, lifting their shoulders in a helpless gesture. "I'd like to dance with you," he said to Ivory.

"Why?" she asked, suppressing a groan of aggravation.

"Why not?" he countered.

"I don't want to dance so would you please leave me alone?" Ivory said, drew in a slow breath and brushed a piece of hair from her cheek with a brief movement.

"Just one dance and I promise I won't bother you anymore," he said. That guy doesn't take no for an answer, Rayanne thought. He'd better hope that Ivory doesn't go off on him. "You're drop dead gorgeous, you know. You are one fine chick," he continued, and he was right because Ivory looked exceptionally so that evening, but this man was exasperating.

Ivory said, "get over it, will you?"

"I'm serious. You're beautiful."

"Thank you very much. Now, will you please just leave me alone," Ivory said. "My friends and I are trying to enjoy ourselves, okay."

The young man stared admiringly at Ivory, then he looked from Rayanne to Dorian and asked, "what about you ladies. Care to dance?"

"No thanks," Rayanne said looking away. He looked at Dorian with the question in his eyes.

"No, but thanks," Dorian said.

The man looked at Ivory, who clicked her teeth and turned away from him. Then he said to her, "Baby, if you could see yourself as others do, you'd kiss yourself." He paused a moment. "Why won't you dance with me? You've danced with every Tom, Dick and Harry in the place. What's wrong with me," he asked, refusing to be offended by the rejection he received.

"For one thing, you ain't Tom, Dick or Harry, besides I'm tired and I just don't want to dance anymore," Ivory said, faking a smile.

"Am I suppose to feel sorry for you?" he asked.

Ivory looked up at the ceiling again, she moistened her lips and she gazed into the young man's eyes. She said, "Feel sorry for me? Of course, I don't want you to feel sorry for me."

"Guilty then?" he asked and without wavering, he returned her gaze.

She gave a short laugh and shook her head. "No, guilt requires a conscience and I'll just bet you don't have one."

With that he dropped his head, laughed and said, "I'm glad you have a sense of humor."

"What would you know about it," she murmured under her breath and thought, he's gonna be a wonderful victim, but it was becoming increasingly more difficult getting to the end of the evening. The man was absolutely tiresome. She said, "who let you in anyway?"

"Okay, okay. I get the picture," he said and with that, the young man turned and walked slowly away, which took Ivory by surprise. He turned a moment to say, "Damn, you're fine though." Then he walked away. It's about time, Dorian thought. Ivory clicked her teeth, Rayanne looked at her and was a little confused by Ivory's expression. Rayanne knew she'd been trying to get rid of the guy all evening, but now that he was gone, she seemed disturbed. There was a reason, Rayanne was certain, she just didn't know what it was.

At midnight, a waiter appeared with a table that held a cake with nineteen candles lit. He stopped at the table where the young blonde, her escort and two other couples, were sitting. The club was suddenly filled with voices singing happy birthday. Afterwards, they ate cake and drank champagne.

Of the people Rayanne met and shared her aspirations, some took her phone number with a promise to assist her with her career and some just promised to call. She excused herself and went to the powder room. On her way, she noticed a tall, well built handsome man with an air of confidence, having a drink at the bar. "Ummm," Rayanne said under her breath. When she was making her way back to her table, a wonderful, totally surprising thing happened. The man approached her.

"Hello," he said after taking a moment to look her over carefully. He had a deep, sexy voice, nice broad shoulders and damn, he smelled good, too. He had medium brown complexion and a smile that he wore only too well. He was the epitome of corporate America. He guided the cigarette that he was holding to his lips, and took a draw. He turned his head away and blew out a puff of smoke. "How are you this evening, Miss Wilson?" His smile revealed white teeth. He took her left hand, looked at her fingers and said, "I take it you're not married or did you remove your ring for the evening." This man definitely has sex appeal, she thought, withdrawing her hand.

"I don't believe we've been introduced," she said looking up into his eyes, slightly taken aback, aware of a powerful jolt of attraction that rushed through her at his touch.

"You're Rayanne Wilson, aren't you?" he asked, "and a lovely creature you are."

"Yes, but I'm afraid that you have me at a disadvantage. I don't have any idea who you are." Ralph Underwood introduced himself and Rayanne wondered what else did he know about her. He said he knew she'd done some acting, was an aspiring writer, and he said he bet she was damn good at it, too.

"Ho, Ho, Ho," she'd said, "a frustrated writer you forgot to add."

"I'm sure that won't last long."

"Let's hope not."

"Nothing is impossible," he said, taking her hand in his again. "So tell me, Miss Wilson, are you married?"

"Are you sure you don't already know. You seem to know everything else about me."

"Actually, I really don't know that much, but I'd like to. As a matter of fact, I'd like nothing better. You certainly are a lovely creature." He paused, "am I repeating myself?"

"No, I'm not married, thank you very much, and yes, you are repeating yourself," she said and was surprised at just how much she was enjoying the attention of this man.

"Are you here alone."

"No, I'm here with friends," Rayanne said, but she was sure he already knew.

"Boyfriend?" he questioned.

"No, girl friends," she went along with him.

"Good, then perhaps there's a chance that you and I can become better acquainted."

"That might be nice," she said. Rayanne knew that Ralph was older than she and the men she'd dated in the past, but he was extremely handsome, intelligent, and he had a wonderful smile. She looked around the room, when she looked at him again, he was staring at her. "Is something wrong?" she asked, a crease in her brow.

He said, "nothing from where I am standing."

"Then why are you looking at me that way?"

"What way is that?" he asked. She looked at him unsmiling, and although she didn't answer him, if she were to guess, she'd say he had something devious on his mind. She glanced away from the look in his dark eyes. "Okay, okay," he said lifting a hand into the air. "You got me. I'll admit it. I was saying to myself, 'self,

I bet under all that calm beats the heart of a wild wantom woman'. Does that come close to what you thought I was thinking?" he asked, an amused look on his handsome face. Dirty old man, she thought and was about to walk away. "You're not leaving?" he said.

"No, I'm going back to join my friends."

"May I?" he asked.

"May you what?" Rayanne knew what he was asking, but she wanted to hear him say it.

"Join you and your friends?"

"If you'd like."

"I'd like very much," he said. As the evening wore on, Rayanne found herself talking easily to Ralph about her work, her goals and her family. In the meantime, she'd learned that he was thirty-five, a native New Yorker, a successful stockbroker at a firm on Wall Street. He was also energetic, fun loving, and charming. He had a real passion for life. It turned out that Ralph and Dorian knew each other. They'd met at a party some time ago and had ran into each other on occasions, but they didn't know each other well. Into the evening Ralph said, "say girls, there was this guy over at the bar who told me you all treated him really cold."

"Which guy was that?" Rayanne asked.

"Some guy over at the bar. He just walked up to me and started talking," Ralph said, a twinkle in his eyes.

"Maybe he had it coming to him," Ivory said.

"He must've because I find you ladies charming," Ralph commented.

"That's what some of them say," Ivory said.

"And others, what do they say?" Ralph asked.

"Something much worse," Ivory said and the girls laughed. Ralph looked questioningly and Ivory replied, "probably that we're ladies with attitudes." The girls laughed again.

"Now, that's thought provoking," Ralph said, then he returned his attention to Rayanne.

Before he could ask, she said, lifting a hand, "You don't want to know what I think," Rayanne said, but she went on to explain, "We love people, we love to have a good time, but we choose who we want to have a good time with. He wasn't one of our choices." Ralph nodded. "Really though, we're not that bad," she assured.

"I didn't think you were," Ralph said, pushed his chair back and asked Rayanne to dance. She accepted, and when they came together on the dance floor, they moved as though they'd danced together for years. He held her gently at first, but as they swayed to the music, his arms tightened around her waist and he became lost in the music.

"Are you married?" Rayanne asked.

"What?" he said, a little taken aback as he was really caught up in the music and the feel of Rayanne's body against his own.

"Do you have a wife?" she said, pushing back enough so she could look into his eyes.

"No, not exactly," he responded, pulling her close to him so that her face rested against his. When he didn't clarify his response, she pulled her head back to look at him again. "I was involved," he began and stopped.

"Was?" she questioned.

"Was," he said without further explanation.

Rayanne had never met anyone as noncommittal and wondered whether she'd ever get anywhere with this man. She tried another approach. "What is your present situation in the romance department?"

"I don't have a present situation."

"What about the woman you were involved with? Where's she now? The relationship just didn't work?"

"Something like that," he said. Here we go again, Rayanne thought, annoyed. She wasn't sure why Ralph was so open about some phases of his life but so tight lipped about others. Ralph, seeing the look on her face said, "Are you upset with me?" She wasn't upset, but she was puzzled as to why Ralph wouldn't tell her anything about his personal life. "I've been talking about myself from the time I joined you and your friends this evening."

"I know, all business. I'd like to know something about you, who you are, what's important to you, your likes, dislikes. Things like that."

"There really isn't much to tell," he said, but she was certain that a man like Ralph could write a book. "My life hasn't been as fascinating as you might think."

"I'd like to be the judge of that," she smiled warmly, looked into his eyes and that look made Ralph want to grant any wish she might have.

"Well, I was married, it didn't work out. I lived with a woman for a while, we had a child. That didn't work either, but all of that was a very long time ago."

"What happened?"

"It's a long story," he said. More secrets, she thought, and Ralph looked at Rayanne for what seemed a long time, but actually, it was only seconds. He said, "As I said, I was married once for a short while. After the marriage failed, I lived with a woman and we had a child. I dated another woman whom I just recently broke up with. She wanted more than I could give, so we thought it best to go our separate ways. She was a nice lady. It just didn't work out. Right now, I'm on my own. End of story."

"What happened to the child?" Rayanne asked and watched as a sad look came into his eyes.

"My daughter and her mother were killed in an automobile accident, and," he said sadly, "if you don't mind, I'd rather not talk about that tonight." Rayanne was immediately sorry she'd pressed and she told him so. "How could you've known. It doesn't show, right?" Ralph said, suddenly joking and just as sudden, he became serious again. "I suppose you could say that I've been unluckily in love."

"It seems you've had your share of tragedies. Are you okay," Rayanne said noticing how the sadness had now covered his eyes. It seemed she'd opened old wounds without meaning to.

"Yeah, it was a mutual decision. We did what we thought was best," he said, "what about you? You've put me through the third degree tonight, so now, I'd like to hear more about you. Is there someone special in your life?"

"I just ended a relationship as well, but I'm beginning to date again. Nothing serious though," she said. That's soon to change, he thought and held her closer as they continued to dance. Rayanne closed her eyes, enjoying the music and the faint scent of the expensive after shave Ralph was wearing. When she opened her eyes, she couldn't believe that the pest had returned to the table, and Ivory looked absolutely mortified. Rayanne smiled to herself, closed her eyes again and continued to dance. When that record was over, she opened her eyes. Another record began to play immediately and to her surprise, she saw Ivory being led onto the dance floor by the man whom she'd despised. It was another one of those slow songs but what surprised her more was what happened next. Ivory was dancing with her arms wrapped around the man's neck and running her fingers through that awful rat tail that hung from the back of his head. When the record was over and the girls returned to the table, Ivory didn't sit. She grabbed her purse and said, "we are leaving."

"We are?" Dorian asked, eyebrows raised.

"What's wrong?" Ralph asked and he looked from Ivory to

Rayanne and back to Ivory.

"You know the guy that I was just dancing with," Ivory said.

"The one you didn't like? "What about him?" Ralph asked, but Rayanne was already out of her seat with her purse in her hand and so was Dorian. Ralph didn't understand what was going on.

"I just Neeted him, so I'm getting the hell out of here," Ivory said, and the girls looked from one to the other and laughed. Ralph was more puzzled than ever.

"What's going on?" he asked.

"Ivory just put Neet on that guy's rat tail," Rayanne explained.

"Neet on his rat tail?" Ralph asked disbelieving.

"That's right and if you all are coming with me, you'd better get a move on," Ivory said on her way towards the door. Neet on the man's rat tail, Ralph thought, shaking his head as they left the club. These ladies are something else. Rayanne allowed Ralph to see them home. Ivory and Dorian said goodnight and entered the loft, while Rayanne and Ralph stood outside the door.

"You're beautiful, do you know that?" Ralph said, looking down into Rayanne's face.

"I'm beginning to think so. You've been telling me that all evening," she said.

"Then believe me," he said, and she blushed and smiled. "I've been devouring you with my eyes from the time I saw you, but do you know what I'd like to do more than anything else right now?" Rayanne didn't answer, she stood against the door, looking at him, "I'd like to take you in my arms and kiss you. I've been wanting to all evening." Rayanne still didn't speak. "What do you think about that?"

"I don't think you'd be breaking any laws," she answered. Ralph took the cue and gently pulled her away from the door. He took her face in his hands and let his lips brush hers ever so gently. He released her, looked into her eyes and when he kissed her again, the kiss was more passionate. He sucked her lower lip and when Rayanne's tongue darted into his mouth, his body jerk with a spasm. When he released her that time, she was dizzy, her head was spinning, and she could tell that he was affected by the kiss as well.

"I'd better go in now," she managed to say, her heart racing out of control.

"So soon?" he asked, kissing her again.

Suddenly, she began to wonder whether she was getting too carried away with this man. Who is he, what kind of man is he, what did she really know about him. She could be opening herself up for a major heartbreak. "Yes, I really should," she said, as the hour was late and she did intend to go to church in the morning.

"Then, may I call you tomorrow."

"I'd be disappointed if you didn't," she replied, trying to keep her voice steady. This man really had an effect on her. Ralph tried to kiss Rayanne again, she placed both hands up against his chest, but ignoring her protest, he pulled her to him and when his lips took possession of hers again, the kiss was fierce, demanding and Rayanne closed her eyes and sighed with undisguised pleasure. The kiss went on and on until she was finally able to pulled away. "You will call me tomorrow," she said.

"Count on it," he said, lingered a moment longer, looking at her, then he was gone. Rayanne entered the loft, stood for a moment with her back against the door, then she joined the others in the living room.

"Come on over here, lover girl," Dorian teased, "and tell us all about it."

"Tell you what, dear," Rayanne said, breezing into the room and plopping onto the couch.

"Yes," Ivory mimicked Rayanne, with a dreamy look in her eyes, "you will call me tomorrow." She then mimicked Ralph, "count on it."

"Ivory," Rayanne said, sending a pillow in her direction, knowing then that Ivory had been listening at the door.

"So tell us about him," Ivory said.

"He's very nice. I like him," Rayanne said. Then she requested that Dorian tell her everything she knew about Ralph. Dorian declared that as far as she knew, he was a nice man, unmarried, she'd seen him around, sometimes with a woman, never the same one twice which made her think that maybe he wasn't serious about anyone in particular. When Dorian told Rayanne what she knew about Ralph, Rayanne didn't know much more than what she'd learned from Ralph.

"Come on. Stop trying to be so cool about this. I know your drawers are wet. Is he a good kisser?" Ivory asked.

"I hope so, because that's one thing that can turn me off in a hurry," Dorian said, crossing her legs and folding her arms across her chest.

"There isn't anything about Ralph that turns me off yet," Rayanne said, beaming.

"I take it he pleases you," Ivory said, giving her a sly smile, and Rayanne contained her enthusiasm as long as she could, before leaping from the couch.

"Yes Lord," she exclaimed, clutching her heart and whirling around. "He's wonderful, simply wonderful." She was behaving like a school girl, and she knew it, but she didn't care. This was a first impression and first impressions were something else. If there was any truth in what they said about first impressions and if Ralph lived up to that impression, he'd be the kind of man she could do some serious bonding with. Rayanne was glowing, Dorian and Ivory noticed. Could she be falling in love. "I had a great time tonight, girls," Rayanne said.

"I'll bet," Ivory said, a wicked smile on her face.

"Now what does that mean?" Rayanne asked.

"Ralph's got your nose," Ivory said, "you're falling for him."

"No," Rayanne lied, and her lips curled into a smile, thinking that it was sinful for her to be feeling that good.

"She's lying," Dorian observed.

"Through her teeth," Ivory agreed. Rayanne sat on the couch between Dorian and Ivory, and looked from one girl to the next.

"You guys are right. I really like him a lot. I've never met anyone like him."

"You ready to get with him?" Ivory asked and laughed.

"I bet you are. I would be, if I were you," Dorian informed.

"But you ain't me and you ain't gonna get none of that," Rayanne said and more laughter followed.

"Guess what guys," Ivory said going through her purse for a cigarette. She held a business card between her fingers as she lit the cigarette. She blew out a cloud of smoke. "I met a couple back at the club tonight. They have their own business, they are agents and they represents models. They said they handle some of the top models in New York." Dorian and Rayanne were excited. "She asked whether I'd ever done any modeling. I told her I'd done a little and they ask me to come in to see them. They said they were certain they could get some work for me. I told them I'm still working on that damn portfolio, but that I've got a good treatment," the words rushing out of Ivory's mouth and when she paused a moment to think, she wished she'd completed that portfolio.

"Yes, and I know you're gonna give it a shot," Dorian said gleefully.

"She said if I was interested, that I should call for an appointment. She didn't seem to think the incomplete portfolio was a problem. Anyway, we'll see where it goes."

"That's great. I know it's important to have a good portfolio to show your stuff, but I'm sure they can work around it. Go for it, girl," Rayanne said.

"I agree," Dorian said and she began to laugh.

"What's so funny," Ivory asked. Dorian laughed some more. "What is it?"

"I was just thinking about the guy with the rat tail," Dorian continued to laugh and the girls joined in.

"I'm sure he's lost that miserable tail by now," Ivory giggled and talked more about the party, about how annoying their friend with the rat tail was and Ralph. "Well, guys," Ivory stretched and yawned, "I think I'm gonna turn in."

"Me too," Rayanne put in and just as they were getting up to go to bed, the telephone rang. "Now who can that be." Not that pervert again, they hoped.

Dorian, still a little tipsy from the drinks she had at the party, said, "You don't think that idiot would be calling at this hour?" She look from Ivory to Rayanne, both of whom lifted her shoulders. "He's crazy, he doesn't care," Dorian said. The phone rang again.

"Please," Ivory said, "allow me." She picked up the phone. "Hello?" she said, not believing that the fool would be so stupid as to be calling again, especially at that hour. If it were he, he'd be sorry, she'd make sure of it. She paused, ready to unleash her fury on him. "Just a moment." Ivory smiled and handed the phone to Rayanne.

"Who is it?" Rayanne asked, but Ivory didn't respond, she just smiled. "Who is it?" Rayanne repeated.

"See you in the morning, kiddo. Goodnight," Ivory said, giving the phone to Rayanne. Dorian looked questionably at Ivory, who whispered to her, "it's Ralph."

"Oooh," Dorian giggled, putting her fingers to her lips. "That didn't take long."

"Nope," Ivory agreed and the two of them went off to bed, giggling.

"Hello?" Rayanne said.

"I hope I didn't disturb anyone, but I had to speak to you before going to sleep," he said.

"Hey," Rayanne said and was pleased that she'd made a good impression on Ralph as he had her. It wasn't that she thought Ralph was out of her league, but he was so much more sophisticated and worldly than any of the other guys she had dated.

"You sound surprised," he said.

"Ivory didn't say who was calling," she said, feeling excitement building up inside of her.

"Were you expecting someone else? I hope I didn't disappoint you." Not only had he not disappointed her, she was pleasantly surprised that he'd call so soon. When he said he'd call her tomorrow, she assumed the call would come later in the day, not at 3 in the morning, Rayanne thought, but she said with a smile, "No, not at all. Where are you?"

"I'm at my apartment, and I wish like hell you were here with me."

"Really," Rayanne said, amused.

"Yes I do. I miss you already. "He paused. "Tell me something. Do you miss me?"

"What kind of question is that?" she asked and began to evaluate the question and the answer took her by surprise. She did miss him.

"It's simple and straightforward," he answered. "Well, do you?"

She inhaled softly. "You're putting me on the spot."

"Not really," he said in a very sexy voice.

Heck no, Rayanne thought. I miss you like crazy but she said as cool as she could, "yes, I suppose I do."

"That's good. Now," he pressed, "do you love me?"

"Love you?" she asked, shaking her head in wonder at what was happening between them. "What is this? Twenty questions."

"Do you practice answering a question with a question?" he teased. Rayanne was silent. "It's not impossible, you know," Ralph said.

"No," she responded, thinking of the warm, wonderful feeling she was experiencing at the thought of him.

"No, you don't love me or no it's not impossible."

"I was answering no to the question of whether it is impossible for me to be in love with you, but," she began, but Ralph interrupted.

"Don't answer it if you're going to say you don't love me, because you see, I think I'm falling in love with you."

Although Rayanne loved hearing the words flow from his mouth, she said, "Ralph, you don't know anything about me. We don't know anything about each other."

"I know what I like, and I like you. Right now, that's enough for me."

"I like you, too," Rayanne admitted.

"That's all right for now, but can we get together tomorrow and get to know each other better?"

"I think that can be arranged." Rayanne went to bed and lay awake for what seemed like hours, her head filled with thoughts, thoughts of her future, how she'd go about making it happen, and with that, there were pleasant thoughts of Ralph. When she finally did fall to sleep, she slept like the dead.

CHAPTER 7

Rayanne was awaken on Sunday morning to the ring of the telephone. It rang two more times before she reached for it and still she was too dazed to speak clearly. "Hello," she said.

"Rayanne?"

"Yes."

"Is this soon enough?" came the sexy throaty voice of Ralph Underwood. She turned over and looked at the clock on the night stand, 8:05 it showed.

"Yes, I guess so?"

"Why don't you get yourself together and ride over to Jersey with me." Rayanne frowned in puzzlement and questioned what's in Jersey, he explained there was nothing in particular. He just thought she might want to go for a ride in the country. They could have breakfast somewhere in between, enjoy the scenery and just spend the day together. "Hey, wait a minute," Ralph said, "let's back up a second. Good morning, beautiful."

"Good morning to you," Rayanne said, lifting herself up on one elbow. "How are you?"

"I'm fine. What kind of plans do you have for today?"

"Nothing much."

"That's good because I've got to see you, woman. I can't get you out of my mind."

"I'd like to see you too," and she meant it. She missed Ralph more than she anticipated.

"So when can we get together?"

"Sometime after two."

"I thought you said you had no plans," he said, thinking six hours was too long to have to wait to see her. Rayanne told him they were going to church and invited him to come along. "To Church?" he asked.

"Yes, you do go to church, don't you?"

"Yes, but I can't make it today."

"Okay then, I'll see you this afternoon."

"Damn, what am I gonna do for six whole hours," he said. Rayanne wished he'd change his mind and come to church with them, but in the meantime, Ralph tried to get her to change her mind and go with him. When he was unsuccessful, he said, "you go to church every Sunday?"

"I try to," she said which was true because she'd practically grown up in the church.

"And, I can't change your mind," he begged.

"I'm afraid not," she said.

"Oh well, I tried," he paused a moment and said, "so tell me Miss Rayanne Wilson, did you enjoy yourself at the party last night?" She told him she'd had a great time and had met some interesting people. He hoped he was one of the interesting ones and she assured him he was. Ralph was one of the most interesting people to enter her life and the thought of how good he looked in his dark suit and white pull over was fresh in her mind. She got goose bumps thinking how that sweater clung to his muscular body when he removed his jacket after they'd danced a while. "I find you interesting, too. You told me that you're a country girl."

"Yes, I was born and raised smack dab in the heart of a little city in South Carolina. I'm a country girl in every sense of the word."

"I've heard that country girls make wonderful wives, mothers and lovers."

"Don't forget that we have a host of other wonderful qualities."

"You're wonderful," he said softly into the phone. She really was something to write home about, he thought. "I woke up this morning feeling very happy," he shared.

"Aren't you always?" Rayanne asked, "why was today an exception? What was so different?" She wanted to know more about this man.

"I met you last night, that's the difference, and the thought of you makes me happy."

"You know what that means, don't you?" she said. "You need me in your life. My mother always told me that a person's needs dictate what makes him happy," she teased.

"You have a very wise mother."

"You get no argument from me," she said and reclined in her bed.

"Rayanne, I've got a really serious question for you."

"What is it?"

"Have your feelings for me begun to resemble love yet?" Oh no, she thought, are we back to that again. He added in his most sexiest voice, "you're just postponing the inevitable, you know." She did care for Ralph. He was an intriguing man, but she honestly couldn't say that what she was feeling was love, at least not yet, she thought and when she told him that, he said, "That's encouraging."

"You are something," she said and looked at the clock again. It was getting late and was time she got up and start getting ready for church. "So, I'll see you this afternoon, then?" she asked.

"Count on it," he said, "I only wish it could be sooner."

"It can be," Rayanne said, wishing more and more that he would change his mind and go with them. She found the more she thought of Ralph, the more she wanted to be with him, but no such luck because he didn't change his mind.

"I'll be there when you get back," he answered.

***

Rayanne went to church and enjoyed the services, but she didn't stand around to fellowship with the members afterwards as she normally had done, nor did she walk the six blocks back to the loft with Dorian and Ivory. She left them at church, took a taxi home, changed into a pair of shorts and top, and she began preparing dinner. It wouldn't be anything elaborate. It would be a simple, but good meal. Rayanne was dashing about the kitchen when Dorian and Ivory arrived, they changed and helped with the finishing touches and when the food was ready, Rayanne left the stove up just enough to keep it warm. She took a quick shower, applied makeup lightly, slipped into a pastel pink mini dress, and she waited and waited. When Ralph hadn't arrived by three-thirty, Rayanne couldn't hide her disappointment. She never could hide her passion and she was as passionate about her dislikes as her likes. Although they sat and thoroughly enjoyed the meal, including a bottle of champagne that Ivory had bought to honor the occasion of having put together enough money to complete her portfolio, Ralph was missed. Almost immediately afterwards, they walked around the block and at six-thirty, Dorian and Ivory got dressed to go to an art showing that was being put on by a friend.

"Are you going to wait around here for Ralph?" Dorian asked.

"Not exactly. I want to get some work done, so I'll use this time to do it," Rayanne said.

"Liar," Ivory said, "you're waiting for Ralph. I wouldn't be sitting around here obsessing over him. Hell, I wouldn't give that nigger the time of day if he stood me up. He could've called, you know."

"That's right," Dorian agreed. "Frankly, I'm surprised he didn't."

"Hey, you two, it's no big deal," Rayanne said. "Why are we talking about Ralph anyway?"

Ivory lifted her shoulders and said, "interesting question." They laughed.

"Come with us. We're going to stop by Luanne's shower for half an hour, then we're going over to the museum for Patti's showing," Dorian said. Rayanne had wanted to go to that showing, but she was so ticked off with Ralph that she knew she'd be miserable and ruin the day for everyone else.

"No, but I'd like you to take a gift to Luanne for me and tell her that I'll call her this week," Rayanne said going into her bedroom to get the gift. She returned to the den and handed the neatly wrapped box to Dorian. "I'm sorry about missing Patti's show but tell her I'll definitely make the next one."

"Patti will be disappointed," Ivory said. Rayanne smiled weakly. "Okay, we will see you later." Dorian and Ivory left and Rayanne was alone to work, to think, to reflect. Her roommates thought she should've been really angry with Ralph, and she was, but what was the big deal? After all, they had only just met. She wasn't in love with the guy. True, he was the only man she'd ever met that made her feel so warm inside just talking with him, but she was not in love with him, was she? Oh well, she thought, you win some, you lose some, but life goes on.

Rayanne wrote to her sister Maxine, then she filled her bathtub almost to the rim and stepped into the tub. She reclined in the hot scented water, closed her eyes and just when she settled in the silky water and begun to relax, the door bell rang. Did they both forget their keys, she thought as she got out of the tub and slipped into a robe? Rayanne opened the door, "Did you two forget your key," she asked, expecting Dorian and Ivory, only to find Ralph standing at the door? He was carrying two dozen roses, one dozen red, one dozen yellow.

"I come in peace," he said with a crooked grin on his face.

"What's with all the roses?" Rayanne, annoyed as she was, was pleased to see him, and she noticed that he was even better looking there in daylight than he was the night before. He explained that the yellow roses were to declare their friendship.

"I don't need to explain the red ones, do I? Rayanne stepped back to allow him to enter, and as he did, he flashed his pearly white teeth. Rayanne looked at him, but she didn't return his smile. "Am I interrupted something," he said, looking her up and down.

"I was just taking a bath."

"Where are the others?" he asked looking around. "Nice place."

"Thanks. Dorian and Ivory are out."

"And, you didn't go with them?"

"No," she said a little taken aback, "you told me you were coming over and I told you I'd be here. I try to keep my word when I tell someone something."

I walked right into that one, Ralph thought and as he studied Rayanne, he said, "Go back and finish that bath. I can keep myself occupied for a few minutes."

"I just need to put something on," she said in an unfriendly tone, then she asked, "can I get you something?"

"No, I'm fine," he said, "but please take off that serious face and hurry back." For a moment Rayanne stared coldly at him, then turned and went off to her room. When she looked back over her shoulder, she thought she saw a slightly worried look on Ralph's face. Good, she thought jubilantly, teach you to make me feel all warm and wonderful inside, then dash cold water on me. Well, she could dash a little cold water herself. Serves him right. She returned wearing a white jumpsuit, a pair of white sandals and her hair up in a ponytail. She entered the living room to find Ralph standing out on the terrace. He turned as he heard her approaching. She was a vision of loveliness. He stared at her, the delicate features of her face and the tempting curves of her body. "You look fabulous," he said.

"You're the most complimentary man I've ever met," she said, managing a little smile.

"I call 'em as I see 'em." Rayanne didn't respond. "Are you upset with me because I was a little late getting here?"

"No, I'm not upset," Rayanne lied, "but you could've called. I came in from church, cooked you a nice dinner, and you didn't even show up."

"I'm here now."

"Yeah, right," was all she could think to say.

"I'm sorry." Ralph gave her a sheepish grin. He walked up close to her, they stood not more than a step apart, staring at each other. He reached for her, but she turned away. "You are angry" he said, and appeared pleased that his tardiness had that kind of effect on her.

Rayanne looked at Ralph and said, "disappointed is more like it."

"And, I think we're having our first quarrel," he continued to sound pleased.

"We're not having a quarrel. I'm just saying that when you saw you couldn't make it at two, you should've called. That's just common courtesy."

"I've upset you, and I'm sorry." he said "Can I make it up to you?"

"No, but please don't make it a habit," she said coolly. She's really angry he thought. What can I do to get back into her good grace. He knew he had to do something. He'd only just met this girl, he liked her very much and he certainly didn't want to lose her. "Look, why don't we do something," she said, interrupting his thoughts.

"What would you like to do?" he asked.

Rayanne, lifting both hands said, "It's doesn't matter. Let's just get out of here." They went to SoHo and as they walked along the streets, they peered into the windows of the art galleries. She'd never been in that part of the city before, but she liked it and when they visited Chinatown, she was amazed, yet again, at all the wonders that city held.

**

Dorian and Ivory left the shower and took a taxi to the museum. When they entered, they were greeted by a tall, slender woman, late twenties with long auburn hair, dark features and startling green eyes.

"Hello Patti," Dorian said, embracing the woman.

"Hello," Patti said, releasing Dorian and embraced Ivory.

"Good to see you, Patti," Ivory said.

"Yes, I'm glad you both could come," Patti said, her lips curled into a smile. "Is Rayanne here?" she asked looking around.

"No, Rayanne is sorry she couldn't be here, but next time she said," Ivory informed.

"Okay," Patti said. "It's good to see both of you."

"This is great, we want to get a closer look at your work," Dorian said.

"You have some wonderful pieces," Ivory glanced around, "you've done some great work."

"I'm very excited and," Patti whispered, "there are several critics here." Her eyes twinkled.

"I know the showing will be a great success," Dorian said. Ivory nodded in agreement. A tall older woman waved a slim hand as she approached them. She stopped short and bided Patti to join her. The woman was accompanied by a small dignified looking man. The gallery was practically filled with onlookers who wandered around viewing the art pieces.

"Please excuse me a moment," Patti said, "Look around and enjoy the show." Then she whispered, "wish me luck."

"Good luck, sweetie," Dorian said and embraced her again. Ivory crossed her fingers and winked at her. Dorian and Ivory admired and appreciated Patti's work.

"Look at this piece," Ivory said of a painting. "She has really captured the passion of this man. Look at those piercing eyes, they seem to reach right out and touch the soul. And that face, there's experience on that face. It's a wonderful painting."

"Yes, she's done a terrific job," Dorian said.

"Which piece do you think we can afford?" Ivory said.

"Ivory, that is so tacky," Dorian grinned.

"Call it what you want, but I just worked my ass off getting enough for my portfolio and I don't have a lot of extra so I can't just walk in an art showing and say 'wrap it,' without some thought as to how much and how I'm gonna pay for a painting."

"Why don't we look around a little more. Too bad Rayanne isn't here to help us decide," Dorian said. Ivory was thinking, too bad Rayanne wasn't there to kick in some of what the piece would cost.

***

As time passed, Ralph and Rayanne became almost inseparable. They saw each other every night, and they learned each others likes and dislikes and they explored the city every chance they got. They took the subway to Coney Island, rode on the roller coaster, the Ferris wheel, they gouged themselves on everything in sight from hot dogs, french fries and onion rings to popcorn, candy apples and cotton candy, and they washed all those calories down with diet sodas. Ralph took Rayanne shopping at some wonderful shops, they ice skated at Rockefeller Center, they frequented museums, and at times, they threw caution to the wind, acting like a couple of kids who were in love for the very first time.

CHAPTER 8

Dorian had finished that semester and had gone out of town with Henry for a few days, Ivory went to San Francisco to visit friends, and Rayanne stayed behind in New York. She was on her way home from work and had gotten caught in the rain long before she was able to get a taxi. When she arrived at her building, she climbed out of the cab, splashed in a puddle that had settled in the concrete, and she ran into the apartment building. She opened the door to the loft and the phone rang. She answered it as Sapphire climbed up onto the chair near her. "Ralph?" she said, shaking the water off.

"You all wet?"

"Yeah. It's coming down in buckets out there."

"I know. I just saw you from across the street."

"What are you doing across the street?"

"I was looking for you."

"Well I'm here, so what are you waiting for." With that, she hung up the phone. Rayanne sat and stroked Sapphire as she removed her wet shoes. Then, Ralph was at the door, and she let him in. Sapphire took one look at Ralph, gave a weak meow, and escaped from the room. Ralph and Rayanne stood facing each other in their wet clothing. "Looks like you're all wet, also," she said.

"I'm afraid I am."

"Let me get out of these things. You might want to give me yours and I can run them down to the dryer. I'll get you something to cover yourself," she smiled. He removed his clothes, wrapped the robe she handed him around himself, tying the sleeves around his waist.

"Mind if I light a fire," he asked.

"No, go ahead," she called back to him. "There are matches on the mantle." Ralph lit the fire and he lay on the floor in front of it. Rayanne took off her wet clothes and threw them along with Ralph's across the rod in her bathroom. She'd take them and dry them as soon as she could get into some dry clothes herself. She stood before the mirror in the bathroom, ran her fingers through her hair and braided it, and when she turned around, Ralph was standing behind her. She felt herself grow tense, nervous, as his body came to rest against her own.

"What are you doing in here," she said as her voice shook.

"I was lonesome for you."

"Were you," she whispered, hoping her voice came out in a normal tone.

"Yes," he said kissing the back of her neck. "You're shaking. Are you all right?"

"No," she replied, and the single word cracked as it escaped her throat. She could feel his breath on the side of her face. They'd been dating only a short while and she'd become very comfortable with him, but at that moment, his closeness made her weak. He turned her to face him, his arms slid around her slender waist, then he took her into his arms and kissed her. The kiss was hard at first, almost bruising. Rayanne extricated herself from him, and for a moment they stared at each other. As they did, she saw desire in his eyes that matched exactly what she was feeling. She lifted her hand to the side of his face, then she let it fall to her side. The blood coursed through her body and instantly she knew she wanted Ralph as much, perhaps more, than she thought possible. They kissed each other again and again as waves of passion pound through her, unmatched by anything she'd ever felt. They kissed until they became rapacious with their needs, and when their kisses just weren't enough, Ralph looked at her and whispered, "my woman. I'm going to make you my woman." He pulled her body against his male hardness. His tongue licked over her lips, and she allowed her tongue to play with his. His fingers came up and cupped her breasts and he kissed each of them through the fabric of her robe. Rayanne moved from him a little, allowing him to untie the sash and peeled the robe from her body and it fell carelessly to the floor. He reached for her again and his lips returned to her nipples. As he nibbled them, she felt the pressure of his teeth connecting with her bare nipples which sent spurts of passion through her body. Ralph's strong hands roamed over Rayanne's silky body, and, in one swift movement, he lifted her up, carried her across the room, and they fell across the bed together. She knew that he was completely aware of how much she was enjoying being with him. It was unbearably thrilling, and she didn't try to conceal her feelings. They kissed and caressed each other until they were overwhelmed with passion. Ralph was completely nude now and Rayanne began placing little kisses on his chest. They made love that night and she was overwhelmed by a combination of pleasure and pain. Rayanne awoke the following morning next to Ralph. She opened her eyes, and saw him propped on an elbow, looking at her.

"Good morning, Beautiful," he said, reveling in the sight of her.

"Good morning," she responded, running her fingers through her thick hair. The braid had come loose during the night and thick locks dangled about her face. "How long have you been awake?" She reached for the covers and drew them close to her neck.

"Not long," he said, admiring her pecan tan complexion, her brown eyes glowing with happiness in her pretty almond shaped face, as she looked up at him and met his warm gaze.

"You should've awakened me," she said, staring towards the window. She couldn't believe what was happening to her. Could she be falling in love, she asked herself silently.

"I didn't have the heart to disturb sleeping beauty," he remarked, unable to take his eyes off her. She's beautiful, the face of an angel, he thought, while Rayanne wondered just how long he'd been watching her sleep. She wasn't used to having a man beside her when she waked, but Ralph was there, it was a long time coming and it felt good. He was smiling down at her. My God, I must look a mess, she thought, trying to move away from him but he held her there. He said, "where are you going? I want you right here with me." Rayanne looked at him, then relaxed in his arms. A warm pleasant feeling enveloped her and at that moment, she knew she cared about this man.

"Baby, making love with you last night," Ralph was saying, filled with the thought of the taste of her on his lips, "was like a pipe dream that I've had all of my adult life. You're the most exciting woman I've ever met. You're wonderful."

"An experienced city man like yourself find a little country girl like me exciting, wonderful. That was how you described me, wasn't it?"

"Yes. You are fantastic."

"Fantastic, too?" she teased.

"Will you cut it out. Let's suffice it to say that you're the best and now you're my woman. You belong to me." She'd liked the sound of possessiveness in his voice.

Later that day Ralph went home, and once he was gone and out of Rayanne's reach, she missed him. She ached for his presence, his arms around her, his lips on hers, she missed all of him. When Ralph and Rayanne fell in love, it burned like a fire out of control.

The months that followed brought about days of adventure and nights of pleasure. They found that they had a lot in common, they shared a fascination with the same things, their relationship blossomed, and when Rayanne returned to South Carolina for a brief visit, Ralph accompanied her, and everyone who met Ralph thought her choice was good.

***

"Oh damn," Ivory said from her bedroom, rummaging through her drawer. She entered the den with the small box that she'd been keeping her money. The box was empty, all the money she'd saved for the past months was gone.

After they searched the entire loft, still unable to locate the money, Rayanne asked, "Ivory, are you sure you kept the money in your room? You didn't put it into a bank?"

"No, I had it in this box right there in the drawer," Ivory said pointing towards the dresser. "I took out some money for groceries and my trip and I left the rest of it in the box in the drawer. It was there yesterday," she said. Then it came to her. She had her answer. Cal had spent the night with her and had seen her take the money from the box to count it. Ivory thought it strange that when she awoke in the morning, he had already left. He'd never done that before, she'd always shown him out.

Cal didn't call or visit for a while after that. Ivory confessed to the girls that he'd been doing drugs. Although she talked about killing Cal when she saw him again and the girls stressed that it was probably for the best if he didn't come back as they would be uncomfortable having a drug user and thief in the house, Ivory didn't appear to share their opinion.

***

The hair that had always hung smooth and silky down Ivory's back was now curly and nappy and clung too close to her head. Rayanne and Dorian noticed it as Ivory rushed passed them and into her room. "Ivory," Rayanne called after her, her mouth hanging open as she followed Ivory into her bathroom. Dorian was on their heels, "Ivory, what happened?" Rayanne asked?

"Look at this," Ivory screamed, lifting the locks, "look what that bitch did to my hair."

"What happened?" Dorian asked, touching Ivory's hair.
"It feels really rough."

"Hannah permed it. I asked her to use very mild chemicals and not to leave it in too long. Do you think she listened, hell no." Ivory looked at her hair in the mirror. "Look at this." She lifted a piece of hair and let it fall again. "What the hell am I gonna do now?"

"How long did she leave that stuff in?" Rayanne asked, examining Ivory's hair further.

"I don't know. She kept running all over the place, trying to do all the heads in New York, and when she finally came back to me, it was too late because this is what I got."

"Didn't she use a timer?" Rayanne asked, gently touching Ivory's hair.

"I don't know. Jesus, what am I gonna do. I have a shoot tomorrow afternoon, but how can I keep the appointment. I can't go any where looking like this," Ivory said. She'd been selected to do a layout for an ad campaign for a cosmetic line, and she'd wanted that job as much as she'd wanted to breathe.

"Your hair always looks so nice, why would you want to have it permed?" Dorian asked.

"I wanted it to look nice so I thought if I had a little curl put in, it would look good. I wanted it to look nice for my shoot but that's out now. I can't go any where looking like this." Ivory lifted her hair and frowned in the mirror at what she saw.

Rayanne looked thoughtful, she knew her own beautician had performed miracles on her hair, so it was worth a try. "Let me give Elayne a call. She's very good, she may be able to help."

"My hair won't take any more chemicals, Rayanne. I'm just going to have to cut this shit off and hope like hell that it grows back," Ivory said, but she loved her hair, she had been growing it a long time and cutting it was the last thing she wanted to do. She usually had it trimmed a couple of times a year, but she never really cut it. "They're never gonna hire me looking like this," Ivory said turning to go to the phone, thinking she'd better call the agency to let them know that she couldn't do the job, that they'd have to get someone else.

"Ivory, wait a minute. Let me at least call Elayne and see whether she can take a look at your hair before you do anything," Rayanne said and waited for Ivory's response. Ivory lifted both hands in complete exasperation, Rayanne left to make the call. Afterwards, they went to Elayne's Beauty Salon. Elayne took one look at Ivory's hair, and said, "Good grief, what happened here? Who did you make mad?" She winked at Rayanne. "Oh, gee, all this is gonna have to go. Come sit in my chair." Elayne smiled at Dorian and Rayanne. Ivory looked back nervously at her friends as she obeyed and sat in Elayne's chair. Elayne sprayed Ivory's hair, pushed her fingers through it, added something from a bottle to saturate the hair from the roots to the ends, then she placed a plastic cap on Ivory's head and sat her under the dryer. Ivory's eyes rolled back and forth as the dryer buzzed. After about fifteen minutes, Elayne lifted the head of the dryer, checked Ivory's hair, started the dryer up again and pulled it back down onto Ivory's head. When Elayne was through working her magic from the shampoo bowl to moisturizers and conditioners, Ivory's hair hung in beautiful bouncing curls without further abuse of harsh chemicals, and the girls were so excited with the results that they pooled their money and gave Elayne a $15 tip and with Ivory's promise to return weekly to have her hair treated until it was back to normal. Ivory had every intention of keeping that promise and Elayne as her beautician. Ivory did that assignment and although she was quite good and she got other calls, she didn't get another job like that for a while. She was faced, once again, with the fact that it was important to have a decent portfolio. Well, she'd have it even if it meant working three jobs because she was still unwilling to borrow the money.

When Ivory had started seeing Cal again several weeks after the money had been taken, the girls told her she should make him return the money. She didn't of course and Rayanne wondered what Ivory was using for brains these days.

77

***

Rayanne awoke at dawn feeling energized, she was going to make something happen and she'd begin by getting an agent. She remembered meeting a man named Harry at a party, with whom she was impressed. They'd talked about her work, her aspirations and interest and he told her he thought her ideas had potential. With that thought, she went to the phone and dialed the number listed on Harry's business card. She was put through to Harry. "Miss Wilson, what can I do for you?"

"You probably don't remember me, but we met at a party at LaVoice's a while ago," she said, knowing he wouldn't remember her. There were only about five hundred people there that night.

"Of course I do. You're Rayanne Wilson, the young lady who's written several wonderful plays, you haven't been successful in placing them yet, but that will change. You've done some acting, but your passion is writing, am I right thus far?" Harry said.

"Yes, I'm that person," Rayanne said, pleased that he'd remembered her, but even happier when he said, her not having been successful in placing her work was about to change.

"Then, yes, I remember you. What can I do for you, Rayanne?"

"Well Mr.," Rayanne began, but Harry interrupted.

"Call me Harry, Rayanne. Everyone else around here does." There was something about Harry that made her feel at ease, and they made an appointment to meet in three weeks. Harry represented a number of clients and at the time of Rayanne's call, his calendar was booked and that included a trip abroad. Harry was wonderful, he was able to make her relax so much so that by the time they ended their conversation, she felt they were old friends.

Rayanne walked out onto the terrace and looked out over the city. Above, the sky was clear and blue and below, the traffic was bumper-to-bumper. She came back in and looked at the clock on the stove. The apartment was quiet at six-fifteen that morning. Ivory and Dorian would be getting up soon, she thought. Ivory was on the early shift at Jacko's that week, and Dorian had a modeling shoot, but that wasn't until noon.

The automatic timer on the coffee maker had already turned itself off and the kitchen was filled with the aroma of coffee. Rayanne put bread into the toaster and began scrambling eggs as she heard Ivory's shower start up. Minutes later, Ivory grabbed her shoulder bag and portfolio with the few good photos she had and rushed towards the front door. "Where are you off to in such a hurry? Aren't you going to have something to eat?" Rayanne asked.

"No, I don't have time. I'll grab a Danish at work, but I'll have a sip of that caffeine," Ivory said. "I've got to be at work a little earlier this morning to put in those hours because I've got an interview at ten." Rayanne handed Ivory a cup of coffee. "I hope this interview materializes into something." Ivory took a sip from the cup.

"So do I," Rayanne said. "Are we doing anything tonight?"

"I don't think so, but let me get back with you," Ivory said, taking another sip of coffee and handed the cup back to Rayanne. "See you tonight." With that, Ivory rushed out the door.

CHAPTER 9

"Ivory, are you coming?" Rayanne called out to her, knowing that Ivory was always the first to start getting dressed but the last to be ready.

"Come on slow poke," Dorian said. They were going to a fashion show and dancing afterwards.

"Be there in a sec," Ivory called out, sitting on the foot of her bed with the small box in which she kept her money, in her hands. She was saving for her portfolio... again. She opened the box, took a roll of bills from it, placing them on the bed. She then took some bills from her wallet, kissed them, adding them to the others bills from the box and returned all of the bills to the box. She placed the box on the top shelf in her closet for the night but tomorrow, she'd put the money into a bank where it would be safe and she'd keep it there until she had enough to get the photos she needed. She would've already had enough to have her portfolio if the money had not been stolen. But, that was a dead issue, and she'd never be that careless again.

The show was a barrage of beautifully dressed women gliding up and down the long runway, camera lights flashing, and all the while, Ivory wishing she were one of those girls. After the show, they had something to eat and went dancing at a nearby disco-theque. When Rayanne returned home that evening, she listened to the single message left on her machine, returned the call to Ralph, removed her makeup and went to bed. Although she had a full day and she was tired, she was unable to sleep. She had ideas for another play racing around in her head, and the first thing she came up with this time which was unusual, was the title. Usually, the title didn't come until further along in the story. "An Early Awakening," she'd whispered into the darkness of her bedroom, and she began to mentally build the story from that point on. The story was about a young boy coming to terms with his desire to become a doctor, during a time when some people weren't even aware of the existence of colored doctors. The death of his grand-mother had consumed him with guilt because he knew she was in pain and he did nothing to help. After storing those thoughts away in her brain, Rayanne felt she could now sleep. Not so, because her mind drifted home to her parents. She was aware that her father was working too hard and that bothered her. Time and time again she mentioned it to her mother, who expressed her concern as well, but always said it was his nature to work hard. Rayanne found that the longer she was away from her parents, the more she missed them. She tossed and turned, but still unable to sleep, she pushed the covers back and got out of bed. She pulled the drapes and peered out of the window at a dark and cold New York night, where the fog moved in and hung over the city like a wet blanket. This was a city where everything moved fast and where the crime rate was the highest in the country, and although she loved the city with all its pluses or minuses, Rayanne couldn't help but wonder what her life would be like had she not left South Caro-lina. She was certain it would've been different. Very different.

Rayanne was awakened by the sound of voices. Ivory and Cal were having an argument and from what she could hear, it was about money. "Get the hell out," she heard Ivory's angry voice saying and the door slammed shut. She got up and listened but there wasn't another sound.

Rayanne went to Ivory's bedroom door and knocked softly. "Ivory, are you all right."

"Yeah, I'm fine, just sleepy."

Rayanne walked away from the door, went into the kitchen and made a cup of herb tea. She sipped from the cup, while chew-ing up a Tylenol PM. She needed to get some sleep because tomor-row would be a busy day at the bank. Sapphire made an entrance and Rayanne picked her up. "Can't sleep either, huh? Come with me and I'll give you a little milk." She walked over to the refrigerator. "This ought to help," she said, poured some milk into a saucer and put Sapphire down to it. She watched as the cat licked up the milk. "You were hungry, weren't you?" When Sapphire was finished, Rayanne walked slowly back to her bedroom. She allowed her heavy terry cloth robe to slip from her shoulders, down her arms to the floor, and she crawled back into bed. It wasn't long before she drifted off to sleep. With the job at the bank and writing, sleep was the one thing she never seemed to get enough of. Sleep was the most precious gift that an exhausted mind could give itself.

Rayanne awoke, blinking and squinting against the sun that streamed through the windows. She shaded her eyes with her hand a moment, then she got up and closed the drapes. After taking a shower, she climbed back into bed, intending to stay there only a few minutes. She pulled the covers close and smiled as her mind drifted to Ralph and the thought of how much she enjoyed their walks, their heart to heart talks and the sharing that took place between them.

Ralph was the only son of parents who separated when he was just a boy. His father raised him and he didn't see his mother again until his freshman year in college. When he told her he didn't need her then, she left again and the last he'd heard, she was living somewhere in California. Rayanne found that aside from that, it was amazing how much they had in common, and how completely happy he made her. She looked at the clock, sprung out of bed at eight-thirty, combed her hair and slapped on a little makeup. Once outside, she got a taxi to work.

***

That evening Rayanne typed a couple of short chapters for her new story, showered, took a container of strawberries from the refrigerator and ran cold water over them. She poured a cup of coffee. The cabinets were almost bare. There wasn't much left on the shelves in the refrigerator either. It was Ivory's week to buy groceries, but she hadn't. She probably forgot again, as she very often did. Rayanne ate the strawberries and sipped coffee while the air dripped with silence. She was amazed at how well the loft was insulated. The traffic could only be heard when a window or the French doors were opened. Nothing from the outside world could enter unless it was invited. She'd spent the night alone in the loft. Dorian went on a deep sea fishing trip with friends, and Ivory was in Chicago, compliments of Patti, where her art show was being held. As Rayanne relaxed and enjoyed the strawberries, she wondered what her mother would say about her eating habit, since she'd always stressed the importance of eating healthy meals. Rayanne picked up the phone and called home. Everyone was fine. She dialed Harry's number and discussed her new project. "Sounds good," he'd said, "it's refreshingly original. Although Harry believed in Rayanne's abilities and never gave up on her, he'd not been successful in locating a buyer for the play she submitted.

The following day, Rayanne put in a full day at the bank and on her way home, she stopped off at the supermarket to pick up some groceries. Ralph was joining her for dinner and she'd make the cabbage and sausage dish he loved so much. She also picked up a bunch of cut flowers. She put the milk, meat and eggs in the refrigerator, and she put the flowers in water before rushing out again, this time to shop for bathing suits. Ralph was taking her on a trip where they would bask in the sun, was all he'd said. He certainly was intriguing.

CHAPTER 10

On a great cloudless day in late October, Ralph and Rayanne walked along the beach hand in hand, in beautiful San Juan. The temperatures were in the eighties, so unlike it was five hours earlier when they boarded a flight from New York, leaving temperatures ranging from 25 to 35 degrees, with the golden sunlight struggling to warm the clear, crisp day. The flight brought them to a warm sunny climate, a tropical paradise, where they would spend five glorious days, engaging in wonderful daily activities and nights of dining, dancing and gambling.

Puerto Rico is a top Caribbean destination because of the easy air access from the U.S., and although Ralph had visited other cities in the Caribbean, San Juan was his favorite and he was certain it would be Rayanne's as well. They checked in at the beautiful and elegant Condado Plaza Hotel and Casino, which offered fabulous dining that would satisfy the varying tastes of people around the world. The hotel also included a casino, and coffee shop as well as a flower and gift shops. Rayanne found that San Juan offered a tourist vast excitement. The night life alone is one that is considered to be legendary, full of glitter. They enjoyed Las Vegas type shows, late night casino action and the discotheques, where the sound of popular American songs drifted through the air for listening and dancing pleasures. Since Puerto Rico is a United States Commonwealth, currency is the dollar and Americans can enter the island without the necessity of Visas or passports, and they can spend the all American dollar all day, every day.

Rayanne and Ralph were relieved to shed their winter clothing for beautiful beaches with silky white sand and water so clear that the coral reefs could be seen weaving back and forth in the ocean. They walked along a secluded part of the beach, and Ralph lifted Rayanne up and carried her over his shoulder out into the ocean. When they emerged from the ocean, they ventured in and out of coves and nooks and gathered sea shells on the shore, and after a couple of hours of enjoying the breathtaking scenery, they stopped off at a nearby restaurant and gulped their food with an urgency to return to the beach. In doing so, they were approached by a representative for one of the hotels that offered a tour the following day. They accepted. It was a timesharing tour, and the trip included a tour of their hotel, a trip to a winery, Old San Juan, a ten minute film and a full course lunch.

Ralph and Rayanne returned to the beach with their sandals in hand, and they watched as the waves rushed up and licked the rocks. "This is incredible," Rayanne said as she stood planted in the sand. It was magical, like anything can happen, the land, the sun, the surf. It was unlike anything she'd ever experienced. They ventured out until the water washed up against their ankles and white foam ran through their toes. "This is a wonderful surprise, honey," she said to Ralph and sighed.

"I'm glad you like it. There is so much more to see, and I want to show it all to you," he said, and they walked along together in silence, their fingers entwined, taking in the many splendors. They stopped walking for a moment and looked into each other's eyes. They stood together, listening to the surf and watching the waves lick at the sand as the tide rolled in and out. Rayanne felt as though she were drifting, being carried away by the ocean. That evening they entered the dining room to the soft murmur of people talking, music playing and beautifully dressed people walking around the vast chandelier room. The maitre d' who greeted them had a quick flashy white teeth smile, he led them to a secluded table near a low open window where they could hear the ocean rushing and slapping against the large rocks, and they relaxed and took in the hotel's wonderful atmosphere. Rayanne looked out and was surprised that it had started to rain and the shower mingled with the surf. The moon was serene and high in the sky, casting a silver reflection on the ocean. "Have you ever seen anything like it?" Ralph asked.

"No, never," Rayanne admitted, noticing that the lights and the moon caused the rain drops to resemble diamonds falling from heaven. They ordered and fell silent and the only sound was the lapping of the waves. The waiter brought them a tall concoction each with a tiny umbrella.

"These look fabulous," Rayanne said before sipping her drink.

"They are."

"You said you were here before."

"Yes, six years ago. The place has changed a lot since then."

"Six years is a long time, and I'm sure the changes are for the better."

"On all counts," he said and fell silent. The salad and shrimp cocktails arrived.

"There are some things about your past that you don't like to talk about much, do you?" she asked, remembering when they first met and he wouldn't say much about himself. Although they'd talked and shared a lot, she knew there were still things he'd kept private.

"I suppose there are some things that should be left in the dark and forgotten past."

"I see," Rayanne said looking into his eyes questioning. One of the things she'd liked most about him was their sharing, but there were times when she knew he could be selfish with his thoughts, that there was still so much she didn't know about him, so much he kept to himself. Ralph looked at her and he took a deep breath. He explained that he brought his wife there on their 5th Anniversary, a second honeymoon. They spent their first honeymoon there and loved it so much that they returned. Problems came up in their marriage, so they came back hoping to recapture what they had.

"This place was paradise for us, a place of magic. The last two years, we were together as husband and wife, but we were going in different directions," he explained.

"I don't suppose it helped much, coming back here, I mean," Rayanne said.

"I don't suppose it did because as it turned out, she got pregnant right here as near as we could figure it, she miscarried in her sixth month and within a year, we were divorced," Ralph said.

His eyes wandered out to the ocean. Rayanne felt his agony and his loss and even though she wanted to comfort him, make him forget the past, she had no words for him. He looked at her and said, "Rayanne, I didn't bring you here for any reason other than the fact that I love this place so much, I love you and want to associate this place with wonderful memories. Please believe that."

"I do," Rayanne said, "and I'm sorry that it couldn't hold all happy memories for you."

"Don't be. We had some great times, but Mary and I were just never meant to be. We tried but it just didn't work out," he said, and Rayanne was amazed that when Ralph spoke again, his voice didn't appear to ring of any remorse. He explained that after the divorce, Mary moved back to Massachusetts to be near her parents. They spoke occasionally by phone, but didn't see much of each other after the move. Ralph had gone through so much in his life. He'd lost a woman he loved and their child in that freak auto accident, he met and married someone who later had a miscarriage and the marriage ended in a divorce. If anyone had experienced a string of bad luck, it was Ralph, but she hoped from now on, he would be happy, and she would do whatever she could to help.

They finished their drinks and dinner mostly in silence, and they went into the lounge and enjoyed the singer's performance. They heard some of their favorite tunes, danced and stole kisses while on the dance floor.

"Have I told you how much I'm enjoying all this, being here with you?" she said, running her arms up around his neck.

"Yes, but you can tell me as often as you'd like," he said and smiled into her eyes.

"When you look at me that way, honey," Rayanne whispered, "you put me in a warm, vulnerable frame of mind, but you know that, don't you?"

When the song ended, he whispered in her ear, "Are we about ready?"

"I am if you are," she responded, and they walked back to the table and collected her purse. She'd talk him into taking one more little walk along the beach before turning in. There was little evidence that it had rained earlier. Rayanne kicked off her shoes and ran across the sand towards the water. Ralph took off one shoe, danced on one foot and alternated until he, too, had removed his shoes. He rolled up his pant legs and ran after her. She looked back, saw him coming and she ran straight into the water. He caught up with her and there in the moonlight, they created an evening that they'd remember even in old age.

***

Just as the sun began to rise and daylight faded the darkness of night, Rayanne awoke nestled in Ralph's arms. He was opening doors within her that allowed her to do things she never thought she'd do. Ralph woke up. "Good morning gorgeous," he said.

"Morning, yourself big guy," she responded and they held each other and enjoyed the quiet for a while. Later they swam in the hotel pool, went into the shops along the strip and purchased souvenirs, and at 12:30 they were met in their hotel lobby by the time sharing representative. They toured a hotel, had lunch and were driven to Old San Juan where they walked over the cobblestone streets, and they enjoyed the many cultural aspects of the city. And, although Old San Juan offered sophisticated and up to date conveniences, you could go back in time viewing the Spanish Colonial buildings with balconies dating back to the 17th and 18th centuries. Many of the buildings housed superb restaurants, craft shops, boutiques, galleries and museums, and, the outdoor air fair was also something in itself, all of which they wanted to see again before leaving Puerto Rico. They rode back to the El San Juan Hotel and Casino where they watched the film and toured another part of the hotel where the rooms and suites were of the finest decor. Ralph didn't buy into the plan, but he took the literature and promised he'd give it some serious thought. They spent their days walking on the beach, sightseeing and doing countless other things that they enjoyed, but, as with anything good, the time had passed much too quickly.

Rayanne awoke early the day before their departure. Ralph was still asleep. She kissed him on his forehead and eased out of bed. She called her parents to let them know that they would return to New York the following day. Then she called Harry. Afterwards, she walked out onto the private balcony and gazed out at the most beautiful stretch of beaches, watching as the palm trees swayed and danced to the silent tune of the early morning breezes. The ocean with its timeless waves came in and out, and the waters looked as though they were divided, one half of the ocean was blue, the other, green. The view was breathtaking.

Rayanne quickly and quietly put on a yellow shorts set over a bikini, she pulled her hair up into a pony tail and placed a yellow headband around her head. She left the room, took the elevator from the 11th floor, walked through the lobby admiring the decor

88

and out to the beach. She wasn't on the beach long before she pulled off her sandals and walked along the edge of the water. She lifted her head, closed her eyes, enjoying the sun on her face and the sound of the ocean. There was something ever so sooth-ing, so calming about the sound of the ocean. Rayanne walked out into the water as it raced back and forth, caressing only her feet at first and as the waves grew, the water, mingling with the fine grains of sand, began to creep up her legs moving closer to her knees. This is wonderful but it will soon be over she thought as she continued to walk along the beach. Then she began to run and as she did, she peeled off her shorts and top, flung them to the ground, and dove into the water. After swimming and playing and just enjoying the water for more than an hour, Rayanne gath-ered her things and began walking slowly back towards the hotel, when she saw Ralph's tall masculine body approaching her.

"You finally woke up, huh" she teased him.

"I missed you," he said. "I looked for you but you were gone."

"I wanted to come out here before it got too crowded. Besides you were sleeping so peacefully, I didn't want to disturb you."

"Baby, next time disturb me."

"I will," she said, facing Ralph.

"Weren't you a little intimidated coming out here alone, dressed like that?" he asked, eyeing her.

"There's nothing wrong with a little fear in your life every once in a while. It makes you feel alive," she teased.

"Oh you are alive. You can prove that by me," Ralph said, and they laughed.

"Tomorrow, we'll leave all this behind," Rayanne looked around thoughtfully, "but it certainly has been wonderful."

"It doesn't have to end tomorrow. We can stay a few more days if you want."

"I'd love to honey, but I suppose we'd better get back to the real world. I have a couple of meetings scheduled for Friday."

"I thought you said you had one meeting," Ralph said raising his finger.

"I did but I called Harry to run something by him, and he wants to meet with me also."

"And, all this has to happen on Friday?"

"Yes, but aside from that, I promised Ivory and Dorian that yes, I'd go to the Lakers-Knicks game with them."

"I thought they both were away."

"Yeah, but they'll be back by then."

"The game is Friday night?"

"Yes," she replied.

"My baby has become a New York Knickerbocker fan," he said.

"Yes, sort of."

"I got you sort of," he joked and took Rayanne's face and held it. "Happy?"

"I'm ecstatic," she answered truthfully, "and you?"

"Very much so. I've never been happier," he replied.

"I'm glad."

"What did I do to deserve you?" he said.

She answered, "you were just born lucky I guess."

"Tell me something. If you had one wish, what would it be?" he asked.

"You can't ask me a question like that." .

"Why not?"

"You can't just give me one wish, you have to give me at least two."

"Okay then, if you had two wishes, what would they be?"

"Family and friends, health and happiness outweighing everything else, I'd wish for the love of the man of my dreams, and a hit play," she answered and smiled.

"You've got me," he said.

"I know that, but I get two wishes, remember, and I want both. In fact, I want it all," she said and smiled wickedly at him.

"And you'll have it. It takes time, but it'll happen."

"I know it will, and I'm being patient. If there's anything that I'm certain about, it's that I'm going to have a successful writing career," she said with conviction.

***

Ralph drove their rented car to Old San Juan, they shopped and took snap shots of the French colonial architecture. They observed the largest cruise ship ports, sneaked into one of the ocean liners and they giggled like two children at their success. Then they were off to other interests in the city where a variety of cultural festivities punctuated San Juan. It was evident that the island was working hard at improving its tourism product as Ralph continued to notice the changes since his earlier visits. They took shots of the lush rain forest, the water falls, wild orchids, the ferns and the towering palm trees. Afterwards, they drove back to the hotel, ate lunch, gambled and later, they walked on the beach. The sun had moved slowly across the sky. Then, it appeared to fall and stopped just long enough to meet the ocean and cast a fiery path that reflected across the waters, extending from the west almost to their feet, where they were planted in the sand, before it suddenly sank and vanished.

Dinner consisted of a dish made of chicken, tomatoes, bits of sausage, mushrooms and water chestnuts. They drank wine, ate chocolate cake for dessert, and afterwards, they visited the casino where Rayanne once again became mesmerized by the one armed bandit slot machines. She went from one machine to another. Afterwards, they took a final walk on the beach where they heard an Ike and Tina Turner's tune playing somewhere in the distance. Sometime after midnight, they returned to the hotel and packed. After breakfasting early and looking out over the ocean once more, they rode most of the way back to the airport in silence, and they purchased a collar for Sapphire before taking the flight back to New York. The plane rolled down the runway and climbed away from the island, leaving Ralph and Rayanne with the thought that they would return, and soon.

CHAPTER 11

Ivory and Rayanne entered the loft wearing sweat suits, after having spent an hour jogging. Although Rayanne had moved into a permanent position at the bank, she continued to write, hoping for that big break. "Sooner or later, something's gotta happen," she told Ivory, removing the towel from her neck and flopping down onto the couch. Her dream of becoming a successful writer was still uppermost in her mind.

"It's just a matter of time, girl," Ivory answered, going into the kitchen to get a bottle of spring water. "Want some water?" she called out.

"Yeah, bring me one." Rayanne replied turning on the stereo.

Ivory returned and sat the bottles on the table. She picked up a magazine from the coffee table, studied the face of the girl who adorned its cover and said, "this is gonna be me one day," she paused, thinking what it would be like to be a top model, known all over the world. Then she said, "I hope."

"Your face is gonna be on that cover and many others one day. Ivory, you're gorgeous so you know it's gonna happen. One day we're all gonna be rich, successful career women."

Ivory had given up working on a temporary basis after having had her appendix removed and bearing the medical expenses alone because the temporary service that she worked through didn't have insurance coverage. She'd learned that in order to get some real benefits, she needed a real job. She applied for the job in an accounting firm and was hired. She'd have insurance coverage even if she didn't have enough money left to buy a pack of cigarettes.

Rayanne uncapped the bottle of water, took a sip from it and opened the newspaper. She gave a couple of sections to Ivory and spread a section onto the coffee table. "Goodness," she said taking another sip of water, "every time I open the paper or put on the TV, all I see is crime. What is this world coming to."

"I don't think it's gonna get any better either," Ivory said.

"It's no telling what the next ten years will bring," Rayanne said, looking at Ivory, and wishing that people would just wake up and live.

"You venture that far. What about next week? To tell the truth, I'm afraid of what may happen to change our lives in the next twenty-four hours."

"I know," Rayanne shook her head sadly, then after a moment she changed the subject, "Are you feeling any better about your job?"

"It's okay," Ivory responded, "at least I've got medical and dental benefits. Oh, I didn't tell you what happened today. You remember Lila?"

"Your new receptionist?"

"Yeah, she's been with us almost six months," Ivory answered. Rayanne didn't realize it'd been that long. "Anyway, you remember I loaned her $600."

"Yeah." Rayanne remembered that Ivory had made a killing on her Income Tax return that year and although she didn't think it was a good idea for Ivory to loan someone she hardly knew that kind of money because it just wasn't smart, Ivory had gone on and made the loan anyway. Ivory explained that the agreement was that Lila would pay her $100 a pay period, $200 a month, until the debt was paid.

"Well, that bitch quit her job a week ago."

"Oh no," Rayanne said, "what about your money?"

"Wait a minute," Ivory paused a minute to turn the page of her newspaper. Rayanne wondered whether she was going to finish this story and would it be that night. She sat silently and waited. "Lila quit a week ago. Wait, I'm getting a little ahead of myself," Ivory said. "She actually resigned over a week ago, but because my boss has been sick and we haven't found a replacement for

Lila, she agreed to work three weeks before leaving. Well, she paid me $100 a pay period as scheduled until she'd paid $300. Yesterday she gave me two post dated checks, one for $100 to be cashed today, and one for $200 dated two weeks from today."

"Okay, okay," Rayanne said, "so you are getting your money back?"

Ivory explained that she sometimes has lunch with Johnny who worked in payroll and who told her that Lila had given him a completed form to terminate her direct deposit. She cashed Lila's first check when she was on her way to work that morning, figuring in two weeks, she'd cash the last check. Well Rayanne thought, she wouldn't be getting all of her money back since Lila had terminated her direct deposit, but Ivory explained that she wouldn't have, but Johnny told her what Lila tried to do, that she owed others and was going to give all of them the shaft. "Guess what I did," Ivory said.

"Lord, I can't imagine, but do tell," Rayanne's curiosity piqued.

"I changed the date on the last check and I went right back to the bank and cashed it too."

"You did," Rayanne squealed.

"You damn right I did. Johnny told me he could hold the change for only a few days, then he'd have to put it through and after that, she'd be getting her check in her hand. In the meantime, I would've been holding a $200 check on a closed account or an account with insufficient funds."

"You didn't. You cashed the second check?" Rayanne smiled, immensely pleased. "This is just too good."

"Isn't it though," Ivory agreed.

"You little devil, but that was a good move, and I'm proud of you."

"That heffa was gonna go back to LA without paying me my damn $200."

"Girl, you're too much," Rayanne said with delight.

"Of course," Ivory said and laughed. "I've got my money but when she's hit with all those returned check charges, she'll know not to fuck with me."

"I'll bet," Rayanne said, and they laughed some more, but their gaiety was short lived, as they were startled when they heard the entrance door slam shut and the sound of Dorian crying.

"Damn him," Dorian said tearfully. Rayanne got up from the couch and rushed over to Dorian with Ivory closely behind her. Dorian and Henry had an argument. He told her he was ending the relationship. "I'm too demanding, he says," Dorian said. "He thinks I'm taking him away from his home and work too much." She shook her head and lifted a hand in exasperation.

"Why that son of a bitch," Ivory said, feeling the anger well up inside her. She couldn't believe it, because after all, wasn't it Henry who was always calling Dorian, trying to control her life?

"What's gotten into him?" Rayanne asked puzzled.

"I don't know. Sometimes he acts at though he can't live without me, then, this," Dorian said looking hurt and confused.

"Try not to let it get you down," Rayanne said as the doorbell rang.

Ivory answered it. "Henry? What are you doing here?" she asked.

"I'd like to see Dorian please," he said, wringing his hands together.

"I don't think Dorian wants to see you," Ivory said with an attitude.

"Please, I just need to see her for a few minutes." The man was visibly upset.

"What did you do to her? Don't you know the girl's in love with you?" Ivory said with a frown on her face.

"Yes Ivory, I do know that, and I'm sorry. I don't suppose I handled things very well. That's why I need to talk to her. If I could see her, I believe we can straighten all this out. Please," he begged. Dorian appeared and Rayanne was on her heels.

"It's okay," Dorian said.

"Are you sure," Ivory said, a hand on Dorian's shoulder.

"Yes," Dorian said.

"Let us know if you need us," Rayanne said, and she and Ivory left the foyer with Ivory giving Henry a look.

When Henry and Dorian were alone, he said, "I was afraid you wouldn't see me."

"Why are you here, Henry?"

"Honey, I'm here to see you. I didn't want to leave things the way they were between us."

"Henry, you just told me you want to end the relationship. How am I supposed to feel?"

"I didn't mean that. It came out all wrong."

"How many ways can you say you don't love me or want to see me anymore?" She headed for the living room with Henry following closely behind. They stood before the window.

"I do love you."

"Then, what the hell were you trying to say to me, Henry? Will you tell me that?"

"I don't know what I'm doing anymore. All I know is that when you left me back there tonight, I felt like my world was coming apart."

"What do you want from me? You want me to show up when you want, but when it comes to something that I want, it's a no go. Is that it?"

"No, that's not it at all. I mean, that's how it appears, but that's not the way it is. I love you, Dorian, very much."

"I still don't know what it is that you want from me."

"I just want you to continue to love me. That's all I can say right now," he said. That's asking an awful lot, Dorian thought.

"You want me to put my life on hold until you decide what you want to do with yours. That's what you want, but do you think that's fair?" Dorian asked.

"No, I don't suppose it is, but I don't want to lose you," he said.

"You don't want to lose Olympia either," she said.

"Yes, that's right, but what I feel for her is nothing compared to what I feel for you." Henry smoothed his hair back. "I want you, Dorian," he paused a moment, "In all the time that we've been seeing each other, we've never had a serious argument." Dorian looked at him, but she didn't speak. "I guess I took it for granted that you'd always be there for me in whatever capacity I needed, but I was wrong, and it didn't occur to me until you said good-bye back there tonight, just how wrong I was. I don't have to tell you how lost I felt. Dorian, I love you, and I need you in my life."

"I feel the same way, but I'm not going to sit around and put my life on hold while you carry on with yours. To hell with that," she spat out.

"I'm not asking you to do that. I just don't want to lose you," he said.

Dorian looked at Henry. Then she walked away from the window and sat on the couch, as Henry followed and sat beside her. "This is all about what you want," she said.

"Baby, I just want you to be patient." He reached for her hands.

"I have been patient, very patient," she said pulling her hands away.

"Just bear with me a while, I promise I'll work things out so that we can be together," he said. Dorian looked at Henry skeptically. "You believe me, don't you?"

"I'm just wondering how much of what you're saying is true."

"All of it. Please believe me." When he reached for her this time, she looked at him a moment before she slowly went into his arms and they kissed. After holding her a moment, he asked, "Are you all right?"

"I am considering all that's happened," she said.

"I know baby, but everything's going to be fine. If we can work this out, I promise to never take you for granted again, and I will always be there for you," he said and when Henry left, he left Dorian with the promise of hope for a future for them.

In the months that followed, Henry did spend more time with Dorian and everything went back to normal, or so Rayanne and Ivory thought until Dorian went on a trip to Mexico and Henry called the night before she returned. That was when Rayanne and Ivory learned that Dorian had made the trip with someone other than Henry. They were surprised when they were sitting around the breakfast table looking at pictures Dorian brought back from her trip. Dorian hadn't told them who had gone with her but when the face of a man who appeared to be Mexican showed up in too many of the photos, they were certain who her traveling companion was. When Dorian was questioned about the mystery man, she said he was just a friend.

"Damn," Ivory said getting up from the table, "this yeast infection is about to drive me crazy. I'm scratching myself raw." Dorian and Rayanne followed her to the den.

"Have you seen a doctor?" Rayanne asked.

"Not yet."

"What are you waiting for?" Dorian asked.

"I've got some of that vaginal cream left," Rayanne said, "but I don't have an applicator. I had that mess a couple of months ago, and I was so glad when it finally went away."

"Hand that cream over. I think I've got an applicator," Ivory said. Rayanne went into her room, got the tube and returned to the den. She handed it to Ivory. "This should work," Ivory said and began reading the label.

"If it's a simple yeast infection," Rayanne said, "but you should still see a doctor."

"Not if this works," Ivory said. "Hey, I want to show y'all my portfolio."

"You got the pictures," Dorian asked excitedly. It took long, hard hours to replace the money that was stolen and to make extra money to complete the portfolio, but Ivory had done it, and she didn't make the same mistake by keeping the money in the loft. When she had saved what she needed, she withdrew the money from the bank and had the pictures done. Ivory rushed off to her room, Dorian picked up Sapphire and stroked her, and when Ivory returned with her portfolio, she sat between the girls and began to slowly flip the pages.

"Oooh Ivory, these are great," Rayanne said.

"Yeah, they certainly are," Dorian agreed.

"I'm pleased with them. Beginning Monday morning, I'm gonna hit all the top modeling agencies in New York and see what happens," Ivory said. Both girls had done some modeling, and although Dorian had gotten far more assignments than Ivory, as yet, their success wasn't as great as either had hoped.

"Well, you've got some sensational shots here," Dorian said. When they finished looking at the photos, Ivory put the portfolio away.

"Knock 'em dead girl," Rayanne said, picked up a book from the table and studied its cover.

"How is that book?" Dorian asked tucking her feet under her body, beginning to do her homework.

"It's good so far. I'm a little more than half way through. We're going to discuss it when we meet next Wednesday," Rayanne answered. She'd joined a book club and they met once a month to discuss a selected book, and she enjoyed the different points of view she received from the group.

After a moment, Ivory said, "Let's go home this weekend," Spontaneity was a big part of that girl's character.

"That's an idea," Dorian said, looking up from her notebook.

"What are we going to do for money," Rayanne asked.

"We'll charge it," Ivory said. "What do you say?"

Rayanne considered for a moment, then lifting her shoulders said, "Sure, that'll work." Ivory still could talk her into doing just about anything. "Should we call and let the folks know we're coming?" Rayanne asked looking from Ivory to Dorian.

"No, let's surprise them," Ivory said.

"That'll work too," Rayanne said.

"It's going to be great seeing your families again," Dorian said looking forward to the trip.

They took a flight out of New York that Friday evening, and Rayanne and Ivory's parents were surprised, but as always, they were happy when the girls came home.

They went to a local night club. The Manhattans were appearing, and the feature artist was a singer the girls hadn't heard of.

"Who is that girl?" Ivory asked, after the artist began to sing.

"Someone said Regina Belle," Rayanne answered and stated, "I've never heard of her but that girl has a dynamite voice. She's going places."

"Good grief, she's blowing everyone else out. That girl can jam," Dorian said. Ivory looked at Dorian and before she could say anything, Dorian said, "I know, I want to be black so bad." They laughed.

"You're damn right," Ivory said. They enjoyed the first set, then they stood and waited on a long line to the ladies room. When they returned to their table, they ordered more drinks, danced between shows and enjoyed the last set. If they thought Regina Belle was good in the first set, the girl absolutely turned out the second set. Late Sunday night, they returned to New York, Dorian had an important message on her answering machine. She was one of a couple of dozen models who'd been interviewed for a shoot in Europe. Many of the girls left after being told they'd be called. The usual story, Dorian remembered thinking. The message on her machine was from one of the top New York modeling agencies, asking her to call.

"It's probably just for a second interview which won't amount to much," Dorian said.

"It's more than that. You're going to Europe, kiddo," Rayanne said. "I'm proud of you."

"I think maybe that's a bit premature," Dorian said.

"I'll bet you're one of the girls who gets the job. I just know it," Rayanne said.

"Take her word for it, Dorian," Ivory put in. "Rayanne usually knows these things. She has good instincts. Besides, what are we going to do?" Ivory said, tilting her head to the side like an elementary school teacher awaiting a response from her students.

"Think positively," Dorian and Rayanne said in unison.

***

Dorian got the assignment and went to Europe, Ivory got the promotion in the firm where she was working and Rayanne's writing was improving. Everything was going well, too well until Rayanne was awaken one morning before daybreak to a persistent knock at her door. Since Cal seemed to be over constantly now, she'd began locking her door before going to bed. Cal was a drug user and a thief and a combination like that was unpredictable. The knocking continued. At first, Rayanne thought she was dreaming. She'd taken a sleeping pill before going to bed that night and she was sleeping soundly. She, dazed from the pill, opened the door and there stood Ivory in her night gown with a frightened look on her face. "Ivory, what's wrong."

"It's Cal," Ivory replied, looking nervously towards her bedroom door, "I..I think he's dead." Dorian had joined the girls and they went into Ivory's room. Cal was dead, only no one knew what had caused his death, at least neither of them did at the time.

Rayanne called Cal's father. It appeared Cal had died of a drug overdose. He'd been using drugs for years, and after they met his father, it appears he was aware of his son's involvement with drugs but like many parents, he couldn't force his son to quit or get help. Cal had kept his drug use a secret, mostly because he injected the drugs under his toe nails, which left no visible marks on his body. And, because of the position Cal's father held with the Police Department, there was limited publicity. Neither, Rayanne or Dorian cared much for Cal, mainly because of the way he treated Ivory, but they certainly didn't want to see him dead.

Ivory changed after that. She didn't joke around as she once did, she didn't go out much with the girls, and she didn't date.

CHAPTER 12

Rayanne's wish to have a hit play came sooner than she expected. Although, she'd hoped it would happen, she was realistic. She knew one had to pay his dues, and something of the magnitude as her hopes and dreams were, took time, a lot of time. She'd known people who'd waited a lifetime to have their hopes and dreams realized.

Rayanne had just celebrated her 23rd birthday two weeks before when Harry called her. "Rayanne," He said, "are you sitting down?"

"Yes, Harry. Why? What's up?" Rayanne asked.

"I think we've found a buyer for your play."

"You what?" Rayanne asked, excitedly.

"We've got some people who are showing interest in, Papa, Come Home," he said. That was the most recent play that Rayanne had written, after having written several that went no where, fast.

"Harry, what exactly does that mean?" her excitement mounting.

"It means that someone wants to buy your play," he said.

"Oh my God," Rayanne was flabbergasted, "I don't believe

it."

"Believe it, honey, because it's true." Rayanne wasn't sure what to say or do. From some of her earlier conversations with Harry, when something like this happens, it was a big step in a writer's career. She hadn't had anything like this to happen to her before, and now that her dream was materializing she was speechless. "Well, if you're interested in looking over the contract and signing on the dotted line," he said. "we'll be in business." Rayanne had given Harry full authority to negotiate contracts for her work. She trusted him and his judgment, implicitly. He asked, "are you interested?" Interested, she thought. Of course, she was interested. When do I sign, she asked herself silently, pinching herself and thinking, could this be true? Are my dreams about to become a reality? "Well," he said, "interested?"

"Yes," Rayanne was finally able to say.

"I thought you might be. Be at my office at nine in the morning and we'll do business."

"Harry," she said. "I don't know what to say, except thank you, thank you so much."

"I'm only doing my job," Harry said, but it was more than that, she thought. Much more. Since she'd met Harry he'd become a friend, and she knew he'd look out for her interests. After hanging up from Harry, Rayanne called her parents and told them her good news. They expressed joy for their daughter, knowing she'd worked hard to make her dream come true. When she hung up the phone that time, she pulled her feet up onto the couch, hugged her knees, and she thanked God.

***

On opening night, the thunderous applause gave Rayanne every indication that the play was a hit, and as if that wasn't enough, the reviews the following morning were phenomenal. That was Rayanne's first big break. The play moved from Off Broadway to Broadway within months and when they held her first reception, the champagne flowed, people were moving around and Rayanne was trying hard to relax. She was so nervous. She shook hundreds of hands, made small talk and smiled until she thought her face would crack. Ralph who'd promised to be at her side that evening, was wandering around, but when he eased up behind her and whispered, "meet me in the powder room," she obeyed, although she wondered why he wanted to meet in such an odd place. She entered the powder room and Ralph took her hand and rushed her into a private area where he introduced her to her first date with cocaine. Minutes after she'd snorted the white powdery substance, she returned to the ballroom where she mingled, danced, told jokes and became the life of the party. Soon after that night, Rayanne quit her job at the bank and the two and a half years that followed brought wonderful and interesting things into her life and the lives of her roommates. They skied in Aspen, spent weekends in Atlantic City, dined in the most exclusive restaurants, traveled extensively and they even hired a housekeeper. It wasn't long before Rayanne began looking into the possibility of purchasing real estate.

***

Ivory seemed to have put men on hold since the incident with Cal. She threw herself into her work, she did commercials, and she received modeling jobs that took her across the country, and abroad. And, as she'd always wanted, her picture was on the cover of every major magazine in the country, and she bought copies and sent to everyone she knew back home. Rayanne remembered teasing Ivory one day before she left for the airport to go on an assignment. She said, "Ivory, your hair don't look so good. You should go back to that hair dresser who fried her hair before and get another perm."

"You must think I'm a damn fool. I still feel like going back there and kicking her ass," Ivory would say each time that subject came up. They chuckled now, only it wasn't so funny then.

Dorian had graduated college, and she was on top of the world in the modeling industry, so much so that she was able to chose the assignments she wanted. And, when it came to magazine covers, it was as though she and Ivory were in competition, because if she was on a magazine cover one month, Ivory was on that cover the next month, and vice versa. Henry still adored Dorian, he certainly was accommodating and that coupled with her own success, could easily have allowed her to be one of those people we see on Lifestyles of the Rich and Famous.

The years that passed brought enormous success for the girls, and at twenty-seven, Rayanne was one of the youngest and most successful playwrights in the City. She'd become the person she wanted to be, everything was going her way, and she was counting her blessings, and in assessing those blessings, she was happy that Ralph was one of them. He was understanding of the restraints on the time she was able to spend with him after her career took

103

off, he was supportive and encouraging, and Rayanne thought that perhaps she'd marry him one day. They talked about marriage, but she'd made it clear about the things she wanted to accomplish before getting married, and Ralph understood.

***

After having had a facial, manicure and pedicure, Rayanne trekked off to find just the right pair of shoes to wear to the Academy Awards. She tried on a dozen or so pairs before deciding on two pairs and at that point, her newly cared for feet were beginning to ache. She had her driver take her home. She rushed into the loft and upon entering, said to Gertie, "have the girls gotten in yet?" Both Ivory and Dorian had been out of town on business but were scheduled back in New York, as they would be flying out to Los Angeles that afternoon for a couple of days of R and R, prior to going to the Awards show. Ralph and Henry would be joining them later for the show.

"Yes, they arrived just a short time ago," the housekeeper replied. "They're getting changed."

"Okay," Rayanne said, looking at her watch and rushing off to get showered and changed herself, "please lay out that black pants suit and the cream blouse for me, Gertie."

"It's done, Miss Wilson," Gertie said, "anything else I can get for you?"

"No thanks, Gertie. But, don't you think it's about time that you start calling me Rayanne," she said. Gertie was a middle aged, stocky built, black woman the girls had hired and who took care of their needs and had settled into their little family. But, Rayanne, the country girl that she was, always felt a little strange when a woman old enough to be her own mother, called her Miss.

"All right, Rayanne," Gertie replied.

Rayanne smiled. "It seems you've been reading my mind again, Gertie," she said, extending her hand towards the bed, indicating the items Gertie had placed there for her. Then Rayanne headed off to her bathroom.

CHAPTER 13

Returning to the loft after seeing Die Fledermaus at the Met, Rayanne and Ralph, Dorian and Henry and Ivory, she had begun dating again, and David, ate the meal Gertie had prepared for them before leaving for the evening. Rayanne had a small chunk of lobster on the tip of her fork and she fed it to Ralph as Dorian observed from where she sat across the table from them. When dinner was over and the girls were left alone, Ivory blew out the candles and they cleared the table. "Did you see my girl feeding Ralph from her fork?" Ivory asked.

"I certainly did," Dorian responded.

"Those guys are really in love," Ivory said.

"Yes, we are. A lot has changed between Ralph and I," Rayanne said, piling dishes into the sink and filling it with water. Although there was a dishwasher, Rayanne sometimes insisted on doing the dishes by hand. She said it kept her grounded. Dorian said she never understood that because Rayanne was one of the most down to earth, grounded persons she knew.

"Why don't we just put them in the dishwasher," Ivory asked, thinking they could let the dishwasher do its job while they talk, do something, anything.

"I don't mind doing them sometimes. Keeps things in their right perspective, somehow," Rayanne said. I can think of a lot of other things I can do to keep things in perspective and doing the dishes by hand ain't one of them, Ivory was thinking. Besides, she'd just had her nails done and she didn't want to soak her hands in dish water. "You don't have to help," Rayanne said, "just sit here and keep me company. I don't mind doing them."

"We may as well pitch in and help or we won't ever hear the last of it," Dorian said and they laughed. "Talk to us about Ralph. Things still seem to be going well."

"Ralph and I are happy. Can't you look at me and tell," Rayanne replied.

"I'll say," Ivory said.

"We decided that we don't want to date other people. We just want to spend our spare time with each other," Rayanne said.

"Sounds like things have heated up quite a bit," Ivory said. She hadn't seen Rayanne go out with anyone other than Ralph the last few years, but Ivory had attributed that to the fact that Rayanne was obsessing with her writing as she'd always done and she didn't have time to devote to any new love interest. Ivory was happy that Rayanne had found the man of her dream. She hadn't and she wasn't sure that she wanted to limit her dating to only one man at that time. It had taken her a while to resume dating after that unfortunate incident with Cal, but now that she was dating again, she intended to play for a while. The one thing she was sure of though was that she would be careful who she became involved with.

"Ralph has been wonderful," Rayanne answered. She'd gone out with other men on occasions since meeting Ralph but those date were casual and strictly platonic. "You guys would know how much Ralph and I are in love if you were ever around. I hardly see you anymore. If you two aren't on a plane to Milan, you are jetsetting to Paris. I believe you guys are in Europe more than you are here," Rayanne teased.

"Are you two thinking of getting married?" Dorian asked, and there was something in her voice that gave Ivory and Rayanne pause.

"I'm not saying that we're gonna rush right out tomorrow and do it, but I think it's getting close. What about you guys?" Rayanne asked. "It's about time that you find a good man and build a good relationship."

Dorian gasped and snapped, which took both girls by surprise, "Perhaps, we're just not ready. Have you thought of that?" With Rayanne and Ivory's mouths hanging open, Dorian continued, "Just because you choose to sleep with one man doesn't mean that everyone else has to. It's a matter of choice."

Rayanne looked from Dorian to Ivory. "I know that. All I was saying is that it's time that we put some seriousness into our lives. We are approaching thirty and," Rayanne said, handing a plate she'd washed to Ivory, who looked hopelessly at the plate before taking it and rinsing it before handing it to Dorian to dry, "I'm not saying that we should settle down today or even this year, but we need to start thinking about where we're going with our personal lives. As far as our goals, all three of us have done pretty much what we wanted to in that area."

"Lighten up, Rayanne. We're living our lives as we choose to, and we're enjoying ourselves, so let's not get into anything heavy tonight," Ivory said, handing another plate to Dorian.

Rayanne was remembering their talks years ago. She didn't expect them to live on some kind of schedule, but she knew that before long she'd want children.

"I want to know who died and left you old mother hubbard, judge and jury," Dorian asked sarcastically and totally unexpectedly.

"Dorian, I didn't mean to come off that way. You know that, and I'm sorry if I've upset you. Maybe we should just drop the subject," Rayanne said, then asked, holding an unwashed cup in her hand. "Is everything else all right with you?" She had noticed that the last couple of times that they had seen each other, Dorian didn't seem her old self.

"Everything's fine."

"And, Henry?" Rayanne asked, as she continued to do the dishes.

"Henry's fine," Dorian replied, giving Rayanne a quick dark look, and Ivory looked at her.

"What's happening with his divorce?" Rayanne asked. Henry had told Dorian sometime ago that he was going to divorce Olympia, but in all the years that followed, it hadn't happened.

"Rayanne, I don't want to get into that okay," Dorian snapped, slamming a stack of plates on the counter and rushing from the kitchen to the den.

"Dorian, what's wrong? Something's bothering you so let's talk about it," Rayanne said, dropping the dish cloth into the sink, following Dorian.

"I said I don't want to talk about it, damn it," Dorian said, her beautiful green eyes flashing with anger. The room grew silent for a moment.

"I just want you to be happy," Rayanne said, walking over to where Dorian stood, looking out of the window.

"I'm happy. I am, and why wouldn't I be. I'm young, I'm beautiful, and I have plenty of money. Why wouldn't I be happy. I have everything anyone could want, so you tell me," Dorian said. Rayanne knew Dorian was right on most counts. Granted, she was young, God knows she was beautiful, and she'd made more money than she'd ever spend, but the question was, is she happy.

"Okay," Rayanne said, lifting her hands and going to sit in a chair across the room, "but let me know if I can do anything."

"I've told you I'm fine," Dorian said, turning away from the window. "Just because you've allowed your life to become one dimensional, don't think that I should do that. You'd probably be a lot happier if you did as I do."

"Oh?" Rayanne said, turning to stare at Dorian.

Ivory, observing from the kitchen, said, "Hey you guys, knock it off!" Rayanne and Dorian had disagreements before, but never like this.

"You should play the field," Dorian said ignoring Ivory.

"That's not what I want to do," Rayanne said.

"Maybe you wouldn't be so damned judgmental if you started living again," Dorian said sarcastically. Rayanne had done all that, she was moving on, and she didn't have a problem dating only Ralph.

"You want to know what your problem is?" Dorian asked.

"Will you two cut this shit out?" Ivory said, looking from one girl to the next, not happy about the direction where the conversation was heading. Thinking a disagreement was one thing but this conversation was laced with venom.

"I wasn't aware that I had a problem," Rayanne said.

"Then, you have an even bigger problem because you don't know you have one. You're being foolish. You believe in giving your heart to one man," Dorian said. "And that's stupid."

"And you believe in giving yours to the whole damn basketball team," Rayanne came back. Dorian looked at Rayanne, her lips began to quiver, then she stormed out of the room. "Good Lord, what's going on here? Did I say something tonight that I haven't said before?" Rayanne said, but she was annoyed at herself for losing control and not handling the situation better.

"Don't worry about it. She'll be okay," Ivory said, putting the dish cloth near the sink before leaving the room to check on Dorian.

"Dorian and I have had little disagreements before, but I've never known her to react this way," Rayanne said when Ivory returned to the room. "Is she all right?"

"She'll be okay," Ivory said, going back into the kitchen and began putting the dishes away.

"Ivory, is there something going on here that I don't know about?" Rayanne asked, following Ivory into the kitchen.

"It'll blow over in a couple of days. It's Dorian's time of the month for one thing, and you know she's evil as hell then," Ivory said and laughed a little. Rayanne knew that was true at one time, only now she didn't agree. She believed there was more. Something else was bothering Dorian.

"I wonder whether Henry has something to do with some of this," Rayanne said. "She has just not been herself lately."

Ivory had always thought of Rayanne as being perceptive and was surprise that she hadn't figured out Dorian's attraction for Henry. "Some of the things I'm about to tell you," Ivory began, "I learned quite by accident."

Rayanne looked at Ivory a moment. "You were snooping again," Rayanne said, not forgetting that no secret was safe from Ivory.

"Of course, but let me lay it out for you. Some time ago, I came across some old photographs in Dorian's room. There were pictures of a little girl who looked to be 6 or 7 years old, and a man and woman. Dorian and her parents, I believe. I asked her about the people in the pictures one day, but she refused to talk about them and she told me to mind my own business. I couldn't get anything out of her. I never brought that subject up again, and neither has she," Ivory said, and there was a pause. Rayanne walked over to the sink where Ivory was.

"So what's the point?" Rayanne asked, a little puzzled, not knowing what Ivory was getting at. She picked up two cups and held them in her hands as she listened.

"When I first saw the pictures, the man looked strangely familiar, but I couldn't put it together. Henry looks almost exactly like the man in the photographs who I suspect is Dorian's father, except Henry is a little younger. You should've seen the pictures. I kid you not, the man in the pictures has an uncanny resemblance to Henry." Rayanne didn't say anything, she just looked at Ivory. "So, are you thinking what I'm thinking?" Ivory asked.

"That Henry represents some sort of father figure for Dorian," Rayanne said, as it all was beginning to make sense. Dorian was a sweet, loving person, but she never talked about her parents which

Rayanne thought, was odd. Did they have some falling out and weren't able to reconcile their differences. Did Dorian's parents know where she was, whether she was safe, or whether she was even alive? Dorian's face had been plastered in magazines across this world, so why hadn't her parents tried to contact her? Rayanne's mind began to wonder whether it was possible to put that family back together again. She was from a close knot family and had no idea what it was like to not be in contact with her relatives. Mamie was the most taxing person in her family, but even she deserved that bonding with her family.

"That's my guess," Ivory was saying.

"I wonder what is the situation," Rayanne said.

"I don't know and I'm gonna leave it that way. She invited me out of her business once, so I ain't no fool. If you would've seen the look on her face when I mentioned those pictures, you'd leave it alone too." Ivory thought for a moment and said, "You know, I couldn't tell whether she was angry, or sad or hurt. Her face went through a series of changes."

"Where did you see the pictures," Rayanne asked, her mind at work. Perhaps there was something with the pictures that would help them learn more about Dorian. As it was, neither of them knew hardly anything. Anytime they asked about her personal life, she'd either become quiet, said she didn't want to talk about it or just changed the subject.

"Oh no you don't," Ivory said but considered the situation at the same time. "It doesn't matter anyway. They are no where to be found now."

"You tried to get another look at them, didn't you?"

"Yes, but only because I thought I could learn something about her. There were some clippings too," Ivory said, "but I didn't get a chance to read any of them."

"There must be something very painful in her past, and since she's never talked about her folks, it makes you wonder." Then Rayanne was struck by an idea. "Do you think Dorian's folks gave her up for adoption? That might explain some of the bitterness and the secrecy."

"Anything's possible. All I know is that she's going through a lot right now. You know she's always said that you and I are the only real family she's got and I believe she really feels that way too. I wouldn't be a bit surprised if she's behaving this way because you're moving out and she thinks our little family is breaking up."

110

"That's ridiculous," Rayanne said, but she hadn't even thought of that. She hadn't thought whether either girl would have a problem with her moving out. "It's not like I'm moving far away. I'll be right around the corner practically. We'll see each other just as often as we do now, we'll just be living in different places. Nothing else will change, Dorian must know that."

"You'd think so," Ivory said, as they put up the dishes. "I'm gonna miss not having you here also, but I'll know how to reach you." They moved back into the den. Ivory sat and propped her feet up on the coffee table. "I've thought of buying a house myself. The loft is nice," she said looking around the room, "it's wonderful, but I want something of my own one day." Ivory hadn't mentioned that before, but Rayanne was glad that she was looking ahead. "I've been thinking about it for some time now. I'm not gonna be doing anything within the next six months or so, but soon."

"I think it's great," Rayanne said.

"Henry's been good to us long enough, and I can certainly afford to do something on my own now." The reason Ivory hadn't made any changes in her living arrangements was because of Dorian. It seemed she was working her way through a legacy of insecurities or something unpleasant left to her by her family. Ivory said, "I feel I need to be here for her for a while yet."

"You think she's gonna be all right?"

"Yeah. She just needs to understand that we're not deserting her. She's going through something difficult right now, and I'm sure she didn't mean to take her mood out on you."

"Never mind that," Rayanne said with a wave of the hand. "I'm just wondering what I can do to help her, to let her know that we will always be there for each other."

"I do think a part of the problem is your moving out, but as you said earlier, I, too, believe that Henry is a part of the problem. He's not getting a divorce after all, but I'm gonna let her tell you about that," Ivory said as Dorian came out of her room and joined them.

"I come bearing an olive branch," she said, looking ashamed. "Am I in the dog house?"

"Of course you're not in the dog house," Rayanne patted the seat beside her on the couch. "Come and sit. We all have our bad days. You are just having two in one," Rayanne said and laughed, knowing the behavior Dorian was exhibiting was out of character for her.

"I was just being childish," Dorian said, "I am sorry."

"This wouldn't have anything to do with my moving out next week?" Rayanne asked, thinking that perhaps Ivory was right.

"No," Dorian lied and her eyes watered over slightly.

"Liar," Ivory said.

"Does it, Dorian?" Rayanne pressed, wanting Dorian to tell her why she seemed so miserable. She wanted to get to the bottom of the situation and, hopefully, help Dorian feel better. Dorian was her friend, more like a sister, and she wanted to help.

"It does seem that everyone I care about leaves me," Dorian said and her eyes became sad.

"I'm not leaving you guys. I'm just moving a few blocks away. We'll still see each other all the time. You and Ivory, gosh, you guys are family, you know that, and I'll always be here for you. I'll just be a phone call away."

"I know, and I'm embarrassed about my behavior," Dorian said.

"No, you just found a way out of helping us do those damn dishes," Ivory said, laughing.

"You got that right," Dorian said, going along with her.

"This girl wants to be black so bad," Ivory said, laughing and shaking her head. Dorian apologized again but was assured it wasn't necessary.

Rayanne told Dorian they became family the day they met and that would never change. No matter where they were in the world, they'd never really be apart because of how they felt about each other. "You'll never be alone," Rayanne said. "Just let me know if there is ever anything that I can do."

"You can stay on here," Dorian teased. "Just kidding. I'm okay, really, just bear with me please." She dabbed the corners of her eyes. "I'm mourning the loss already."

"I'm not dead yet," Rayanne said and laughed.

"I know, but I'm going to miss you an awful lot," Dorian said, as her eyes glistened with tears.

"Dorian," Ivory began, "we'll always be friends. We love each other, nothing's gonna change that. The thing to remember is that although we may not always live under the same roof, we'll always be there for each other. If I'm on the other side of the world and one of you guys need me, just say the word and I'll be here in a heart beat. You know us. We're the Manhattan Trio, we've got staying power," Ivory laughed a little. "That may not be a good choice of words, staying power, but you know what I mean." Dorian didn't say anything, she sat and looked from one girl to the other, listening.

"I'll miss you guys too," Rayanne said, "but I'll be right down the street and my home, as always, is your home." Dorian still didn't say anything, but she smiled. Rayanne gave her a hug and was happy to see that the sadness that had clouded her eyes previously was replaced by happiness. "We'll always be there for you, Sis. Okay?"

"Right on," Dorian said.

"Oh hell," Ivory said looking from Rayanne to Dorian, and tossing her hands into the air.

"Tell us about your new home," Dorian said after a moment.

"My new home," Rayanne said looking up at the ceiling. "It's pretty and airy. The condo is in a high-rise with a view of Central Park. It's nice. You gals are gonna love it." Dorian and Ivory sat and listened and were excited as Rayanne filled them in on her new real estate purchase. One week later they gave Rayanne a moving out party and the week that followed, she moved into her new condo.

The condo was done in luxurious fabrics, cool soft colors with huge windows that provided wonderful views of the city by day, but spectacular by night where the city was ablaze with a multitude of lights. The walls contained trendy art pieces. As a house warming gift, the girls gave Rayanne the piece they'd pooled their money and purchased at Patti's first art show.

One evening shortly after the move, Rayanne was sitting on the side of her bed. She picked up the telephone and dialed a number. "Hello?" came the smooth, silky voice of Ralph Underwood.

"Hello yourself. How are you?" Rayanne asked.

"Okay," he answered, "and you?"

"I'm great. Tell me, Mr. Underwood, are you in a wish granting mood tonight?" she asked.

"That depends."

"Oh?"

"You know I'm just kidding. What's your wish?"

"Are you sure because it's going to take some generosity to fulfill this girl's wish."

"I'm in, so tell your fairy godfather what wish he can grant you. Your wish is my command," he said.

"I wish to spend the night in your arms."

"Your place or mine?"

"I'll be there in an hour."

"I'll be waiting," he said.

113

Rayanne arrived at Ralph's apartment that evening wearing a full length fur coat, the Christmas present he'd given her two years before, the same Christmas that Dorian received a diamond bracelet from Henry and Ivory, a Rolex watch from whomever it was that she was seeing at the time. Rayanne also wore a pair of black pumps and a single red rose caught between her teeth. She let herself in with her key. Ralph was sitting on the couch with one leg propped up on the arm of the chair and one leg hanging in front of an open fire. He wore only a short silk bathrobe. She walked up to the back of the couch and kissed him on the neck. "Hi," she said.

"How are you?" He pretended to be less than enthusiastic. "You're late," he said, closing his eyes and inhaling her sweet, soft perfume.

"Is there anything I can do to make it up to you?"

"Oh, I don't know. I'll have to think about that," Ralph said, pretending to pout.

"Well," she said coming around to the front of the couch and letting the coat slip to the floor. "I hope you don't take too long to decide."

"Why? You going somewhere."

"You tell me," she said, standing completely naked before him.

Ralph opened his eyes. "Baby," he said, catching his breath, and at the same time, a log fell in the fireplace, sending sparks up the chimney but they were unmatched by the sparks Ralph felt inside. He reached out and touched her about the waist, allowing his hands to slide down to the curve of her hips. He was shaking his head. "You are beautiful."

"Am I forgiven?" she asked.

"Oh yes, yes." He pulled her to him and looked up into her eyes. "My God woman, do you have any more ammunition in that arsenal of yours?"

"I won't tell. I like keeping little surprises for you."

"Never a dull moment with you." He pulled her down onto the couch. He loved her freshness, her energy, her spontaneity, and she loved the time she and Ralph spent together. They were so much a part of each other's lives and they shared so much. She'd always felt that the substance of a good relationship is sharing everything, the good, the bad. She ran her fingers through his hair, thinking they enrich each other's lives that way, and sharing their lives together meant everything to her.

"Ralph, we have what so many other couples are frantically

114

trying to find, we make waves. You and I are one big wave together, and we are riding the crest of it right now."

"How did you get so smart to be so young," he asked, pulling her closer to him.

"Oh I don't know," she said, kissing him on the forehead, and nestling against him. How perfect they were together, she thought and when she slept, it was well, with pleasant thoughts.

Rayanne opened the window early that morning to find a dark dull day in winter, the time of year when the clouds hung low in the heavens. On that cold, cloudy day, the wind hissed, tossing her thick long hair as she breathed in the crisp air, watching the skyscrapers reaching for the sky. She pulled the burgundy terry cloth robe close to her body, she tied the belt and look down to the streets, hearing only the traffic as the vehicles came and went. The parked vehicles were blanketed with a layer of snow, but because the streets in New York were always busy, the snow had already turned to slush. Rayanne was thinking how much she loved the city. With all its pleasantries and gory, she was fascinated by the bright lights and big city atmosphere, the horse drawn carriages and her many strolls along Central Park. She sighed and looked at Ralph. He was still asleep. She ran a comb through her hair, set the computer to print her latest project, and when the laser printer shot out the 108 page script, she turned off the machine and climbed back into bed. "Where have you been?" Ralph asked, sleep in his voice.

"I got up to print some material," she responded, smoothing the covers up against her chin.

"You got a busy day planned?"

"It's too early to think about that right now. Ask me later," she said, snuggling up closely to him.

"Let Henry know that I got those hockey tickets for him, will you?" he said.

"He'll be thrilled," Rayanne said, she kissed him on the lips, and they slept until noon.

***

Ralph arrived at Rayanne's three bedroom condo punctually at 7:30 that evening to escort her to the theater for the premier of her latest play, The Ice is Melting. Ralph was a regular Billy Dee Williams, wearing his black tuxedo, and Rayanne, the epitome of a young, rich, society woman. She was radiant in a red short and

115

tight taffeta dress with matching floor length pleated skirt over it that was opened just enough in front to expose the fitted dress. Her red shoes and purse, and diamond earrings that hung an inch below her ear lobes, completed her ensemble. "Hello, gorgeous," Ralph said as he took in her entire frame. "You look wonderful." He took her in his arms and kissed her on the cheek.

"You're handsome tonight also, honey. What's this," she asked accepting the envelop that he handed her.

"Just a pair of tickets to the opera next week." She put the tickets into a drawer in a table in the living room. "Do we have time for a drink," he asked, lighting up a joint.

"I don't think so," she looked at her watch. "We should be at the theater and in our seats at least by 7:50, since the play starts promptly at 8."

"Come take a hit of this with me. It will put you in the right mood for the evening."

"No Honey. You know I don't mess with that stuff anymore."

"I know, baby, but tonight is special," he coaxed.

"Yes it is, but no thanks. Let me get my wrap and I'll be ready to go. "Ralph finished the joint without trying further to persuade Rayanne to join him.

Their limo stopped in front of the theater. Traffic moved up and down the streets, bumper to bumper and the street was jammed with people entering the theater to see the play. Rayanne and Ralph met Ivory and David and Dorain and her date, the Mexican whom they hadn't met previously but recognized from Dorian's Mexican vacation photos, at the theater. They were also joined by Harry and his wife, Cinnamon. They sat through the three act play and they enjoyed it and when the final curtain was down, they knew the play was a success. Rayanne had another hit on her hand. Everything went well until they caught sight of Henry and Olympia. Although no one mentioned it, Dorian, who was usually a chatterbox, was extremely quiet. "Are you all right?" Rayanne whispered to her. Dorian nodded her head that she was, but after the play and dinner at one of New York's finest restaurants, they went to Rayanne's condo for drinks. Everyone noticed Ralph and Dorian doing a lot of cocaine. Another thing that was noticed was the way Dorian completely ignored her own date, and instead, was hanging all over Ralph. Dorian kicked off her shoes, asked Ralph to dance, he obliged, and she wrapped her arms around his neck. They swayed, with closed eyes, to the music that someone was playing on the white baby grand piano located in a corner of the huge room. They whispered to each other and laughed out loud as though they shared a secret that the others weren't privy to. They danced to one song after the other and at times close to the point where it became embarrassing for Rayanne and her guests. During one of those dances when Ralph was holding Dorian a little to close, he suddenly opened his eyes and noticing that they were the center of attention, he disengaged himself from her, held her with one arm and lifted the other in the air. "What's going on, guys, "he said in a slurred voice. "This is supposed to be a party."

"You two seem to be the only real party animals here," Ivory said, angry at the distasteful manner in which her friends were behaving.

Ralph looked from one face to the next, then his eyes came to settle on Rayanne's. He pulled away from Dorian's grip and made his way to a stool at the bar. "Party poopers," Dorian giggled and sat in the chair next to Carlo, who was her date.

Harry, medium height, stocky built, middle aged man and his wife got up and walked over to Rayanne. He said, kissing Rayanne on the cheek, "Congratulations on another great piece of work." Harry had gone out on a limb, had invested time and even some of his own money to assist in getting Rayanne's career started. When Harry and Rayanne met, he not only liked her, but he believed in her and her talent, and he really appreciated her perseverance. Rayanne worked hard, she dedicated herself to her craft, and she deserved the success that came to her.

"Thank you, Harry," she responded. "Thank you for everything."

"You are welcome. Goodnight, now," he said.

"Goodnight Harry."

"Congratulations, Rayanne and goodnight," Cinnamon said. She was a petite woman with short blond hair, vibrant blue eyes and she had a quick warm smile. The twelve years they'd been married were good ones and two daughters completed their home. Rayanne walked them to the door.

Soon afterwards, other guests left and as Ivory and David were preparing to leave, Ivory approached Rayanne and said, "You have done it again, my friend. Congratulations, sweetheart. "I'll call you tomorrow."

"Thanks, girlfriend," Rayanne said and they embraced. "And thank you for coming, David."

"I enjoyed the play, and it was nice seeing you all again," David said.

"Are you coming, Dorian," Ivory called out.

"I may as well. It would seem the party's over," Dorian snapped.

When Rayanne and Ralph were alone, she picked up and emptied the ash trays, piled the glasses into the dishwasher and turned it on. She returned to the living room, walked up to the sliding glass door and looked up at clouds that were thick and white and heavy with the promise of more snow before long. Rayanne pulled the drapes shut and went into her bedroom. She heard the shower running. Ralph had begun removing his clothes from where he sat at the bar earlier, because his tie was on the bar, his jacket hung across the back of the stool, his shirt was on the floor in Rayanne's bedroom and his socks were on the floor near the bathroom. Rayanne removed her clothes, pulled on a bathrobe and was pinning up her hair when she heard the shower door opened and the sound of water more pronounced.

"Rayanne, come on in. The water feels great," Ralph said. When she didn't respond, he called out again, "Honey, what's taking you so long?" Rayanne took a pillow and a blanket from the linen closet and toss them onto the couch. She went back to her bedroom and used a hairpin to hold in place a piece of hair that hung loosely about her neck. Then she walked across the length of her bedroom to the shower, she opened the door and as she did, Ralph reached for her.

"Don't" she slapped his hands away. Ralph blinked and withdrew his hands.

"What the hell is the matter with you," Ralph asked stunned.

"You really had more than you could handle tonight, didn't you?" she said.

"What is that suppose to mean?" he asked, looking a little puzzled.

"Ralph, you're so stoned that you're not even aware that you are," Rayanne said, noticing that he was taking a shower without removing all of his clothes. "It's been a long time since you've taken a shower with your drawers on." Rayanne turned away from him and said over her shoulder, "when you're finished cleaning yourself up, you can sleep on the couch. I'm going to bed." She went into her room, slid open the glass door to the whirlpool, turned on the water, and shook in a light fragrance bath salt. Moments later, she climbed into the whirling currents of hot water and settled back into the tub while the rippling water pampered and relaxed her. She allowed her thoughts to drift. She wasn't happy with Ralph or Dorian at that moment but basically, she was a happy person, happy where life had taken her. She was a successful writer, a businesswoman and she was still relatively young. The first run of the play had gone very well and she was extremely pleased. Where would her life take her from that point. She closed her eyes and allowed the water, coupled with the classical music that filtered through the bathroom intercom, to do their job. It caressed and soothed her and removed the tension that had settled around her shoulders. When she climbed out of the tub, Ralph was sitting on the couch partially dressed.

"Don't you think we should talk about this?" he said.

"I'm too tired and I'm not going to waste the time. We'll talk in the morning."

"Why was everyone so angry?" Ralph asked and the look on his face told Rayanne that he really didn't have a clue as to what provoked the attitude that he received from the guests.

"You really don't know, do you?" she asked.

"No, I don't. All I know is that Dorian and I were dancing, just having a little fun, and the next thing I knew, everybody was looking at us strangely, then they all left. I don't understand." Rayanne knew that Ralph acted that way because of the drugs, and she knew that no matter how hard she tried to talk with him about it, there'd be no reasoning with him in his present condition.

"Ralph, I'm tired. We'll talk about this in the morning. Goodnight." With that Rayanne went off to bed. When she awoke the following morning, Ralph was gone.

***

Rayanne wore a white sequined gown and Ralph wore his black tuxedo, to the opera that evening. They accepted a program and were ushered to their seats. There were a number of familiar faces and they smiled and bowed in recognition. Moments later, the lights dimmed, the curtains were drawn and the program began. After several arias and at intermission, Ralph excused himself. Tiffany Berrington, a friend of Rayanne's sat in his seat. Rayanne had met Tiffany at her book discussion group and they had become fast friends. They were also on the Board of Directors of a major media corporation, and they'd even contemplated going into business together.

"Tiffany," Rayanne said, surprised to see her friend as she slid into Ralph's vacant seat, "I didn't know you were here tonight."

"I didn't know you were either until I saw Ralph a moment ago," Tiffany said.

"She's good, isn't she? Wonderful voice," Rayanne said of the opera singer.

"Yes she is," Tiffany said, and added, "we loved the play last week. Great opening night."

"Thank you. We thought it went well," Rayanne said and after some discussion about the play, she asked, "are Ted and Liza here?" Tiffany was married to Ted, and Liza was their ten year old daughter.

"Ted is here. He's right over there," Tiffany said, pointing in his direction and they both waved to him, "but Liza is at a sleep over at a friend. She's not much for the opera, she says the singers hurt her ears." She and Rayanne chuckled.

"She'll get into it a little later."

"I'm sure she will." Tiffany was wearing a blue gown that matched her piercing blue eyes that sparkled with excitement as she said, "have you given anymore thought to what we talked about? I know we could make it work."

"Yes I have. I should have a definite answer for you in a couple of weeks."

"Remember, this is a situation that we can go into where we call the shots and run it as we please. Each of us has contacts that will help greatly in getting this project off the ground and running in no time. We can't lose," Tiffany said and Rayanne silently agreed. She knew what Tiffany said was true, but she also knew that it would be a lot of responsibility and hard work starting a business, and she wasn't sure how much time she'd be able to devote to the company. If she became involved in this business venture, she wanted it to work out. "We can do it," Tiffany said.

"You don't have to convince me. I know we can if we commit ourselves. I just wonder whether we're going to have the kind of time it's going to take to get a new business started."

"We'll find the time. This will be our own personal baby. Think about it some more and we will talk."

"To tell you the truth, I've been thinking about it a lot, but I'll get back to you, soon," Rayanne assured her.

"Great." Tiffany changed the subject. "Are you going to be available for that meeting in the morning?" Tiffany's position as Vice Chairperson on the Board allowed her the opportunity to assist in the decision making process of the scripts selected for television movies.

"With the people from L.A.?" Rayanne asked. "I thought you were taking that meeting."

"Yes I am, but I'd like to have you there with me on this one. I want to get this deal finalized," Tiffany said.

"I'll be happy to accompany you, but I'm sure it won't be necessary. You are a much smarter negotiator than I."

"Two heads are better than one."

"I'll be there," Rayanne said as the lights began to dim.

"Great. I suppose I had better get back into my seat. See you in the morning," Tiffany said and she left just as Ralph rejoined Rayanne.

"Hey you," Rayanne said as Ralph sat.

"Hey yourself," he said. He looked at her and asked, "How is Tiffany?"

"She's fine."

"That's good," he said and they sat quietly through the second part of the opera. When the singer concluded her final number and curtsied, she received a standing ovation and "encore" could be heard across the house. The singer did one last song and the program came to an end. The theater emptied out onto the street, and people went in different directions. Ralph quickly got a taxi.

"Would you like to stop off for a drink or something?" Ralph asked.

"Not tonight. I've got a meeting in the morning and I need to prepare," Rayanne responded.

"Okay, are we going to your place or mine?" he asked.

"Just drop me off at my place," Rayanne said, closed her eyes and rested her head against the back of the seat, "and I'll call you in the morning." Ralph and Rayanne hadn't spoken since the night her play opened and he was thinking that Rayanne was still a little perturb at him over what happened that night. He wanted to be close to her again, but he also knew not to rock the boat, and give her the time she needed. She'll come around soon, Ralph thought or he hoped.

"Are you sure you don't want to have just one drink?" he asked.

"No, really, I can't. I've got a couple of things that I need to review tonight."

"This is against my better judgment, but if this is what you want."

Rayanne knew Ralph didn't like her being angry at him. She opened her eyes, looked at him and said, "what if I cooked you dinner tomorrow night?" She smiled and placed a finger on the tip of his nose. "Would that make up for tonight?"

"I was thinking about taking you to that favorite restaurant of yours, but whatever you want is fine with me." He paused a moment. "But just so you know, I'm not happy about this," he said and laughed.

"I'll make it up to you. Deal?" she asked.

He looked at her and said, "deal," and he kissed her on the lips, happy that she no longer appeared to be angry at him.

CHAPTER 14

Rayanne had gotten home not more than a half hour, from a late afternoon tea party that was held at a friend's home, when Ralph arrived that evening. She greeted him at the door wearing over her red silk panties and camisole, a matching see through negligee that swept the floor as she walked. She also wore red fish net hose and red spiked heels. A classical tune playing on the stereo in the background. "Oh, it's you," she said, pretending she was expecting someone else as he entered. She closed the door and walked into the den with Ralph following.

"Yeah, it's me. Who did you expect?" he asked, thinking how wonderful she looked and enjoying the scent as he exhaled the fragrance of the perfume she was wearing.

"I thought you were the other guy," she teased.

"Oh, I must have the wrong apartment. The girl I came here to see tonight is the girl I planned to take on a little trip. You see, I have two open round trip tickets to Bermuda."

Rayanne turned to him, turned him around and pushed him towards the front door. "Let's start this evening all over again," she said, laughing while opening the door. He laughed but obeyed. "Now, you go back out and ring the doorbell again. I'll answer, and we'll go from there." She pushed him out of the door and closed it behind him. The doorbell was silent. What's taking him so long, she thought. She'd give him another thirty seconds. Silence. She opened the door to find Ralph walking away. "Ralph," she called after him, "where are you going. Come back here." He looked back, smiled but continued to walk away. Where is he going Rayanne thought as she dashed into her bedroom, slipped into a robe and rushed back towards the door. She remembered once before when Ralph was in one of his moods and she toyed with him this way, he'd left and she didn't see or hear from him for three days. I'd better catch up with him, she thought, but as she flung open the door, Ralph was standing there smiling.

"Gotcha," he said pointing a finger at her, and glided back into the condo.

"Why you...you," she said.

"Now do you want to start this evening off right," he asked, a crooked smile on his face. She nodded, yes. "Teach you to play games with me," he said and laughed that warm wonderful laugh, a laugh that was like music to her ears.

"You won this time," she said, but she thought she'd get even with him later. She'd teach him to play games with her, too.

"Okay, here we go," he said. She nodded again. "Hi, baby," he said.

"Hi," she replied, following his lead. "It's so good to see you," she said.

"Now that's more like it. Oooh," he said, marching up to the fireplace and rubbing his hands together in front of the opened fire, "it is cold out there tonight."

"Let me get you something to warm you up a little. A cup of coffee will knock that chill right off." She was about to go off to the kitchen.

"Not just yet," he said and pulled her to him. "Sit and talk with me for a while." He removed his top coat, threw it across a chair, and as they sat on the couch together, he wrapped his large arms around her, and, as usual she was painfully aware of the broad shoulders and the strength of this man.

"You doing all right," he said nuzzling her neck.

"I'm fine," she said, "I was just thinking about my book reading tomorrow night. We will be discussing an oldie, *Weathering Heights*."

"My man Heathcliffe," Ralph said, continuing to nuzzle her neck. After a moment he said, "Don't you want to hear about the trip?"

"Yes, please tell me about the trip, to Bermuda, did you say?" she asked and thought how wonderful it would be to go somewhere and bask in the sunshine at that time of year.

"Yes, but there's not much to tell," he said pretending to play the island down. "We'll be staying at a little place called the Southampton Princess Hotel. The hotel has elegant accommodations, edged with palm trees, silky white sand and air that is heavily fragrance. There is a golf course, tennis courts. You name it; sun, clear blue sky, and gorgeous beaches, just a little touch of paradise."

"Ummm," she said when he was finished. "I can hardly wait." Rayanne kissed Ralph lightly on the lips. They sat quietly and watched the fire flicker. The fire and the candles made the room cozy and warm with Tchaikovsky's Swan Lake playing softly in the background. "I cooked dinner here for you tonight. You don't mind, do you?" Rayanne had learned how to cook early in life and she enjoyed it, and what's more, she enjoyed cooking for Ralph, preparing tasty dishes for him. She also learned what he liked to eat and on occasions, she would surprise him with one of his favorite meals.

"No, that's fine with me. Something smells good, but I thought you were going to be busy most of the day," he said.

"I thought so too, but I finished sooner than I expected."

"You no sooner get one play in the theater before you are off and running with another. You are a born workaholic." He paused a moment, "so what do you call your new masterpiece?"

"Out of the darkness," she answered.

"That sounds ominous."

"Yes, but quite the contrary. I'll tell you about it in a minute, but first, come with me, I have a surprise for you." She pulled him up from the couch, and they went into the kitchen. "I'll let you have a little taste. Just enough to whet your appetite," she said, running a finger down the side of his face. And what a handsome face she thought. Ralph obeyed, following her into the kitchen. Rayanne had made Beef Wellington and the works, and although Ralph loved her cooking, there was something else he wanted to talk with her about and when he voiced it, she asked, "what about us?"

"Some permanency. I think we should get married."

"You do?" Rayanne questioned, but she was not surprised by his statement. He'd been dropping hints for some time, and, whenever he did, she indicated that she'd think about it.

Ralph said, "yes, I do."

"Okay, I'll think about it."

"You've been thinking about it for the past three years now," he reminded her.

"Here taste this," she said after cutting off an edge of the meat, and cooled it with her breath before sticking it into his mouth. She awaited a response.

"Rayanne, I'm serious about this," he said, chewing and swallowing the meat. "I don't want to live alone anymore. I want us to be together."

"I know." She paused a moment trying to find the right words. She'd given him an acceptable answer each time he'd approached the subject of marriage, but tonight she couldn't find the right words. Instead she said, "What do you think." Seeing the puzzled look on his face, she said, "about the meat?"

"Delicious, but when are you going to give some serious thought to my proposal?"

"Soon my darling, soon. Come back with me and relax. Dinner will be ready shortly." She poured each of them a glass of wine, and they sat on the couch. Rayanne fluffed some pillows, put them under his head and undid his tie. She kneeled on the floor beside the couch, untied his shoes and lifted his feet up onto the sofa. She massaged his feet and told him about the play.

"It is a story about a young boy who was diagnosed as having stomach cancer. It tells of the pain and agony the boy and his family endured, the fact that the man of the house was unemployed, they were unable to afford insurance and when they thought they'd give up although they never really lost faith, the cancer went into remission, the father became employed again, and the story has a happy ending."

"How do you do it," he asked when she finished the story.

"Write?" Rayanne asked.

"Yes. How do you do it? How do you come up with the titles and all the other stuff that goes with it?" he asked, his head cocked to the side.

"I suppose you could call it using my imagination. Honey, I write about things that are happening in the world today and just flavor it with my own imagination, characters, a little humor, compassion, sensitivity and it usually works," she conveyed.

"I'll say and you've got a hell of a track record to prove it." He counts on his fingers, "*Papa Come Home, The Ice Is Melting, Hanging On By A Thread, An Early Awakening* and now, *Out Of The Darkness.* Honey, you are a phenomenon," he said, thinking Rayanne certainly was a woman who had everything going for her, beauty and brains.

"I've giving some thought to my next play. I'm thinking about writing about three young girls in the big city falling in and out of love, relationships and especially jobs. Working here a day, there a day, quitting without notice, whenever the mood hits," she described and laughed thinking how easy it would be to write that script. It would be like a chapter from her own life, but not to forget Dorian and Ivory's.

"Wait a minute, do I know the girls who you're basing your characters on?" Ralph laughed.

"I think you do," Rayanne said and laughed too.

"That'll be a killer," he said, "a real piece of work." Meanwhile, Rayanne's mind went to Tiffany and the business venture they'd discussed. They aspired to start up a typing service. He noticed that she was distracted and interrupted her thoughts, saying, "But before you get involved in writing another play, I think we should get away for a while." He knew that once she got involved in her writing, everything else took a back seat. She'd commit herself to the project totally. "I want to take you some place nice and warm, where you can unwind and relax. When would you like to go," Ralph said.

"It doesn't matter. Just as long as we're together," Rayanne said almost absentmindedly.

"You've got more than that play on your mind. Come here," he pulled her close to him, "and tell me what else is going on inside that pretty head of yours?" he said, the crease deepening along her forehead.

"Tiffany and I have been running an idea around in our heads. Tell me what you think?" she said sitting up on the coach. Ralph sat up also, he, looked into her eyes and listened. She told him about the project and after dinner, they returned to the den with their coffee. Ralph didn't touch his coffee until it was just barely tepid, and Rayanne wondered why he just didn't ask for iced coffee since he always seemed to like it best when it was cold.

"I know you could make it work, but with your schedule, do you think you're going to have the time to run it?"

That had been her exact thinking, but she said, "We could make the time, honey. We've been giving some serious thought to this and I think I want to do it." Rayanne found that, the more she talked about the business idea, the more excited she became.

"Then what can I say. Go for it," he said. She loved this man's supportiveness of her and the career choices she made. Recently, she'd been recognized as a young savvy businesswoman, and Ralph wasn't threatened by her independence nor was he intimidated by her aggressiveness or accomplishments. If anything, her talents endeared her to him. He was wonderful, he was thoughtful and he should be rewarded, she thought. She'd indulge him, pamper him, spoil him and make all of his fantasies come true. And, as she turned her full attention to him, Ralph thought, what an incredible woman.

The following week, Ralph and Rayanne would spend a week in Bermuda. She'd never been there before, but everything Ralph had told her about that island was true as well. Ralph received a call from his office before the week was up, and as a result, he cut his trip short and returned to the city. Ivory and Dorian were able to join Rayanne, and they spent a couple of days sightseeing, shopping and enjoying the island.

That winter, *Out of the Darkness*, opened on Broadway and became Rayanne's biggest hit of all. The play evoked so much emotion that there was hardly a dry eye in the audience.

CHAPTER 15

Dorian and Ivory arrived at Rayanne's condo a little after ten that Saturday morning. "What are you two doing here at this hour?" Rayanne said, allowing them to enter and they headed back to her bedroom. "I could've had an attitude, you know." Rayanne hardly ever had an attitude. She was very even tempered.

Dorian asked, "what are you planning to do today?"

"I was just finishing up some contracts for the office," Rayanne explained.

"How is business at Raytiff," Ivory asked. That was the name of the new business Rayanne and Tiffany started six months ago. Things were going very well, and Rayanne thanked the girls for sending business to them. "Of course," Ivory said.

"So what's up?" Rayanne asked. "How are you guys doing?"

"We thought we'd go by the club and play a little tennis, do a little shopping and have something to eat," Dorian said looking through Rayanne's closet, tossing a blouse, a belt and a scarf onto the bed. The girls still searched through each other's closets and borrowed things from each other. It was an old habit that they never broke. Ivory and Rayanne sat on the bed. Dorian walked over to the dresser and checked her makeup, eyeing her face closely, gently touching the areas under her eyes and the corners of her mouth.

"What are you looking for Dorian?" Rayanne asked noticing

that she was paying a lot more attention to her face than usual.

"Wrinkles," Dorian replied.

"Girl, please," Rayanne said.

"I have told her a million times that wrinkles are a long way off, but if she keeps worrying, that's a sure way to get them," Ivory said.

"That's for sure," Rayanne agreed, but she had noticed dark circles around Dorian's eyes on occasions.

Dorian pinched her cheeks which immediately colored into a healthy pink. She turned away from the mirror. "I'm trying not to use as much makeup."

"You really don't need to wear any. Your complexion is beautiful," Rayanne said.

"Do you really think so," Dorian asked, and Rayanne and Ivory assured her that it was true.

"I bought a new racket yesterday," Rayanne said, changing the subject.

"You did. I need a new one, myself," Dorian said, and turned back to the mirror and applied a little mascara.

"Yeah, I'll bet. You need a new tennis racket like you need a hole in your head, Dorian," Rayanne said, then she looked at Ivory, "you're quiet today. What's going on with you?"

"I met a man," Ivory said, getting up and walking over to the magazine rack. But, that wasn't anything new. Ivory was always meeting a man, only she hadn't dated anyone on a steady basis, with the exception of David, since Cal. David was the first man she'd dated, since Cal's death, and now, another man. "This is the real thing this time."

"Yeah, this is the real deal," Dorian agreed, running a finger over an eyebrow.

"What's so special about this one?" Rayanne asked.

"She's in love with this one," Dorian said, looked at them and back to the mirror.

"Dorian, please shut up," Rayanne said and threw a pillow at her.

"But it's true," Dorian said, picked up the pillow and threw it onto the bed.

Rayanne got up and stood behind Ivory, where she sat on the foot of the bed and wrapped both arms around her. "So what's wrong with my big girl," she asked as she'd never seen Ivory like that. Ivory was a happy person, a person who constantly celebrated life. Nothing was unobtainable to her. She could bring excitement to trivial things, she was delightful and energetic and above all, Ivory had an undying love for people. "What's going on with you?"

"Oh nothing," Ivory said with a wave of her hand.

But Rayanne knew that wasn't true. She remembered once when they were in elementary school and one of their classmates, who was less fortunate, didn't have money for lunch, Ivory gave that classmate her own lunch money. There were times when she missed the bus and walked to school because of doing something to help an elderly person or someone else who needed help. That was Ivory. The happy go lucky, fun loving girl that she was, was now different and Rayanne was concerned. She didn't want her to return to the depressed state she'd experienced after Cal's death. "I have never seen you like this. I don't see you guys for a couple of weeks and you go crazy on me. Come on, spit it out," Rayanne said.

"Rayanne, I met this man," Ivory said.

"Okay. I think I understand that much. Is he making you unhappy?"

"No, absolutely not."

"He makes you happy then?"

"Yes, very happy."

"Then I don't understand," Rayanne said removing her arms.

"I met Desmond two months ago and we liked each other right away, but I was involved with David, and you know David. He's been so good to me, he helped me put it back together all those years ago, so I didn't want to hurt him." David was patient and understanding of Ivory when she was going through that rough time, and she appreciated him very much.

"I can understand your loyalty to David, but obviously you must feel something special for this Desmond, who I'm just hearing about now for the first time," Rayanne said.

"I fell in love with Desmond," Ivory said, matter of fact.

"So what's wrong with that? He's not married is he?" Rayanne asked, and Ivory shook her head no. "You said you love him, he makes you happy, and he's not married. So what's the problem? Do you love David also?"

"I'm not in love with David, if that's what you mean, but he's a great guy, and he doesn't want to let me go," Ivory said.

"I'm sure he doesn't, but it really isn't his call, is it?" Rayanne asked. When Ivory said she felt she owed David more than that, Rayanne said, "You guys dated, you had some good times, but it's over. You're moving on."

"When I met Desmond, there was just so much chemistry between us. I've never felt this way about anyone. I want to spend the rest of my life with him and I told him so," Ivory said.

"Okay," Rayanne pressed.

"David and I were together two weeks ago, and I told him I thought we should start seeing other people. Well he hit the ceiling, said he wasn't interested in seeing other people, and he said he doesn't want me to see anyone else either."

"You didn't tell him you wouldn't date anyone else, did you? Rayanne asked.

"Well sort of."

"Ivory," Rayanne said, not totally surprised knowing Ivory's devious nature.

"It's all very confusing. Anyway, I have a strong attraction for David. We are compatible in many ways, but I thought maybe I was making a mistake limiting my dating to just one man." Ivory seemed confused, but she tried to explain, "there was a time when I thought of ending my relationship with Desmond because I felt I owed David so much, but I couldn't stop seeing him, Desmond, I mean. We have a lot in common too. We talk about everything. He's wonderful," Ivory said.

Rayanne was more confused now than ever. "Ivory you said you are in love with Desmond, he is the apple of your eye. You care about David, but you are not in love with him, then what's the problem. Desmond sounds like a man who's after my own heart."

"David has been great. He's in love with me," Ivory said.

"I understand that Ivory, but you have to make a decision."

"I know," Ivory said thoughtfully.

"You love Desmond, David will just have to take a hike," Rayanne said, then there was a pause.

"It's the age thing," Dorian said, when Ivory didn't respond.

"What age thing?" Rayanne asked and laughed. "Oh, is he one of those older gentlemen."

"That might've been better. Rayanne, I'm 28," Ivory said. Rayanne raised her eyebrows, waiting for Ivory to continue. Desmond's only 20, and I'm in love with him. Just these last few weeks alone he's made me happier than I've ever been."

"Ivory, if you love him and he makes you happy, I don't see the problem. I think you should go with it", Rayanne said, lifting her hands in the air.

"Be honest with me, Ray. What would you do if you were in my shoes?" Ivory asked.

"Ivory, I am in your shoes. Well, vice versa," Rayanne said.

"That's different. Society is always more accepting of an older man and younger woman than the other way around. What will people think?"

Rayanne asked, "since when have you cared about what people think?"

"I suppose since I met Desmond."

"Ivory, you really have to live for yourself. Your happiness is what's important. This is life and life is for living, giving and experiencing everything. Passion, pain, happiness, sadness, successes, disappointments, all of it. This is no dress rehearsal, Ivory," Rayanne said, "this is what's happening now."

"God, when I'm 50, he'll only be 42."

"Yeah, and when you're 60, he'll be 52. What's the difference. Someone said to me once, do the things today that make you happy because a hundred years from now, we'll all be dead and it won't matter. Be happy, girl. Look at us. We've got it all. We are right where we want to be."

"I am happy," Ivory said half heatedly.

"Then, don't go bring in obstacles where there are none. Take today for what it's worth and go with it. That's my motto." With that Rayanne gave a little laugh. Her friend had really fallen in love.

"Yeah." Ivory got up from the bed, and headed towards the kitchen, then she turned at the door and said, "I like that. A hundred years from now, we'll all be dead and it won't matter," Ivory laughed that infectious laugh and her beautiful face lit up. "So are you gonna get dressed or you gonna lay around here all day?" Ivory said going towards the refrigerator. Rayanne laughed and shook her head.

"I'll say the chick is feeling better. She's hungry," Dorian said finishing her makeup. She removed the beret from her hair and the blond hair fell, cascading down her back.

"That girl wants to be black so bad," Ivory called out over her shoulder.

"Where in the world did she meet someone with a name like Desmond," Rayanne whispered to Dorian and they laughed, as Ivory entered the kitchen.

"I heard that and it's none of your damn business" Ivory snapped in good humor.

"Yeah the girl is back," Rayanne said.

After playing a couple of games of tennis, they sat in the steam room an hour, each had facials, their nails manicured, then they ate lunch. Afterwards, they went to Tiffany's where Ivory ordered a set of china, Dorian bought a pair of diamond earrings which she vowed she'd have Henry reimburse her later, and Rayanne purchased three business suits, one navy, one beige and a black one, and blouses to match each suit. She also purchased a baby blue chiffon dress, which she intended to wear to the opera in two weeks, to see Madame Butterfly. This dress she'd keep, unlike times in the past when they wanted something for a special function, and, at Ivory's prompting, went into an expensive shop, charged something fancy only to wear it, have it cleaned, if necessary and returned it after the function. But now, they'd arrived. They could afford any dress in the store, they could wear it once and hang it in the closet for all eternity, if they chose. They no longer had to resort to that kind of tactic. When they arrived at Bloomingdale's, Ivory attacked the racks and within minutes, she held a half dozen items over her arm, which she immediately began trying on. She was a girl on a mission, as Rayanne and Dorian watched with raised eyebrows. They got a kick out of shopping with Ivory. It was an adventure just watching her switch jackets and skirts with others that didn't match and come out of the dressing room, shocking the girls, making them hysterical with laughter. Some of the outfits made Ivory looked like someone who'd wandered onto earth from some other planet. Before the girls ended their day pampering and buying things for themselves, each girl bought a special gift for the others, which was something they did often.

CHAPTER 16

What a day, Rayanne thought. It was rainy and very cold. The weather was behaving like a spoiled child and it was making everyone miserable. She wasn't just pissed off with the weather. There was another reason for the bad mood she found herself in when she awoke before daybreak. She received a call from home telling her that her brother, Josh, had been arrested for disorderly conduct. He'd been drinking, he went out, had gotten himself into a fight and had been arrested. By the time she received the call, Josh was out of jail, but, the situation had put her parents under a lot of stress. Why does Josh keep doing things like that, she thought.

She and Tiffany had rented a suite of offices on the upper East side, they had hired an office manager and four typists. It was a busy and hectic time and when things finally slowed down, summer, her favorite time of year for traveling, was over and she had missed it. Nevertheless, she decided she was going to treat herself to some real fun anyway. It was time. She decided to go out and drink and dance and just let her hair down for a change. And, she did, and only after she'd drank and partied until she was completely worn out, did she decide to get a taxi home. She left the club, and walked out onto the street, but before she could get a taxi, some stranger walked up to her and demanded she give him her purse. Well, she thought, that purse belong to her and she had no intention of turning it over to him. He had other plans, however, and when she put up resistance, he struck her in the face with his fist and flung her to the ground. The police were called and she filed a report, but she knew nothing would come of it. Dozens of people were mugged or killed in the city daily and as far as the city was concerned, she was just another statistic. She was so sick of the violence.

As she drank coffee and chewed up two aspirins, she thought, that mugger had better be glad that she was tired and almost drunk, otherwise she would've creamed him. And, that was true. Rayanne had grown up with brothers who really knew how to defend themselves, they'd taught her and had taught her well. But, she was caught by surprise and was totally defenseless, and she had lost. She was so upset when she went to bed that she had trouble falling asleep, and what little sleep she did get, was not restful. With all that had happened in her life lately, it was no wonder that when she woke, she had a bad headache and was in a foul frame of mind. She sat on the couch, put her feet up and waited for the pills to work. She tried to form in her mind what needed to be done that day, but exhaustion took over and she dozed off. When she awoke later, the day had dawned clearer and sunnier than it had been in weeks.

Rayanne got up and touched a button and as the drapes opened the length of the wall, the room was flooded with light. She gave the sky a measuring glance, then she sat at her desk and made notes on things she needed to do at the office and at home. She was so busy that she'd become a list person and without her lists, she was lost. There was something else that had been occupying her mind lately. She wanted to take some time to think about going back to school. Ivory and Dorian had gotten their Master's, but she hadn't been able to find the time to go back herself. Soon, she thought. When her lists were completed, she dressed in a pair of white wool slacks, a white silk blouse and a coral wool jacket. She slipped her feet into a pair of white ankle boots, picked up her purse from the bed and headed out. She stepped out of a taxi in front of Elayne's salon where she went every Saturday to have her hair and nails done. She sat in the chair and a cup of black coffee was place on the table in front of her. She took a sip and settled back and allow Elayne to take care of her. As she was receiving the French manicure, Rayanne thought how wonderful it was having something as simple as that, done. As she closed her eyes, she thought of the lists she'd made which she left on her bed. She tried to reconstruct the lists in her mind. The only things she could remember were the drapes and comforter she wanted to order.

***

Although the afternoon sun was amazingly clear for that time of year and the sun was so bright it hurt her eyes, Rayanne could see the clouds rolling across the edge of the sky, gathering in the east, and she wondered whether it would snow again soon and cover the city in a soft blanket of whiteness. She spent much of that day on the telephone, but that was the way it had been. She'd been moving nonstop the past few months and as she was contemplating where she'd spend the holidays, the telephone rang. It was Ivory. A new club had just opened and she thought they should check it out. They'd meet first for dinner, then on to the club for dancing.

Rayanne went into the bathroom and stared at the bruise on her cheek. Yes, she'd been the victim of yet another mugging and nothing was new. The mugger, of course, wanted her purse, and she, as usual, put up resistance, and pow. She got it again. Right in the face. As Rayanne looked at her face, she thought a little make up would probably cover up the bruise so that it wouldn't be too noticeable. She gently washed her face, patted it dry and applied a light layer of pink facial mask. There were times when she liked doing some things for herself. Afterwards, she laid out a short straight black skirt and a black and white blouse. Then she rinsed the mask from her face. She put on a moisturizer, poured herself a cup of coffee and laid back on the couch to read the newspaper. Crime was on the rise. Something had to be done, she thought.

At dinner, although Dorian was having one of her favorite meals, she hardly touch her food, and, wasn't she getting thinner, Rayanne thought. She looked up to see Ivory staring at her. "What happened to your face?" Ivory asked.

"Oh, it's nothing," Rayanne tried to brush it off with a wave of the hand.

"It is something," Ivory said looking closer. "Your face is bruise and it looks swollen."

"I was mugged again last night," Rayanne confessed.

"What," Ivory said, her face clouded with concern.

"Yeah. Some guy wanted my purse again and as usual, I refused and pow," she said aiming a fist at the side of her face. "You know the routine."

"Rayanne, I keep telling you. It's just not smart to try to fight off a mugger. Give them what they want no matter what it is. It's

137

not worth your life or having them use you as a punching bag. These people are crazy out of their heads, all drugged out," Ivory said. "You know what they say about living in New York. You have to keep mugger's money on you at all times. It sometimes saves your life. Are you okay?"

"Other than being thoroughly pissed, I'm fine." Rayanne laughed a little and when both, Ivory and Dorian looked up questioningly at her, she said, "Sometimes I think I walk down the street with a huge stamp on my forehead that reads, 'hey mug me. I'm an easy target'."

"It's nothing to joke about. You could've been seriously hurt," Dorian said.

"That's right," Ivory agreed.

"I know, but I'm okay," Rayanne said.

After dinner, they left the restaurant and when they arrived at the club, they jumped out of the taxi and entered. The music was jumping, the club was filled to its capacity and the dance floor was crowded. After some time, the girls found three available seats at the bar where they sat and ordered drinks. "This place is slamming," Ivory said, moving to the music and checking the place out.

"I'm serious," Rayanne agreed, enjoying the music, moving from side to side on the bar stool. Before one record ended, another began.

"I love that song," Dorian said, to Philip Bailey's Chinese Wall, that was playing. She got up from the stool and danced her way to the floor with Ivory and Rayanne behind her. They danced together until three men joined them on the dance floor. They danced until two in the morning, stopping only to take a sip from their drink glasses.

In the taxi home, Dorian took a small container from her purse and snorted the white substance from it. "Dorian, what are you doing," Rayanne's whisper came out in a hiss.

"I've told her about this shit until I'm tired. I don't understand why she feels she has to do this shit," Ivory said, then looked at Dorian. "We offered to help you but you say you don't have a problem. You don't think cocaine is a problem? Dorian, that shit kills."

"Dorian, you have to cut this out. It's no good," Rayanne warned.

"I do this because it helps me to keep my mind off of things," she said.

"What things, Dorian?" Rayanne asked.

"Just things," Dorian said and laugh. "Why do you guys think I've got a problem?"

"Because you damn well do," Ivory said through clenched teeth. "I don't want you to die and I'll be damned if I'm gonna watch you kill yourself."

"I am not going to kill myself," Dorian said.

"Oh no," Ivory spat out.

"Dorian, we just want to help you," Rayanne said more gentler this time.

"Listen to me girls. If you don't blow my high tonight, I promise I'll talk about my so called problem tomorrow," Dorian said. The taxi pulled up in front of the loft, but because of the condition Dorian was in, they didn't want her spending the night alone, since Ivory had moved in with Desmond. Rayanne gave instructions to the driver to take them to her condo, where Dorian spent the night.

The entire condo, except the kitchen, was carpeted in white. The walls and the drapes were also white as well as the baby grand piano. That was Rayanne's pride and joy. The condo had a living and dining room, kitchen and breakfast nook. Down the long hall were the master bedroom, where her king sized bed was almost lost in the huge room, and two other bedrooms, one of which was turned into an office. The condo, space wise, was not the loft, but it had plenty of room and Dorian could stay as long as she'd like. Before Ivory left, they helped Dorian get settled in the spare bedroom. It seemed Dorian had kept her word and hadn't touch the stuff. At least that was what Ivory and Rayanne thought, and they were happy.

***

Night was just beginning to fall when Rayanne dashed out of the office, took a taxi and met Dorian and Ivory at a mid-town restaurant. She hadn't seen the girls in a while and she'd missed them. Each of them had a glass of white wine and did some catching up over dinner. "So, how are you guys doing?" Rayanne asked.

"Great," Ivory said. "What about you?"

"Busy as usual."

"You're always busy," Ivory said, "you should give yourself a break, take it easy."

"There's still so much that I want to do," Rayanne replied. She was still a workaholic and the girls knew it.

Dorian said, "How are the folks doing?"

"They're fine. They sent you guys their love when I talked with them earlier," Rayanne answered and asked, "How are things going with you?"

"I am fine," Dorian replied.

"What about Psycho?"

"Who?" Dorian asked, with a little frown on her face.

"You know who she's talking about," Ivory said and sipped her drink.

"Oh Carlos," Dorian said and smiled, "I see him occasionally."

"Why? I would no more see a man who beats me," Rayanne said, "than I would a rattlesnake." There had been other reports of Carlos abusing Dorian, the question was why did she allow it. Why would she want to be with someone like that.

"I've told her but do you think she listens to me? She likes a man who tries to tear her eyes out," Ivory said taking another sip from her drink. "I would've kicked his ass to the curb long ago."

"Carlos is a good man. He's just jealous," Dorian said in defense of Carlos.

"I just wouldn't stand for that crap," Rayanne said.

"Carlos is really a nice guy. Sometimes, I just push him too far," Dorian explained.

Ivory clicked her teeth, lit up a cigarettes and blew out a cloud of smoke. "All right, all right, so what's new with Henry. Is he or isn't he filing for divorce?"

"I don't know what Henry is going to do," Dorian said.

"What are you going to do?" Rayanne asked.

"I don't know. I am still in love with him, but I am getting tired of him and his broken promises."

"So what are you gonna do about it, be his mistress for the rest of your life?" Ivory asked.

"Didn't I just tell you that I don't know what I am going to do," Dorian replied.

"Dorian, you've waited on Henry long enough. It's time that he crap or get off the pot. You don't need this," Rayanne said.

"That's right, he's been blowing smoke for ten years. Hell, I'd get rid of him and Carlos and get on with my life," Ivory said.

"Oh really?" Dorian said.

"Hell yeah," Ivory fired back.

"Dorian, Henry really needs to make some decision, You've put your life on hold, hoping for some kind of future with him. He needs to do some thing," Rayanne said.

"I tell you what. Since you can't seem to take control of your own life and make some decisions where your own future is concerned, then I'll make the decision for you. Kick Henry's ass out, tell Carlos to get a life and you, my friend, should wake up and live." Ivory said.

"If I remember correctly, it wasn't long ago when you were in the same situation, or at least you couldn't decide which man you wanted."

"The situation was completely different. My problem was that I didn't want to hurt anyone," Ivory said.

"Ivory, give me a break, will you," Dorian said. "I just want you to answer one thing for me."

"What's that," Ivory asked.

"Where are we spending Thanksgiving this year and who's bringing the turkey?"

CHAPTER 17

The phone rang at a quarter to nine. Rayanne almost always did not open an eye on a Saturday morning before 10:30. She thought about letting the machine pick it up, but she answered it instead. It was Ivory. She was scheduled to go to California on assignment and wanted to let Rayanne know. "When are you leaving?" Rayanne asked.

"I have got an 11 o'clock flight," Ivory responded, "today."

"Today?"

"Yes. In just a couple of hours. They want to do a shoot in Los Angeles, would you believe, tomorrow of all days. Can you imagine that? And, from there, we go to San Francisco. I should be back by Tuesday. Wednesday, the latest."

"Well, have a good trip," Rayanne said. "You talked with Dorian lately?" That was another reason for Ivory's call.

"You'll need to keep an eye on her while I'm away. Desmond will as well."

"Of course, I will," Rayanne said, her head still in a buzz due to lack of sleep. The Typing Service was getting so much work that Rayanne and Tiffany hired additional typists in order to be able to fulfill all of the contracts, and Rayanne was working on another play. "Ivory, when you get back, I think we need to have a serious talk with Dorian. I'm really worried about her. She needs help," Rayanne said.

"It's been bothering me, too," Ivory said. Both Rayanne and Ivory had noticed that Dorian had started using an assortment of drugs. She'd even smoked crack in their presence a couple of times. They'd talked with Dorian, reaffirming her of the dangers of abusing drugs with Dorian always promising that she'd cut back, but she never promise to quit.

"What's wrong, Ivory?" Rayanne asked, after Ivory was quiet for a moment.

"Dorian got into a little trouble last night."

"What happened?" Rayanne asked, sitting up in bed. She wondered whether Ivory was still upset about Dorian and Ralph's most recent production. It seemed whenever they all got together anymore, Dorian and Ralph did drugs, got carried away and became even more flirtatious with each other. During those times, Dorian would flirt with anyone who wore pants, but the night in question was two days ago when the girls and their dates went to the MET to see the Nutcracker. Afterwards, they went to one of their favorite night spots for an evening of dining and dancing. Dorian kept insisting that Ralph dance with her, ignoring Carlos again, and although he didn't appear to object at that time, he voiced his true feelings later. Dorian's action was innocent and harmless, and Rayanne and Ivory, both, knew that one day Dorian would get into a jam with someone who didn't really know her.

"It seems Carlos objected to the way she and Ralph were behaving."

Carlos had seen them cut up before, but Rayanne said, "Why? Has something happened?" She turned in bed, putting her feet on the floor. Ralph stirred in bed beside her, but he didn't wake up. "He didn't hurt her?" Rayanne asked.

"He sure did. That son of a bitch whipped her ass, and she looks like hell this morning."

"What?" Rayanne sprung out of bed and was on her feet. "Where is he now?"

"Oh hell, you don't think he'd still be here after what he did, do you? He was out and gone last night before Desmond and I got here."

"Has Dorian seen a doctor?" Rayanne asked, her voice filled with concern.

"No, she hasn't. Her face is all black and blue, and she says it hurts like hell but that it's not as bad as it looks. I think she'll be all right," Ivory assured Rayanne.

143

"Ivory, are you sure?" Rayanne questioned.

"Of course, I'm sure. She's got a steak on her face right now and it's looking better."

"I'm coming right over," Rayanne said.

"There is no need," Ivory informed. "Dorian is meeting Henry for lunch in a couple of hours."

"How is she going to explain those bruises to Henry?"

"She told me she's gonna tell him she was mugged."

"Lord," was all Rayanne could say.

Ivory looked at her watch. "Rayanne, I've gotta get out of here or I'll miss my flight."

"Okay. Let me talk with Dorian. You have a good trip and don't worry about Dorian. We'll take care of her."

"Take care, and I'll see you when I get back," Ivory said, and she handed Dorian the phone. After talking with Dorian and being assured that she was fine and she would call Rayanne when she returned from lunch, Rayanne hung up and sat down on the side of the bed. She was in deep concentration when she felt the pressure of Ralph's hand pulling her to him.

"Get back into bed, woman," he said. Rayanne obeyed. She was silent as she lay in bed. "Who were you talking with so early in the morning?" he asked, snuggling closely to her. Rayanne relayed her conversation with Ivory to him. "What are you talking about?" Ralph asked, finally opening his eyes and looking bewildered.

"Apparently Carlos got fed up with your little performances, and he showed Dorian just how much he didn't like it," Rayanne said.

"What did he do?'

"He slapped her around, and she's black and blue."

Ralph let out a little whistle, "Is she all right?"

"She said she is, but I still don't like it. He had no right hitting her."

"Honey, Dorian's a big girl. She can take care of herself," Ralph said.

"That's not the point, and obviously, not true," Rayanne said. "If it were, Dorian wouldn't be at home black and blue with a piece of steak on her face right now."

Ralph propped himself up on an elbow and stared dismally at Rayanne. "What do you want to do?" he cocked his head to one side to listen.

"I wanted to go over there, but she's meeting Henry for lunch."

"That should be interesting," Ralph said snuggling up to her and for the first time she thought she was seeing a different side to Ralph. He certainly seemed a bit insensitive to the situation, especially since he was one of the participants of which that situation grew out of.

Rayanne could certainly understand why Carlos reacted the way he did about Ralph and Dorian. She'd probably react the same way if she didn't know them. "You two do tend to get a little carried away when you do that stuff, and I've noticed that you guys are doing more of it, all the time," Rayanne said, looking thoughtful.

"Why don't you call it what it is. It's cocaine or coke. It's not a dirty word. You don't have to treat it that way," Ralph said, a frown creasing his brow and the smile lines that appeared in his face had seemed more pronounced.

"I know what it is, Ralph, and I wish I didn't have to deal with it at all, but it's there staring me in the face and it concerns me, okay," she said.

"Why are we talking about this now?" he asked.

"Because it's important. Honey, drugs kill," she said and when he didn't answer, "I love both of you very much, and I sort of have a desire for us all to grow old together."

"Rayanne, I'm not an addict, I'm not hooked on the stuff. I just do it sometimes. I can quit anytime I want," he said and Rayanne wondered how much of what he was saying was true.

She said, "I sure wish you would want to."

"I can't see what the big deal is."

"Ralph, drugs are a big part of the problems we're having in this country today, and if we, as adults, don't take some responsibility for ourselves and educate others, then we are doomed. I need you to promise me that you're going to do something about the drugs."

"You're serious, aren't you?" he asked, laying very still.

"Yes, I am."

"Okay. Okay, I will."

"Promise?" she asked.

"Scout's honor," Ralph said, lifting two fingers to his temple, in a boy scout's salute. Then, he said, "now, can we go back to sleep." As Rayanne lay there thinking about the situation, she knew she couldn't stand by and do nothing, but how could she help when she wasn't sure that her friends wanted the help she was offering. Suddenly, she heard Ralph snoring, nestled there beside her. She

145

looked at the clock and although it was still early, Rayanne couldn't get back to sleep.

CHAPTER 18

The hour was late but the cocktail party was in full swing. It was Labor Day weekend and Rayanne and Ivory were throwing a party before Rayanne returned to school. Rayanne was planning to take a course in public speaking. Dorian had flown to Paris three days earlier to spend two glorious weeks, which she referred to as a mini vacation, with Henry. Henry was still married, he insisted he was getting a divorce without involving Dorian more than was necessary, and he was being as discreet and protective of her as he could be. He just hadn't gotten the divorce as he'd said and he hadn't married Dorian.

The food was catered to the condo, the guests milled around, getting acquainted, dancing and listening to wonderful numbers being played by an elegantly dressed woman who sat at the piano, while bursts of laughter punctuated the conversation. A combination of cigarette and marijuana smoke mingled and drifted across the room. Some of the guests munched on food, some did lines of cocaine while others gorged themselves on liquor or wine or whatever was available at that hour. Rayanne and Ralph danced closely, their bodies molded and kept perfect pace as he kissed her on her lips. When the kiss ended, Rayanne smiled and Ralph whispered in her ear, "You're so beautiful." Rayanne had lightened her hair to a reddish brown, and she wore it high on top of her head, with wisps about her neck. Her dark brown eyes sparked with happi-

147

ness and excitement. She wore black spiked heels, black silk nylons, a black sheer sleeveless top and a floor length black shirt, slit high up her thigh. "I love you, honey," he said, holding her close. She closed her eyes, enjoying the dance. Ivory and Desmond were dancing and chatting and Rayanne was thrilled to see how happy they were.

Ivory was about to take a hit of a joint that was being passed around when the phone rang. She was dressed in a white floor length dress that covered her throat up front but it plunged dangerously close to her behind in back, and she wore white pumps and white accessories. The one thing that was in keeping with her name was that Ivory almost always wore white. It was her favorite color, if you can call white a color. She detached herself from Desmond and answered the phone on its third ring. Rayanne had smoked a little grass and had tried cocaine once but it didn't appeal to her and knowing it was an addictive drug and that if it didn't kill you, it could make your life a living hell. That made her decide early on that the only high she wanted was the high she got from her man, the high she got from her writing and the high she got from Rum and Coke. Ivory beckoned Rayanne to the phone. She moved away from Ralph and smiled as she approached Ivory, but her smile vanished when she saw the expression on Ivory's face. "What is it?" Rayanne asked.

Ivory handed her the phone. "It's your mom." Ivory put her hands to her mouth and moved to Rayanne's side. That was one of the phone calls that would change the course of Rayanne's life.

"Mama, what's going on?" Rayanne asked, knowing whatever it was, it was serious for her mother to call at that hour.

"It's your daddy, honey. He's in the hospital."

"The hospital, what's wrong with daddy?" she asked and walked into another room, away from the noise and the crowd, and listened as her mother shared the news with her. Ralph walked over to Rayanne. "How is he, Mama?" Rayanne asked visibly upset. She listened some more, and said, "are you okay?"

"Don't you worry about me, I'm fine. We just have to be strong for your daddy and trust in the Lord," her mother said.

"I'll be there as quickly as I can," Rayanne said. When the conversation ended, she lifted her head and tears rolled down her face. She explained to Ralph and Ivory that her father had a heart attack. "Mama said the doctors are optimistic, but he's not out of the woods." She wiped away the tears.

"I'm sorry, baby," Ralph said taking her into his arms. "Is there anything I can do?"

"No, but I've got to go home," Rayanne advised.

"When do we leave?" Ivory asked.

Rayanne called Mamie. She got the answering machine. "Mamie, this is Rayanne. If you're there, please pick up." No one answered. "Mamie, please pick up the phone," Rayanne said fighting back the tears that threatened to flow again.

Ivory snatched the phone from Rayanne's hand, saying into the mouth piece, "Mamie, pick up the goddamn phone. This is no time to be pussy footing around. This is serious business. Pick up the goddamn phone, will you." Mamie had never liked receiving late night or early morning phone calls. Her philosophy was that such calls always brought bad news, and that whatever it was that had happened, she couldn't only not do anything about, it would be wise to get a good night's sleep in order to be able to handle the situation when she did receive the news. Rayanne left a short message on the machine informing Mamie that she would be taking the first available flight back home, since all she could get on that holiday weekend when Ivory called the airport, was a standby flight. At 9 O'clock the following morning, Rayanne boarded a plane and was on her way to South Carolina. Upon arriving at the airport, she rented a car and drove directly to the hospital.

The hospital was a little different than she remembered when she had her tonsils removed when she was eight years old. Twenty years was a long time and things do change, but the nurses were the same. They were crisp and businesslike in their white uniforms and the air of professionalism went along with it.

Rayanne entered the waiting room on the 4th floor, her eyes scanning the room until they met those of her mother's. Rayanne was the youngest of three brothers and two sisters, and everyone was there except Mamie, whom she had tried to reach the night before. Mamie was divorced four years ago, and she lived in New York with her thirteen year old son, Jeremy. Rayanne didn't know how Hank had managed to stay married to Mamie for as long as he had because she was a royal bitch. I guess love does make you do crazy things and loved her, he did, Rayanne thought. She rushed over and embraced her mother. "How are you, mama?"

"I'm fine, baby. How's my girl?" her mother responded.

"I'm okay. What about daddy? What are the doctor's saying now?"

"Take that buckle out of your brow," her mother smiled and lifted a hand to touch her daughter's cheek. "Your daddy gave us quite a scare, but he's doing a little better."

"I'm so glad. And you? Are you sure you're okay?" Rayanne questioned as she and her mother stood holding each other.

"Darling, your mama is fine," she assured Rayanne.

As Rayanne looked at her mother she thought how strong this woman is, she was a tower of strength. She greeted other family members as a nurse entered the waiting room, Mamie and Jeremy accompanied her. Each one, with the exception of Ruth, was allowed to spend only a couple of minutes visiting Raymond, as he was in Intensive Care. Ruth and Raymond had been married almost forth-two years, and although they were strong, proud parents, with only a high school education, they were bound and determined to see that each of their children received an education.

Raymond's vital signs were improving. Although the prognosis was good and everyone was optimistic that he'd recover fully, Rayanne was worried and the rest of the day went by as though she were under water. She only remembered her father being seriously ill once and that was when he had pneumonia. She was only seven at the time, but she could tell by the look on the faces of her relatives and the hush that covered the room when she entered the house, that her father's condition wasn't good. Rayanne entered a room filled with flowers, and at the sight of her father, she felt something deep in her chest hurt. He looked so weak, she looked away quickly after making eye contact with him, blinking back the tears.

"We ain't gonna have none of that," Raymond said opening his arms to his daughter. She smiled and embraced him. She was very frightened and worried all those years ago when he was sick, and she was very frightened and worried now.

CHAPTER 19

"**D**addy doesn't look good," Rayanne commented as she and Mamie sat across from each other having coffee in the hospital cafeteria.

"Daddy is sick, Rayanne, he just suffered a heart attack. How do you expect him to look," Mamie responded.

"I don't know. It's just been so long since I've seen him looking so helpless," Rayanne said. Her father had always represented strength to her, a super human, in her eyes, her childhood hero and in her heart, she was still daddy's little girl.

"People are going to get sick, Rayanne, it happens, and daddy is no exception. This is just a part of life, but he's going to be fine, I'm sure," Mamie said. Rayanne was quiet. She'd always thought that her father worked too hard, he worried too much and the words rest and relaxation were not in his vocabulary. "Don't go thinking anything negative, Rayanne, because if you do, mama will pick up on those vibes and the last thing we need is to have both of them sick," Mamie said and Rayanne stared at her, but she knew Mamie was right. Their mother appeared to have a sixth sense and it was always at work. While growing up, they thought their mother could read their minds as there wasn't a thing they could get away with no matter how they tried to disguise it.

Mamie was the oldest of the girls and the second to the oldest child. She was a head strong, complicated woman whose business acumen was strong, but her personal life was always in shambles. More than ten years ago, Mamie began working in an agency as a Medicare supervisor. She created, developed and implemented programs for her agency of which she received promotions and awards. She'd made some smart business investments which allowed her to acquire a substantial amount of property in South Carolina and when she divorced Hank, she hit him hard for child support, adding to her already sizable bank account. Mamie had further demonstrated her greed for money and power when she quietly pulled some strings and had gotten herself on public assistance, thereby receiving a hefty check each month. She had the Midas touch. Everything worked in her favor. As the saying goes, everything she touches turns to gold. She played the numbers, and she even hit on occasions. She was becoming more financially able year after year. What she lacked though was compassion. There were times when Rayanne didn't know whether Mamie was schizophrenic or just plain crazy. Perhaps both, Rayanne thought, but she asked, "how is Jeremy doing in school now?"

"He's doing much better since I put a belt to that ass of his last month," Mamie answered.

"You whipped him?"

"Yes, I strapped his ass big time and why shouldn't I?"

"I'm a little fuzzy on something here," Rayanne said. Although she believed the adage, spare the rod and spoil the child, Mamie wasn't guilty of that adage. Rayanne only wished that Mamie would communicate with Jeremy some way other than with a belt.

"Now why doesn't that surprise me," Mamie said with a hint of sarcasm.

"I was thinking you might get better results by talking to him. He's a teenager, Mamie"

"He's also my son, and he's got a hard head."

"He's probably going through a difficult period right now, but that'll pass."

"And, another thing," Mamie said, ignoring Rayanne, "he's girl crazy. That's what it is. The boy is girl crazy."

"Jeremy is thirteen years old," Rayanne said.

"Yeah, thirteen going on thirty," Mamie said.

"He's a teenage boy. Which teenage boy isn't girl crazy, unless he's got some sort of problem. He's just a typical, red blooded American boy."

"You ain't lying, but check this out. I came home from work a couple of weeks ago and instead of him being at the next door neighbor's house where he was suppose to be, I found him at the apartment with some little gal, and I don't have to tell you what I found." Rayanne was trying not to appear shocked. "Hell, at the rate he's going, I'll be a goddamn grandma long before I'm forty." Rayanne hadn't thought of Jeremy being sexually involved at this stage in his life. "You know, that boy is fucking, and he doesn't even have pubic hair yet," Mamie declared. Rayanne wondered what one thing had to do with the other, and when she asked, Mamie fired back, "What kind of a question is that?"

"What I meant, Mamie, was how do you know that."

"What? That he is fucking or that he doesn't have pubic hair?"

"Pubic hair. Actually, I suppose the other must've been pretty obvious."

"What are you talking about?" Mamie asked.

"Nothing, Mamie. To be honest, I don't even know why I said that." Rayanne knew from past experience that it didn't take much to set Mamie off, and when she became angry, her anger ran rampant. Therefore, she decided to change the subject. "I wonder how long they'll keep daddy here."

"You know daddy. He's a toughie. He'll be back on his feet in no time," Mamie said, and Rayanne hoped that was true. She had to believe that her father would be all right.

"I'm telling you. Daddy'll be out of here in no time. Hell, it'll take more than a couple of doctors to keep him here more than a few days," Mamie said trying to reassure her sister. "Daddy can be pretty feisty when he wants to be." Rayanne smiled weakly, but she had to agree. Soon, Mamie returned to the subject of Jeremy. "I don't know what I'm going to do about Jeremy. His head is so hard, he won't listen. I'm just so afraid that he's going to get himself into something awful out there. New York is just not the place for him. He's trying to keep up with what's going on out there in the street, and what he's picking up isn't good. Things that he doesn't even begin to understand. He's losing the battle, Rayanne, and I'm afraid he's losing miserably."

"What are you going to do?"

"I don't know." Mamie sighed. "I really don't know."

"You know you can always move back here," Rayanne said, offering the best advice that she could at the time.

"Who, me?" Mamie was incredulous.

"Yes," Rayanne answered.

"Where did you get such an idea?"

"Mamie, you just expressed concern about Jeremy living in New York. Well, the pace here is slower, you'd be better able to keep an eye on his activities and most of the family is here, and I'm sure they'd help look after him."

"I certainly wasn't thinking about moving back here." Mamie hesitated a moment before saying, "At least, not yet."

"Exactly when were you thinking of doing it?" If the situation was as Mamie had said, she had to make some decisions. It appeared Jeremy was growing up fast, and chances are, he wasn't going to put his life on hold to wait for his mother to do something. Mamie had better take charge of this situation before it got out of control.

"There must be some other option."

"Think about it, Mamie. The change might be good for both of you."

"My God, Rayanne, be realistic. That's just about the last thing I need, besides, what would I do back here?"

"You could be giving your son a chance to live," Rayanne said. Mamie was incredibly smart and talented. She had resources that she hadn't even tapped into yet. She had money, power, and prestige, where she was employed, and those things were seductive and satisfying, but she could move here, set up some sort of business and still do well.

"That's an idea, Rayanne, and I'll shelf it for later, but what do I do right now? I need help with that boy now."

"I'll do whatever I can to help."

"Rayanne, I can hardly believe these kids and what's going on in their minds today," Mamie said. "It's shocking." Rayanne understood what Mamie was trying to say because she also thought that a part of the problem was that a lot of the kids don't look like kids, they don't act like kids and they certainly don't think like kids. Most of them want to be grown without being capable of accepting responsibilities of an adult. Jeremy, for instance. Anyone who didn't know Jeremy, wouldn't think he was only thirteen. Jeremy probably didn't thinks he was thirteen.

"Sister, I think you'd better get your priorities in order," Rayanne said. Mamie didn't comment. "Jeremy is a kid inside of a man's body. He's gonna love the girls, and they're gonna love him back, and no matter how we preach abstinence, kids are gonna have sex. We're gonna have to deal with it." Before she could finish, Mamie interrupted.

"All I know is that I don't want that boy climbing up on top of some little gal, thinking he knows what he's doing, when he really doesn't, and getting his ass in a world of trouble. I don't need any crap like that. And another thing, I don't intend to pay no damn child support. Hell, I can hardly afford to take care of Jeremy and myself," Mamie said and Rayanne had to laugh.

"Who are you trying to kid? You have money up to your behind so money isn't a problem."

"That's not the point, Little Miss Fort Knox," Mamie said. "Do you realize how much it takes to raise a child? And, everything that Jeremy wants costs like hell."

"I know that. I was joking," Rayanne said half heatedly.

"I don't joke when it comes to my money, and it is mine, and mine is the operative word here. I worked hard for it, and I don't intend to support half of New York. Those young gals take their little fast asses out there, get a little piece, enjoy the hell out of it, and they go back for more. I reckon some of them see where more got them. The same place it got me," Mamie said, remembering when she'd gotten pregnant with Jeremy and how she and Hank didn't get married until she was in her eighth month. She'd never forgiven Hank for delaying their wedding and she'd never forgotten it either.

"Mamie, I understand what you're saying, but what I'm talking about is worse than getting some little girl pregnant. I'm not trying to minimize teenage pregnancy, it's a growing concern in this country. What I'm saying is that some of these kids' little hormones are on fire, so we've got to keep the lines of communication open, get into their minds, listen to what they are saying, talk with them and hope they'll listen. We can't give up on them. We've got to keep trying to do whatever it takes to reach them. We also have to talk about practicing safe sex," Rayanne said and added, "I hope I'm not sounding as though I'm saying these kids are bad and all they want to do is have sex, because I don't mean it that way, and I'm not condoning sex either, but we should make them aware that there are alternatives. We shouldn't overlook anything. They need to know that if they're going to have sex, they should exercise some responsibility and protect themselves and their partners," Rayanne said. Mamie had a worried look on her face. "Mamie, we are the adults. Kids don't come with instructions. We have to work with them, teach them. We can't depend on anyone else to do the job for us."

"Yeah, right," Mamie said and the statement bordered on sarcasm.

"I'm serious. This is nothing to fool around with."

"I know and while we're talking, let's keep in mind that these are kids we're talking about," Mamie said.

"I'm not losing sight of that. Why do you think I'm so concerned? The situation would be a little less frightening if we were talking about adults. It's the kids that I'm mostly concerned about. It's up to us to try to mold them and guide them because they're the ones who aren't going to be using their heads when they meet some young thing," Rayanne said, looking thoughtfully at her sister.

"They'll be using their heads all right, Mamie said. "Only it won't be the one up top."

"It's a job, it ain't gonna be easy, and we may not like the options that are available to us."

"I have no intentions of moving back home right now, if that's what you are getting at again. There's got to be another answer," Mamie said, looking at Rayanne. "I wonder whether John and Christen would let Jeremy stay with them for a while."

John was the second oldest brother. He'd met and married Christen after they graduated college seven years ago, and although they wanted children very much and it wasn't due to lack of trying, Christen didn't conceive. That had been a big part of Christen's problem and what had caused her to lean so heavily towards alcohol. She was a good person, you couldn't ask for a better sister-in-law, but there were times when she was moody as hell. John, an assistant principal and Christen, who worked in the school system as well, lived in a three bedroom, ranch style home. The entire house was beautifully furnished, with the exception of one room which was left empty with the hope of one day making it into a nursery. "I don't know. You'll have to talk with them," Rayanne answered. "I thought you talked with them about this last year."

"Yeah, but Christen wasn't too happy about it, and John will only do what she wants." Rayanne didn't comment. "Would you talk with them for me? Christen likes you. I think they'd do it if you asked them," Mamie said.

"Mamie, I'm not getting involved in that. This is something that you need to take care of."

"Well, correct me if I'm wrong, Miss, but didn't I hear you say you'll help?"

"I said I'd do what I can to help," Rayanne corrected.

"You are so damn selfish. You are so caught up in your own little world that you are not willing to lift a finger to help anyone else," Mamie spat out.

"That's not true and you know it. You are just pissed because I won't ask John and Christen to raise your son when he has a living mother and father. Well, I am sorry but I don't think John and Christen are the answer to the problem. You have got to decide what's best for your son. I can't find a home for Jeremy, but I will help if you can come up with a viable solution," Rayanne said, and Mamie stared at her with unblinking eyes. "Mamie, if you spent less time trying to become the wealthiest person in New York and more time being a mother, you might not be having this problem." Rayanne knew Mamie didn't like what she was saying, but she continued. "Sometimes we can't have it all when we have children. We have to give up something, make sacrifices. Kids are wonderful, we have to spend time with them, and we have to remember that time is not a renewable resource. We can't replace it or make it up in anyway at all, and we certainly can't pass our children off to someone else when trouble comes."

"Where do you get off at saying something like that? It's not like that at all, Rayanne, and you know it. I'm not trying to shun my responsibility. John has been telling mama and daddy how much they want a child," Mamie said.

"They want a baby," Rayanne stated, "there's a difference in wanting a baby and having someone else's child who is half grown. It just isn't the same."

"Don't get damn technical with me," Mamie said.

"Look, Mamie," Rayanne threw up her hands in exasperation, "you talk with John and Christen and if you all can work it out, then it's fine with me."

Mamie was quiet but Rayanne knew her mind was at work. Mamie's mind was always at work. She said, "If Christen was any damn good, she would've given my brother kids a long time ago."

"Why do you think it's Christen's fault that she hasn't gotten pregnant?"

"Because John is a Wilson and us Wilsons are fertile. Shit, we are full of babies. I thought you would've had at least one by now yourself," Mamie said. Rayanne looked at Mamie. "It's not as if you haven't been having your little house painted. By the way, did you bring that fine ass, Ralph home with you?" Mamie asked, changing the subject. Mamie had met Ralph only once when Rayanne invited her to join them at a play, but she remembered him.

"No, I didn't," Rayanne answered.

"I would've never left something that good looking behind."

"What do you expect me to do? Carry him around in my pocket?"

"I would," Mamie admitted, laughing. Rayanne looked at her. "You ask, so I'm telling you."

"I don't think that's necessary," Rayanne said, nonchalant.

"You don't huh? You will learn sooner or later, little sister," Mamie said bitterly, "that you can't trust these men. Especially the fine ones."

"Mamie, Ralph and I wouldn't have much of a relationship if we didn't trust each other," Rayanne said, trying to ignore Mamie's statement.

"A word to the wise, as they say," Mamie said, a smirk on her face. Why was it that Mamie always thought that she knew just a little bit more than anyone else, about everything, Rayanne wondered. "I know what you are thinking," Mamie said, "you're thinking that I think I'm right. It's not that I want to be right, Rayanne. I just don't want to see you get hurt."

"There's an element of risk in most things," Rayanne said.

"You are and always have been the eternal optimist."

"Mamie, I'm not stupid, but I'm also not going to live my life worrying about what some man is doing when we're not together."

"Some man? I thought Ralph meant more to you than that."

"How'd this conversation get turned around to me? I thought we were talking about Jeremy."

"I'm just saying don't put too much trust in one man. You tell me. Who trusted anyone more than I trusted Hank, and look where it got me. You see what he did to me," Mamie said. Rayanne wondered if Mamie had ever thought that maybe she asked for some of what happened. "Hank got tired of me, he split, and that's all there was to it."

"I don't know that it's any one person's fault when a marriage fails," Rayanne said.

"It was all his fault. I did everything for the man, and he walked off and left me anyway, and for some old ass broad. The bitch is older than Hank. Hell, she's almost as old as mama."

"I don't think age had anything to do with it," Rayanne replied.

"Obviously," Mamie said. Everyone in the family thought it was uncharacteristic of Hank's behavior to just walk out like he did, but they also knew that Mamie stayed on his back. And, as far as trusting him, she was always nagging and suspicious, even when there was no reason to be. She'd made the man miserable by showing distrust and jealousy, but Rayanne didn't think that Hank ever stopped loving Mamie. She simply made it impossible for him to live with her. If she'd only thought to put his happiness before your own insecurities, she would've been pleased with the dividends, and Rayanne had told her as much. The two women sat quietly for a moment. Mamie needed time to formulate her thoughts, to reflect on what Rayanne had said to her. Once she accomplished her goal, she said, "So, little sister is teaching big sister the facts of life." Rayanne smiled, but she didn't say anything. She was thinking that Mamie was at the top in her professional life, but her personal life plunged deeper with each relationship. Mamie looked up to see Rayanne looking at her, and she smiled. "What?" Mamie asked.

"I was just thinking," Rayanne said, resting her elbows on the table and clasping her hands about her chin.

"What about?" Mamie asked.

"You and how you went about preparing for Jeremy when you were pregnant. You read all the books on babies, painted the nursery and crib yellow, bought records of the sound of rain and the ocean and played them while carrying him and after he was born, to keep him calm and peaceful, which I might add, was great. Mamie, you're quite a woman when you want to be."

Mamie looked at Rayanne, tilted her head to the side, smiling. "That's quite a compliment."

"Well, it's true. But it's only when you," Rayanne pointed a finger at Mamie, "want to be." They laughed together. This was a rare occasion for the two of them to share anything, even something as simple as laughter, but laughing was good, for both of them.

John and Jeremy entered the cafeteria and joined the women at their table. "What's up, mom, aunt Rayanne?" Jeremy said, leaning over to give Rayanne a hug and a kiss on the cheek.

"Hey, Jeremy? What you been up to?" Rayanne said, running her arm affectionately around his shoulders.

"Just hanging out with uncle John," Jeremy answered.

"You're not giving uncle John and auntie Christen a hard time, are you?" Mamie asked.

"No, mom", Jeremy responded, wrinkling his nose.

"Jeremy is a good kid," John said as he sat forward in his chair, clasping his hands in front of him on the table, "I thought the two of you were going home."

"We were, but we stopped off here for coffee," Mamie answered.

"How was daddy when you left him, John?" Rayanne asked. Her talk with Mamie had allowed her to put her thoughts about her father aside momentarily, but they were back and the thought of it brought the crease back to her forehead.

"He seems to be holding his own," John answered.

"And mama?" she asked.

"I was finally able to talk her into going home and getting some rest," he answered.

"Good. She's been here ever since daddy was brought in," Rayanne said.

"Yeah, but she's okay. You know mama," John said. "She's the strongest woman I know."

"She's upset about daddy, but mama is fine," Mamie concurred.

"Maxine is driving Mama home and she'll stay with her until you get there," John said.

"Maxine looks fantastic," Mamie said changing the subject.

"She does," Rayanne agreed, "she's looking like her old self again." Maxine was the sister between Mamie and Rayanne. She was short, pretty and shapely. She was a lab technician at the hospital. Her marriage to Joseph Duncan, who was a plumbing contractor at the time, produced two sons, Bobby and Bruce. The marriage was a good one, she thought. She was made to feel special, she was an equal partner in the decisions made in their lives. She loved Joe and felt he loved her just as much which is why she was devastated when, one day out of the blue, Joe ran off, leaving her alone to raise the boys. Maxine later filed for divorce, Joe didn't contest it and her marriage of nine years was dissolved. Her devastation was short lived, though because shortly afterwards, she met and married Marcus Richards and a year and a half after that union, Maxine gave birth to a baby girl, Marcia Raylyn. Maxine and the kids realized later that when Joe left, it was the best thing that he could've done for them.

"Maxine and the kids are fine. That Marcus is one helluva nice guy," John said.

"That damn Joe," Mamie said, "I heard that he hasn't given Maxine any support for the boys or herself since he left."

"I don't think Maxine wants anything for herself but surely Joe should be doing something for the boys," Rayanne said.

"And it's not as if he can't afford it," Mamie said. "The man was a shit contractor."

"Plumbing contractor," John attempted to correct her.

"I know what he does," Mamie spat out, "but the point is that the guy made good money then, and I'm sure he still does. Joe always had a knack for making money so I'll bet he's got plenty. Another thing, whatever went on between he and Maxine was one thing but to neglect his kids is wrong," Mamie said, and Rayanne agreed. "I don't know what some of these men are thinking. Hell, we don't make these babies alone. Oh, they are there for the making but not the finish. It takes a real man to hang in there for the long haul."

"We're not that bad," John avowed.

"Speak for yourself," Mamie said.

"I am," John said.

"Look at the record here. Hank and I got married, had a baby, we got divorced. Maxine and Joe got married, had two babies, they got divorces. Two out of two marriages of your sisters failed and we weren't at fault. What do you say to that," Mamie said not giving John an opportunity to respond. "These guys just walked off without a word. I wouldn't rush into it, Rayanne, if I were you. Look around, have a good time, but put off getting married for a while," she finished.

"At least Hank didn't drop the ball. He takes care of his son," John said winking at Jeremy who smiled and returned the wink. Then to Rayanne, "Don't let her scare you off, baby. Marriage, like anything you really want, takes work. There are some bad apples out there, but that goes both ways."

"I know that," Mamie said, "but you know most of you guys are full of it. You just can't be trusted. Irresponsible jackasses."

"Who are we talking about?" John asked.

"I'm just talking in general," Mamie answered.

"I hope you're not worried about Maxine. She's good, happy as can be," John assured them.

Mamie had to agree, "That girl hit the jackpot the second time around."

"Marcus is a good man," John said. "I think it's wonderful how he relates to all of them, especially the boys. They are a family now, and it's plain to see that the kids adore him."

"Mom, give me a couple of dollars," Jeremy asked, interrupting their conversation.

"What do you want a couple of dollars for and is that any way to ask for it?" Mamie asked.

"I'm sorry, mom. May I have a few dollars, please?" Jeremy

161

rephrased the question. "I want to get a soda and a candy bar."

"When you can't ask for things any better than that young man, you need to have a job and your own money," Mamie said, handing the boy a ten dollar bill. Jeremy thanked her and rushed over to make a purchase. "That boy," she said.

"Give the kid a break, Mamie," John said.

"I don't want Jeremy growing up thinking he can get anything he wants, anytime he wants. And another thing, he needs to have manners. A kid without manners is something to deal with. He'll grow up being a jerk. Speaking of jerks," Mamie said, "does anyone know where Joe is now? Maxine said the last she heard, he was in Florida or was it Georgia? I don't know, but I know one thing. He is the most exasperating men that I know." Rayanne tried not to be judgmental, but Joe was high on her list of exasperating men as well. "Well good riddance to him," Mamie finished.

"Mama said daddy likes Marcus also," Rayanne said, wringing her hands. John noticed her mood as he watched her from across the table. He reached out and took her hand in his.

"I know you're worried about daddy, sweetheart, we all are, but we've got to hang in there for both of our parents."

"That's what I've been telling her," Mamie said and suddenly she was distracted and John and Rayanne saw who had captured their sister's attention. This woman will never change, John thought. "Who is he?" Mamie asked.

"That's Larry."

"You know that wonderful specimen?" Mamie asked and inhaled causing her breasts to heave.

"Yeah, we play ball together," John answered. He and Larry had also gotten together on occasions for a beer, they'd even gone on fishing trips. "Larry's a nice guy."

"Well, introduce me," Mamie ordered.

"I can, but just so you know, he's married and has two precious little girls," John said.

"John, I didn't ask for his resume, I just asked to be introduced to the man."

John bided for Larry to come over. Larry was handsome in a rugged kind of way, he was tall, well built and had a nice set of brown eyes, that added to his attractiveness. He was about thirty-four, and he moved with the grace of an athlete when he approached them. "Girls, this is Larry Jacobs. Larry, these are my sisters, Rayanne and Mamie. They live in New York." Jeremy approached them and John finished the introduction. "And this is

Mamie's son, Jeremy."

"Pleased to meet y'all. I hope the reason you're here is nothing too serious," Larry said.

"Daddy had a heart attack," John explained.

"I didn't know that, man. I'm sorry," Larry said. "How's he doing?"

"I'm gonna get more coffee, anyone want some," Rayanne said getting up from the table.

"No, I'm fine," Mamie responded. Both Larry and John also said no, and Rayanne walked away. "It happened late last night," Mamie said to Larry, "but he seems to be doing pretty good."

"Is there anything I can do?" Larry asked, genuinely concern.

"Just good thoughts and prayers," John said.

"You got it. I hope he'll be okay."

Mamie craned her neck to see where Rayanne was. She wanted to be sure Rayanne was unable to hear her. "Daddy's not out of the woods yet, but the doctors are optimistic."

"I'm glad to hear that," Larry said. "We'll keep him in our prayers."

"Thank you, Mr. Jacobs," Mamie said.

"Please, call me Larry," he said. Rayanne returned to the table with a cup of coffee that she didn't touch once she sat it down. She didn't want coffee or anything, she was trying to keep busy, to keep calm.

"What are you doing here? Is everything all right with you and your family?" John asked Larry.

"Yeah, everything's fine. I had to get a physical for the job." He looked at his watch. "So I reckon I had better be getting on back."

"Okay, Larry, take care," John said.

"You too, and hang in there, man," Larry said, extending his hand to John.

"It was nice meeting y'all," he said to Mamie and Rayanne, "you too, my man," he said to Jeremy. "I hope the next time we meet won't be under similar circumstances." Then he left.

"A nice man," Mamie said.

"A married man," John reminded her.

"And thank you, John," Mamie said and John looked confused, and she explained. "For not referring to me as your oldest sister. That's the first time you introduced me and didn't say, 'this is my oldest sister, Mamie.' I was so sick of you always doing that to me." Mamie and John laughed. Rayanne's mind was elsewhere.

"Rayanne, would you loosen up a bit." Rayanne looked from Mamie's face to John's. How could she explain how she was feeling. How could she relay her thoughts and fears without bringing everyone else down. Her father was in his late sixties and he was ill, and to Rayanne he seemed very different, so unlike his usual self. Rayanne had always been a person of divine faith and a positive thinker, but she knew that life could change drastically, within a split second and at that moment, she felt helpless, wondering whether her father would ever be the same again.

CHAPTER 20

Although only three and a half miles separated the hospital and the family house, the drive seemed much longer. At first, Mamie couldn't shut up about Larry and what a nice man he was. When she said she wondered what it would be like to date him, Rayanne reminded her that not only did the man have a living, breathing wife, but he had two children as well. They rode the rest of the way in silence with Mamie sporting a secretive smile. Rayanne didn't have to ask to know exactly what was on her mind. The same as always. Men.

Rayanne pulled into the driveway and stopped the car. She unhooked her seatbelt and sat for a moment to take in the beauty of the yard. It was picturesque, colorful, a place of beauty. Her mother had spent a lot of time working in the yard, making sure that there would always be colorful flowers, and sure enough, the yard held burst of colors year round. Mostly chrysanthemums lined the edge of the yard on either side of the house, a sprinkling of zinnias were still evident as well as other fall and winter flowering plants. Her favorite flowers that bloomed early spring which she missed most because she didn't spend much time home during that time of year were the azaleas and the white dogwood trees. The lawn that was manicured and still green, held a mother duck and three babies that sat near the white bird bath that stood in the center of the front yard.

Mamie had already gotten out of the car and was standing on

the porch, looking impatient by the time Rayanne removed her bags from the trunk. Rayanne set her bags onto the driveway, walked across the lawn and picked up the paper. She tucked it under her arm and used her old key to let herself and Mamie in. Rayanne stood on the threshold and took in the view. Their home had been remodeled since all the kids had grown up and left home. Where there were four bedrooms, a living room and a kitchen that doubled as a dining room, the house now had only three bedrooms, but a formal dining room and a large family room were added. The furniture was old but still in good taste, and the house was immaculate. Ruth always kept it that way, and as the saying goes, you could eat off of the floors in her home.

Rayanne and her siblings were blessed with parents who had an enormous capacity to love and that love was not limited to family and close friends, they showered their love on anyone who'd accept it. When Rayanne and Ivory brought Dorian home for a visit, Dorian was adopted by each family. They fell in love with her, and she them. Dorian still didn't talk much about her own family so her past was still something of a mystery, but she made a quick connection with Ruth and had promised to visit as often as she could. And, in doing so, she and Ruth became close and Dorian shared more with Ruth than she did anyone. "If you're not going in, would you move aside and let me," Mamie said, interrupting Rayanne's thoughts. They entered the house. Ruth had set the table in the dining room and the kitchen, because when the entire family gathered, one table wasn't enough to accommodate them all.

The house was filled with wonderful odors of food. Rayanne had managed to keep her figure during the years. She was a trim, 5 feet 7 inches frame, but her mind had already began to calculate the calories and the pounds that would settle in some unwanted place on her body, if she weren't careful as she eyed the food on the stove. Her stomach would have no choice, she thought as the smells invaded her nostrils. "Mama," Rayanne called out, "you're cooking?"

"Yeah, some of everybody's favorites," Ruth answered, stirring the collards.

"I thought you came home to get some rest," Rayanne said, noticing that the sleepless nights her mother had recently gone through showed on her face, yet she moved about the kitchen with what appeared to be untouched energy.

"Honey, I ain't done a think but cooked a little something,"

Ruth said and Rayanne thought, a little something. She had roasted two chickens, made stuffing, collards, browned rice, black-eyed peas, candied yams, peach cobbler and corn bread. There was even a slab of ribs cooking in the oven. This was no feat for Ruth. This meal wasn't even to compare with one of her Sunday dinners when all of the children were still at home. She'd prepared almost twice that amount of food on Sunday mornings when the children were growing up, and she'd be fresh as a daisy, teaching her Sunday school class at 9:30 every Sunday morning.

"I wish you wouldn't push yourself this way. There are enough of us around to take care of the meals." Ruth heard her daughter, but she didn't mend her pace, finishing up what she was doing.

"If you wanna make yourself useful," Ruth said to Rayanne, "make another picture of tea. I need to pull them ribs out of the over. And Mamie, you put another water picture and some glasses on the table." Within an hour, everyone gathered around the large dining table where Ruth asked the blessings before they were seated at both tables to eat. Ruth always felt that a family should eat at least one meal a day together, even if only for a half hour, it kept families together.

Although Rayanne hadn't eaten since lunch and the smell in the kitchen made her mouth water, she toyed with the food and realized she was no longer hungry, once it was on her plate. After dinner, she excused herself and went into her bedroom to call Ralph. She was a little surprised that he hadn't phoned her. She flipped the switch that flooded her bedroom with light that poured from the cut crystal with brass plated base lamps. The rose pink comforter and shams were simple elegance and the pink organdy matching sheers and tie back drapes cast a soft spell across the room. She dialed the number, got his machine and left a message.

When Rayanne returned to the hospital that evening, it was difficult, but she was successful in convincing her mother to stay home that night. Rayanne was surprise at how much her father seemed to have improved from when she'd seen him earlier. She was happy, so much so that she found herself humming to a tune that played on the car radio on her way home. Everyone had gone to bed except Ruth and Mamie. Rayanne informed them of Raymond's improved condition, then she asked her mother about Josh. "You know Josh," Ruth said, "still drinking like a fish.

"Is he, Mama?" Rayanne and Josh were the youngest of the siblings and they'd been very close growing up. Josh had earned a degree in engineering at Clemson, but he didn't put it to much use most of the time because of his drinking. However, he'd managed to hold onto his most recent job at the power plant in Georgia. Josh was smart. He'd been an honor student from his sophomore year until he graduated college, but as they say, women and alcohol can destroy a good man. In Josh's case, it was the latter.

"Yeah, your daddy and I done talk to him until we're just about blue in the face, but it don't seem to do no good." Rayanne knew Josh was an alcoholic, although he'd never admit it. She also knew all too well that alcoholics rarely admit that they are.

"He needs help, Mama," Rayanne said, a frown creasing her forehead. She heard Mamie clicked her teeth and was about to leave the room.

"You turning in?" Ruth said to her oldest daughter.

"I may go out for a while. I'm not sure yet," Mamie said as she left the room.

Ruth nodded and gave a half smile, then said to Rayanne, "You're right about Josh, and we're trying, but it's hard."

"I know," Rayanne said, looking thoughtful.

Ruth reached across the kitchen table and rubbed Rayanne's hand. "Don't you worry yourself about Josh. He's gonna get the help he needs. He'll be all right. Me and your daddy are gonna see to that, so don't you worry. And get that buckle outta your brow. If you don't, you're gonna look old before your time."

Rayanne smiled and said, "You always say that I know and it's true," Ruth said.

"What about Ruby," Rayanne asked. "What's going on with her."

"Ruby is fine until Josh gets on her nerves. Then, it's a merry go round. One week she's there, the next she's gone," Ruth said, shaking her head. She got up and took a plate of spare ribs, rice and collards from a pot that was sitting on the stove keeping warm, and she sat the plate of food on the table in front of Rayanne. "I put a little something aside for you, seeing you didn't eat much supper."

Ruth was about to pour a glass of iced tea, but Rayanne took the glass from her hand and poured the tea herself. "Mama, you're too good to us."

"I don't mind honey."

"I know and I hope you know that we appreciate everything you do for us," Rayanne said and her mother smiled and nodded her head back and forth. Rayanne took a sip from head back and forth. Rayanne took a sip from the glass of tea and returned to

168

their earlier conversation. "Ruby is a good girl, and I can't say I blame her when she splits on Josh when it becomes unbearable. Living with a drunk is no picnic."

"I know it. Shucks, Josh is my son and I love him dearly, but sometimes he comes in here so sloppy drunk that I want to just walk right out and give him the house," Ruth said, looking at Rayanne, who wiped her mouth and thought, that'd be the day when Mama turned away from any of her children for any reason. "Josh isn't all bad. He's as nice as can be, he is smart, and he could be doing so much more with his self, but that drinking, Lordy, Lordy. We're gonna do the best we can, and we'll leave the rest in the hands of the Lord and let His will be done. You know, honey, we don't get to pick out the kind of families we get no more than we can clean germs," Ruth said, and Rayanne thought her mother had never uttered truer words. She pushed her plate away and took another sip of tea. "What else is bothering you? I know you're worrying 'bout your daddy and Josh, but something else seems to be troubling you."

Ruth always seem to know when something was going on with her children. Rayanne didn't want to tell her what was bothering her, but she didn't want to lie either. She looked at her mother. "I was thinking about Dorian."

"What about Dorian," Ruth asked, concern in her voice.

"Dorian has a drug problem, Mama" Rayanne said and she didn't stop talking until she'd told Ruth everything.

"I don't know why she wants to do a darn fool thing like that, and such a pretty girl. Lord have mercy. Well, honey, the important thing is that we be there for her. It's hard to help when the person you want to help doesn't want it. We just gotta let her know we love her and that what she's doing is not just hurting herself, but all of us who love her. And, we gotta pray." Rayanne felt much better after they talked and she thought how much she was going to miss her mother when she returned to New York.

***

Mamie hung up the phone and entered the family room wearing a long blushing pink night gown with matching robe and slippers. She had her long black hair pulled back and twisted into a ball at the back of her head. Although Mamie was a little on the plump side, she was very attractive and very aware of the effect she had on men. "What are you two talking about," she asked and without waiting for an answer, she walked out onto the back porch, closing the door behind her.

Ruth looked at Rayanne, smiled and shook her head. "Honey, I forgot to tell you that Ralph called you while you were at the hospital. Said he was gonna call you back." The phone rang again and Mamie rushed in and scooped it up.

"Hello," she said in her sexiest voice. She looked at Rayanne, handed the phone to her and returned to the porch. It was Maxine. The phone beeped during their conversation and when Rayanne answered, it was Ralph calling back. She quickly ended the call with her sister promising to call her back and she talked with Ralph. She was excited. She'd seen him less than twenty-four hours ago, but it seemed an eternity. She'd missed Ralph and told him so.

"I miss you too, baby. How is your father?" he asked.

"He's improving. He looked even better tonight when I saw him."

"I'm glad. Now, when are you coming back here?"

"Sounds like someone misses me," she said, her smile broadening as she pictured his handsome face. Ralph had been so much a part of her life the past nine years that she could hardly remember what it was like before they met.

"You got that right," he replied.

"Well, I'm not sure, honey. That depends on how well daddy gets along." Rayanne relayed a good night to Ralph from her mother who waved to her as she left the room.

"So I've got you all to myself now," Ralph said.

"I'm afraid so," Rayanne chuckled softly. When he told her he hoped all goes well so she could hurry back because he couldn't handle living in that big city without her much longer, she felt warm and tingly all over. "Why don't you think about coming down for a few days," she asked, thinking it would be great if he came down for the weekend. "The family would love seeing you again and it would be good for you to get away from the city for a little while."

"I may just do that," he said, "because this loneliness ain't happening." They talked a half hour more, then Rayanne hung up and went to bed.

Dorian and Ivory flew down for a couple of days and Dorian spent a lot of time talking with Ruth. Ruth was always easy to talk with. Even when Rayanne was in high school, her friends sometimes came over just to talk with Ruth. But, as it turned out, Ralph didn't make the trip. Rayanne drove Ivory and Dorian to the airport and upon returning home, she visited her Aunt Bessie who was her father's older and only sister. Although Aunt Bessie was in her late 70's, her faculties hadn't been dull by age.

Rayanne spend a week at home after her daddy had been released from the hospital. The night before her departure, she packed her suitcases, and she called Ralph, but got his answering machine. She walked out onto the front porch. She stretched her hands out against the railing that framed the porch and she watched the moon as it edged it way across the sky to mark the judgment of time. She watched as the stars twinkled, making their presence clear and in doing so, Rayanne wondered for the first time, whether the stars communicated with each other, and if they did, what did they talk about, what did they say to each other? Did they experience emotions, did they have secrets of their own?

There was just a hint of fall that chilled the air and as Rayanne sat in the porch swing, she began to think about returning to New York. She also thought of her parents and thinking for the first time that although she missed Ralph and wanted to see him badly, she didn't want to leave her parents. She was immersed in her thoughts, when Mamie said from the door, "you all set for the trip back to New York in the morning?"

"I suppose so," Rayanne said, reservation flooding her voice. "Aunt Bessie said she was hoping to see you before you leave."

"Oh my goodness," Mamie said with a groan, putting her hands up to her face. "I meant to stop by to see her. How is she?"

"She's worried about daddy, but she's okay. Still as sharp as ever." It was true. Aunt Bessie was amazing. She ran her house alone, kept it immaculate, did her own banking and shopping, but got someone to drive her where she needed to go. That was the only thing that'd changed about her. She no longer drove. "I took her to the grocery store yesterday and she wouldn't even let me push the shopping cart. No ma'am, she pushed that thing up and down those aisles herself," Rayanne said chuckling. After a moment, she fell silent.

Mamie noticed Rayanne's silence and said," you still worrying about daddy?"

"Yes, that too, but I was thinking about something Aunt Bessie said today. She told me Stevie stole from her the last time he was home." Mamie didn't doubt it, given the situation he'd created for himself.

"I don't even speak to Stevie when I see him. I try to avoid him whenever I can."

"He's your cousin," Rayanne said.

"That's not my fault," Mamie said stiffly and Rayanne could

understand her feeling that way. They knew that Stevie was using drugs and his career had gone to pot. He'd literally become a bum, but blood was thicker than water.

"It breaks Aunt Bessie's heart to see her only child's come to this. Uncle Steve had never gotten over the way Stevie Jr. turned out."

"Stevie Jr. is a trip and I'm going to stay as far away from him as I can, and I certainly don't want him any where near my son. Jeremy doesn't need that kind of influence in his life," Mamie sneered. "He needs to get it together with his grown behind."

"It's such a waste. Stevie is an intelligent, good looking man who had everything going for him. He had it all. It is amazing how a person can be on top of the world one day and rolling around in some gutter the next."

"It's about the choices we make," Mamie said.

"Yeah," Rayanne said, her voice trailing off.

"So what were you so engrossed in when I came out here?" Mamie asked, changing the subject. Rayanne looked at her, puzzled. "It seemed like something was on your mind."

"Not really," Rayanne replied.

"Don't give me that. I bet I know what or should I say who was occupying your mind."

"Then why don't you tell me. That way, we'll both know," Rayanne said in good humor.

"Don't be flipped with me. You were thinking about Ralph. I'd even go further and say that you're worried about him. Hell, I would be. Your father was hospitalized after having had a heart attack, you've been here two whole weeks and he hasn't brought his ass down here not once and you're suppose to be the love of his life."

"Looks like you've gone into mind reading," Rayanne said, laughing softly.

"But I'm right, aren't I?" Rayanne didn't respond. "You don't have to say, but I'm sure I'm right. Just a woman's institution," Mamie said and walked over to where she could face Rayanne and leaned with her back against the railing.

"You and your woman's intuition," Rayanne said, pushing off in the swing with her head back against the chair.

"Maybe it's a little more than that," Mamie continued.

Rayanne stopped the swing abruptly and asked, "What are you getting at, Mamie?"

Mamie threw her hands up in the air, "Hell, never mind. It's none of my business what goes on between you and your man. If what he does or doesn't do is all right with you, then it's fine with me. It's your business, not mine."

"You could've fooled me," Rayanne said.

"I'd be a little suspicious myself though," Mamie said and smiled wickedly at Rayanne.

Rayanne thought she'd better take this head on or Mamie wouldn't give up. She'd pick all night, trying to get a rise out of her. So, unless Rayanne faced her and let her know under no uncertain terms that she should mind her own business, it would go on and on. "Suspicious about what," Rayanne said. "Mamie, Ralph is a man. He is a busy man and aside from that, he has a life of his own. But just in case you hadn't noticed, he and I are not joined at the hip. We can live independent of each other."

"Rayanne, the man hasn't bothered to put in an appearance in all this time. Are you telling me that you haven't asked yourself why at least once?" Mamie sneered and it was more evident than before that her bitterness over losing Hank was turning her cruel. And, even if Rayanne had wondered why Ralph hadn't made the trip, she'd never admit it to Mamie. Mamie walked over and sat in the swing next to Rayanne. "If he was my man, he'd have a helluva lot of explaining to do."

"Divorcing Hank certainly has made you bitter. Just because he walked over you doesn't mean that that's a way of life for women, because it's not. God," Rayanne said shaking her head, "I pity the next man who gets involved with you because you're gonna kick his behind for everything Hank did and things you thought he did." Rayanne was almost sorry she brought up Hank's name. He was a soft spot in Mamie's heart. She knew Mamie still loved him, that he'd probably always be Mamie's strongest weakness, and any comment that was the slightest bit negative, would hurt Mamie, but she didn't care. She just wanted Mamie off of her back. That was her only weapon and she used it when necessary. There were lots of things on Rayanne's mind. Ralph, of course was one, but there were her parents, and at that time, they were the ones who were uppermost in her mind. As she thought about it, she looked at Mamie and was about to apologize but she found Mamie looking at her with clenched teeth.

"You bitch," she hurled, "how can you be that cruel?"

"Look, I'm sorry, but you just wouldn't let up. We're leaving here tomorrow and I'm concerned about Mama and Daddy. As far as Ralph is concerned, sure he does some things that I question, but I don't speculate about what he might be doing and make myself miserable. Ralph and I are free to do as we please, date other people if we choose to, whatever. It just happens that we don't choose to," Rayanne informed.

"What black man is going to allow his woman to date other men?" Mamie asked, with raised eyebrows.

"Ralph doesn't allow me to do anything. Each of us is our own person. We make our own decisions and we control our own happenings. We don't dictate what the other can or cannot do. We are not control freaks. That's a mistake a lot of couples make." Rayanne seemed to have gotten through to Mamie.

Mamie sat back in the swing and crossed her legs. "Okay, if that's how you see it." She reached into her pocket and pulled out a piece of gum, removed the wrapper and stuck it into her mouth. "Speaking of men, I thought I would've seen Larry again by now."

"Who?" Rayanne asked, with a crease in her brow.

"Larry. Larry Jacobs, the guy we met at the hospital."

"Is that who you've been going out with," Rayanne asked, looking in Mamie's face, and she was surprised when Mamie nodded, yes. "You know that guy is married."

"Are you making a point?"

"No, just an observation and I think you ought to leave that alone."

"Rayanne, I learned a long time ago that if you don't step out and take chances, nothing will ever happen. I don't want to mess up his home life or marry him. I just want to have a little fun, that's all," Mamie said but Rayanne knew nothing in life was that simply with Mamie. As possessive as she was, she'd have that man jumping through hoops.

"You'll have that poor man flying to New York so often that he'll probably start buying stock in an airline," Rayanne said and Mamie chuckled.

"Larry had called earlier, but he was doubtful whether he could get out tonight. I looked up his number in the phone book and if I don't hear from him in the next half hour, I'm going to call him."

"Oh no you won't," Rayanne said disbelieving.

"You damn skippy I will," Mamie assured her.

"Girl," Rayanne said shaking her head, "you're too much. This is not New York, you know. This is a small town and you know how people talk."

"Who gives a damn," Mamie said. Rayanne wanted to tell her to be careful, that they also had family who live there, besides,

174

Jeremy had met Larry and knew he was married.

"Jeremy is observant, and you might want to be careful what you impart to your child."

"Come go for a ride with me," Mamie said.

"Where are you going this time of night when we've got a plane to catch at the crack of dawn?"

"Are you going or not?" Mamie asked, ignoring Rayanne's question.

"No I'm not, but where are you going? Not to Larry's house, I hope."

"That's none of your business," Mamie said jokingly, with her hands on her hips, "you don't want to go, don't ask no questions." Although Rayanne felt that Mamie was making a big mistake, she was grown. Rayanne looked at her with a frown on her face. "Life hurts, doesn't it," Mamie said and Rayanne agreed. Lots of things in life hurt. Dating a married man could be a very painful experience. Rayanne had gone that route and had experienced that pain first hand. It was a dead end street, and she vowed never to make that mistake again. "Rayanne," Mamie said, pulling Rayanne back to the present, "If I die tonight, this world wouldn't own me a damn thing. Know why? Because I've done it all. I haven't just thought about it, I've lived and I don't intend to stop, at least not now." Rayanne knew the type of personality that Mamie had. She was possessive and clinging and she didn't need to get involved with no man who was married. She'd make his life miserable. "It could turn out better than you think," Mamie was saying. "Anyway, I won't know if I don't try, will I."

"Hey, if this is what you want to do, then go for it," Rayanne said, then she got up and went into the house.

From the bathroom, Rayanne heard Mamie come into the house, spoke with someone on the telephone and left. Rayanne stepped into the shower, shampooed her hair and rubbed her favorite soap all over her body. She blew dried her hair, set it on a few large rollers and went to bed. Once in bed, she had trouble sleeping. She looked at the clock on the night stand. A quarter to 1. An hour later, she was still awake. There was a soft tap on her door, Mamie poked her head into the room and switched on the light. "I thought I was gonna have to send a posse for you," Rayanne said, blinking under the light.

"Oh yeah," Mamie smiled wickedly, "is Jeremy here?"

"It's a fine time to ask," Rayanne said, shielding her eyes from the light with her hand.

"Is he here or not," Mamie asked, losing patience.

"He's here. Maxine and Marcus brought him shortly after you left."

"Good. I'll see you in the morning," Mamie said, flipped the light off and closed the door. Rayanne turned over in bed and before long, she was awakened to the soft buzz of the alarm clock. Within four hours, she'd returned to the hustle and bustle of the fastest moving city in the world, and her life there, the life she'd love so much, but she knew before hand that it wouldn't be the same.

CHAPTER 21

Rayanne went through a stack of mail that Yvonne had piled in a neat stack on the desk, and although her accountant took care of most of her bills, she still wrote checks to cover the underground parking space where she kept her 1984 black Corvette, and she wrote sizable checks to charities for Abused Children, Battered Women and the Homeless. She replied to RSVP invitations, and went through the junk mail. She'd been inundated with mail of no consequence and when she was finished, she laid down her pen and went into the kitchen to have breakfast. The food that had looked so tempting when Yvonne first laid it on the table before her, had lost much of its appeal. She ended up pushing it away and after making several phone calls, she started a new play. However hard she tried, it was difficult to concentrate. Her mind was occupied with her parents. She reviewed her previous notes, organized then reorganized them, jotted a few sentences, looked at them, then crossed them out. After several repeats, she put on her Reeboks and walked around the block. A nice vigorous walk had always proved successful for her writer's block in the past.

When she returned to the building, she met an elderly woman with beautiful gray hair and friendly blue eyes. The woman was accompanied by a small dog with a leash attached to its collar. The woman introduced herself as Maggie. Her dog, Cha Cha, and she'd just moved into the building a week ago. Rayanne introduced herself and she informed Maggie that she'd just returned from a business trip. She learned that Maggie had lived on Long Island with her husband before he died, then she moved to Florida with her daughter a couple of years, but had missed New York so much that she purchased a condo in Manhattan. They talked almost an hour when Rayanne returned to her apartment. She remembered thinking what a nice lady Maggie was.

Rayanne sat at the desk and picked up the pen again, but still, the words didn't flow. She pushed the pen and pad aside, sat deep in her chair and sighed. Her father was released from the hospital two months ago and although he appeared to have recovered fully, there was something about the way he looked that Rayanne couldn't put out of her mind. She couldn't hardly concentrate on anything else for thinking about her parents, her father in particular. She dialed a number. "Hey, Mama," Rayanne said when her mother answered the phone.

Ruth, knowing her daughter well enough to know why she was calling, said softly, "Everything is fine here, honey. How are you?"

"I'm fine, just checking on y'all," Rayanne said, not wanting to let her mother know how worried she was, but her own voice betrayed her and before she realize it, she asked, "Is he all right?"

"Yes, he's all right." Rayanne wanted to ask whether her father was still working as hard, but she refrained, trying to shut out the mental picture of him toiling from dawn to dusk, growing older and more worn day by day. "And, yes, your daddy's still working hard," Ruth answered her daughter's silent question.

"Daddy should take it easy, enjoy the grandchildren and just chill out."

"I got you chill out. Raymond ain't gon' let nothing stop him," Ruth said and it was true. She knew her husband better than anyone and she knew that he liked being busy. Ruth had always said that she didn't think Raymond would live long if he didn't have his work. He liked doing things that were meaningful.

"Daddy acts like he's on somebody's clock. Mama, I wish you would talk to him. He's killing himself and why. Y'all certainly don't need the money," Rayanne said, but she knew as her mother did that her father was set in his ways and once he made up his mind to do something, he rarely ever changed it.

"Honey, some of us have to do our own chores. We don't have some one to drive us around, or cook and pick up after us," Ruth teased but when Rayanne didn't respond, Ruth said." All joking aside, we're all concerned about your daddy, but you know how bull headed he can be. And, I can just see that buckle in your brow right now, so take it out," Ruth said and laughed. Rayanne laughed a little too. "I love your daddy, too, he's the only man I ever loved, and I'll be the first to say that he does work too hard, but I ain't never tried to change him in all the years I've known him and I ain't gonna start now. I ain't got no right trying to do nothing like that."

"But Mama," Rayanne protested.

"Honey, I don' talked to your daddy and he knows how I feel about all them long hours he's working, but how he wants to go about living his life, is up to him. I want my man, but I want him happy."

"All right." Rayanne knew she'd never be able to convince her mother otherwise. "You're wonderful, Mama."

"Sure I am. I'm your mother, ain't I?"

"You most definitely are," Rayanne said and after a moment, asked, "You all right?"

"I'm fine," Ruth replied, and Rayanne wondered. She knew her mother liked protecting them. "Everything's okay, thanks the Lord."

"I don't know why I can't shake this feeling of uneasiness." It was silly but she felt that as long as she was at home, nothing bad would happened, but from the moment she stepped on the plane, leaving South Carolina, she began to worry and felt that each time the phone rang, it was bringing bad news. It was silly, very silly, but that was how she felt.

"You're a worry wart, that's why. You worry about everything. You'd worry or feel responsible if there was one of them earthquakes in Africa." Ruth paused. "Things are gonna happen, but we can't live looking for bad things around every corner. We gotta have a little faith, live life to the fullest and trust in the Lord. No matter what happens, however bad it might be, God will give us the wisdom to know what to do and the strength to do it." All of what Ruth said was true and Rayanne was the first to agree, but an earthquake in Africa, she thought and smiled. "Worrying ain't gonna do but one thing for you. It'll make an old lady out of you before your time. Take it from me. Oh, did I tell you," Ruth said changing the subject, "Maxine is planning to go back to school in the evenings. I'll help Marcus look after the children. By the way, when are you gonna settle down and give your daddy and me some grandchildren?"

"I don't know," Rayanne responded.

"You don't know? You ain't getting any younger, you know."

"No kidding?" Rayanne came back, joking. "I'm just not ready yet."

"What about Ralph, is he ready?" Ruth pressed.

"He's been for some time now, Mama. He's waiting on me," she said and suddenly an uneasy feeling came to rest around her shoulders again. Maybe it was simply because she was tired.

"Well, don't wait too long," Ruth said, then asked, "how's that other daughter of mine?"

"Mamie and I talked a couple of weeks ago," Rayanne replied, knowing that wouldn't go over well with her mother. If her mother had her way, Rayanne would be calling or seeing Mamie everyday.

"Y'all live right there together. You oughta be talking more than that." Rayanne and Mamie didn't talk much because it was always Rayanne who initiated the calls and even when she did, Mamie was either too tired, too busy or on her way out. Often times when Rayanne tried to get her but couldn't and left a message on her machine, Mamie seldom bothered to return the call. So, what's the use, Rayanne thought. "You know Mamie. She's got her own little world mapped out and she ain't gonna let nothing bother it, but she's my daughter, your oldest sister and I love her as you ought to. She just likes doing things her way." It was more than that but that was Mamie's business, Rayanne thought, and the less she had to do with it, the better. "I talked with Jeremy day before yesterday," Ruth continued, "and I don't think it's a good idea for no thirteen year old to be staying in no apartment by his self like that."

"I agree, Mama, but I thought Mamie had taken care of that. Just one more thing that Mamie was suppose to do but didn't. Anyway, I will call and check on them," Rayanne promised before they hung up.

The following afternoon Rayanne had guests over for dinner, Ivory and Desmond, Dorian, Henry and Tiffany and Ted, one other couple and Ralph, of course. She also invited Maggie but she had to decline because of a previous engagement. Yvonne was on vacation and Rayanne prepared the meal which consisted of a leafy salad, white potatoes and steaks to bake on the grill, candied yams, cole slaw and baked beans. She'd even baked a couple of sweet potato pies for dessert. Rayanne was in the kitchen when Dorian appeared. "Hey, hey, hey girl," Rayanne said, swaying to the music that oozed into the kitchen from the terrace. "How's it going?"

"Things are good. You?"

"Everything's everything," Rayanne answered. "What are they doing out there?"

"They're talking stock options and golf at the club," Dorian said, and making quotes with her fingers, added, "boring."

"Aaah," Rayanne said and laughed.

"Where's Yvonne?" Dorian asked.

"She's on vacation," Rayanne said, busy tearing lettuce apart for the salad.

"And you put all this stuff together yourself?"

"This is nothing," Rayanne said, dipped a piece of lettuce into a bowl of salad dressing and stuck it into Dorian's mouth.

"Ummm, this is delicious." Dorian picked up a stick of carrot, dipped it into the dressing and took a bite of it. "This is so good. New dressing?"

"It's just a little something I threw together. A package of dressing mix, a dash of salt, pepper, accent, a little mustard, blend it all together and this is what I got. So, what have you been up to?"

"I've been fine," Dorian said and it was true. Because of the nagging or encouragement of Ivory and Rayanne, she'd gotten the help she needed with her drug problem, and she looked good. "I've got that fashion show tomorrow night. You know the fund raiser for the Heart Association. You coming?" Dorian asked with raised eyebrows.

"Yeah, I'll be there," Rayanne popped a piece of cucumber into her mouth. "You look great, girl."

"I feel good," Dorian replied. "How are things going with you? Are you still writing?" Rayanne admitted that the ideas were not coming as before, nothing she could sink her teeth into and get the juices flowing, she informed, a frown on her face which Dorian noticed. "You're just having writer's block, but that'll pass." But what she didn't know was that Rayanne was more preoccupied with what might be going on back home than she was with her writing career, but she smiled and nodded, yes.

Ivory joined the girls in the kitchen. "What are you two talking about?"

"And how are you, too," Rayanne said and laughed.

"Girl, my body is here, but I left my head out there somewhere," Ivory mumbled because Dorian had stuck a piece of lettuce dipped in salad dressing, into her mouth.

"Isn't that good?" Dorian asked.

"Ummm yeah, delicious, what is it?" Ivory asked.

"Just a little something I whipped up," Rayanne said, she checked the rolls in the oven, removed them and sat them on top of the stove and said, pointing to the top cabinet, "grab a dish from that cabinet over there." Ivory brought the dish over, slid the rolls from the sheet into it and covered them. "Dorian has the fashion show tomorrow night," Rayanne said," The one sponsored by the Heart Association."

"Oh yeah, that's right. What time ?" Ivory asked and tore off a piece of bread.

"Eight," Dorian answered, removing a dish of coleslaw from the refrigerator.

"Who's gonna eat all this food," Ivory asked, moving her hand in a sweeping gesture. "You've got enough here to feed an army." She picked up another piece from the salad bowl and Rayanne looked at her.

"Ivory, you're munching all over the place. You pregnant?" Rayanne asked, a smile on her face.

"You'd like to be an aunt again, wouldn't you?" Ivory made fun of Rayanne. "Well no. I ain't pregnant."

"I Just asked because you seem to have quite an appetite," Rayanne said eyeing Ivory and continuing to smile.

"Gal, please," Ivory said just as Ralph poked his head through the door.

"Girls, what's going on in here," he asked. "The steaks are ready and the party's outside."

"We're coming. Come girls," Rayanne said, picking up a couple of bowls of food, "grab a dish and take it out to the terrace." The unfortunate thing was that by the time the food was moved out to the terrace and they began to eat, it started to rain.

CHAPTER 22

Rayanne met Ralph in the lobby of the building on Wall Street where he worked. When he approached her, long gone was his tailored suit, shirt and tie that transformed him from an average guy to Corporate America. He'd changed into a pair of white slacks, tan pullover and a pair of white sneakers. Rayanne was comfortably dressed in a pair of yellow slacks, a sleeveless yellow blouse, white sneakers, and she wore her hair in a pony tail. They first had a glass of iced tea at an out door restaurant, then they took a taxi to the dock where they boarded a small boat and they ate dinner while circling the City. They watched the lights on shore as they twinkled and almost vanished as the boat moved further away from shore.

It was a lovely summer night and the breezes that came off of the water was cool and pleasant. Ralph and Rayanne stood close to each other and watched the moon light as it cast a silvery path across the water. They strolled around on the boat, listening to soft music played by the band that was set up on the stern. When they docked, they ran off of the boat, hand in hand and came upon an ice cream shop. Ralph chose chocolate chip, Rayanne had buttered pecan. "Yours look delicious," she said.

"So does yours."

"If you give me a lick of yours, I'll give you a lick of mine," she said and when she looked up at him, he was smiling wickedly, as he handed the cashier a bill to cover their purchase.

"That was a dangerous statement," he said.

"You know what I meant," she said, laughed and punched him gently in the ribs.

"Now she's trying to kill me." He was holding his chest pretending to be in pain. He put his arm around her shoulders and they walked along the sidewalk. They'd been rushing so much from the time they met that neither had inquired about the kind of day the other had. Rayanne asked. "It was crazy and busy," he replied, remembering how hectic his day was before they met, "and yours."

"Not bad," she said, looking up at him as they continued their walk, hand in hand, enjoying the evening breezes. "You want to talk about it?" she asked, noticing his perplexed look.

"Maybe later."

"You sure," she continued to look at him.

"I'm sure," he replied, as they strolled along the street.

After a while, Rayanne looked at Ralph again and asked, "are you tired?"

"No, why do you ask?" he questioned, the look grew more perplexed.

"I'd like to go over to Broadway and walk around a little, but if you're not up to it, we don't have to."

"No, I'm fine."

"Interested?"

"Sure," he said.

"Ralph, really, we don't have to if you don't want to," she teased.

"What's do you mean? I said I'm fine. I know I'm a little older than you but,"... he began.

"A little older?" Rayanne continued to tease, "a little older?"

"All right, so I'm almost ten years older, but I'm not ready for a rocking chair," he said, sounding annoyed.

Rayanne looked at Ralph, he looked tired and she was already sorry she'd teased him. "Honey, I was only teasing. I hope I didn't offend you. That is the last thing I'd want to do, is hurt or offend you Ralph." She stopped and held his hand tightly so that they faced each other. "Are you upset?" He didn't respond. "Ralph, I was just kidding." He looked at her, but he still didn't respond. "Ralph, I'm sorry. I had no idea you were so sensitive about your age." He freed his hand and turned to walk away, but Rayanne rushed after him, caught his arm and turned him around to face her again. "Ralph," she said, looking very serious.

"Gotcha," he said, pointing a finger at her and laughing out loud.

"What?" she said.

"I said gotcha," he repeated, threw his head back and laughed. Rayanne smiled then, shook her head and punched him in the arm. "I got you that time, didn't I? Honey, I'm approaching middle age but I don't have a problem with that. Why? Because I'm all man. Maybe I won't be so quick to say that in 30 years but right now, I'm pretty confident. My health is good, I've got a young beautiful woman by my side. I've got nothing to frown about. Hell, life can't get much better than this," he said looking at her. He laughed again, caught her hand, and they resumed walking and before heading to her condo, they browse in some of the 24 hour shops on Broadway. Then Ralph offered to get a taxi.

"Why don't we get the bus?" Rayanne said.

"All right." Ralph looked back and saw the bus coming up behind them. "If you want to catch the next one, we've got about a minute to cross the street and get to the corner because it's coming," he said, and he started to run. Rayanne hadn't mentioned that she'd run track while in high school. She sprinted, caught up with him, cut across in front of him, and caught his hand. They ran across the street between traffic, with horns honking and wheels screeching. "Hey, you," Ralph yelled, "we've got to be careful. Haven't you heard about these crazy New York drivers. You're going to get us both killed."

"Shut your mouth and run," she said, holding his hand and laughing. "Come on, you're such a baby."

"Maybe, but I'm your baby," he said, almost out of breath. They reached the corner ahead of the bus and Ralph was breathing heavily when they boarded and found seats.

"Let's ride to the end of the line and back," Rayanne said.

"All right," he said and Rayanne snuggled up next to him, rested her head on his shoulder and closed her eyes. He looked down into her face and asked, "Happy?"

She opened her eyes, looked at him and answered, "Very."

"Me too," he whispered. "I love you."

"Me too," she said.

"You too what?" he teased.

"Me too love you," she answered and linked her arm through his.

185

After a moment Ralph said, a puzzled look on his face, "where did you learn to run like that." Rayanne laughed, and nestled closer to him as they rode in silence, watching the city unfold before their eyes.

They arrived at the condo, and spoke with Maggie as she was leaving the building, walking her dog. "Get back safely," Rayanne said to her and she could tell that Maggie was something with the young men in her day. Because even now, her eyes shine brightly as she flirted outrageously with Ralph. In the condo, they had a glass of wine. Rayanne attempted to get up from the couch to check her messages, but Ralph stopped her, pinning her down with his arms. When Ralph left in the morning, Rayanne listened to her messages. Ivory called to say she'd be out of town a few days, and the other two calls were from her mother. Her father had been hospitalized again, he'd suffered another heart attack and at 2:15 that afternoon, Rayanne was on her way back home, thoughts and guilt consuming her. She wished she'd checked her messages last night.

This attack was far more damaging than the first, and Raymond looked much older than when Rayanne had last seen him. He stayed in the hospital ten days that time and during that trip, Rayanne took time to reflect. She took long drives in the country, she worked with her mother in the yard, and she gave a lot of thought to what she wanted to do with the rest of her life. She had been blessed. God had bestowed many wonderful blessings on her. She looked to God for guidance throughout her life and she'd continued to look to Him for answers. She'd found that even when she was having the best of times, her thoughts were centered on her parents and their well being. She considered the possibilities and when she made her mind up, the decision wasn't a difficult one. It became crystal clear to her one day as she sat alone at the lake beyond her back yard, and two weeks after her father was home from the hospital, Rayanne returned to New York. She spent several months finalizing some business, selling her part of the Typing Service to Tiffany, she lined up other projects and by the end of January and after some tearful goodbyes, she packed up and moved back to South Carolina.

CHAPTER 23

The first six months, after Rayanne returned to South Carolina, passed quickly. She was able to persuade her father to allow
the handyman he'd hired to do more of the work on the property.
Her father had built several houses while they were growing up
and those houses were being rented and from time to time, repairs
were necessary. Although, the handyman was working out very
well, it didn't last long, because in no time, Raymond was doing
most of the work again, himself. However, Rayanne noticed a vast
improvement in his condition. He appeared to turned over a new
leaf, thrived on hard work, but she also knew that if he wasn't
careful, he'd run into trouble again.

***

Rayanne returned from a trip to New York that was both, business and pleasure, and she was thinking that although, she and
Ralph saw each other every three weeks, if there was a flaw in her
decision to return to South Carolina, that was it. She missed him
terribly. On her way home that day, she stopped off at a local
Chevrolet dealership and purchased a new black Corvette for herself, and, although over great protest, she also purchased a dishwasher for her mother. Ruth had always washed her dishes by
hand, and if she had her wish, she would've kept that tradition
alive.

Rayanne had almost forgotten how beautiful it was in South Carolina during the fall. She took long drives in the country and marveled at the wonders of mother nature, how she made her appearance. The leaves, as she observed in the late afternoon sun, set off bursts of colors in the woods, dazzling crimson, harvest gold, reddish yellow, deep brown, while others were still green, fell and mingled playfully, creating a colorful blanket as they landed beneath the trees. Looking out over the fields, she couldn't remember a time when she didn't enjoy the splendor of nature. Its beauty and tranquillity stood there before her to see and enjoy, and as she took a deep breath of clean, satisfying country air, New York seemed so far away. She'd also forgotten the warm and friendly way people at home greeted one another, a smile, a friendly wave of the hand, while New Yorkers concentrated more on what they were doing and where they were going, rather than concerning themselves with the people around them. People differ from state to state, but it was times like those when Rayanne really appreciated the wonderfulness of home.

Rayanne was thirty-two, unmarried, childless and living back at home with her parents, but before long, she settled in and began to enlarged her comfort zone, and as time passed, she'd begun to write again, sometimes until the early morning hours. The only problem was that she wasn't satisfied with anything she wrote. She hadn't been successful in finding the atmosphere that was conducive to allow her creativity to take hold and emit wonderful words that evolved into wonderful pages and wonderful plays.

***

Spring made an early appearance that year. The birds were chirping, the grass was greener and the flowers were blooming. The bees were buzzing around by day, while stars winked and flirted in the moon lit sky, as songs drifted through the windows from the cars that sped by. Love was in the air. There was something about spring and love that made Rayanne think of Ralph. He'd come down on Friday and it would be good to see him. She really missed him, she missed him a lot.

Ralph and Rayanne went to Swan Lake, where the aroma given off by the magnolia and yellow jasmine touched the air softly and wonderfully, and as they circled the lake, they kissed in every secluded place they came across. They crammed a lot into Ralph's short stay and before he left, he met Aunt Bessie, who liked him but told Rayanne later that he was a rascal, had that look in his

188

eyes, she'd said, which Rayanne thought was interesting because that was exactly what Maggie had said when she met Ralph. Anyway, it was a good visit, only it was too short, much too short.

Rayanne stood on the steps of the front porch and looked at her watch. Ralph's plane left for New York more than four hours ago and she was sure he'd reached his destination. She walked down the steps and wandered across the yard, engrossed in thoughts when her mother called out from the side door, "Rayanne, telephone."

It's probably Ralph, she thought, rushing across the yard and breezing into the house. She took the phone and gave her mother a kissed on the cheek. "Hello." She paused. "Ivory. Hey girl, what's up?" When Ivory started talking, she did so a mile a minute. She and Desmond would be married the second Saturday in June, and of course, Ivory, Dorian and Rayanne would plan the wedding. Rayanne was as excited as Ivory, if that were possible as they discussed the wedding, and on the day of the blessed event, Ivory was an exquisite bride in her Dior gown with its 20 foot train. And Desmond, he was dashing in his tuxedo.

The colors Ivory had chosen were pink, yellow, blue, peach, green and lilac, all with white, and Dorian and Rayanne's Maids of honor gowns were a rainbow as they took in all the colors of the six Bridesmaids gowns. As Ivory repeated her vows, Rayanne looked over at Ralph. Although, he was in his early forties, hair graying at the temples and his hairline receding a little, he was still as handsome as any man there. As Rayanne continued to look at him, she wondered if it was her imagination or was Ralph avoiding eye contact with her. There were other times during that visit when she thought he looked a little uncomfortable and it was puzzling, however, all of her apprehensiveness dissipated later when Ralph came up behind her, whispered, 'I love you,' in her ear, kissed her, and led her away from the others. Ralph's kiss had been magical the first night they'd kissed and it still was.

Within a year, Ivory gave birth to a beautiful 6 pound 8 oz. baby girl. She named her Stephanie Lynn, and when the baby was christened, she was blessed with Rayanne and Dorian as Godmothers, but the year that followed didn't produce a husband for Rayanne as they had planned.

***

Ruth and Raymond celebrated their 50th wedding anniversary. Ralph and numerous others were invited and although most of them attended, Ralph didn't make the trip and that was the first of many disappointments to come. For years, Ralph had been devoted to Rayanne, so much a part of her life, but what had happened to change that. Wasn't the old adage, absence makes the heart grow fonder, true anymore? Absence certainly didn't seem to make Ralph's heart grow fonder. He'd missed his last two visits, and Rayanne was concerned. She wanted answers and if Mohammed wouldn't come to the mountain, the mountain would be on a flight that day, to see Mohammed.

Her plane arrived at La Guardia Airport at 4:15 in the afternoon, she took a taxi to Ralph's apartment, she showered and as she finished, she heard his key in the lock. "Hello," Ralph called out after he saw Rayanne's jacket hanging over the back of the couch.

"Hello," she answered.

"Who's there?" he pretended to not recognize her voice, while tiptoeing towards the bedroom.

"Why don't you come in and find out." He entered the room and rushed over to embrace her, but not before she thought she saw his eyes quickly scanning the room. She had some questions for Ralph and she wanted answers, but those questions would wait. Tomorrow is another day, she thought. That night would belong only to them.

About 10:30 that morning, Rayanne woke up alone. She got out of bed, pulled the sheets off, and put on fresh ones. She picked up the soiled sheets and as she did, she noticed something on the floor. Upon closer inspection, she saw that it was a condom wrapper. She was stunned, but after the initial shock, everything that happened that year had now made sense. She wasn't stupid, she knew it was possible that Ralph could be seeing someone else, but for some reason, she didn't expect to find out this way, if at all. He was having his needs satisfied there. No wonder he was able to spend more and more time away from her.

Rayanne finished the bed and as she pulled out a blouse that she'd hung in his closet the night before, something else caught her eye. It was a scarf that she'd misplaced, one that she didn't like very much, yet she had to wonder why would she have worn that scarf to see Ralph, and why hadn't he brought it back to her.

Ralph returned with groceries, prepared breakfast and poked his head into the bedroom. Rayanne wasn't there at the time but moments later she returned, wearing running clothes. "There you are," he walked over and kissed her.

190

"Miss me?"

"Yes, but did you have to ask?" When he was greeted with silence, he said, "Where did you go?"

"I went for a run."

"I wasn't sure what to think when I came back and found you gone."

"I'm here now and to tell the truth, that run really stirred up my appetite. Let me wash up, and I'll be out in a few minutes," she said heading to the bathroom.

"May I join you?" he asked and he caught her hand.

"Why don't you finish up here. The sooner I get back, the sooner we can eat," she said leaving the room with a silent Ralph staring after her. As she undressed, she was experiencing an emotion that she hadn't dealt with much in the past. Jealousy. She was feeling jealousy toward some woman who was screwing her man, and she didn't like it. She showered and when she returned, Ralph was sitting at the table waiting for her. "Something smells good," she said.

"Was it something I said?" he asked, looking at her.

"What?" Rayanne said, sitting across from Ralph.

"Did I say or do something to upset you?"

"Why do you say that?"

"Well, something has changed since last night, so tell me. What is it?"

"I'm just a little tired, I suppose," she lied.

"Are you sure that's all?"

She smiled, stood up and bend over the table. "Of course, what else could it be. Now come here you." She caught him by his ears and pulled him to her until their lips met. Ralph had slept with another woman. It had happened and there wasn't a thing she could do about it. But, she was with him now and she would make the best of it. She was glad he'd had the good sense to use protection with the other woman, because he certainly didn't with her.

They spent the next couple of days in each other arms, shutting out the rest of the world and they were happy, but the flight back home was anything but a happy one. Rayanne thought of Ralph, how they'd come together and became one, but she wondered who he'd be sleeping with that night, or the nights afterwards.

She picked up her car from the long term parking at the airport and was driving home when she saw several police cars, lights flashing, and sirens wailing. As she eased by, she saw three young, black males, handcuffed and being herded towards a police car. She didn't know at the time what had happened, but she did know that whatever it was it meant trouble for someone.

Rayanne arrived home and carried her bags inside, and as she entered the house, she felt tired, her shoulders knotted and tense. She looked out of the kitchen window and saw her father, unloading firewood from his truck. Her mother was in the kitchen making dinner. "How are you, Mama?" she asked as she peered through the door to the den. She put her bags down. "Is that Josh in there?"

"Yeah, Ruby kicked him out again," Ruth said, taking a pan of biscuits from the oven. "We gon' let him stay here 'til he gets himself straight."

"Oh Mama," Rayanne said, remembering the last time that happened, Josh was there more than six months and when he left, they had to replace a mattress and the carpet in that bedroom because of his urinating in bed.

"Honey, it wont be long," Ruth said, reading her daughter's mind.

Rayanne picked up her bags and walked towards her room. "Whatever," she said. She just didn't have the energy to deal with Josh and his drinking problem today. The situation with Ralph and living with an alcoholic brother were just two of many negative episodes to monopolize her life.

CHAPTER 24

Rayanne finally decided to go back to school. She picked up literature from the University of South Carolina, and after reviewing it, she enrolled the next semester, and not only did she find the courses challenging and stimulating, she met some nice people too. Two women whom she met that lived in Columbia and were in her Psychology and Math classes, were close to her own age. Brenda, a young black woman, with two teenage sons who lived with her, wanted to be a licensed Realtor. Hilary, also black, wanted a degree in business, was happily married to Ben, and they had a ten year old adopted daughter, whose name was Jessica. The women quickly struck up a friendship and in no time, it was as though they'd always been friends. The day when Rayanne had shared with Brenda and Hilary the episode when she last visited Ralph, Brenda said, "well at least the son of a bitch is playing it safe." Rayanne liked Brenda, she was more like Ivory than anyone Rayanne had ever met. After classes one day and as they were about to part, Rayanne called out to them. "My brother's baseball club is having their annual banquet next Saturday night. If you all can make it, I've got tickets." Rayanne laughed and pulled some tickets from her purse.

"That's next Saturday?" Brenda asked. "I don't have any plans. I'll take one."

"Jessica has her dance recital, and we have some plans afterwards, so I don't think we're going to be able to make it," Hilary said.

"Okay," Rayanne said and handed a ticket to Brenda. "Say hello to Ben and Jessica and tell Jessica I said break a leg." Then, they got into their cars and drove away.

The drive home was relaxing. It gave Rayanne time to think about the exercises they had in class and she made mental notes of questions she'd ask in her next class. When she arrived home, her father was in the yard mixing paint. He looked tired. "Hey daddy," she said.

"How you doing, daughter?"

"I'm good, but what about you? What are you doing?"

"I'm mixing up some paint. Old Miss Jamison had a grease fire in her kitchen yesterday and the walls got messed up some, mostly behind the stove. I done replaced the woodwork, but now I wanna get that painting done or she'll worry herself to death." He stopped to looked up at his daughter, "how them classes going?"

"The classes are fine, but I'm worried about you, daddy. Why don't you let someone help you with this?"

"You know what they say, daughter. If you want somethin' done right, you gotta do it yourself."

"Where is Josh?" she asked, looking around. Her father pointed towards the house. Josh had an engineering degree, certainly he could do a little carpentry and painting work, she thought, but it didn't take long for her to know why Josh couldn't do that job or any other job at that time.

Rayanne entered the house, and found her mother in the den folding clothes, but Josh was no where in sight. "You're home early," Ruth said.

"Yeah, they canceled my last class. The instructor left sick. How are you, mama?"

"I'm fine. How was school?"

"Pretty good," Rayanne said and asked, "Mama, where is Josh?"

"He's back there in that room, drunk. I'm telling you, Rayanne, somethin' gotta be done," Ruth said shaking her head.

The following morning before class, Rayanne spent time getting information from a local Rehab center and over the next several weeks, Josh went every day. The treatment lasted 30 days and when it ended, it looked as though Josh was trying to put his life back together.

***

Sometime during the month of December and only four days

194

before the winter school break began, Rayanne came in from class and her mother had several messages attached to the wall where the phone hung in the kitchen. Her first call was to Aunt Bessie, who needed to see her, the second call was to Harry, who gave her more bad news. He couldn't get a buyer for her last play, but what else is new, Rayanne thought. She then called Ivory. Now Ivory was the one person who could always cheer her up, but not this time. "Rayanne, It's Dorian," Ivory said and she sounded tired.

"Dorian? What's wrong with her?" Rayanne was alarmed.

"She's drinking a lot, she's doing coke again, and I'm worried about her." Rayanne could hear concern in Ivory's voice. "I don't know what's going on with her right now. I can't seem to reach her anymore, Rayanne."

"I'll get a flight out tomorrow morning."

"Don't you have classes?"

"I have only one class tomorrow, and I can make that up later," Rayanne assured.

"Okay, I'll see you tomorrow then," Ivory said and added, "thanks Rayanne."

"No problem," Rayanne said sincerely, "she's my friend, too."

"Are you going to let Ralph know you're coming? That way he won't have any more surprises waiting for you," Ivory said and snickered, remembering Rayanne's discovery when she'd visited Ralph the last time.

"If I have time, I'll see him. If I don't, then it won't make that much difference, will it?" Rayanne said.

"I'm scared of you, girlfriend," Ivory said and they both laughed.

***

A major storm was threatening outside to unleash its ugly fury, but it was mild in comparison to what Rayanne felt inside when she saw her Aunt Bessie and learned that Stevie had attacked her and took money from her. Her first thought was to take Aunt Bessie to the emergency room, but she assured Rayanne that she was not hurt. Rayanne could tell just by looking at Aunt Bessie that she must've put up a struggle because her fair complexion was splashed with horrible, dark bruises. She was seventy-four and although she shouldn't have to suffer any kind of abuse, she certainly shouldn't have to suffer at the hands of her own son. Aunt Bessie told Rayanne that she didn't care that Stevie was her only child and that she loved him very much, she didn't want him back in her home again until he learned to behave like a man. Since he

195

returned this time, the TV from the bedroom was gone, a clock radio, a set of silverware and money from Aunt Bessie's purse, which was at least a couple of hundred dollars, since she always wanted to have a little something handy. "Never know what might come up," she always said.

Rayanne was so upset that it was hard to think. She took a deep breath to study her erratic breathing and after getting some control, she asked, "Where is Stevie now?"

"Said he was going back up the road. Anyway, I ain't seen him since this morning," she said and swallowed and Rayanne could see that it was with difficulty.

"Come Aunt Bessie, I think we should go to the emergency room and have you checked."

"No, I don't need to see no doctor, but I'll tell you one thing. This was the first time that he's scared me. You know, I think he would've hurt me if I didn't let him have the money." She told Rayanne she was more frightened than anything. In the end, Rayanne took her to the emergency room and afterwards, Aunt Beside agreed to spend a couple of days with the Wilsons. Violence was mounting, it was becoming a major concern. People were attacking one another every day which was bad, but when sons attack their mothers, that was despicable.

Rayanne packed a clothes bag and an overnight case. When she finished, she heard Josh coming in through the back door. His condition had improved, he had come a long way the past couple of months. He was holding down a steady job, he'd returned to the world of the living, and Rayanne was proud of him. They sat at the kitchen table and talked, and it reminded her of old times. In the early morning, she was on a flight to New York. Seeing Ivory at the airport was like dejavue, as Rayanne's mind immediately returned to when she first arrived in New York and Ivory had met her at the airport. How different it all was then.

On the ride to the loft, Ivory filled Rayanne in on what had been happening. Things were good with Ivory and Desmond, she loved the house they'd bought on the island, and Ivory had done all the decorating. Dorian had continued to live in the loft as Henry had never demanded anything from her except time, when he wanted to see her. He was still with Olympia and two other girls had moved in with Dorian.

When they entered the loft, they were equally surprised, perhaps even shocked by its condition. The place that had once been a regular showplace was now in a state of disarray. Old newspapers and clothes were strung over the couch, the table, on the floor, and there were dirty dishes everywhere. Not only was the loft in an extremely bad condition, Rayanne and Ivory were more shocked and sadden by Dorian's appearance upon entering her room. Dorian looked and smelled as though she hadn't had a bath or washed her hair in what may have been days, perhaps weeks. The girl who'd once been filled with vim and vitality, was reduced to someone who appeared to have just walked out of skid row. Dorian looked at Rayanne and Ivory as they approached her. She closed her eyes a moment and when she opened them again, they were catlike in her face. She looked tired, her face was drawn, and what about Sapphire, Rayanne thought as she looked around. They later learned that Sapphire, however old she was, had gotten out of the apartment and no one seemed to know where she was, and Rayanne didn't ask. Dorian's condition was already fragile and she didn't want to put any unnecessary strain on her. They later packed a suitcase for Dorian and the three of them went to Ivory's house for the night.

It was wonderful to see Desmond and Stephanie Lynn waiting for Ivory when she returned. Desmond met them at the door with the baby in his arms. He extended greetings to Rayanne and Dorian, he kissed his wife affectionately and she took the baby from his arms. "How is my little girl? Was daddy mean to my baby?" Ivory jokingly questioned Stephanie Lynn, who was nearly two years old and who nodded yes in agreement that her father had been mean to her. "Bad daddy," Ivory said, kissing Desmond on the lips again as they entered the house.

Ivory had a great, four bedroom, split level home. The house was tastefully furnished. The decor was mostly in peach, dark green and panel. The foyer, dining room and kitchen were wallpapered and the living room was painted a shade slightly lighter than peach, the family room was done in dark paneled walls, two of the upstairs bedrooms were wallpapered, while the others were painted a soft lovely pastel. All the bathrooms were wallpapered. Rayanne and Dorian each took a bedroom and after dinner, Rayanne called Maggie and after having been settled in, the girls talked at length into the night.

The following day Dorian was admitted to a drug rehabilitation center. She still wasn't able to understand why everyone was abandoning her, although Rayanne and Ivory spent most of the previous night trying to assure and reassure her that what they were doing was necessary and that they loved her.

The counselor who spoke with Rayanne and Ivory informed them that they wanted to work with Dorian at least two weeks without her having any visitors. There was a reason for that they'd said. Rayanne and Ivory spent the entire day at the center with Dorian because they knew it would be at least two weeks before they could see her again.

Ralph and Rayanne got together that night and although it'd been weeks since they had been together, seeing each other was as good as it'd ever been. Before they said good-bye, each had promised they wouldn't allow as much time to come between their visits. This was a promise that they vowed to keep.

On the plane trip back home, Rayanne was haunted by the dark circles that surrounded Dorian's eyes, she'd lost a lot of weight and she looked awful. Rayanne didn't realize she'd been crying until the passenger in the next seat asked whether something was wrong, handing her a tissue. "No, why do you asked?" Rayanne said.

"The tears on your cheeks," the passenger replied. "It appears you've been crying."

"Thanks," she said accepting the tissue, "I guess I was." She wiped the tears away.

Rayanne called the center that evening and was assured that Dorian was settling in. She'd eaten a little breakfast and a good portion of her lunch. Rayanne felt some relief and she called Ivory and they talked at length between tears. Sometime later that evening, she received a call from Brenda. There was a Psychology exam scheduled for Thursday, and she thought if Rayanne was in town, she might want to take it. Rayanne was glad for the call and she certainly would take the exam.

Rayanne called the center daily and she and Ivory spoke regularly. The counselor informed them that Dorian's condition had improved some over the past several days and they could visit the following weekend.

CHAPTER 25

Maxine turned into the driveway and waved to Rayanne and her father, who were sitting on the front porch. She drove around to the back of the house and parked her car. "Hey Maxine," her mother called out to her as she headed towards the house. "Come on in and have something cold to drink." Ruth stood holding the door open for Maxine.

Maxine embraced her mother and said, "How's it going, Mama?"

"Pretty good, and you?" Ruth answered.

"I'm great," Maxine said.

"What about Marcus and my grandchildren?" Ruth asked, filling the glasses with ice and took a pitcher of lemonade from the refrigerator.

"They are fine. Bobby got two A's and Bruce got B's. Let me help you with that, Mama," Maxine said, taking the pitcher from her mother's hand.

"That's not too shabby, but remind them that grandma pays for A's only," Ruth said, setting the glasses onto a tray and they joined Rayanne and Raymond on the porch.

"Marcus took the boys to Bobby's soft ball games," Maxine informed.

"Marcus takes up so much time with the boys. You got yourself a good man in that Marcus, honey," Ruth said. It was true and Maxine felt blessed in many ways.

"There's an envelope on top of the refrigerator for you, Maxine. Don't forget to take it when you leave," Raymond said.

"Thanks daddy," Maxine said, still a little embarrassed about accepting money from her parents to help support her boys, but they'd insisted on helping her since Joe ran off and left them, and forgot to look back. The money was some that was collected as rent from the houses their parents owned, and although it was only $300 a month, it helped. The family didn't feel it was fair that Marcus should be the one to take on the responsibility for the boys, although he'd vowed to do so from the day he fell in love with Maxine and married her.

Rayanne laid down her pen and pad and accepted a glass of lemonade that Maxine handed her. "Thanks."

"Bruce was accepted at Clemson," Maxine announced, sitting on the steps to the porch.

"Clemson? That's great," Rayanne said.

"Yes. He'll enroll in their engineering program this fall," Maxine said, beaming with pride.

"My, how time flies. Seems like just yesterday when that boy was running around in his diaper and now he's almost a man," Ruth said.

"He's still in diapers," Raymond teased.

"Daddy," Rayanne said, shaking her head and laughing.

"Raymond, don't be so hard on the boy," Ruth said.

"You gotta be hard on them if they're gonna amount to anything," Raymond said.

"You weren't hard on yours and they turned out all right," Ruth said.

"Wonder what happened to Josh," Raymond said, avoiding his wife's eyes. He knew she didn't like his speaking badly about any of their children.

"Raymond, we're talking about Bruce," Ruth said, "not Josh."

"I was only joking about that. I think Bruce is gonna do real good," Raymond said.

"Yeah, "Ruth said, "that young man's got a bright future ahead of him."

"I was hoping he would've picked one of the schools that offered him a scholarship," Maxine said, sipping her lemonade.

"If you're worried about money, Maxine, there's a lot of financial assistance out there," Rayanne said.

"Yeah, we're looking into that," Maxine said. "Bruce wants to go to Clemson and I think it's important that a person gets to make these choices. He visited several schools, all good schools and some with full scholarships, but Clemson is his choice and if that's where he wants to go, then that's where he should go."

"I agree, it's a good school, and I understand they have the best engineering program. Don't worry about it. Everything will work out. It always does," Rayanne said, thinking it was good Maxine felt that way because it makes a big difference for a child to be able to go to the school he really wants to instead of where he has to.

"Something else bothering you, Maxine?" Raymond drained his glass and held it up for his wife to refill.

"No not really," Maxine lied.

"You may as well come on out with it. Any body can see you got something on your mind," Ruth said.

Maxine was quiet, looking out across the yard, a far away look in her eyes. "Bruce has been asking about his daddy a lot lately, and I don't really know what to tell him," she replied.

"Tell him the truth. Don't be lying to them. Joe Duncan lived here all his life, and if the boys don't learn the truth from you, they're gonna hear it from someone else," Ruth said.

"What does he want to know about that jack leg anyway?" Raymond asked.

Rayanne got up and went and sat on the steps beside Maxine. "All kinds of things," Maxine said, "why he left, was it their fault, whether he loved them, things like that. I always told them that he went away because he didn't want to live here anymore. I didn't want my kids feeling responsible for something that jerk did. Anyway, after a while, they stopped asking, but now that they're getting older, they're curious again. Joe has never loved any one but himself, but do you tell that to the children?"

"No, of course not," Ruth said, sympathetically.

"You just tell them the truth about the bastard," Raymond said.

"Raymond, you hush up now. Can't you see that this thing is troubling the girl?" Ruth said.

"Yeah, but those kids shouldn't be thinking that their daddy's some Saint," Raymond said. "The boy are old enough to know the kind of man Joe is. He certainly was vile and nasty when he was married to you Maxine and the way he ran off like a coward and never looked back, I don't believe he's gonna ever change. You should tell them that their daddy wasn't perfect and that they don't want to be anything like him. Those boys aren't stupid, they'll understand."

Maxine looked at her watch and said, getting up and taking another sip from her glass, "I gotta pick up Marcia Raylyn from her dance class. You know how that child gets when I'm late."

"Tell that little lady she's getting slack. She hasn't called me all week," Ruth said.

"She hasn't? Oh my goodness, she is getting slack. I'll tell her what you said, Mama. Do you want me to take this tray back into the kitchen?" Maxine offered.

"No, you go on and don't keep my granddaughter waiting," Ruth said. "And Maxine, you take it easy. All this will work itself out."

"I know, mama. Thanks," Maxine said, and she kissed her parents. "I love both of you."

Rayanne and Maxine sat their glasses on the tray and walked around the house to Maxine's car. "There's something else going on with you," Rayanne said.

"You know me so well," Maxine said, getting into her car. "Come ride to the store with me."

"What about Marcia Raylyn?"

"This won't take long."

Rayanne got into the car. "You heard from Joe?" He was the only one who could upset Maxine that much.

"You know he's a minister in Florida, right?" Maxine stated and Rayanne nodded. "Well, I hear he's coming here to be the guest minister in a couple of months, in our church, and with his new wife. Can you believe that?"

"He's coming where?" Rayanne asked. "Here? Joe's coming back here?" Rayanne asked and Maxine nodded. "Why is he doing that?" Maxine lifted her shoulders and shook her head. "Apparently, Mama and Daddy don't know. They're going to hear about this sooner or later." Maxine knodded her head up and down, but she didn't answer. "Maxine, you are going to tell them before he gets here, aren't you?"

Maxine stopped the car in front of a neighborhood store and without switching the car off, said, "I'll be right back." Moments later, she exited the store, got back into the car, carrying a single bag. She unscrewed the cap off a bottle of beer, turned it up and took several large swallows from it before replacing the cap.

"Good God," Rayanne gasped.

When Maxine had calmed down sufficiently, she explained that her friend, Althea, the church Program Coordinator, drove to her house with the news the moment she was asked to book Joseph Duncan to speak at the church.

When they pulled back into Rayanne's yard, they got out of the car and Maxine deposited the near full beer bottle into the trash can that sat in the back yard before getting back into the car. As she was about to drive off, they noticed a car stopped in the middle of the street near the house and the driver was talking with a young man who was walking along the street. "Just look at that. Dealing drugs right there in the middle of the street, in broad day light," Maxine said, and Rayanne agreed, silently shaking her head. When the guys noticed that they had the attention of the two women, the driver said something to the guy who was standing against his car, and he drove away. Maxine said, "I've got to go. I'll call you later."

"All right drive safely," Rayanne said and Maxine drove away. Rayanne walked around to the front of the house and watched the young man who was talking to the drug dealer until he was out of sight.

Maxine called at 9:45 that night. "Sorry I'm just getting back to you, but I had lots to do, grocery, picking up things from the cleaners, looking over homework."

"That's all right. I just got home myself. I was visiting Aunt Bessie," Rayanne said.

"She's all right?" Maxine said and added, "it's a damn shame how Stevie treats her, isn't it?"

"You doggone right. He needs his behind whipped." They never would've thought Stevie would turn out the way he did and although they knew it was mostly because of the drugs, that was no excuse.

"I've seen what that stuff does to people. It ain't a pretty picture."

"Yeah, I know, but what's going on with you, Maxine?"

"Where do I begin," Maxine said with a shaky laugh.

"Any where you like," Rayanne offered.

"Rayanne, it just pisses me off so damn much," Maxine began, "it makes me so doggone angry that he has these kids, and he ain't doing shit for them. I feel guilty as hell using Marcus' money to do things for Joe's kids. I know Marcus doesn't mind, but it's the principle. How can anyone be that nonchalant about his own kids. They're great kids, wonderful kids, but do you think he cares." Maxine was distraught.

"When he comes here, you should tell him how you feel. Let him know the kids have questions. Talk to the man, Maxine,"

Rayanne said.

"He has always had a happy go lucky carefree life. I think it's time that he pays the piper."

"Don't let it get to you like this. You keep this up and you'll end up as bitter as that sister of yours," Rayanne teased, however, she was thinking that Maxine was acting just as Mamie would.

"Your sister too, mind you," Maxine said.

"That's not my fault," Rayanne came back, and they laughed.

"I think I'll call Mrs. Duncan."

"No Maxine, don't call her. Go by and see her. Look her in the eyes and talk to her. I am a sucker for communications. Besides how bad can it be?"

"Let's just say like mother, like son," Maxine joked, but she agreed to go and see Mrs. Duncan.

"Do your part, Maxine and if Joe doesn't want to be involved in his children's lives, then that's his loss."

"Marcus is pulling into the driveway right now," Maxine said, "let me put his dinner on the table. I'll talk with you tomorrow."

"Take it easy," Rayanne said and hung up. She picked up the mail from the table and as she look through it, she saw that there was a letter from Maggie and a smile touched her lips.

CHAPTER 26

Rayanne and Brenda met at the party. Brenda was introduced to John and Christen, and she immediately began referring to John as her big brother, as well. The room was filled with mostly baseball players, the majority of them were accompanied by a female, and the message their eyes sent to the unattached women was synonymous. It clearly said, hands off, and neither Rayanne nor Brenda had any plan of invading their territory, and from the size of some of those women, they could definitely count on it. Rayanne and Brenda danced a couple of times with some of the men who showed up alone. When they were seated, Rayanne noticed Brenda watching two men, who sat across the table from them. One man was paying a lot of attention to Brenda, as well. She was attractive, short and thin, but shapely. Her complexion was light, she had large dark brown eyes and dimples that made large indentions in her round face. She wore her hair long and curly on top and short and tapered in back. Brenda was separated from her husband, but neither had filed for divorce. She was good natured, easy going and a lot of fun.

The center was decorated with colorful streamers and balloons, and a banner that stated Congratulations Teams, hung from the ceiling, extending from one side of the center to the other. The tables were set up in long rows that seated 100 persons to a row with a break between every five tables. There were at least 700 people present. The festivities began with a buffet dinner, then the trophies were presented to teams and individuals for that season's performance, and dancing followed. Rayanne and Brenda sat at the table with John, his wife and some of their friends, and the table was set up with bottles of vodka, rum and scotch.

There was a buzz across the room as they ate. A friend of John's approached the table, spoke to John and Christen, asking about their parents, and Rayanne recognized him as the man she met when their father was hospitalized after having his first heart attack. Although Larry was there with his wife, Rayanne wondered how Mamie would've reacted had she been there. Brenda pushed her plate away, lit up a cigarette and smiled, her eyes nearly closed. Rayanne didn't know Brenda very well, but she knew her well enough to know that she had something devious on her mind, and although Brenda and Ivory had absolutely no physical similarities, the girls reminded Rayanne of one another. "You see that old fart over there?" Brenda said, with a nod of her head.

"Which one?" Rayanne asked, looking at the men across the table.

"The one to the left."

"Yeah, what about him?"

"He's been sitting over there drinking our brother's liquor all night."

"So?"

"So? Hell, liquor is expensive. Besides, he's got a flask over there that he's only touched once. He poured himself a drink and didn't even offer anyone else," Brenda said with a smirk on her face.

"Well, he can only drink a stomach full," Rayanne said laughing.

"Yeah," Brenda said putting out the cigarette and her lips curled into a smile. "You wanna have some fun?"

Rayanne asked, "What's on your mind?"

"Pass me that flask."

"What?"

"Pass me that flask," Brenda repeated.

"Why? What are you going to do?" Rayanne asked, she looked at Brenda, then at the men across the table as she reached for the flask.

Brenda smiled broadly when one of the men turned to look at her. "Not yet," she whispered.

"Oops," Rayanne said, slowly withdrawing her hand and she took a sip of her rum and coke. The man returned his attention to the dance floor.

"Now, quick," Brenda hissed, "grab it." Rayanne quickly grabbed the flask and handed it to Brenda who emptied it and replaced its contents with iced tea. Brenda is so much like Ivory, Rayanne thought, remembering once when Ivory had just started a new job and wanted to go out of town, but knowing she wouldn't be given permission to take leave, she devised a plan, telling her supervisor a relative had died and she needed to attend the funeral. She'd talked Rayanne into typing up a funeral program on the none existing person, complete with Ivory and her family's names listed as surviving relatives. Needless to say, Ivory took off and returned with the fraudulent funeral program in hand, a beautiful flowering plant and sympathy card on her desk awaiting her return and with no one the wiser. Rayanne didn't feel good participating in the deception, but Ivory had asked and she'd done it.

As time passed and the liquor bottles were empty, the man held his flask under the table, poured a shot into his cup and looked around. Rayanne and Brenda pretended to not notice when he took a sip from his cup, but they snickered as they caught a glimpse of the strange look on his face as he looked into his cup. "Fixed him," Brenda said. At 1:30, Brenda and Rayanne left the party.

***

Rayanne flew to New York, where she and Ivory spent the day with Dorian. Those two weeks that Dorian was in rehabilitation made a big difference, and although Dorian looked much better, she still had a long way to go. Rayanne went back home feeling good about Dorian's progress and she returned to New York every other weekend while Dorian was being treated. She even attended one of the sessions along with Ivory where they learned that Dorian's parents had died in an auto accident when she was ten, and she'd suffered greatly. No other family available, a friend of Dorian's parents took her in, but shortly afterwards, that couple divorced, leaving Dorian on her own again to suffer the trauma of another loss. Before the accident, she was a happy child and before she slept each night, she made her parents promise they'd always be together. When her parents were killed, Dorian was devastated, and she went into one foster home after another, until she was sixteen when she ran away from Detroit and came to live in New York. Never forgiving her parents for leaving her, Dorian carried around with her the pain and insecurity of the loss. She was working through what she felt was betrayal and abandonment, but therapy was helping. Dorian had taken odd jobs that enabled her to put herself through high school and shortly after arriving in New York, she'd met Henry who looked so like her father that she'd transferred her feelings for her father to him, but Henry took the relationship a step further and they became lovers. It was brought to light through therapy that Dorian never was in love with Henry. She only saw him as a father figure. Her breakdown resulted from a combination of the lost of her parents, her friends and when Ivory and Rayanne moved out of the loft, she felt she was losing her family all over. She was further devastated when Henry took up with another woman, but still never divorcing Olympia and never marrying her. The loss was too much for her. Ivory and Rayanne's families were supportive of Dorian and although it was obvious that she was improving, Rayanne and Ivory noticed something different in her eyes. They just weren't sure what to make of it.

CHAPTER 27

Scott and Rayanne met one day literally by accident. She was running late one rainy morning for a Psychology exam scheduled for 8:45. The rain wasn't coming in a downpour, it was a constant drizzle, just enough to create havoc for drivers. Rayanne had found that more accidents seemed to occur when the weather was pleasant and suddenly got hot or when it rained. She drove the 40 miles to Columbia, and although the highway was wet, she made good time. However, someone once said that something always seems to go wrong to slow you down when you're already late, and sure enough, once in town, she was caught by every light. But each time she stopped, she'd grabbed her notes from the seat and reviewed them. She looked up a moment, and saw that the light had changed and the traffic had already begun to move. Engrossed again in her notes, she took her foot off of the brake pedal and pressed down on the accelerator, not noticing the vehicle that was stopped in front of her. She ran her Corvette in to it. "Oh, No," she said, tossing her notes onto the seat and letting her head drop to the steering wheel. She couldn't believe how careless she'd been. She lifted her head to see the young man from the vehicle that she'd just hit approaching her. She got out of her car. "Are you all right? I'm so sorry," she blurted out. "That was very careless of me."

"Yes, I'm fine, I accept your apology and yes, you were careless. I'm Scott Christopher," the man, said extending his hand. "Are you all right?"

"I'm fine," she accepted his hand. "I'm Rayanne Wilson. Are you sure you're all right?"

"I'm fine now, but I'm certain that by Friday, I'll need a good neck rub," Scott Christopher said as they both looked at the minor damages each vehicle sustained.

"Excuse me," she drew her eyes away from the vehicles and looked questioningly at him. "What did you say?"

"I said I'm fine but that I could use a neck rub by Friday," he repeated, his eyes holding hers deliberately. She swallowed and looked quickly at her watch. It was 8:25.

"It doesn't look like we have a lot of damages here, so if you're sure you're all right and if it's okay with you, I'll give you my insurance company and you can have whatever repairs done that are needed. I'm scheduled to take an exam in about 20 minutes and I need to be getting to class, if that's all right with you, of course," she said.

"Just give me your phone number Rayanne Wilson and I'll call you."

"I really appreciate this," she said, calling out her phone number while getting into her car.

He wrote the number down, smiled and said as she drove away, "drive carefully, Rayanne Wilson." Scott Christopher's pecan tan, broad shouldered frame stood - at least 6 feet 2. He appeared educated, he was handsome and his dark brown eyes were hypnotizing.

Rayanne arrived for class exactly one minute before her professor closed the door and began to administer the exam. Brenda and Hilary were there and they appeared eager to get started and have it behind them. After an hour, those papers were taken up, they had a 20 minute break, then they were given the second part of the exam. At 12 O'clock, it was over, and Rayanne, Hilary and Brenda went to Appleby's for lunch. Rayanne told the girls about the accident she had, but assured them she was fine. She even talked a little about Scott. "How do you guys think you did on that exam? It was a monster, but I think I did okay, "Rayanne said sipping tea from her glass.

"Yeah, it was tough, but I think I did all right, also," Hilary said.

"I did my best," Brenda said, stuffing a piece of baby back rib into her mouth. "I thought it would never be over." After a moment, she said, "I sure hope I passed that test because I don't want to have to take that one again."

"You got that right," Rayanne agreed, eating her salad.

"If I get the full 10 points on that classical conditioning question and the 5 points for the question on the 3 main forces in a man's life, than I think I've got an A on the test," Hilary said.

"I don't know that I'll get an A, but if I get a high B, I'll be satisfied," Rayanne said. She knew she had done her best also, therefore she'd just wait and see what the results were.

"That was the question about the id, which is an instinctive force, the ego, an executive force that contacts the world of reality; and the superego, the superior disciplinary force, right,?" Brenda asked.

"Yeah," Hilary said. She was a tall, thin, well groomed, sophisticated woman, with light colored skin and grayish eyes that were hidden behind a pair of horn rimmed glasses. She was attractive, although not considered pretty. Her morals were very much in tact, she was an intelligent woman, but somewhat naive.

"Then I think I did okay on that question," Brenda said, letting out a sigh of relief. "Anyway, I'm not gonna sweat it. We're gonna know the results soon enough."

Sipping her tea and wiping her mouth, Hilary asked, "what are y'all doing while we're on break?"

"I don't know, I'm doing some volunteer work at a center for the elderly a couple of days and I may go to New York a few days," Rayanne said, "what about you two?"

"Working. I can't afford to do anything else right now," Brenda said, signaling the waitress for more tea.

"Ben and I are going to be taking care of some things around the house and spend a little time together. Jessica will be visiting Mama," Hilary said. Then looking at Brenda, she asked , "How are the boys?"

"They're fine. I just want them to grow the hell up and get out of my house. I want some time for myself," Brenda said and although she was just kidding around, Hilary didn't think so.

"What do you mean? They are your children. You should want them around forever," Hilary said.

"Get real, Hilary, shit, no one wants their kids around forever," Brenda said but Rayanne could've challenged her on that point, because if her parents had their way, they'd have every one of their children living in their house until they all died.

"I can't believe you said that," Hilary said to Brenda. "I want Jessica to always be with Ben and me. I know that's not going to happen, but I can wish can't I?"

"Look," Brenda began, "I don't give a damn how any one else feels, I'm just telling you how I feel. Hell, you've got one child and a husband who takes care of both of you. I've got two boys and no husband, so the equation is a little different. You walk in my shoes a year or two and see if you don't change your mind." Brenda certainly reminds me of Ivory, Rayanne thought.

"People are different," Hilary said.

"Yeah." Brenda removed a pack of cigarettes from her purse, stuck one between her lips and lit it.

"Have you thought about getting back with your husband?" Hilary asked. Rayanne knew, as she looked at each of them, that Hilary was treading on thin ice bringing up Cardell's name, but she didn't say anything. Brenda opened her mouth to curse, thought better of it, and closed it again. Brenda still loved Cardell, she'd told them as much, but she'd also told them that since they'd been separated, and she'd started dating again, that she liked it. She'd said that one on one relationships worked for some people, but it didn't work for her. When Brenda met her husband, she'd loved him and wanted to spend her life with him. She even said that even though they'd been apart for years, they were still friends and saw each other occasionally.

"Cardell has a weakness for good looking women, I like a lot of money. I look good and he makes good money, so it works for both of us, as long as we don't have to live together," Brenda said.

"And, she uses her beauty like a shovel digging for gold," Hilary said.

"I adored Cardell," Brenda said, "and I thought he was crazy about me. It turned out that he was just plain damn crazy. He ran around on me, you name it, he did it. One night I was coming home from dropping off the boys at my mother's when I saw his car pulled into a hotel parking lot. I made sure it was his car, I called a girlfriend and asked her to get a cab to the restaurant across from the hotel. When she got there, I used my spare key, took Cardell's car, brought it down to Winn Dixie and left it there. I wanted to see what kind of lie he'd invent. You see girls, it was my 8th anniversary and I had on my expensive dress with my teddy laid out at home, a great dinner in the oven and a bottle of the Don, chilling, waiting for the two of us to celebrate. Well he had other plans. Anyway, I moved the car, dropped off my friend, and I came home. I threw the food in the garbage, took off my party dress, and I drank almost a bottle of champagne. My nose bled all over the place. You know, it was my anniversary, not hers. When he finally got in, he told me something about stopping at the mall to get me a gift and when he came out, the car was gone."

"Did he have a gift?" Hilary asked, and both Brenda and Rayanne rolled their eyes towards the ceiling.

"Of course he did. He had to give credibility to his story, and besides, Hilary, hello, it was our anniversary, remember," Brenda said.

"So what was it?" Hilary asked and Brenda and Rayanne looked at one another.

"What the hell difference does that make. The point is that nigger was cheating on me, he was lying about it and was trying to cover his tracks," Brenda said.

"Men, what are we gonna do with them? We can't live with them and we can't live without them," Rayanne said, shaking her head and sipping her iced tea.

"Your man cheats on you too?" Hilary asked Rayanne.

"Which one doesn't?" Rayanne asked, putting her glass down on the table.

"Not all of them," Hilary said firmly, finishing her lunch and wiping her mouth.

"Yeah, I'm sure you're right," Brenda said with disbelief.

"If you think Ben cheats on me, you're wrong," Hilary said emphatically, her feelings hurt.

"Don't get uptight, Hilary. The important thing is what you think and how you feel about your man," Rayanne said.

"You're not saying Ben is fooling around too?" Hilary asked and Rayanne was a little taken aback.

"I'm not saying anything," Rayanne said. "I don't know what Ben is doing. I don't even know Ben. I just think it's important how someone feels about his given situation and that it shouldn't matter what anyone else thinks. Your and Ben's relationship certainly seems to work and that is what's important," Rayanne said.

"Ben makes me very happy," Hilary said, merrily.

"I heard that," Rayanne said.

Brenda was thoughtful, "I've never had anyone who's ever made me feel that secure. I've had a few who cared, but I've never felt secured enough to think that he only wanted me," Brenda said.

"Don't you feel any better about yourself than that," Hilary said and Brenda stared at her.

"It's not even about that. I've been involved, I have trusted, loved, tried to be loved. Hell, I've tried it all, I wanted it all; a husband, kids, a nice home, a car, money in the bank. I've tried to have those things, but I've failed miserably. The only good thing about my life are my children, Chris and Devin. They're my successes," Brenda said smiling, "and they really can stay in my house until they are old and gray."

"I knew that all along, Hilary said with a smile.

"And you were right," Brenda said.

"It seems there was a lot of love between the two of you at one time," Rayanne said, feeling for Brenda.

"Can't you two all work through this and put your lives back together," Hilary said, "for God's sakes, he's your husband."

"I've given Cardell more chances than he deserved. He cheated on me and I sent his ass packing. It's been that way for a while now and I'm happy." Brenda says she's happy, Rayanne thought, but the look in her eyes told a different story. "You know Cardell and I never talked about that night and the real reason why I sent him packing. He didn't get in until 4 O'clock the next morning, so he thinks I was angry because he pulled an all nighter on our anniversary. Don't ask me why I didn't tell him what I knew. I suppose I was too hurt, too embarrassed, or just too much in love. I could never have minimized that," she looked wistfully. "He meant a lot to me. Foolish, huh?" Brenda said.

"Not necessarily. I suppose you did what you thought you had to do," Rayanne said.

"What I should have done was gotten up close and personal with his ass, but I didn't." Brenda lifted her shoulders and looked a little lost. "What would you have done?" She asked Rayanne.

"Gotten up close and personal with him," Rayanne said and smiled. Then she thought a moment. "I don't know how I would have handled that. I guess that depends."

"On what?" Brenda asked.

"A lot of things I suppose, I don't know. I just don't know. One has to actually be in that situation to know how they'd handle something like that. I sure hope I don't have to find out," Rayanne said.

"What about you, Hilary?" Brenda asked.

"I don't know and I don't want to speculate. I am not one to tempt fate," Hilary answered.

"I was young and foolish at the time, but I don't know if I would handle the same situation differently today. When I'm in love, I'm a fool. Now, all I want to do is have a good time. I make sure that the guy protects me from the stuff that's out there and I go with it," Brenda said, then she added, "these men lie so that it really doesn't matter any more."

"And, you said you still see Cardell?" Hilary said incredulously.

"Every chance I get," Brenda laughed. "What can I say, the man is good."

"I always viewed love and commitment as prerequisites for sex," Hilary said.

"You must be one boring bitch," Brenda said. She was so like Ivory, Rayanne thought. Independent, strong, opinionated. God was she opinionated.

"That maybe true, but I'm happy," Hilary said.

"Where's your sense of adventure. You want all of life's little uncertainties to be made clear. You want complete order. I like living, and the more on the edge it is, the better," Brenda said.

"But if you live your life taking chances just for the sake of a good time, excitement without any real meaning, you will suffer the consequences," Hilary said.

"Hilary, I'm not a fool. I know what I'm doing. Maybe I'll settle down one day but for now, if I make mistakes, I'll live with them," Brenda said and for the first time while talking with Brenda, and Rayanne thought of Mamie. Those two certainly had the same philosophy about living but that was where their similarities end.

"It doesn't have to be that way," Hilary said, cupping her hands in front of her.

"Everything is already fucked up," Brenda said, looking sad a moment. "I've been through hell trying to deal with one man. I used to walk around so engrossed in my own dilemma that I didn't know what was going on around me. I've been fucked, fucked with and fucked over, and I don't need any more of that. I'm doing what it takes to make Brenda happy. Besides, Cardell is not out there playing dead. He wasn't when we were together, so you know he ain't now." After a moment she said, "Anyone up for going to Atlanta this Saturday."

"What's happening in Atlanta?" Hilary asked.

"Us," Brenda replied simply. "We could leave early Saturday morning, do a little shopping, hit a club or two and drive back Sunday morning, whatever. Are you with me?"

"Sounds like it could be fun," Rayanne said. "I don't have any plans for this Saturday."

"I could go this Saturday also. Ben can take Saturday to do what he needs to and Jessica is spending some time with my mom," Hilary said.

"Oh hell, I'm practically all packed and ready to go, but I don't have any money. Damn, I'll be glad when school is over. Then I can sell some houses and make some real money," Brenda said.

"All these great plans and no money," Hilary said. Rayanne chuckled softly remembering other shopping sprees, events at the Koger Center, plays, movies or whatever, with Brenda always using her credit cards.

"When has not having any money ever stopped me. I've got plastic," Brenda said lifting two credit cards from her purse.

"Credit cards are good to have when you're in the lurch, but you charge everything," Hilary said. "I'd much rather pay cash because the interest on those cards is so darn high."

"Then what do you suggest I do for cash when I don't have any?" Brenda asked.

"Brenda, do you realize how much money you're wasting when you shop by credit card. You're paying for the use of that money, and you're paying a very high price," Hilary said.

"So, sue me," Brenda said. "I'll tell you what, when I get out of school and sell you a big ass house, then maybe I'll start buying with cash, all right? But until then, it's plastic, plastic and more plastic. If that ass hole at work would pay me what he owes me, I could shop with cash on this trip. I loan him a couple of dollars and that jitterbug won't pay me back for nothing. He keeps putting me off," Brenda said looking perplexed and it reminded Rayanne of the time when Ivory had experienced a similar situation. She relayed the incident to the girls and immediately, she saw the wheels in Brenda's head turning. "That's it," Brenda laughed, "I know what I'm gonna do. I'm gonna send him a post card, telling him that I need my money and I expect full payment by the middle of the month. That'll give him two weeks," she said.

"Brenda, you can't mean that," Rayanne said. "A post card?"

"Yep," Brenda said and the girls knew she'd already made up her mind. "That'll get him up off his ass and do what he's suppose to." Rayanne knew that was true. From what she'd heard about Joey, he was a very private person and if he got something like that in the mail, he'd be mortified. Rayanne looked at her watch.

"Girls, I guess it's settled. We're going to Atlanta. Now, I've gotta be getting home."

"So do I," Hilary glanced at her watch. "Jessica will be there soon. I'll see you girls later. And Brenda, you are a good person, you are very pretty, and you could have a monogamous relationship with any man you want, so I'm not gonna give up on you.

You deserve so much better."

Brenda stood up and when she did, she was confident again. That gleam was back in her eyes. "Honey," she said, "don't worry about me. If you were half as happy as I am, you'd go into cardiac arrest. I may live to want the lifestyle that you have, but believe me, I don't want it now. I'm fine. Really, I'm good to go."

"Well it's your life," Hilary said, lifting her hands.

"That's what I've been trying to tell ya," Brenda chuckled, they paid their checks and left the restaurant.

Rayanne arrived at the Senior Citizens' Center a quarter to 4 and just as she was about to enter, she remembered that Mrs. Shapiro had only four Sudafed tablets left in the box the day before. She quickly ran down to the grocery store and purchased two boxes. She didn't think to check the contents before leaving the store. She entered the home and Mrs. Shapiro's eyes lit up. She was fine, but her sinus problem was driving her crazy. Rayanne opened the first box and discovered it was empty. She opened the second box, got a glass of water and gave two tablets to Mrs. Shapiro. Rayanne returned to the store, walked up to a male cashier, explained what happened and told him she needed to replace the empty box of Sudafed. The Assistant Manager, doubling as cashier, looked at the box in Rayanne's hand, but he continued to wait on other customers as though he hadn't heard her. After waiting five minutes, she repeated her story and he said, "I'll be with you in a minute." Rayanne waited some more. Then she looked at her watch, thinking of all the things she had to do that afternoon. She looked at the man as he began ringing up items for yet another customer. She slammed the empty container on the counter, went to the shelf, picked up another box of Sudafed, checked its contents, and she left the store, calling over her shoulder, "Don't worry, you don't owe me anything."

"She returned to the Center, gave the Sudafed to Mrs. Shapiro, and after spending some time with her, she read fifty pages of Crime and Punishment to Mrs. Gordon and Mrs. Shapiro. She assisted Mrs. Hunter in getting started on her new 250 piece puzzle. She left the center after praising Mrs. James on her progress on the afghan that she was crocheting. When she arrived home, her father was in the backyard struggling with a wheel barrel. He was trying to push it, filled with concrete onto the back of his truck. She parked her car, quickly got out, dropping her bag and a book onto a chair on the back porch and rushed over to her father. "Daddy, what are you doing?" Sometimes her father made her angrier than anyone else. Parents always said their children had hard heads, but that was kind compared to what she was thinking about her father. "Why are you doing this by yourself." She helped him dump the cement into the back of the truck, and in doing so, she was wondering where was Josh.

"Look at your hands. You gon' get dirt in them nice clothes you got on there," he said. Rayanne thrust her hand into his overall pocket, pulled out a handkerchief, and wiped the dirt from her hands. She pushed the handkerchief back into his pocket, picked up her purse and books from the porch and headed into the house. Ruth was in front of the TV mending socks, while watching the 7 O'clock News, and from the odor in the kitchen, she was making something good for dinner. There was a definite hint of apples and cinnamon in the air.

"Hey honey," her mother looked up at her daughter.

"Hey Mama," she said, her eyes flashing back and forth to Josh.

"I baked a couple of your favorite pies today," Ruth said.

"Oh my, pumpkin pies," Rayanne teased. She hated pumpkin pies.

"Bite your tongue. I also baked a couple loaves of that yeast bread you like so much."

"I think I'll have a piece." She looked again at Josh, who was sound asleep in a chair in front of the TV. "Why isn't Josh helping daddy?" she asked, taking her things to her room.

"Just got in here. Said he been looking for work," Ruth said, as Rayanne returned to the kitchen. "Josh, Josh," Rayanne heard her mother call out, as she headed for the kitchen to cut Rayanne and herself a piece of yeast bread. "Josh, go on outside and see what your daddy wants you to do."

"I'll go out later, Mama. I don't feel like it right now," Josh stirred in his chair.

And as though something snapped inside of her, Rayanne walked quickly over to Josh and stood a foot away from where he sat sprawled back in the chair. She placed both hands on her hips, bending down to face him, saying, "you ought to be ashamed of yourself. Get your behind up out of that chair and go help daddy." Josh was drinking again and it was a disgusting sight. "All you want to do is drink and lay your lazy behind around the house all day." Josh opened his eyes half way, squinted, blinked then focused. "Get your butt up out of that chair, find your way outside and see what daddy wants you to do."

The look on Rayanne's face must've told Josh that she wasn't fooling around. "All right, all right," he said getting up from the chair on unsteady legs, "you don't have to yell." He staggered out of the house.

"You don't seem to understand anything else," she turned to find her mother looking at her.

"Come on in here and sample this bread," Ruth said, "and let me tell you about Oprah. That girl had a show on today like you wouldn't believe."

"Oh yeah," Rayanne said, taking a deep breath before sitting at the table.

"Incest. That's what it was about and it was somethin'. It's a shame what some folks do to their own children," Ruth said, and they enjoyed the yeast bread and iced tea, while Ruth talked about the show. Rayanne admired her mother, they were as close as any mother and daughter could be. It was a relationship they, both cherished and as she thought of Josh, she wondered what was it about mothers that made them want to protect their young, even when their young wasn't so young. In fact in the case of Josh, the young was old enough to be a grandparent.

CHAPTER 28

It was 8 o'clock Friday night. Rayanne was sitting on the front porch sipping a glass of rum and coke and enjoying the smell of the flowers as their fragrances floated by in the early evening breezes. Although the yard was picture perfect, Ruth was always doing something to improve it. The stereo was on in the living room, and *How Will I Know*, Whitney Houston's latest song, was playing. Another hit, and such a classy lady, Rayanne thought, looking up at the umbrella of twinkling stars, searching for the big dipper. The phone rang, interrupting her thoughts. She got up, went inside and answered it.   "Hello?" she said.

"May I speak with Rayanne Wilson, please?" the caller said.

"This is she."

"How are you?"

"I'm fine. Who is this?" Rayanne didn't recognize the voice.

"How quickly she forgets."

"I'm sorry, I don't recognize the voice. Who is this?"

"Well, it's Friday, and I believe I'm due a neck rub. May I collect?"

"Mr. Christopher," she said, now remembering, he was the man she'd run into on her way to class that rainy morning.

"No, Mr. Christopher is my daddy. I'm Scott."

"How are you, Scott?" she asked and wondered whether he was all right. Was he hurt?

"I'm fine, just need a neck rub?"

"What ?" She said.

"The neck rub. Remember we talked about it a few days ago," he explained.

"Oh yes. I do remember now," she said as her mind returned to the day of the accident.

"So, how about it?"

"That's fine. I have to tell you though that I don't have a lot of practice, but I will do my best."

"That's good enough for me. Can I come over?"

"Where are you? Do you know where I live?" Rayanne asked.

"I can be there by 9, if that'll make a difference."

"You don't know where I live."

"You're right, but I follow directions pretty well," he said and he waited, when she didn't respond, he asked, "What do you say?"

"I guess it'll be okay." Before she hung up, she gave him directions, and within 30 minutes, Scott's dark green truck slowly pulled up into her drive way. Rayanne invited him in and offered him a drink.

"No thanks, I don't drink," he said.

"Uum, that's nice."

"What can I say. I'm a nice kind of guy." He was staring at her hair. "You've got pretty hair. I'm a hair freak, you know."

"Really?"

"Yeah. I like a woman with a head full of pretty hair. After a moment, he asked, So what you been up to?"

"School mostly," she replied.

"What are you studying?"

"I'm taking some Psychology courses, and dabbling a little in real estate but I'm not sure what I want to do."

"A lady who's doing it all, huh? You're gonna sell me a house," Scott asked.

"That would be nice, but I'd really like to do something else. I'd like to sell something important to kids," she answered. She was concerned with the violence that was on the rise, and she told him so. It was getting worse across the country.

"What would you like to do about it?"

"It's a long story."

"I'd like to hear it sometime," he said, looking into her eyes, "you are a very pretty lady. Tell me, is there a Mister around?" he asked, pretending to peek around the corner.

"You waited a fine time to ask, don't you think?" she smiled.

"Better late than never, besides with me, it's first things first."

"So tell me about yourself, Mr.," she corrected herself, "Scott?"

"I'm in the construction business. I build large houses."

"That ends my career as a Realtor. Doesn't appear that I'll be selling a house to you."

"You never know. I also like cars, fast cars, race cars. I work on them in my spare time. I do a little racing some time too."

"That must be exciting."

"It is. Gives me a real rush. All that speed, all that power, you know," he said and Rayanne could see the excitement in his eyes. "I also coach a little league softball team," he finished and from the smile on his face, she knew this was a man who enjoyed what he was doing.

"You do keep busy. You enjoy it, don't you?" she asked. Scott was intelligent and interesting and there was something about him that made her want to get to know him better.

"I never do anything I don't enjoy."

"Never?" she asked.

"Well almost never," he said and they laughed as Ruth appeared at the door.

"Oh, I didn't know you had a visitor," she said, and Rayanne introduced her mother to Scott. "Do you live around here, young man," Ruth asked.

"Yes ma'am, across town on Manchester," he answered, and before Ruth left the room, she'd learned who his family was, what he did for a living, the church he attended and that he'd never been married.

"It was nice meeting you, young man, and you must come again. You might want to come go to church with us some Sunday," Ruth said, extending her hand at the end of their conversation.

"Yes Ma'am I will. It was nice meeting you too, Mrs. Wilson, and I hope to see you again soon," he said, shaking her hand.

Sometime later when her parents had gone to bed, Rayanne heard Josh staggering in. She and Scott talked until after midnight. She talked about her family, friends, school, her relationship with Ralph, and Scott talked about his son, Donnie and his mother, Frannie, whom he'd lived with before their relationship went bad. He'd even shared with her the times when Donnie's mother had told him that he wasn't the boy's father. Rayanne listened silently. "I've never been a 100 percent sure that Donnie is my son. I want him to be, I treat him like he's my son, and in my heart I'm his daddy. At least I'm the only daddy the boy knows,"

Scott said.

"You could find out if you really want to know," she said. "There is DNA."

"Oh, what's the use. I love the kid."

Rayanne smiled. "How old is he?"

"He's two and he's a great kid," Scott smiled.

"You have pictures?" Rayanne asked.

"Sure do," he said, taking out his wallet and opened it to the photo section.

"He's adorable," Rayanne said, leaning over, getting a look at the picture.

"I wish his mother thought so," he said, and Rayanne caught a glimpse of sadness in his face, the pain in his eyes, vivid. "He's with his grandma most of the time."

Rayanne could see that he was deep in thought. "What's wrong, Scott?"

"I was wondering whether I'm gonna be able to collect on my back rub," he said lightening the conversation.

"I thought it was a neck rub," Rayanne corrected.

"Okay, a neck rub then."

"Where would you like to sit?"

"Right there between your legs is fine with me," he said.

"In your dream," she said, and patted the floor beside her feet. When he was seated, she began massaging his neck. As she did, Scott thought how easy she was to talk to. He hadn't felt that comfortable talking with anyone he'd just met as much as he did her. "You have great hands. You sure you haven't done this before?"

"I said I didn't have a lot of practice," she answered.

"Oh, so you have done this before," he said and after a moment, "tell me something? What are you doing here when that man of yours is a thousand miles away?" She explained the circumstances that brought her home. "And he didn't follow you back here," Scott said. "I say he's a fool."

"Was he suppose to give up his life, his home, career and come live in the South just because I did?"

"I would have if I were he," Scott replied and Rayanne's hands became still. She felt a little uneasy by what he'd said, but she also felt strangely exhilarated at the same time. She was also thinking that was exactly what she would've done if Ralph had wanted her to. And, as if Scott had read her mind, he said, "You love this Ralph guy, don't you?"

"What kind of question is that?" she asked.

223

"Just a question. Am I being too personal or too nosy?" he smiled. Nosy, she thought, tightening her hands around his throat pretending to choke him. "I get the message," he said and they laughed. After a moment's silence, he said, "I think you and I are having a tremendous bonding experience." He turned his head to look up at her, "No, really," he said, "we are bonding. It's like we're old friends." Rayanne had to admit, she liked him and it did seemed like they'd known each other much longer.

At 1:10, Scott was leaving, but before he left, Rayanne agreed to have dinner with him the following evening. She went to bed and as she dozed off, the phone rang. She answered and Ivory said, "Hey girlfriend."

"Ivory, hey," Rayanne said, her mind leaping to Dorian, was she all right. "What's going on?"

"Everything's fine. Dorian's good," Ivory said, "but I've been thinking about you."

"I'm fine. Had a little fender bender a couple of days ago, but everything else is fine," she said. "I tried to get Dorian earlier but got her machine."

"She went out with friends, dinner and a show perhaps," Ivory said and when she questioned Rayanne about school, Rayanne told her she'd gotten all B's that last semester but felt she could've done better. "Are you sure you're okay," Ivory asked.

"Yeah, I'm great," Rayanne said breathing a sign of relief that Dorian was okay.

**

Rayanne was studying in the den as she heard Ed McMahon introducing a contestant on Star Search. The young girl began to sing and soon, she had Rayanne's full attention. The girl was no more than eleven or twelve, but what a talent. Her competitor was good, but Rayanne knew who'd win, and sure enough, Shanice Wilson received four stars which was the highest score one could get for their performance, and of course, she did win.

Rayanne put her books away at 3:30 and was about to take a nap when Maxine called. She'd met with Joe's mother and learned that he didn't want a meeting with Maxine and the boys. He was a different person now, he had a new life, a new wife and he was moving on. Rayanne knew that Maxine was angry as she imparted that information to her. She also knew that Maxine wouldn't stop at that, and that the one thing Joe didn't stay with her long enough to learn, was that Maxine didn't just get even, that girl got ahead, no matter how long it took. That must've been the day for her sisters to call because no sooner than she hung up from Maxine, Mamie called. She believed that Jeremy's girlfriend, April, was pregnant. She'd rambled on about not supporting that girl or her baby. Mamie sometimes put the cart before the horse, and this was one time when Rayanne hoped that was the case.

At 6:45, Ralph called. He wouldn't be coming next weekend as planned, he was going on a fishing trip. Rayanne was disappointed and expressed it, but after the initial disappointment, she said she understood and looked forward to seeing him the following weekend.

Scott arrived at exactly 8:30. They went to a steak house for dinner, then a movie, after which, he brought her home. But on the way home, Stranger by Jeffrey Osborne was playing on the car radio. When Scott learned how much Rayanne liked the record, he stopped his car in the middle of the street and walked around to her side of the car. She was baffled when he opened the door and reached for her hand. She got out of the car and they danced in front of his car in the middle of the street. After arriving home, they sat on the front porch and Rayanne realized that not only was Scott very romantic, but he was a great conversationalist. After a while, they became quiet. It was a lovely night and they enjoyed the quiet. When Scott spoke again, he interrupted her thoughts, "I thought about you a lot today."

"What?" she asked, blinking.

Scott looked over at her, "Where did you disappear to? I hope I'm not that boring."

"No, of course not. I'm enjoying your company very much," she said, thinking he must've sensed her trepidation. She was looking forward to Ralph's visit next weekend. Now he wasn't coming until a week later and it was wreaking havoc on her concentration. She felt she'd already waited an eternity to see Ralph and to be told that there would be a longer wait just didn't sit well with her. She squared her shoulders, looked at Scott and told him what was bothering her.

"He's going on a fishing trip?" Scott said.

"He's going to be out in the middle of the ocean," she said, "and I'm not real fond of that much water."

"That nigger must be a bigger fool than I thought. Doesn't he know he can go fishing anytime?"

"It's not that important. I'll see him the following weekend," she said trying to mask her disappointment.

"It is important. You're upset. You need to talk about this, otherwise it's gonna stress you out and we don't want that." He paused a minute. "So, if you wanna talk, I'm here, and if you'll let me, I won't go away until you feel better."

Rayanne looked at Scott and smiled. "Thanks, but I'm okay. Ralph says he can't make it. So, if he can't make it," he can't."

"But it don't work like that. There was a time when I would've thought so, but not anymore. Anytime two people are in love, nothing is impossible. If you wanna see that joker next week, you call him and tell him so. Sounds to me like he made up his mind, then he called and told you. Don't let him call the shots. You two are in this thing together, so you two should decide together."

"I'm not going to force the issue if he doesn't want to see me," she said half heartedly.

"Then, all I can say is, it's his loss. If I had a lady like you, she'd never have to feel second best to anyone or anything," he said. "Especially not to a fishing trip."

Rayanne looked at him and she was really glad they had met, however unfortunate the circumstances. After a brief silence, she said, "The woman you lived with, what is she like?"

"Frannie?" he looked up at her questioningly.

"You're so sensitive and caring," she said, "I wonder why would she let you go."

"The usual story, I guess. Our goals changed, we drifted apart," Scott said.

"That simple, huh?"

"That simple."

"Do you miss her?"

"I did," he said matter of factly.

"And now?"

"Well you know what they say. Some people come into our lives and leave quietly, while others leave an imprint on our souls," he said. She wondered had anyone affected him as greatly as the latter and asked. Scott answered looking up at the stars. "She was the most beautiful woman I'd ever seen, and I fell in love with her at first sight. Would you believe I took a sewing class years later because she was the teacher."

"When did you meet this woman?" Rayanne asked, a wrinkle in her brow.

"Oh, didn't I tell you. I was in the 5th grade, if that helps," Scott said and laughed softly.

"Scott, you are too much," she said pushing his shoulder.

"You should've seen some of those little stuffed animals that I made. They were so cute," he said, and they laughed so loud that Rayanne thought they'd wake her parents.

"That's adorable."

"You think so, huh?"

"Yes I do," she said, and they laughed some more. She turned her head to look at Scott but was shocked to see that he'd stopped laughing and was staring at her. "What is it? What's wrong?" she asked softly.

"I just love that hair of yours. Did I tell you before that I'm a hair man?"

"Yes, you did," she said smiling at him.

"I enjoy all women. I think they are precious and beautiful, and they should always be treated that way. The important thing is that they should know they are appreciated, but," he held up a finger, "I think women are most beautiful with a head full of pretty hair."

"And, you are a regular romantic."

"I've been called worse. Besides, what's wrong with being romantic?" he said, looking at her. Only days ago, they'd been total strangers but that night, their friendship broadened, and as he studied her face, he toyed with the idea of kissing her, but he immediately discarded that thought. He'd liked the way their friendship was progressing, and he wasn't going to do anything to jeopardize its course. However, his thoughts were his own and at that moment, he thought if he could hold her in his arms just once, it would stay with him a lifetime. As they talked and learned more about one another, they were surprised as the moon and stars began to vanish and the sun prepared to wake up the sky.

CHAPTER 29

The rain was beginning to fall softly the morning that Scott drove Rayanne to the airport. It reminded her of the day that they met. She watched the drizzling rain as it settled and glistened on the highway. Scott seemed moody when he arrived that morning. Although she tried to drag out of him what was wrong, he only said something had gone wrong at one of the sites, he'd left it at that, and they rode most of the way in silence. "When will you be back?" Scott asked as he drove into the parking lot at the airport.

"In a few days," she replied.

"Will you be seeing what's his name?" he asked. Rayanne didn't reply, she just looked at him. "Of course you will. What a stupid question," he said.

Rayanne didn't answer his questions, instead she said, "I'm gonna miss you, Scott."

"Yeah, I'll miss you too." He got out of the car, removed her suitcase and they entered the airport. He saw Rayanne board the plane and he watched until the silvery glimmer disappeared in the sky.

The trip to New York was non stop and quick and that evening Rayanne, Ivory and Dorian had dinner. Dorian was very quiet and when asked whether she was all right, she began to cry. "You are too good to me," she looked from Ivory to Rayanne. "I don't deserve your friendship." Ivory and Rayanne looked at each other, not sure what she meant.

"We are family, aren't we? We're suppose to be here for each other, right?" Ivory said reaching across the table and took one of

Dorian's hands in her own.

"I know and both of you have been terrific," Dorian continued to cry, looking from one girl to the other.

"Dorian, you're terrific as well. We haven't been any better to you than you've been to us," Rayanne said softly, "we love each other."

"Yes, but I've been awful. I've not been the friend to you that you've been to me. I've betrayed you in the worst way," Dorian said, her eyes darted to Rayanne's face then back to the table. "It's true."

"What are you talking about?" Rayanne wondered whether Dorian was as well as they'd thought. "You're like a sister. You've been a very dear and sincere friend too."

"It's Ralph," Dorian interrupted.

"Ralph?" Rayanne voice was low and controlled and although the look on Dorian's face made her not sure she wanted to know the answer, she had to ask. After all, hadn't Dorian avoided looking at her most of the evening. "What about Ralph?"

"Ralph and I," Dorian blurted out, paused, her lips quivering, "we've been sleeping together."

Ivory frowned and looked at Rayanne. "Dorian, what are you saying?" Ivory got up, looking from Rayanne's shocked expression back to Dorian. For a moment Rayanne was unable to speak or think, she could only look at Dorian with a wrinkled brow expression.

"I'm sorry, Rayanne," Dorian said. "We didn't mean for it to happen." She dabbed her eyes as Rayanne's expression changed from wrinkled brow to opened mouth shock as the realization of Dorian's words found their way to her brain. Ivory looked at Rayanne, bewildered, she closed her eyes, when she opened them, she could only stare at the ceiling and shake her head helplessly.

Ivory signaled the waitress and paid the check. "Come on, let's get out of here," she said and they went back to the loft. Rayanne sat in shocked silence. The words had hit her like a hurricane, jolting her, replacing the wonderfulness she'd felt toward her friend and Ralph with something that was horrible. Although Rayanne felt as though she were caught in a maze, her mind began to work and as it did, her thoughts raced like a fire out of control. Dorian explained how her and Ralph's relationship got started, Henry's divorce that never happened, her learning that Olympia, not Henry, owned the apartment complex, the magazine, the other properties. Olympia owned everything, including Henry. Dorian wasn't able to work out her disappointments and feelings of abandonment until she had gone into therapy. Rayanne swallowed hard after hearing the story, then breaking her silence, she asked, "when did you start sleeping with Ralph?"

Dorian looked at Rayanne, then Ivory and then she turned her gaze to her hands that she was wringing in her lap. "It happened quite innocently one night," Dorian began.

"How does a friend fuck another friend's man, innocently?" Rayanne asked and not only did she shock Dorian and Ivory with that outburst, she'd shocked herself, as well. The room became silent. Rayanne got up and walked away from Dorian. When she turned, she looked directly at Dorian and said, "Go on, answer my question."

Dorian took a deep breath to steady herself. "I was feeling really low. All of my friends had left me, I'd lost Henry, and I was all alone. I called Ralph up and told him what had happened between Henry and me. He knew I was feeling badly and he invited me over. We had a couple of drinks and we talked. It got late, Ralph invited me to stay over, he didn't want me to be alone. I stayed, we drank some more, one thing led to another, and, oh God," she said as the sordid picture came back to her and the tears started all over again, "we made love. Ralph was so gentle and loving. I haven't had anyone to treat me that way in a long time," she said.

Ivory's eyes rolled towards the ceiling again as she mumbled, "Oh shit," under her breath.

Rayanne felt a shiver go over her body at Dorian's words. She composed herself as much as she could and said, " Of all the men that you know, all the men you've been involved with, why did you have to pick Ralph to go to bed with? Why would you do that to me? Why?" Dorian hung her head in silence. "Answer me," Rayanne shrieked, "why Ralph?"

"Rayanne, I'm sorry. It wasn't something we planned," Dorian said. "We didn't intend for it to happen. Please believe me. I was at a very low point. I'm sorry."

"Why does it always have to be about you?" Rayanne asked. "You go out and screw my man, how do you think this makes me feel? I trusted you," Rayanne said and began pacing back and forth, pushing her hair back on her head. "I can't believe this is happening." Then she turned suddenly to Dorian. "Did you stop to think what this would do to our friendship, my relationship with Ralph?" Tears now rolling down her cheeks.

Ivory went to Rayanne and embraced her. "Take it easy," she whispered.

Rayanne freed herself from Ivory and walked back over to Dorian. "When did this happen?"

"When?" Dorian looked confused.

"Yes, when? Oh don't tell me. It's happened more than once," Rayanne said, "hasn't it?" Dorian didn't respond. "Hasn't it?" Rayanne screamed at her.

"Yes," Dorian said and began to cry again, deep, raking sounds escaped and filled the room.

"Just how long has this been going on?" Rayanne asked, ignoring her cries.

"Can we talk about this a little later," Ivory said seeing the effect the argument had on both girls.

"No, Ivory, I wanna know right now, how long my supposedly good friend and my man have been sleeping together," Rayanne said.

"A couple of years," Dorian answered, after staring at Rayanne a moment.

"What?" Rayanne said, walked on unsteady legs and dropped in a chair. The room was silent once again. Ivory looked perplexed, Dorian looked lost and Rayanne looked as though her world was coming to an end. It was clear now why Ralph sometimes could not make eye contact with her. No wonder. Then something else came back to Rayanne's mind. "That blue scarf of mine, the one you loved so much, Dorian. Where is it?" Ivory looked even more perplexed as she looked from Rayanne to Dorian.

"Blue scarf?" Dorian was baffled. "I don't know. I know the one you are talking about, and I love that scarf but I don't know where it is I have looked everywhere for it."

"Have you checked Ralph's closet lately?" Rayanne spat out the words. She'd seen the scarf in his closet when she'd visited him several months ago, but she couldn't remember how it had gotten over there. There was something about it being there that had bothered her, but after a while, she put it out of her mind.

"Rayanne, I'd do anything not to have had this happen," Dorian said. "I know what you must think of me."

Rayanne looked at Dorian. "No you don't. You couldn't possibly know." Fresh tears welled up and rolled down Dorian's cheeks.

"What are we gonna do?" Ivory said sitting on the couch, her head in her hands.

Rayanne looked at her. "I'm gonna call the airport, and I'm taking the first flight back home. That's what I'm gonna do."

"Rayanne," Ivory said, going over to her, "please don't leave like this. Stay at least until tomorrow and let's talk this through. There's so much at stake here."

"It's a little late to try to salvage a friendship when something like this has happened," Rayanne said.

"But we can't just walk away and leave things the way they are right now, not like this," Ivory said.

"You watch me," Rayanne said, she got up and strutted over to the telephone. Ivory went and sat beside Dorian. Rayanne hung up the phone, walked over to the French doors, opened them and stepped out onto the terrace. It was cold outside and that was exactly what she was feeling inside, but she was in so much pain that she didn't notice the chill in the air.

"I thought you might need this," Ivory said, coming up behind Rayanne, placing a coat around her shoulders. Rayanne shivered, but it wasn't from the cold. "I'm sorry, Rayanne, and for the record, I didn't know. God, I had no idea Dorian had reached that point." Ivory looked out over the city. "Something awful has happened here and it can't be undone, so we have to deal with it. But what do we do? I don't know why something like this happened, but I do know that everything happens for a reason. It's not going to be easy, but we've got to find a way to get pass this. Tell me, girlfriend, what can I do to help. Desmond and I are here for you, for whatever you need." One of the things Ivory admired most about Rayanne was her strength, but she knew this would be difficult to handle. Her friend was going through pain that had reached down and touched her soul, and she didn't know what to do to help her. "I know you're hurting now, you're angry and you will be for sometime, but there is an answer to all of this, the answer to this whole mess is time," Ivory said.

Rayanne turned and faced Ivory. "So what do you suggest I do until enough time has passed to drive the pain away? Am I suppose to just forget what she's done, act like nothing's happened? Is that what I am suppose to do?" Rayanne's anger mounting. "What I should do is go back in there and kick her ass into next year."

"Yeah, you could do that, but what good would that do," Ivory said.

"It would make me feel a hell of a lot better," Rayanne stormed. Then she said a little more gently, "Ivory, you have no real sense of how I'm feeling because it didn't happen to you."

There was silence between them. After a while Ivory said, "What are you thinking?"

Rayanne took a deep breath. "I was just thinking that I can't stop this from happening. I can't stop it from being true, can I?"

Ivory sighed and said, "No you can't, none of us can. I just wish I could bring some sense to this whole mess." Ivory wrapped her arms around herself. "I was thinking it might help to remember that Dorian was going through a lot. Dorian isn't innocent in this, I know that but understand how something like this could happen. I just didn't think it could happen to us, but it did happen and it can't be undone. It is a horribly dilemma. The truth is, we are all broken, torn apart by this," Ivory said and her voice cracked, "but we have got to find a way to put it back together again. At least we've got to try."

"Ivory, honestly, what would you do if this happened to you?"

"I'd kick both of their asses all over New York. That's what I'd do, but that's me talking, not you. You're the sensible one. If I were to blame anyone, it would be Ralph." And, Rayanne thought. She'd placed all the blame on Dorian. She didn't screw up everything by herself. She had plenty of help. Ralph was right there in the middle. He shouldn't have allowed this to happen. He was aware of Dorian's fragile condition, yet he took advantage of it and he worsened the situation. Rayanne thought of Ralph and all the times he'd disappointed her, the way he avoided eye contact with her at times, and his general attitude. As she thought of him, her heart split into a million pieces, and she wondered whether it would ever be whole again.

"You know, Ivory," Rayanne began, "something like this had to happen. What we had was so perfect that one of us was bound to screw up."

"It was perfect," Ivory agreed as they stood on the terrace in the cold, and after a moment's hesitation, she said, "So what are we gonna do?"

"I don't know," Rayanne replied, "I can't get a flight out until tomorrow, so it looks as though I'm stuck here for the night."

"Good," Ivory said, thinking it would give them a little more time to talk.

Rayanne and Dorian spent the night at Ivory's. When Rayanne went to bed, she buried her face in the pillow, then rolling over onto her back she opened her eyes and suddenly the words came back to her, "Ralph and I, we've been sleeping together." The words echoed in her mind and she knew she'd never be able to forgive Dorian or Ralph. Family and friends were important, but trust was also high on the list of things that were important to her.

The flight back to South Carolina was long. Rayanne adjusted her seat, closed her eyes and tried to sleep. She was tired, emotionally drained and consumed with pain, literally sick with misery and pain. When she returned home, she found a message from Ralph, but she didn't return his call. At first everything seemed at a standstill. For three days, Rayanne would get up, get dressed, went to school, although unable to concentrate, returned home at the end of the day and repeat the cycle. After a while, the days began to go by quickly and since she refused to take calls from Ralph, letter came from him and began to stack up on the dresser in her bedroom. She left the house one day, running blindly towards the lake behind their house, tears rolling down her face. She'd cried so often after her trip to New York that it was a wonder that she still had tears left to cry. It was there at the lake as the sun began to fade and night was coming fast, that she realized that although she felt pain throughout her body, she had to pick herself up and move past her misery, and, she forced herself to do just that. Her grades were good, she was keeping busy, she exercised and she was able to smile on occasions. As time passed, the one positive thing that happened since that awful night in New York was that Dorian met, fell in love and married a Frenchman, and they'd moved to France. She sent Rayanne an invitation and a note with more apologies, by way of Ruth, because she knew Rayanne well enough to know she would not read any mail from her. Dorian wanted Rayanne to be with them for the occasion, but she was doubtful that Rayanne would be a guest at the event. Rayanne did send did a gift, but she didn't attend the wedding.

***

Trouble never seemed to come alone. Raymond had given them another scare, another heart attack. Josh had gone into yet another detox center, stayed sober for several weeks, but the usual story, he'd started drinking again. When Ruby kicked him out that time, along with it was a promise that she'd never have anything to do with him again, and, of course, that meant he'd moved back in with the family one more time.

CHAPTER 30

After church and dinner, Rayanne's parents and Aunt Bessie visited one of Ruth's childhood friends who was in the hospital and who lived just down the street from the Wilsons. There had been talk of Abigail's daughter coming from Washington, D.C., and moving Abigail back with her. Abigail had been mugged in her own neighborhood and she'd been badly beaten. Ruth and some of the other neighbors had taken care of the widow until she came down with pneumonia and it was necessary to have her hospitalized.

When the house was quiet, Rayanne sat in her bedroom and stared aimlessly out of the window. Mamie called and the conversation was based on one major question. Could Jeremy and Little Charlotte come and live there for a while. "It won't be for long. Just until I can decide what to do about this situation," Mamie had said, and she'd made it perfectly clear that she wouldn't be calling if she didn't really need the favor.

"What a way to ask for a favor," Rayanne said, and pointed out, "If that is the reason for your call, then you could've saved yourself the dime."

But, Mamie went on as though Rayanne hadn't spoken. "Jeremy will take care of himself and the baby and he can help out there around the house."

"Mamie, Jeremy is a teenager. He isn't going to want to be tied down with a baby. My schedule is pretty full right now and Mama isn't physically able to look after a teenager and a 3 month old baby," Rayanne explained; however, Mamie couldn't see what harm it would be for them to live there and look after each other. Rayanne tried going through it once more, but before she finished, Mamie hung up. The phone rang again. It was Ralph. He'd run into some problems at work, been laid off, he'd said, and he was afraid he might even be terminated. Downsizing, he told Rayanne but she wasn't sure she believed him. He had been with the Wall Street firm for many years and had done quite well, and Rayanne thought if the firm was really downsizing, it would take a drastic cut to let someone as productive as Ralph go. She knew he was still doing drugs and if he was laid off, the drugs would be the reason. After she hung up from Ralph, she turned the radio on to a station that played slow, soulful ballads. She switched on her computer and begun to write while tunes by Johnny Gill, Howard Hewitt, Patti, Levert, and Keith Sweat played softly in the background. Then the record by Babyface about paying the rent and buying the clothes played, and Rayanne could never remember feeling as lonely as she did at that moment. She'd spent time alone before, but now, she was lonely and there was a difference. Shanice Wilson's record played and just as she'd thought, the young girl had become a success story.

Rayanne wrote for hours as the soft music continued to play. Scott called, he was coming over. At 6:30, she showered and slipped into a shorts set. She left the house through the back door, wandered around the yard and watched the storm cloud pass across the sky. It was hot and muggy and the look of the clouds promised rain. She walked to the end of the backyard where the trees began, and she took the path that they'd cut as children, to the lake. It was picturesque the way the trees and wild flowers cast reflections on the water. With a little work, this would be the ideal setting for writing, she thought.

The lake was special for each of the Wilson children. When Rayanne was a young girl growing up, she'd go out to the lake just to be alone, on occasions, taking her favorite doll with her. Growing up in a house with five siblings caused one to seek refuse from the others on occasions. The lake was a place of solace, a place where she could be quiet, talk to her doll or to reflect, as well as plan. She'd decided there at the lake that she'd go to college, which college she would attend, and what she wanted to do with her life.

She even thought about the kind of man she wanted to marry and the number of children she would have. There were other times when she and Ivory sneaked off to the lake to read love letters that some boy from school had written to one of them or both. They'd read the letters and sighed, their hearts filled with love, and together they composed responses and slipped them into the waiting hands of the boys who'd written them the day before.

Rayanne found a small clearing near the lake, and sat. She thought of her conversation with Mamie, she thought of Ralph and Dorian, and she thought of her life since returning to South Carolina. She thought of many things. She also thought of her oldest brother, Samuel, the effect he had on her life, and the thought of him made her smile a little. Sam, as Rayanne almost always referred to him, had encourage them to always do their very best to literally go out on a limb, to take risks. Rayanne smiled as she thought once when Sam had tied an old tire to the end of a rope, climbed out onto the thick limb of a large tree that extended out over the lake and had tied the other end of the rope to it, allowing the tire to swing back and forth over the water. At first, no one was brave enough to use it, but after Sam's coaching, each of them was soon swinging out over the water, enjoying their new game, although taking many spills before managing to glide out over the water and return safely to land. Needless to say, the swing became their favorite summer sport, and not only did Sam gain the respect and trust of his younger siblings, he was looked upon as their hero. Sam had a way of making everything right. But that was then and this is now, Rayanne thought, and life may never be that simple again.

Rayanne got up, looked around her and when she turned to leave, she saw Scott approaching. "Hey there," he said, reaching her and looking around, "this is nice. I didn't know you had your own private lake down here."

"Yes," Rayanne replied. "I love it here. It's a great place to think."

"What do you think about when you're out here?" he asked as they walked slowly back towards the house.

"Everything. The past, the present and the future," she said looking at him. "So what've you been up to?"

"Work mostly, but where've you been. I've been trying to get you all week."

"I've been kind of busy. School, the center, writing," she said as they rounded the house and mounted the steps. "Do you want to go inside or sit on the porch a while."

"The porch suits me," he answered and conveyed, "I just met your father."

"He didn't offer you a drink, did he?" Rayanne asked, smiling at him

"As a matter of fact he did."

"You didn't accept?"

"You know I don't drink," Scott said looking skeptically at her, and she thanked God that Scott didn't drink. Her father had done that with Ralph, who accepted the beer, and although her father never did say, his opinion of Ralph changed after that incident. Her father had a way of doing that with any man his daughters brought home to meet them. He didn't approve of anyone drinking and anytime any of his children did so, they had to keep it hidden from him. Somehow, her mother knew, she knew everything, but her father didn't. That was a fatal mistake Ralph had made with her father.

They sat on the porch and it wasn't long before Ruth appeared with a picture of lemonade and two glasses filled with ice. Rayanne inquired about Abigail's condition. "Abbie ain't much today. Don't know how she is gonna fair off this time. She's still scared half to death after she was robbed," Ruth said and told Rayanne that Abbie's daughter, Tangy was there. She asked about you."

"How is Tangy?"

"She's doing good, expecting her second baby," Ruth said and smiled at Rayanne who understood that look only too well.

"Mama please don't," Rayanne said, lifting her hand to quiet her mother and letting her know that she didn't want to entertain any questions about when she was going to have a baby. Please, at least let me get a husband first, Rayanne thought.

"I didn't say anything," Ruth said.

"But you were thinking."

"Well, you can't blame a mother for thinking," Ruth said with raised eyebrows. Then she turned to Scott. "How was service at your church today, son?" When Scott said it was fine and told her what the sermon was about, she smiled, telling him it was so nice seeing him again as always and she disappeared into the house.

Scott and Rayanne talked as the day faded into night and as it did, there was a change in the temperatures. It became a cool night for such a warm day. After a while, Rayanne became quiet, and Scott asked, "What's going on inside that head of yours, tonight?"

"Oh, nothing much," she said and when Scott looked directly

into her eyes, "I'm all right."

"This is Scott. You can talk to me." He'd gotten to know her, her likes, dislikes, her moods. "You never did tell me about your trip to New York," he explored.

"That was months ago. Why are you asking me about that now?" she asked, not wanting to think about New York, more less talk about it. There were too many unhappy memories of New York.

"Something happened there?" he pressed for details and although he was certain she wouldn't tell him, still he had to try.

"What makes you think something happened?" she asked, with a frown on her face as she looked at him.

"Because, you've changed. You haven't been the same since you came back," he said.

She studied him for a moment. "It's a long story, and I don't care to get into it right now," she said and looked away, but not before Scott saw what he thought was fresh pain in her eyes.

"It might help to talk about it," he coaxed, ignoring the strange sensation in his stomach as he watched the crease deepened in her brow. "It's usually you who gets me to talk.   Whenever I do, I always feel better." It was true, Scott had valued Rayanne's friendship and he talked to her about everything.

"Scott, I know you want to help and I appreciate it, but it's a little embarrassing for me to discuss something like that with you."

"You don't have to be embarrassed about discussing anything with me."

"Leave it alone, will you," she begged.

Scott hated the way she was shutting him out, but he thought he'd better not push, he didn't want to run the risk of killing off the friendship before it had a chance to grow, only she looked so sad suddenly. "We have a relationship here. We're suppose to talk about what's bothering us."

"We do not have a relationship. We've had a few dinners and a couple of movies, but that doesn't constitute a relationship," Rayanne stated.

"Well excuse me," Scott said and slapped his arm, then quickly added, "hold that thought and let's go inside. These mosquitoes are eating me alive." They went into the living room, and sitting in front of the TV set, he said, looking at his watch, "Why don't you put it on Channel 7. Wild Kingdom will be on in a few minutes." She obeyed and sat beside him. "So you don't think we have a relationship, Huh?"

"We have a friendship," she said flatly. Scott had wanted more than friendship when they'd met but since Rayanne was firm in her decision, he'd given up and accepted what she was willing to give.

"Friendship," Scott said the word slowly, "I like the sound of that. Now that we've established that we're friends, let this friend help. Let's talk about what's bothering you."

"I don't think so. Look," she said trying to divert his attention, "Wild Kingdom is coming on."

"It might help," he said, pushing her hand down, ignoring her last statement.

"It may not," she came back. Scott looked at Rayanne for a moment, she lifted a hand to silence him, got up and she made herself a Rum and Coke and returned to her seat. Scott sat quietly beside her, his back against the couch. During a break in the program, Rayanne asked, "How old are you, Scott?"

Scott looked at Rayanne. He could tell she was serious, only he didn't understand the question. "Where's that coming from?" he asked.

"I'm just curious," she said, "and, you've never said."

"Maybe I didn't say because it's not that important. Besides, you never asked," he said matter of factly.

"I'm asking now."

"Okay, I'm twenty seven."

She knew he was young, but he wasn't as young as she'd thought, and for some reason, she was pleased. Then she asked, "You wanna know how old I am?"

"Not really. Why? Do you want to tell me?"

"I'm thirty-six."

"Okay."

"I just thought you might wanna know."

"Age doesn't matter to me, I hope it doesn't bother you. I'm a man and the last time I noticed, man was spelled m-a-n not a-g-e," he said confidently and smiled. He was young, Rayanne thought, but wise. They watched the program and when the last segment was over, Scott looked at his watch. "May I have a neck rub before I leave." Rayanne was in deep concentration, she didn't hear his question. "Hey," he nudged her shoulder with his, "where are you?" Rayanne was baffled as she looked at him. "What about a neck rub, please," he repeated, lifting his hands as a dog would lift his paws, begging. Rayanne looked at him a hint of a smile touched her face. He sat on the floor beside Rayanne's legs and she began to massage his neck, his shoulders and his temples. "God, you've got the best hands. Have you ever thought of going into the business," he teased, "you sure got the right touch." Rayanne remained quiet. "You think you can control yourself just a little," he continued to tease. Rayanne continued the massage, but she still didn't speak. "Hey you, talk to me, please say something. The silence is killing me." Scott tried to turn his head to look at her, but she held his head, preventing it. Then they heard the key in the back door lock and she knew it was Josh and the way he was fumbling with the lock, she knew he was drunk. She stared at her glass of Rum and Coke that sat on the coffee table. Scott twisted his neck from the pressure that she was suddenly applying. When she was certain that Josh was too drunk to open the door, she got up, went into the kitchen and opened it for him. Josh staggered in just as Rayanne had suspected he would. She helped him to a chair and draped a blanket across him, hoping he'd sit and sleep off some of the alcohol before going any further. She'd been bailing him out of one situation after another for some time and here she was, helping him in yet another situation, but now, her patience was wearing thin. The last episode that landed him in jail was three weeks ago when one of Josh's pals had gotten into a fight with someone, Josh thought the only way he could help his friend was by blocking the highway so that his friend could catch the man. Well, when the authorities learned of Josh's involvement in the incident, he lost his driver's license and he went to jail. It was Rayanne who'd posted bond to get him out. He'd promised all the way home that he was never going to touch another drop and he'd kept his promise the entire fifteen minutes it took her to drive him home from jail. Then he was off again, only to return later pitifully drunk.

Rayanne heard Josh in the bathroom. She picked up her glass of Rum and Coke, walked into the kitchen and poured it down the sink, it was at that moment that she decided never to drink anything alcoholic again. Now, if only Josh would make the same decision and stick to it. As her thoughts raced around in her head, Rayanne found herself feeling responsible for Josh's drinking. Why was it that she felt responsible about things of which she had absolutely no control. What kind of personality allowed that kind of thinking. She really should see someone about that, she thought, returning to join Scott. "I wish he wouldn't drink so much," she commented, as she resumed the massage she was giving to Scott.

Scott tried to turn his head to look at Rayanne, but again she held him in place. "I know it bothers you, Rayanne, understandably so, he's family. We wish we could do something to change the ones we love who are hurting themselves and us, but we can't always. When I find myself caught in a situation like that, I talk about it. The more we talk and deal with it, the quicker the healing begins," Scott said and Rayanne wondered what was he talking about. All that couldn't be just about Josh's drinking. He continued, "Some people come by hurt and disappointment first hand and some a little further along, but it doesn't make it any easier if it involves people we love." He turned to look at her. This time she didn't try to stop him. "It's not always easy, but you don't have to go it alone. You got family, you got friends and you got me. You've always got me."

"We are talking about Josh, aren't we?" Rayanne asked looking at him.

Scott looked at her, a weak smile on his face. "Yeah."

Rayanne, still not sure the conversation was just about Josh, said, "It's awful seeing him like that."

"Yeah, I know," Scott agreed.

Although Rayanne had shared many things with Scott, there were still things she'd kept to herself, burdens she suffered alone, but now she asked herself why. Scott had always been supportive and understanding, and hadn't he always offered to help. That night as she looked at him, she decided it was time to share her misery with him, her worries about her Father, Josh, and the situation involving Dorian and Ralph. "Ralph and I have had our ups and downs as couples do, but the one thing I thought we had was trust," Rayanne began. "I trusted him especially his love for me, but all that's gone." Her voice was just above a whisper, she tilted her head to the side and the wistful look on her face made Scott believe that she was remembering better times.

When she finished the story, Scott couldn't believe that Ralph would stoop so low. How could he have done something like that to Rayanne, Scott thought. He shook his head. "You got a lot on your plate, but you're handling it really well," he said. What could he do to make her feel better, he wondered, unconcerned about the pain that cut deep in his own heart at the look in her eyes when she was thinking of Ralph. That look alone told Scott one thing. With all that Ralph had done, Rayanne still loved him and because she did, she'd forgive him, but none of that was important at the moment. All Scott could think of was comforting her.

"It may look that way on the outside, but underneath I'm struggling to hold it together," Rayanne said. "Can I ask you to be patient and understanding with me until I can get past this."

"Whatever you need, baby," he said and sat on the coffee table facing her. "Hey, I've got an idea." He changed the subject, "Patti and Bobby are coming to the Township next week. Interested?"

"Yeah. I love Patti and Bobby. They're the best," she paused, then, "so are you, Scott." Scott was great, sensitive and caring, and she was proud to call him her friend.

"You can you know," he said softly, looking away from her.

"I can what?" she frowned.

He looked directly into her eyes. "Trust me, love me, count on me, whatever. It's safe," he said and she found herself just feeling warm and lucky, lucky to have him in her life. He'd assured her of his sincerity, he seemed to turn his full attention to the dismantling of her life, and he promised to stand by her while she put her life back together, piece by piece. "It might help if you understood how I really feel about you."

"I think I do, but I need to do this by myself," Rayanne said. "Life has a way of throwing us lemons."

"Well you know what they say. You make lemonade."

Once when he said that to her, she asked, "does the same principle apply when life throws you a curb?" His response was simply that you hit it out of the ball park. She had laughed about it then, only she didn't feel so much like laughing now.

He looked at her. "You're a bright beautiful lady. If there's anyone who's knocked off her feet, gets back up and walks away the wiser, it's you," Scott said very honestly. "Rayanne, always remember that people come in and out of our lives like Grand Central Station. Some leaves a moment in the soul that can last forever, and then there are those who just quietly go away."

A wave of tenderness swept through her. "Get over here and let me finish that neck rub before I change my mind," she said and laughed. After a moment, he quietly said, "I love you, you know."

"No you don't. You just think I need to hear it," she said, but she'd never appreciated him more than she did at that moment.

"You want to hear it too. I'm gonna tell you something. You're saying one thing, but I know that you have love for me hiding in there somewhere," he said pointing a finger towards her heart." He was like a candle in the darkness, Rayanne thought, and she really cared a lot about him.

"Scott, you're something else. You make me feel grateful for today and eager beyond anything I can imagine about tomorrow, you give hope," she said jokingly, but it was more true than ever, she realized.

"Spoken like a true poet," he said.

"No, you're the poet in this family. Now get on over here," she ordered, he obeyed and for a while, they sat motionless and listened to the sounds of the night, cars honking, crickets creaking and dogs barking, adding to the melody.

CHAPTER 31

When you have good health and happiness, you should count your blessings because as time passes, changes occur. Some good, some bad, others, devastating. Rayanne had been deceived in the worst way, she was the only one of the trio who hadn't yet married, and Josh was in rehab centers more than he was out, but nothing had prepared her for the shock and the incredible sense of loss that enveloped her when her father died.

Rayanne had accompanied Tiffany to a meeting in San Francisco, where Tiffany was recognized as an enterprising young businesswoman. Although Rayanne had sold her partnership, the business still bore the name RayTiff, and Tiffany had invited her to come with her.

Rayanne returned three days later on a hot summer's day to find her father alone in the yard, working as usual. He looked tired, perspiration stains had soaked his long sleeved shirt that he wore rolled up, and Rayanne wished once again that he wouldn't work so hard. Rayanne hugged her father as he tried not to soil her clothes. She tried to get him to come inside, but he wouldn't and as she was about to enter the house, she met her mother bringing out a pitcher of lemonade and two glasses, and she knew, from her mother's expression that she, too, had tried but failed to get her husband to quit work at least until it was cooler. "Where is Josh?" Ruth asked.

"I thought he was out here with you Raymond," she said, looking around the yard, trying to catch sight of Josh. Rayanne was going towards the house, when she heard her mother ask, "where did Josh get to this time?"

"He's laying around there in the house," Raymond said, climbing down from his truck and wiping his forehead with the back of his hand. "I don't know what to make of him no more. He's got such a good head on his shoulders and it bothers me to no end to see him just throwing his life away like that."

"Come on over here and sit with me for a while." Raymond sat. "Here," Ruth said, handing him a glass of lemonade, "have something to drink. It's nice and cold."

Raymond took a sip of lemonade, closed his eyes and said, "next to you woman, this is the closest thing to heaven." Ruth blushed and fanned her hand at him. He took a handkerchief from his pocket and wiped the sweat from his face and neck and took another sip from his glass. "This really hits the spot," he said.

"I thought it would." She leaned close to him and whispered, "Who knows, you might get a notion to make it up to me later."

"You better believe it," he winked at her, "your man ain't dead yet."

How lucky they are, Rayanne thought, observing her parents from the kitchen window, to still be so much in love after all those years. She turned away and smiled as she checked her messages. She was going to change, then she'd watch the Oprah shows that she'd recorded while she was away. Before she reached her room, she heard a sound. Was someone snoring? She stood still, listening. There was that sound again. She walked towards it. "Josh," she called out, walking towards his bedroom. Rayanne entered the room and saw Josh sitting in a chair behind the door, his head thrown back. He was sound asleep. She approached him. "Josh." The air surrounding him wreaked of alcohol. "Josh, wake up," she said shaking him by the shoulder. Josh opened one eye just a slit.

"Rayanne, hey. What's going on?" his words slurred as he focused on her.

"What are you doing in here?" she asked.

"I just came in a little while ago. I'm gonna go back out in a minute," he said, frowning up at her.

"I think you ought to be getting a move on."

"Rayanne, I'm hurting so bad right now. Just give me a few minutes more, okay?" He'd been drinking more than usual and making a habit of sitting around and wallowing in self pity. Didn't

246

he know what he was doing to himself, the family? Didn't he care? "Just give me a little time to get myself together," Josh begged, shifting in the chair. Upon a closer look, Rayanne saw an ugly gaping scar on the side of his head, and his jaw was swollen.

Rather than guess at what had happened to Josh this time, Rayanne asked, "what happened to your face?" Josh was thirty-eight, just two years older than she, but because of the way he lived, he could easily have passed for forty-five, even fifty. "What happened to you?" she repeated.

"It's nothing to worry about." He tried to get up. "Phew, this thing hurts like hell." He rubbed his jaw.

Rayanne kneeled down, took Josh's face in her hands and said, "Josh, your jaw may be broken. You need to see a doctor. Go, clean yourself up and let's go to the emergency room."

"I'll be okay. It hurts but it'll be all right. I just need a couple of Tylenols."

"You need to see a doctor. The folks don't know about this, do they?" She asked, continuing to eye his face.

"No, I don't think they even know that I'm here."

"That's what you think," Rayanne said and Josh just looked at her, hoping it wasn't true. Neither of them wanted their parents to see his face in that condition. They worried enough as it was. Josh cleaned himself up and waited at the front of the house, while Rayanne drove around, picked him up and drove him to the hospital. Josh told her that some man had accused him of going with his wife and had belted him a couple of times.

Josh's jaw was fractured, but not broken, thank God. He was treated, they left the hospital and returned home just after 9. They pulled into the driveway and were surprised to see so many cars there on a Monday night.

"Looks like everyone's here," Rayanne said and snickered as Josh growled. She parked the car and they sat a moment.

"Someone must've seen us at the hospital and told mama and daddy. It looks like they done call everybody," Josh said.

Rayanne snickered, again. "Oh well, we may as well go on in and face the gang," Rayanne continued to laugh at Josh, who didn't want to go inside. He was embarrassed about the condition of his face, but Rayanne knew if he didn't go in and at least let everyone know he was all right, they'd probably worry even more. "You know, Josh," she said, "if you choose to live your life this way, you have to face the music." Rayanne giggled some more.

"You sure I can't go in through the side door. I'd sure like to avoid the questions," he pleaded.

"You get no help from me brother, dear. So come on in and face it." As she put her key into the lock, the door opened suddenly and there stood Maxine, teary eyed and a Kleenex in her hand. "Maxine, what is it? Has something happened to one of the children? Marcus?" The questions rushed out of Rayanne's mouth.

Maxine shook her head, tears rolling down her cheek. "No, Rayanne. It's daddy."

"Daddy? What's wrong with daddy? Is he sick?" Rayanne asked, walking quickly pass Maxine towards her parents' bedroom. "He's been doing too much. I keep telling him that, but he doesn't listen," Rayanne said over her shoulder to her sister.

Maxine rushed after her, caught her arm, turning her around. "Daddy's dead, Rayanne," she said and as the words slammed into Rayanne's brain, she felt frozen. Her head began to spin and the last thing she remembered was a scream tearing its way out of her throat. She awoke in the middle of the night in her own bed, not knowing how she'd gotten there, and she tried to recall the earlier events of the evening. When she tried to move, pain shot through her head, disabling her.

"You lie back down and rest, child," Aunt Bessie said from the chair beside Rayanne's bed.

"Aunt Bessie, is that you?" Rayanne tried to focus in the dim light, "what are you doing here?" she asked, easing herself up on an elbow, meeting the tormented expression on Aunt Bessie's face as she began to remember. It was like a kick in her stomach. "Daddy's dead," Rayanne said.

"Yes," Aunt Bessie answered and Rayanne lay back and cried softly into her pillow. Aunt Bessie hardly ever left her side. When Rayanne recovered some, she asked about the rest of the family. They were holding up as best as they could under the circumstances, Aunt Bessie informed. Rayanne learned that her father fell in the back yard, he'd suffered another heart attack and by the time Ruth was able to get help, it was too late.

"It's my fault," Rayanne said, shaking her head.

"Why do you say such a thing, child?" Aunt Bessie asked. "Ain't nobody's fault."

"If I were here when daddy got sick, maybe I could've help and daddy would be alive."

"Now child, you listen to me. What happened here today didn't have nothin' to do with you. Was the will of the Lord, and you got to get that in your head," Aunt Bessie said. "This is the

Lord's work. It hurts us, but we gotta accept it." Rayanne was silent, but she knew if she'd been there, she would've been able to help, and for that, she'd also feel guilty. Aunt Bessie talked with her during the night, rubbed her hands, comforting her as best as she could.

As the sun began to wake up the morning, Aunt Bessie left the room once and returned with a glass of warm milk and two pills that she pushed into Rayanne's mouth. Although dazed for the most part, Rayanne could hear the door to their home opening and closing throughout the morning. When she woke in the early afternoon, Aunt Bessie was still there with her. Rayanne closed her eyes, a vision of her father in her mind and fresh tears rolled down her cheeks. She looked at Aunt Bessie, sitting with her, strong and brave and it was at that moment that she realized that through her own sorrow, she'd forgotten how the death of her father had affected her Aunt. My God, Rayanne thought, her father was Aunt Bessie's only brother. How traumatic this must be for her. "Aunt Bessie, I'm sorry," Rayanne said, reaching for her aunt.

"I know my child, I know." Aunt Bessie understood and she held Rayanne in her arms as if she were a baby.

The days that followed were almost unbearable, but each time Rayanne caught sight of Aunt Bessie, her faith and strength were renewed. The day of the funeral, there were so many in attendance that it was impossible to fit them all in the church. More mourners were outside than in and flowers were delivered by the dozens, to the house and the funeral home. Ivory, Desmond, their two children, and Dorian and her husband attended the funeral. Although Rayanne didn't expect him and Ralph did call and send a telegram expressing condolences, he didn't make the trip.

Rayanne and Dorian had spoken only by telephone and only after Raymond's death, but they hadn't seen each other since the night of the confession and although their visit started out strained, Ivory, Dorian, and Rayanne used some of their time catching up. Before Dorian and her husband departed, Rayanne told Dorian she appreciated her being there. Dorian knew that was true, but she also knew that Rayanne wasn't even close to welcoming her back into her life.

CHAPTER 32

Scott found that he was angry at Ralph as he watched Rayanne agonized over the loss of her father, and although a lot had happened to put distance between Ralph and Rayanne, Scott knew that she needed Ralph at that time, more than ever. Scott would never forget the effect Rayanne's vulnerability had on him. The night after the funeral, she'd cried like a lost, frightened child and all he wanted to do was comfort her, help her, remove the pain completely, if he could. He would've done anything to make her world right again.

Most of the family left a couple of days after the funeral, but Mamie stayed a little longer and when she left, Jeremy and Little Charlotte were left behind, with a promised that she'd return within two weeks for them. But, the weeks turned into a much longer period. Mamie seldom called, and when she did, she kept putting off picking them up. Rayanne felt really bad for Jeremy. Since she'd come from a home of loving supportive parents, she could only imagine what Jeremy must be feeling. Mamie had never demonstrated any real love for Jeremy. She constantly put him down, telling him he'd never amount to anything. There were even times when she assured him that he'd never have been born if it'd been up to her.

The weeks that followed Rayanne and Jeremy talked and they became close. She introduced him to young people at church, people in the neighborhood, she took him shopping, taught him to drive and she helped him get his driver's permit, then his license. Jeremy was a good kid, at first, but as the saying goes, nothing lasts forever.

As September came in and Jeremy and Little Charlotte were still there, he enrolled at the local high school to complete his senior year. Rayanne knew that not many teenage boys could be relied upon to care for an infant, and Jeremy was no exception. As it turned out, Little Charlotte would wake up in the middle of the night, crying and there was no way to know how long this would've gone on had it not been for Ruth and Rayanne, who got up and took care of the baby. By that time, Rayanne was counseling teenage girls three times a week, putting in lots of time at the adult care center, writing and she was still going to school. She also served on several committees at church. She loved the children and it wasn't bad having a teenager and a baby in the house, but her hands were full. Some evenings when she arrived home, she'd be so tired that all she could do was shower and go straight to bed. One of those nights when she'd just gotten into bed, the baby began to cry. She opened her eyes but lay there and waited, thinking maybe Little Charlotte would go back to sleep or Jeremy would look after her, but instead, the baby continued to cry. Rayanne threw back the covers and went into the room that they'd set up for Jeremy and the baby. She picked up the baby and checked her. Jeremy must not've changed the baby for hours, she was soaked, and as Rayanne looked around the room, she noticed Jeremy's bed was still made. Where is he, she wondered as she changed Little Charlotte, gave her a bottle and put her back to bed, where she slept through the remainder of the night. She didn't know when Jeremy had gone out or why, but he still wasn't in when Rayanne got up after 3 a.m. to check on the baby.

Rayanne made breakfast and waited for Jeremy to come into the kitchen. She wanted to talk to him before he went to school. She looked at her watch. Jeremy should be up by now, she thought. Rayanne got up from the table, went to his room and gently knocked on his door. "Jeremy." When she didn't get a response, she knocked again. Still no response. She entered the room and turned on the light. "Jeremy," she approached his bed. "get up or you're going to be late for school."

"I don't think I can make school today, Aunt Rayanne," Jeremy said shielding his eyes from the light that flooded the room.

"Why? What's wrong?" she asked.

"I don't feel so good."

"Does something hurt?" she went over and touched his forehead. "I don't think you have a temperature." She left the room and returned in minutes with a thermometer, but Jeremy was asleep. He's probably not sick, just sleepy and no wonder, Rayanne thought. He'd spent most of the night away from home. She got dressed and gave instructions to Madeline, the young lady whom she'd hired to look after the baby and keep her mother company, what needed to be done, before she drove to the University. She called home midday to check on everything and learned that Jeremy had gone out with someone an hour ago and hadn't returned.

As Rayanne drove home that afternoon, she thought of her mother. The woman who once had enormous strength and insight, had changed. The change occurred shortly after her father died. She'd never seen her mother cry. Ruth had mourned and grieved, but she didn't cry, even at Raymond's funeral. Rayanne didn't witness tears from her mother until one night about a month after her father had died. She'd just checked on the baby and was returning to her room. As she was passing her mother's bedroom door, she heard her say, "Damn you, Raymond, why did you have to die and leave me? What am I gonna do without you? I miss you so. Oh, Raymond, why, why?" Not only was Rayanne surprised by her mother's cries, she felt completely helpless. She didn't know what to do to help her mother with her grief. The one thing that she did know was that she couldn't go in at that moment. She'd watched the pressure build up in her mother daily, she'd been keeping it all inside. Once when Rayanne had tried to get her mother to talk about her father's death, she'd said that death was a part of life and that we had to accept it. Only Ruth hadn't accepted it. She'd kept it inside and had suffered as a result. As Rayanne stood by the door, she knew her mother needed to cry. More than anything else, her mother needed to cry. She kept watch over her mother during the night, and she appeared to be sleeping peacefully, but to Rayanne's amazement, she awoke the following morning to the smell of breakfast. Her mother had gotten up and cooked breakfast and was folding a bunch of towels she took from the dryer. "Wow," Rayanne said, as she entered the kitchen. "What's all this?"

"Breakfast. What do ya think it is?" Ruth said, with her usual quickness that Rayanne admired so much.

"You must've gotten up at the crack of dawn," Rayanne said.

"About an hour or so ago," Ruth remarked, continuing her

chores.

"You certainly have been busy this morning. Breakfast, laundry, my goodness," Rayanne said, piling her plate high with grits, eggs, bacon and even a piece of toast. She ate heartily, and as she did so, she watched her mother. "So how are you doing this morning, Mama?"

"Just fine, honey, and you?" Ruth replied, but Rayanne noticed Ruth's actions contradicted that reply. She was doing everything at twice the normal pace.

"Mama, are you okay?" Rayanne asked, feeling uneasy.

"Your mama is fine, just busy, got a lot to do today," Ruth responded, only Rayanne wasn't so sure.

"You don't have to worry about all of that. Madeline will help," Rayanne said, then to Madeline, "right Madeline?"

"Right," Madeline replied. Ruth didn't comment. She gave Madeline a dark look before she picked up a stack of folded towels and left the room. Before Rayanne left that morning, although her mother appeared to be her old self, she asked Madeline to keep a close eye on her mother.

The weeks that passed, Rayanne and her mother visited her father's grave and she watched her mother become a different person. One morning in late November, when Rayanne didn't have any classes, a call came in from a doctor's office, reminding Ruth of her appointment the following day. When she hung up, she wondered what was wrong with her mother, why was she seeing a psychiatrist and why wasn't she told. Rayanne called Maxine and told her about that phone call and was surprised that Maxine knew. Ruth had been going through periods of depression over the loss of her husband and to add to her dilemma, her best friend, Abigail, was moving out of town. "Rayanne, I didn't tell you because you have enough on you," Maxine said and it was true, but Rayanne would've preferred being told up front.

Rayanne arrived home late one night after she and Brenda had gone out to dinner at a jazz lounge restaurant. She got into bed and it seemed she'd just closed her eyes when Little Charlotte began to cry. She waited a moment, thinking either her mother or Jeremy would see to the baby, not so. The baby cried out again. Rayanne got up and found that the baby had a slight temperature. She gave the baby some children's Tylenol, changed her and shortly afterwards, Little Charlotte was smiling and kicking her tiny feet and hands. The thing that made her angry, though, wasn't the fact that she had to get up and see to the baby, but the fact that Jeremy was no where in the house. Within an hour, the baby was back in bed and Rayanne called Mamie but as she suspected, she got the answering machine again. She left a message and Mamie returned the call from work the next morning. Rayanne expressed concerns about the hours Jeremy was keeping and the crowd he was running around with. She told Mamie that there was a lot going on in the streets in South Carolina as well, and that she thought it would be a good idea if Mamie made some other arrangements. Mamie didn't see it that way, of course. She'd been tied down with Jeremy all of his life, she wanted a little time for herself she wanted to live a little. "Besides," she said, "I don't see what harm it would be for them to stay on especially since Jeremy will graduate soon, not to mention his helping out around the house."

Rayanne didn't mention the fact that Jeremy was hardly ever at the house. "Mamie, Mama isn't doing that well, and I really don't have time to look after Jeremy, the baby and continue with the things I need to do." Rayanne was in for yet another surprise when Mamie told her she'd talked with Ruth and had convinced her that if Jeremy stayed in New York, something awful would happen to him, and, of course, Ruth, feeling the way she did about family, assured Mamie that it wouldn't be a problem for Jeremy and the baby to stay on until Mamie made other arrangements. Well it was settled. The following night, or rather early morning, Rayanne heard Jeremy go into his room. She got up, went to his door and paused a moment before knocking and entering his room. "Jeremy, it's nearly three in the morning. Where've you been?" she asked.

"Just hanging out," he said, pulling his oversized sweatshirt over his head. He sat on the side of the bed, kicked his shoes off, allowing them to drop to the floor with a thud.

"Your little girl was sick earlier tonight." She tried not to show her anger.

"What's wrong with her?"

"She's all right now, but she had a temperature earlier."

"I'm glad she's okay," he said, almost nonchalant, "I'm gonna turn in now, Aunt Rayanne. Goodnight." Little Charlotte was Jeremy's daughter and Rayanne would like to think he'd be a little more concern. "Jeremy, where are you? What's going on with you? This is not the first time that you've disappeared during the night and returned in the wee hours. I know you're young and it's difficult being a parent, especially at your age, but you've got to take some responsibility. If the baby had become seriously ill and I were not here, I don't know what would've happened. Mama isn't able to take care of the baby." Rayanne paused as Jeremy appeared not to be paying any attention. "Jeremy, are you listening to me?"

"Yes, Aunt Rayanne."

Rayanne looked at him and sighed. "You go on to bed, but we're going to talk about this." She left the room, closing the door behind her. For sometime she'd wanted to talk with Jeremy about his strange comings and goings, times when he'd come in, wandered around in his room, and she'd hear him leave again, to get into a waiting car, something he'd been doing more and more. On one of those nights, the baby was fussier than usual and Rayanne rocked Little Charlotte until early morning when she quieted down and went back to sleep. A few weeks later, a similar incident occurred, but that time, instead of someone else picking him up, Jeremy had gotten into his own black Corvette, the one Rayanne had given to him when she'd bought a new one, and he drove away. Rayanne became increasingly more concerned about Jeremy and the company he was keeping. She'd heard he was hanging out with a known drug dealer, and she was surprised when she arrived home one day to find Jody Brown sitting in their home. Jody was older than Jeremy, he was bad news and if she had her way, guys like Jody Brown wouldn't be a friend of Jeremy's and he certainly wouldn't be invited into their home.

Jeremy was feeling abandoned, deserted by both parents and was in search of himself, his own independence, but what he found was something entirely different. Rayanne was afraid that without some intervention, he'd be selling or using drugs himself, possibly both. She talked with Jeremy, not as some domineering person, but like an aunt, someone who cared, and, although she didn't condone some of the things she suspected he was doing, she didn't criticize him. Jeremy had a lifetime of hearing negative things about himself and Rayanne certainly wouldn't treat him that way, but she did take a hard line with him, letting him know what she expected from him and what he could expect from her. In order that they coexist, it meant working together, and no one said it would be easy.

Rayanne and some friends were planning an evening out. They'd meet at a friend's house for snacks, a little girls' talk and a couple of games of cards. She was about to leave the house when Jeremy approached her. He'd made plans to go out as well, he'd said, and he wanted to know whether she would look after the baby. She'd been accommodating whenever she could, but tonight, she needed to get out for a little R&R and shoot the breeze. "You're out every night, Jeremy. You're gonna have to cancel your plans this evening because I'm going out." Rayanne knew Jeremy was upset that he'd have to stay in, but she had no idea how desperate he was until she went into the bedroom to kiss the baby goodnight, and she caught him giving the baby Robitussin to make her sleep. Rayanne yelled at him so loud that he dropped the bottle, spilling its red liquid content all over the carpet. When questioned, Jeremy swore that he'd only given the baby a half teaspoonful of the medication, but Rayanne called the doctor anyway and needless to say, she canceled her plans for the evening and she told Jeremy that under no circumstances should a similar situation ever occur again. Little did she know at that time, that she'd be spending even more evenings at home taking care of the baby.

As Rayanne sat quietly rocking the baby that night, she thought how her life had changed. Family was still a priority. She'd wanted a husband and children one day but she had no idea she'd suddenly have two children thrust upon her without the benefit of having a husband. Her life was becoming more of a stand still, but Jeremy's though, was wide open.

***

"What you got there," Ruth looked up from where she was hanging curtains in the kitchen and asked, as Rayanne entered the house with a couple of packages in her hand.

"Just a few things for the baby," Rayanne answered, she paid Madeline and after she left, Rayanne helped her mother with the curtains, while informing her that she'd gotten an A and 2 B's, Brenda got 2 A's and a B, and Hilary, 3 B's.

"You girls are doing good. Won't be long now before y'all will have all this behind you."

"Yeah, a few more semesters and it will be over," Rayanne said after putting the last tieback in place, "come and let me show you what I've got."

"Let's see what you got that little lady this time," Ruth said, grinning. She was having a good day, she appeared to be her old self and Rayanne was glad.

"Okay," Rayanne said, "I got her a few things." She took the items from the bag.

"Oooh, how pretty. Why, I don't know which one I like best," Ruth smiled, looking at the dresses.

Little Charlotte was just beginning to walk and for a beginner, she was as graceful as a swan and as time passed and her graceful-ness continued, Little Charlotte lost that name and she became Swan. She was Swan to everyone, well everyone except Mamie.

Jeremy was on the telephone, which wasn't unusual, but what made Ruth and Rayanne pay attention was that he'd made three phone calls to three different girls, saying the exact same thing to each of them. "What's up, baby? You know I've been thinking about you all day. Yeah, I'm crazy about you, baby, and I'd like to see you this evening. Are you with that? I thought we could get together, you know, have a little pizza, something to drink and chill." Rayanne and Ruth looked at each other, shook their heads, laughing and after Rayanne picked up Swan from her playpen, they left the room. Jeremy was eighteen, popular and handsome. He stood over six feet, his complexion was medium brown and he had jet black wavy hair that he wore cut short. Rayanne was sure that, even at his early age, he'd left some broken hearts be-hind.

Just when Rayanne thought everything was going to work out, she began receiving letters from school. Jeremy was missing classes. When he was there, he didn't pay attention, never turned in his homework or he was disruptive in class. "What's going on, Jer-emy?" Rayanne said to herself, "what are you doing with your life?" When Jeremy came in that night and went into his room, she followed him. They had to talk, but it was late and he looked tired sitting on the bed. "Jeremy, you and I need to talk, but obviously this is not a good time. You get some sleep, but we will talk tomor-row," she said and as she left the room, she was beginning to ques-tion giving him her old Corvette. Was it a mistake? He'd kept strange hours almost from the time he came to South Carolina, but he kept worst hours now that he had his own transportation. She'd wanted Jeremy to have nice things, things a teenage boy would want and deserved, and Rayanne had no problem giving him those things, but some things had to change.

Rayanne returned to her room and unable to sleep, she opened the newspaper. What is happening to the people in this country, in the world? The drugs, the shootings, rapes and robberies and other types of crime, you name it, we've got it, and not just here in this country, but in our own back yards, and to people we know. Something's got to be done to make the world a better, safer place to live and bring up our children.

CHAPTER 33

"**H**ere comes that lying ass Brenda," Hilary said.

"Shhh," Rayanne said in a hushed tone, "she'll hear you." They were sitting in Quincy's having lunch after class. Brenda came through the line, tray in hand, to join Rayanne and Hilary. She saw someone she knew and stopped to talk. "The girl just likes to have fun," Rayanne said.

"It's more than that," Hilary responded.

"You're not jealous, are you?" Rayanne teased, putting her elbow on the table, her hand cupping her chin.

"Absolutely not, but I'm concerned that she's involved with all those guys, sexually," Hilary said, putting emphasis on those guys and sexually.

"Brenda's not stupid. She knows what she's doing."

"I know she's practicing safe sex and all but it still bothers me, her falling into bed with every man she meets," Hilary said, clearly disgusted.

"Hilary, I don't think it's like that at all," Rayanne said in defense of Brenda.

"I don't see why not. You don't even have to guess at what she does, she puts it all out there for you."

"You know Brenda, she jokes a lot," Rayanne said. She'd gotten to know Brenda pretty well and although she knew Brenda was having some fun, Rayanne felt that she was more talk than anything. "She's not had the best life you know, been kicked around a lot you know. Now, I think she's just trying to have a little fun."

"She seems happy enough to me."

"She's trying to be, but looks can be deceiving. You know," Rayanne said after a pause, "although she hasn't said so, I think she still loves Cardell."

"What?" Hilary said incredulously. "Do you really think so?" After considering what Rayanne said, she asked, "Do you think they'll get back together?"

"I think she's still in love with him, but I don't know whether they'll get back together. I hope they will," Rayanne paused, "if that's what Brenda wants."

"I don't have anything against Brenda. Heck, I like her, but the woman has no morals," Hilary said.

"Brenda's all right," Rayanne said as Brenda approached the table and sat.

Each girl piled her plate high with salad and had a glass of iced tea. When they were all seated back at the table, Brenda said, "So, what's up with you guys?"

"Things are going okay with me, but the questions is, what's up with you, girlfriend?" Rayanne asked.

"Did she really ask me that question?" Brenda said. "My question is do you really wanna know?"

"Oh heck," Rayanne said, "why not? Let's just live dangerously for five minutes."

"I don't know if I want to hear this," Hilary said, putting a fork of salad into her mouth.

"Well, let me tell you anyway. Last night," she began, pointing to a hickey on her neck, "I got this little love flower? Jason gave it to me," Brenda said and took a sip of tea.

Rayanne said, "I thought you were seeing Matt last night," while Hilary stared at Brenda.

"Wait a minute and let me tell you what happened," Brenda said, the girls were all ears. "Matt, with that big black ass of his, called me yesterday, and I agreed to see him. I asked him to call me before coming over. I wanted to take a little nap so I could be fresh for him when he arrived. Well, Jason decided to stop by."

"Is he the nineteen year old?" Hilary asked.

"He's older than that now. Do you think I got older but he didn't?" Brenda answered, looking at Hilary with her mouth hanging open, "wrong."

Hilary clicked her teeth and said, "He's still just a boy."
Rayanne and Brenda laughed.

"I know one thing, that so called boy's got his act together. He
sizzles," Brenda shook her body so that her breasts jiggled. "Just
look at y'all." She laughed at Rayanne and Hilary, "a bunch of
nosy old women."

"Okay, don't tell us. See if we care," Rayanne said biting into
a piece of dill pickle.

"Oh hell, y'all care. You ain't shitting me?" Brenda said and
laughed.

"You may as well get on with your sordid little story," Hilary
said, "you know you're dying to."

Brenda, her eyes sparkling said, "As I was saying," she dabbed
her lips with a napkin, "Jason stopped by just as I was getting out
of the shower. He was just sitting there in my living room looking
at me, then he started licking those sexy lips of his."

"His lips or your lips?" Hilary asked, perched on the edge of
her seat.

"His lips, Hilary, his lips," Brenda said. "Then he poked his
tongue out at me and sort of wiggled it."

"Where were the boys?" Hilary asked.

"They spent the night with my mother," Brenda said, winking
at Rayanne.

"Hello," Rayanne said, and gave Brenda five.

"Jason got up from his chair, got down on his hands and knees
and crawled over to me," Brenda informed.

"What did you do then?" Hilary lifted a fork of salad to her
mouth, not noticing the salad had fallen off and she pushed an
empty fork into her mouth. Realizing what she'd done, she laid
the fork on the plate.

"I didn't do anything. He did it all. He kissed my feet, licked
my legs up to my knees, and then," Brenda said and filled her
mouth with salad, chewed slowly on it and made the girls wait
until she swallowed and washed it down with a couple of sips of
tea. Brenda looked at Hilary and burst out laughing?

"Are you going to finish this disgusting story?" Hilary asked.

"Sure," Brenda said, taking another sip of tea. Rayanne snickered as she knew Brenda was enjoying the mileage she was getting out of telling that story. "Then he opened that wonderful mouth
of his," Brenda continued, "and started sucking my knees." She
paused. "Have either of you ever had your knees sucked?"

"My goodness," Hilary whispered as she caught her breath,

and peered over the rim of her glasses. Hilary was usually a little behind in her thinking being the prude that she was, but at that moment, her thinking was right with the others, and the implication of what Brenda was saying, spurred her imagination.

"Yeah, I have," Rayanne said, " and, it's not bad."

"Not bad? Try, it's freaking good," Brenda said, and she looked at Hilary, "what about you old lady?"

"This is your story," Hilary spat out.

"Uh uh. Scared of her," Brenda said, and she and Rayanne laughed. "Anyway, Jason was turning me on, and he hadn't even laid his hands on me yet. Can you guess what happened next. The phone rings and who do you think it is?"

"Matt," Rayanne and Hilary said in unison.

"Damn right. So I go into the kitchen to answer it and there I was standing, just leaning against the table with my back towards the door, talking with Matt when all of a sudden, Jason comes up behind me, puts his arms around me, and kisses my neck. Then, he rubbed my stomach and he sucked my ear lobe," Brenda said, her eyes closed.

"Were you still talking with Matt while all this was going on?" Hilary asked, disbelieving.

"Yes, Hilary, some people can do more than one thing at a time."

"I asked a simple question," Hilary said, tearing off a piece of roll and popping it into her mouth.

"Yes, I was still talking with Matt," Brenda took another sip from her glass. "Then he came around and faced me, Jason, that is. He pushed me back onto the table, opened my robe and we had the best time."

"Couldn't Matt tell something was going on," Hilary asked.

"Matt was talking dirty to me, so I suppose he thought my moans and groans were meant for him," Brenda answered.

"You didn't allow Jason to make love to you there on the kitchen table," Hilary said.

"No, we didn't make love at all that day. Does that mean my virtue is still in tact?" Brenda teased.

"Hardly," Hilary snorted, and they laughed. "Rayanne thinks you're still in love with Cardell," Hilary changed the subject.

Brenda's smile faded and she looked serious a moment, "why would you think that?" she said to Rayanne.

"Because it's true," Rayanne answered, and she was just as serious as Brenda had been.

"That's water under the bridge now," Brenda said sadly.

"Not necessarily," Rayanne said. She knew Brenda's relationship with Cardell didn't have to be over, not if they loved each other enough.

"Look, it's over all right," Brenda said. "Believe me, girls, it's over. Why are we talking about Cardell anyway?" Brenda was about to go to the dessert bar. Whenever she wanted to avoid a subject, she'd walk away or she just would not talk about it.

Rayanne reached out and caught her arm. "Wait, Brenda. Let's talk about this a minute."

Brenda looked hard at Rayanne, and accepted coffee from the waitress. "What is it that you two want to talk about?" she asked, looking at each girl.

"We want to talk about you," Rayanne answered.

"We've been all through this. Cardell and I separated after all possibility of reconciliation was explored."

"But you two never divorced," Rayanne said.

"No, and I really don't know why, the children I guess," Brenda said.

"You probably gave up too quickly, just as you always do when something doesn't go your way. You," Hilary began, but Brenda cut her off.

"I hope you're not judging me now about things I did at a time when you didn't even know me. Look, I went through hell. It wasn't easy back then," Brenda said and it was obvious she was hurt.

There was a slight lull, then Hilary reached across the table and took Brenda's hand. "Brenda," she said, "I just want you to be happy, that's all."

Brenda stared silently at Hilary, then she said, "I didn't say anything, but Cardell did come by last week, we talked, and he mentioned us getting back together."

"That's wonderful," Hilary said.

"Don't go jumping the gun. I simply said we talked. It would take a lot of changing on his part, which I'm not sure he's ready or willing to do. I'd have to make some adjustments myself." Brenda lifted a finger and said, "don't let those imaginations run away with you. It'll just make all of us unhappy. So let's forget it. It's kinda late for Cardell and me so lets close that subject. I'm still hungry," she said, getting up again.

"Hey, wait a minute," Rayanne said, "if there's a chance to put your marriage back together, to bring the father of your kids back home, don't you think it's worth a try." Rayanne liked Brenda, she was a good person, usually a happy one, Rayanne thought, awaiting a response, but none came.

"He wants to get back with you. Doesn't that tell you he still loves you and he's changed," Hilary said.

"No, it only tells me he wants to control my life. He knows I'm having a good time, so he wants to get me back under his thumb with my head in the sand," Brenda said. "I've always been really vulnerable to Cardell, but I've learned to be a little more cautious. This time I'm trying to make my decisions with my head and not my heart. That man has hit me with a hard dose of reality more than once," she said remembering times when he'd say let's get back together, and she'd be all for it, even after what he'd put her through, and he'd change his mind again. Brenda shook her head, not wanting to remember and said, "never mind."

"What happened?" Hilary asked.

Brenda wrapped her fingers together and stared down at them. She took a deep breath. "One minute he talks about getting back together, I start to show interest and try to get close to him, then he backs away. He does that shit to me all the time. I don't know what it is with him. Confuses the hell out of me." She threw her hands into the air, "Anyway, it's no big deal and there's no use talking about it," Brenda said.

"It is a big deal if you love him and want him in you and your kids' lives," Rayanne said softly.

"I don't think I want to take the emotional risk," Brenda said.

"Everything involves risk, but it might be worth it. Talk with the man. Find out what he wants, let him know what you want and see whether you guys can work it out. Give the man a chance," Rayanne told her. Brenda smiled and shook her head negatively. "Aah, give the man a chance," Rayanne repeated.

"I've given him lots of chances," Brenda said.

"Give him another," Rayanne said, smiling slightly.

"What if it doesn't work out? What if he hurts me again?"

"What if he doesn't? He does make you happy, doesn't he?" Rayanne asked.

"He's made me just as unhappy," Brenda came back. Hilary remained silent through the exchange.

Rayanne understood Brenda's dilemma, but she felt if there was an ounce of hope for that situation, then Brenda should go for it. "I know what you're going through," Rayanne was sympathetic.

"Obviously, you don't, Rayanne, or we wouldn't be having this conversation," Brenda said.

"There aren't any guarantees, but I think it's worth a shot," Rayanne said.

Brenda slid out from behind the table, stood up, lifted both hands and said, "I can see that the only way I'm gonna be able to get something else to eat is to tell you two what you wanna hear, especially you, Rayanne. I'll think about it. That's all I can say, and right now, I'm still hungry." With that, Brenda left the table.

"Are we still going to New York on that shopping trip?" Hilary asked when Brenda returned.

"I'd like to," Rayanne said, "but I'm not sure. Brenda? What about you?"

"What?" Brenda said, slightly distracted.

"Are you going to New York on Thursday?" Rayanne asked. "I can go if I get a baby sitter. Madeline won't be able to stay over night and Mama has just not been herself lately." That was another thing about Rayanne's life that had changed drastically. She couldn't just pick up and go as she'd done in the past. She had to make sure that someone would be looking after her mother and Swan, since her mother was depressed because Mrs. Abigail was moving that day, and she couldn't depend on Jeremy to do anything.

"How are Jeremy and the baby?" Hilary asked.

"Swan," Rayanne smiled, "she's great, but Jeremy, what can I say. He's a teenager."

"You now know what it's like to be a mother," Brenda said, "and about that New York trip, count me in. I ain't got no money as usual, but my plastic still works." She still depended on her credit cards. Her motto was live and enjoy yourself as much as possible today and pay later. Always pay later.

"This woman charges everything. Ben lets me have one card which I use primarily for gas. He cut the others. He's concerned about the interest rates being ridiculous and he's right, but that one card is fine as long as I'm going in the direction of Bloomingdale's."

"I know that is right," Rayanne said.

"I've always wanted to shop at Bloomingdale's," Brenda said, "and Macy's." There are lots of great stores in New York, Rayanne thought as she remembered previous years when she'd shopped as if shopping was going out of style. She'd had the good fortune of being driven to stores of her choice, by her own private driver, and taken home again with lots of shopping bags filled to the top with every thing imaginable. That was the life, it was wonderful, but that was in her past.

"Are we still driving my van?" Hilary asked.

"That would be great," Brenda said. "Rayanne, I hope you can make it. I've got my heart set on this trip. What is the limit on that credit card of yours, Hilary?" she asked.

"$5,000."

"That's a nice piece of change," Brenda said, "I'd go wild if I had $5,000 on my credit card. I'd spend as much as my plastic would allow. Hell, life's a bitch, but this way, I can have my cake and eat it now, and when I die, I want to owe everyone, even Jesus Christ."

"Mercy," Rayanne said and laughed.

"Isn't she just too much," Hilary said, laughing but Rayanne had to agree.

Brenda looked at her watch, "I gotta run girls. I wanna go home and finish my paper that's due on Wednesday, and I wanna see what Victor Newman is up to today."

"I think he's gonna divorce Nicki, don't you," Rayanne said, tossing her napkin into her plate.

Hilary looked from one to the other, asking, "How many of those soaps do y'all watch anyway." She wasn't a regular soap watcher, herself. Rayanne admitted recording and watching Young and Restless and As the World Turns, while Brenda kept up with Young and Bold and Beautiful.

"I don't see how you do it. I don't have the time," Hilary said.

"It's escapism for me," was all Brenda said before they departed, and Rayanne thought, that's what they were becoming for her as well.

Rayanne arrived home just as the moving truck pulled away from the curb in front of Abigail Brunson's house, with her belongings. The street in front of Abigail's house was crowded with neighbors who met there to say good-bye to Abigail and her daughter before they departed for D. C. It was a sad farewell, but not only was the departure sad, it angered Rayanne and her family. They knew Abigail would not have moved if she had not been the victim of that brutal attack. The attack had been so violent that she was afraid to walk down the street in her own neighborhood, afterwards.

CHAPTER 34

When it looked as though Jeremy and Swan had become a permanent part of the Wilson's household, Rayanne knew it had been no accident. It had all been a long, calculated, well orchestrated plan of Mamie's. She'd worked on Ruth and had gotten her wish. It was quite an adjustment listening to music that was so loud that the walls seemed to vibrate, the sound of a baby crying in the middle of the night, and groups of teenagers streaming in and out of the house, day in and day out. At first, it wasn't bad. At least it was tolerable. They kept reasonable hours, Rayanne and her mother made snacks for the kids, and they enjoyed the renewed life in the house. It was reminiscent of how it was when Rayanne was a teenager and her friends came in and made themselves at home. Unfortunately, after a while, Jeremy's friends called and dropped in all hours of the day and night, and Jeremy's odd hours recurred and he almost totally shun all responsibilities as a father.

Rayanne couldn't help feeling that Jody Brown had more of a negative affect on Jeremy than anyone else. When she first met Jody, she didn't have a good feeling about him. He looked like trouble, acted like trouble and another thing she found disturbing was the way Jody looked at her. She mentioned it to Jeremy one day and he simply said, "You're a fly lady, Aunt Rayanne. You can't blame Jody for liking what he sees." Mercy, Rayanne remembered thinking. Jody was only several years older than Jeremy, and it was embarrassing the way that boy allowed his eyes to travel over her body.

Jody came by one day, wandered into the kitchen and asked for a drink of water. He was wearing his hat backwards, his pants was so far below his waist that the crease of his behind could be seen, and he wore designer sneakers that were only strung up half way. Rayanne poured a glass of water for him and asked why he wore his pants that way.

"This is the nyle," was Jody's responded.

"What?" Rayanne asked, not knowing what he meant.

"It's the nyle," he repeated. There was that word again. "Everybody's wearing 'em like that."

"Are you saying this is the style?" Rayanne asked, extending her hands in his direction, thinking that the young fart couldn't even pronounce the word. There were a number of distasteful things about Jody that sent her mind racing, and she had to wonder why Jeremy would want to associate with him.

***

Madeline announced that she was getting married and moving out of state with her husband and as a result, there was the task of hiring someone else to look after the baby on an almost full time basis, and although unfortunately, and the fact that a lot of time had passed, Rayanne still hadn't had that talk with Jeremy. As she entered the house that day, she was thinking that she'd certainly make that a priority. She'd put it off long enough. However, as fate would have it, the talk would still have to wait because as she entered, her mother called out to her. "Rayanne," Ruth, looked up from where she was mending a pair of Josh's slacks, "I want us to sit and talk when you have a little time."

"Sure Mama, what do you want to talk about?" Rayanne asked, looking at her mother and seeing her as she'd never seen her before. Ruth was not wearing a scarf on her head as she'd done the past several months and to Rayanne's surprise, her mother's hair was completely gray. The six months after Raymond died had certainly had an impact on Ruth. "How are you mama? You had a good day?" Rayanne reached for the mail that lay on the table.

"I sure did. I talked with your daddy today," she said, a smile curling her lips.

"What?" Rayanne said, whirling around and dropping the mail from her hands.

"Oh, did you see that letter you got from that agent of yours?," Ruth said.

"Yeah, Mama I did," she replied and picked up the mail that had splattered across the floor. She also noticed a letter postmarked from France. She knew it was from Dorian and she'd put it with the others that were unopened in her dresser drawer.

"Well go on, open it."

"I will, Mama" Rayanne answered, "but that can wait." Rayanne knew from the size of the envelope that she laid on the table that Harry had shopped her play around, couldn't get a buyer and was returning it. She was in touch with Harry often, and she knew what the letter would say. He'd said the same thing the past six years, since she returned to South Carolina. "Mama, what did you say a minute ago?" Rayanne asked.

"About what, honey?" Ruth said, almost childlike.

"You said something about talking with daddy?"

"Talking with your daddy? What are you talking about, girl? Your daddy's dead." Ruth looked at Rayanne, an odd expression on her face. Rayanne was confused, dumbfounded. She knew she'd heard her mother correctly, she also knew that her mother had said and done things in the past several months that were strange. Something was wrong. Very wrong, but she decided not to press.

"Don't give up, Rayanne. Don't give up on your dreams," Ruth was saying. "You're a good storyteller. You always were since you were a little girl. You were real successful in New York, and you'll be again too," she lifted one finger, "just you wait and see." The one thing that had remained a constant with her mother, even though she'd had better days, was that her faith in her children never ceased. Rayanne sat in a chair in front of her mother.

"You sound just like daddy."

"Your daddy and I were together a long time, over fifty years and if he hadn't died, we'd still be together. When you live with someone that long, you became like one. Your ways become that person's ways." As Rayanne observed her mother, she noticed that her eyes were red and swollen and surrounded by lots of wrinkles. Her mother had never looked her age before, but she did now. She knew how much her mother had missed her father and Mrs. Abigail. Rayanne took her mother's hands in her own. "It'll be all right, Mama. It'll be all right." Rayanne released her mother's hands and took a deep breath. "So what did you want to talk about?"

"Rayanne, you got a lot of responsibilities on your shoulders. You done spread yourself sorta thin, and I wish there was more I could do to help you."

"Mama, you help me much more than you know. The best thing is that you're here for me and the kids every day. That is what's important to us."

"I know that's how you feel, but what I want to talk to you about now will be one less burden you'll have to bear later on."

Rayanne was puzzled. "What is it, Mama?"

"I want the two of us to plan my funeral."

CHAPTER 35

Scott called at half past nine that night, there had been another robbery in the neighborhood, and she told him how ticked off she was about it. Afterwards, he shared with Rayanne, the frustrations of his day, Frannie was on his case again, demanding more money for Donnie. Scott didn't have a problem with doing whatever was necessary for the boy, but he knew there was more to it. Frannie was running around, hanging out in the streets and she'd gotten back on the kick of telling him that he wasn't Donnie's father. He told Rayanne he didn't have a particularly good day but had hoped hers was better. Rayanne wasn't that lucky, in fact, her entire week never left the ground and to top it off, Madeline was getting married in less than a month and not a single person who'd applied for the job was suitable. In addition, Jeremy had punched a boy at school over some little girl and it had gotten him suspended. She'd told him many times that he should keep his possessive tendencies in check, but did he listen, no. Rayanne shared with Scott some of the things Jeremy had been doing, some of the people he'd been hanging out with and that she'd found marijuana in his room. Jeremy had changed. He was a man in that he was eighteen, but he still behaved like a spoiled child. He spent hardly any time with the baby, he didn't do any chores and he'd become brazen and disrespectful, but what bothered Rayanne most was that Jeremy had started lying. He lied when the truth would've served better. She had to put a stop to some of his shenanigans.

"Now," she said after revealing all to Scott, "have I sufficiently ruined your day?"

"No, and I want to be with you when you confront him," Scott said. Rayanne was thankful for his support and told him so but this was something she had to do. He impressed upon her how unpredictable teenagers can be, especially when they're involved with drugs, big money and felt cornered, having that lifestyle threatened.

"I appreciate that, Scott, but I'll handle it."

"Okay, but I'm here if you need me," Scott said and when that was settled, he asked, "What about Peters? You still seeing that tired old man. I thought you would've given him his walking papers by now."

"The man's name is Peterson... Pe-ter-son," Rayanne pronounced each syllable, then added, "and no I haven't given him no papers yet."

"Not yet, but soon. Kick that old dude to the curb," Scott chuckled, but Rayanne didn't comment further. She'd run into Billy Peterson almost a year ago, after she'd broken up with Ralph. She and Billy had began dating again and the sad part was that he hadn't changed much from when they dated as kids. Billy and his wife had divorced after fifteen years of marriage and although he didn't satisfy all the things Rayanne craved, he wasn't married and considering the men that were available, she continued to see him. She knew Billy loved her and she cared for him, but there were no fireworks for her in that relationship. She didn't experience any of the things she did when she was with Ralph. Ralph, she thought. "I wonder who he's messing over now," she said, but what difference did it make. He was out of her life and it would stay that way.

***

Rayanne received her Master's on Friday and later, she and Scott went to the movies and saw Boys N The Hood. When he dropped her off that evening, she checked on Swan and her mother, but as usual, Jeremy was no where in sight. She went into the den, and she began reading the paper. She looked at it, unable to concentrate, she tossed it aside again and looked at her watch. "Where is he," she said, getting up and going into her bedroom. She looked out of the window. The street was practically deserted except for an occasional car passing by. She heard a car slowed down. "Is

271

that Jeremy," she said but the car passed on by. Rayanne waited up for him until midnight, then she went to bed and drifted off into a troubled sleep to a Whitney Houston's tune on the radio.

The hour was late when she heard Jeremy come in. The phone began to ring as she climbed out of bed. She went into the kitchen where Jeremy was getting something to eat. The phone rang again, only it had a different sound and it was not the phone that hung on the kitchen wall. Jeremy pulled a phone out from his jacket and answered it. "This is 'J', speak to me," he said, taking the sandwich from the refrigerator that Rayanne had left for him. Rayanne waited and listened while Jeremy carried on a conversation. "Hey, baby, what's up?" he paused, "I'm fine, just getting a little something to eat before turning in. That sounds good to me. Say, that was a phat outfit you had on today. It was slamming." He listened. "Look, babe, can we get back to that a little later," he said and listened again. "No, baby, it ain't like that. Now see, you didn't even have to go there. Everything was cool until you said that," he paused. "Oh so it's like that, huh." Another pause. "You want to talk about this tomorrow?" he paused again. "Well, if that's how you feel, that's fine with me." With that he clicked the caller off. "You still up, Aunt Rayanne? What's up?" he said, sitting at the table, and beginning to devour the sandwich.

"There was a robbery in the neighborhood today," Rayanne said and Jeremy said he'd heard about it. "It's not the way it use to be," she said more to herself than to Jeremy. She looked at him, "It's kinda late to be coming in on a school night," Rayanne said setting the tea pot on the stove before she sat across the table from Jeremy.

"I was just hanging out with my boys," he said.

"Jody doesn't go to school. You do."

"I didn't say I was hanging with Jody."

"Jeremy, you didn't have to. Jody seems to be the only person you hang out with anymore, never anyone your own age. He certainly doesn't seem to be doing anything with his life?" Rayanne got up to make herself a cup of tea.

"He keeps busy. Jody's got his own thing going. He's in business for himself practically."

"Jeremy, I don't care what Jody is doing. I'm concerned about you."

"Why, I'm fine, Aunt Rayanne," Jeremy went on excitedly, "Jody's got this truck and he makes these runs twice a week and he makes plenty."

Rayanne sat thoughtful, then she asked, "when did you get a mobile phone?"

Jeremy looked up at her, got up, took several cookies from the jar that was in the cabinet. "Yesterday," he answered, shoving a cookie into his mouth.

"Those phones are not cheap. Where are you getting that kind of money?" She asked.

"My mother." He took another bite out of his sandwich.

"I know what your mother sends you," she said and her mental calculations told her that with buying school supplies, clothes and shoes, there wasn't that much left.

"It sounds like you've been talking with my mother." Jeremy got up to get a glass of milk.

"She called this morning," Rayanne said.

"Why is she all up in my business anyway? She didn't want me with her so I wish she would leave me the hell alone," he snapped.

"Does your mother know you talk like this?"

"She would if she talked to me." He sat and placed the glass on the table.

Rayanne sipped her tea, set the cup back on the table and folded her hands. "Have you changed your mind about the prom?" she asked.

Jeremy stopped chewing, looked at Rayanne, resumed chewing and replied, "No, I haven't."

"Why don't you want to go to the prom?" Rayanne asked.

Jeremy got up and pulled a couple of towels from the roll that hung over the sink. "I just don't want to," he answered, annoyed and sat.

"Why, Jeremy? That kind of event is usually a landmark night in young people's lives. Why would you want to miss it?"

"Aunt Rayanne, that kind of thing is for kids." Jeremy turned his glass up and gulped down the milk. "Besides, you don't want to talk about no prom. So why don't you say what's on your mind," he said going back to the refrigerator to refill his glass with milk.

"I would, Jeremy, but it's difficult to talk to a moving target," she said. "I wish you would sit down. Your buzzing around is making me dizzy." She gave a little laugh.

"Cute Aunt Rayanne, but I wish you would cut me some slack. I just want to eat and go to bed. I've got school tomorrow."

"I don't think so," she said, looking at him.

"Excuse me," he said, lifting his eyes to meet hers.

273

"I said I don't think so. Jeremy, why didn't you tell me what happened at school today?"

"What?" he questioned.

"I believe you heard me."

Knowing his aunt had her facts right and that she wasn't one to play with when it came to education, Jeremy decided not to stretch the lie he'd been about to tell. "I didn't think I needed to," he said.

"Jeremy, I need to know when you've been kicked out of school for whatever reason." She paused and took a deep breath before going further. "Graduation is less than two months away. Have you given any serious thought as to what you're going to do when that happens?" She'd asked that same question of him since he came to live with them, but she'd never gotten an answer, at least not a satisfactory one. "You do plan to graduate?"

"Sure I'm going to graduate, then I suppose I'll get a job."

"What kind of job do you think you're going to get?" Jeremy didn't respond. "Do you not know how difficult it is to get a decent job even with a college degree? It is tough, very competitive, and I'll tell you something else, the job market is not at its peak right now. It's going to be hard carving out a place for yourself. It is going to be next to impossible to get a decent job without a decent education. That's why I always stress staying in school and getting something here." She poked her finger to the side of her head.

"I've got this friend who's going to hook me up," Jeremy said, taking the last bite of his sandwich and wiping his mouth with the back of his hand.

"Are we talking about Jody Brown again?" Rayanne asked.

"What's wrong with Jody? he asked and as if he were struck by a new thought, "I sure hope you don't think Jody had anything to do with those robberies because he didn't. He's an all right guy," Jeremy said and he may believe that, but from what Rayanne had learned, Jody didn't have a conscience. He was someone Rayanne wished Jeremy didn't spend so much time with. Jody was trouble, with a capital T.

"I hear Jody is a drug user, he's ruthless and the only thing he cares about is making a dollar for himself any way that he can. I think he's bad news. "

"Aunt Rayanne, you don't even know Jody, not really, so I don't know how you can say that."

"He's been around enough for me to have formed an opinion

and that is what I see. I'm just telling you how it looks through my eyes," she said. Jeremy did not respond and she continued, "let me give you my opinion about something else. I found something in the house, specifically in your room and needless to say, I don't like it and my opinion is that it's not going to continue."

"What," he looked at her with a challenging stare, but he felt his heart skip a beat.

"Marijuana," she said flatly.

"No kidding," Jeremy said and half laughed, "so Uncle Josh don't just hit the bottle, he's smoking grass, too?" Jeremy stuck another cookie into his mouth and emptied his milk glass, again.

"No. Josh drinks like a fish granted, but he doesn't do drugs and even if he did, he'd never bring drugs into this house," Rayanne declared and she was absolutely sure of that fact.

"At least you're giving him the benefit of the doubt," Jeremy said.

Rayanne didn't know what that was suppose to mean. They'd been nothing but supportive of Jeremy and they had trusted him, but he'd done things that cause her to change her trust. "Jeremy, I've tried to look at things from your point of view and be understanding. I know you're young and you've had some tough breaks, but you can't expect every one to feel sorry for you and you wallow in self pity when you've done something wrong and have been caught. You've got to start taking responsibility for yourself and your daughter. You are a father. That was a choice that you made, and you've got to start acting like a responsible parent. That child needs a father. She has no mother, so in essence, you represent both parents for her. Mama and I don't mind helping out but from now on, I want you to take an active role in your daughter's life, spend some time with her. Let her get to know you." Rayanne shook her head, got up and put her tea cup into the sink. "What I'm going to say has nothing to do with trust, but fact." She turned to look at Jeremy. "I know you're involved with drugs. You've gone so far as to bring drugs into this house." When Jeremy tried to protest, she closed her eyes and raised a hand to silence him. "I believe drugs are hidden in this house right now." She knew that it was the drugs that was behind the late nights, his strange comings and goings and some of the other peculiar things he'd been doing. She searched Jeremy's face. He was quiet. "You will not, and I repeat, will not do those things here and I mean it. I love you very much, Jeremy and I mean that too, but I've got to do what's best for all of us. I will not allow you to subject this family to any foolishness. It just doesn't make any sense."

"That's an interest analogy, but your little scenario is all wrong. I don't do drugs, I don't sell drugs, nor have I brought any drugs into the house," Jeremy spat out. Rayanne knew he was lying, but she had no intention of arguing the point.

"Okay, that's good to know, and in view of that, I'm putting you on notice that a crew of cleaning people will be in here tomorrow. They will clean this place from top to bottom, they will uncover a lost needle, and they've been instructed to destroy anything they find that does not come under the order of household goods. And, they will return randomly on a regular basis and do the same thing." Rayanne sat back in her chair and watched Jeremy's reaction. Although he tried to play it off, it was obvious that he was feeling trapped, and just as Rayanne thought, he'd been lying all along, because long after Rayanne checked on Swan and was back in her own bed, she could hear Jeremy rummaging through his room. She hoped he'd have the good sense to get some sleep because he would be getting up in the morning and going to school, and she'd be with him. There'd be no more of his hanging out all night and not go to school the next day. No more pretended illnesses, when, in fact, all that was wrong was that he was burning the candle at both ends. She'd see to it that he stayed in school until he graduated. She didn't believe in using friendship for gain but this is one time she was glad she'd gone to school with the person who was now principal at the High School where Jeremy attended, and she was glad they had remained friends and had kept in touch.

Although, Jeremy's contention was that Jody was an all right person, what happened two days later established Rayanne's prior conviction. Jody must've crossed someone, or as the songwriter wrote, he must've done somebody wrong, because according to the paper, during the early morning hours, a car passed through Jody's neighborhood and shot up his house and car. Rayanne noticed that Jeremy looked a little spooked while reading the article, and she hoped that he'd think about what happened to Jody, what could've happened and have an attitude adjustment. As time passed, they did become close again, and although she did follow through with having the house cleaned randomly, to her surprise and joy, nothing, out of the ordinary, turned up.

***

Rayanne was teaching two courses at the University. She was

grading papers and watching, Our *Voices with Bev Smith* one evening when the phone rang. She answered it and when she hung up, her hand shook as she dialed John's number. Jeremy had been arrested on drug charges. John was going to meet her at the county jail after Maxine picked up Ruth and Swan and took them to her house for the night. Ruth didn't have a particularly good day, and Rayanne didn't want to leave her and the baby home alone. Mrs. Marshall, the new nurse whom Rayanne hired, was wonderful, but she' gone to Atlanta to be with her daughter who was having a baby any day, and she hadn't returned yet.

As Maxine was taking Ruth and Swan with her, Josh came up the driveway, staggering. Maxine looked at Rayanne and shook her head. Josh caught one of Marcia Raylyn's ponytails and tried to play with it, but the child pulled away. She loved her uncle Josh, but like the others, she didn't like to be around him when he was drinking. Rayanne stood aside and allowed Josh to enter. She heard him bump into something, making his way to wherever he was going. "I think I ought to stay here with Josh," Ruth said, looking nervously towards the house.

"He'll be all right." Rayanne was hoping that was true, but she didn't have time to worry about it at that time. She knew that if he didn't burn the house down, he'd be all right.

"You sure he'll be all right by his self?" Ruth asked, still looking back toward the house. Rayanne assured her he'd be fine, telling her mother she'd see them later that night or in the morning, depending on how things went with Jeremy. Ruth appeared satisfied and went with Maxine willingly.

The county jail was filled with people of all ages, and although a higher percentage of them were black, the majority of them were young, black men. John and Rayanne, after a couple of hours of waiting, were met by their attorney. They couldn't do anything for Jeremy that night, but he'd be released in the morning. It was difficult leaving Jeremy locked in a cell overnight, but it couldn't be helped. Rayanne debated calling Mamie that night or waiting until morning. She decided she'd wait, knowing from past experience that Mamie wouldn't answer her phone at that hour.

Rayanne was exhausted as she approached her street, but instead of turning into her own driveway, she passed her house, heading in another direction. Scott was surprised when he opened his door and saw her standing there. He stood aside, allowing her to enter and they began to talk, which they did for some time. "Scott, I'm so sick and tired of all this. I'm fed up to here," she said marking herself at the throat. "I'm so tired of being everything to everyone." She got up, paced back and forth, then she walked over to the bookshelf and scanned the books before returning to her seat. "I know I'm feeling sorry for myself, wallowing in self pity, but tonight, I don't care. I'm just sick and tired." Scott didn't say anything. He wanted her to do whatever was necessary. "I've always been there, haven't I? I think I've been dependable," Rayanne looked questioningly at Scott.

Scott was thinking there should be a limit, a time to say yes and a time to say no, a time to act and a time to come to your senses and let others accept responsibility for themselves, but he said, "You still are."

Rayanne sat next to Scott on the couch and said, "I don't know why Jeremy would do such a thing," she took a deep breath. "This is pure nonsense."

"I know, baby. These kids are so unpredictable," Scott said.

Rayanne shook her head, then she mentioned the state Josh was in when he arrived home that evening. She ran her fingers through her hair and said, "but I can't even think about Josh right now." She got up and began pacing the floor again. "I hate the thought of Jeremy being in that place all night. I feel I need to be doing something." Rayanne was feeling helpless, like a caged animal.

"There's nothing we can do tonight," Scott said.

"Yeah, you're right," she said, and she turned and walked into the bathroom. She removed the hair clip from her hair, pushed her hair back with her fingers to make a tighter ponytail, then she returned to the living room. "Thanks for letting me cry all over your shoulders. You've done enough for me for one night." She laughed a little, "I think I can handle things from here. Now, I'm gonna get out of here and let you get some sleep. Thanks again." She turned to go to the front door.

"Why don't you stay here tonight?"

"You're a sweetheart, and I appreciate the offer, but I'd better get on home."

"Why? Your mother and Swan are at your sister's, we can't do anything to help Jeremy until in the morning, so why do you think you need to go home?" Scott asked, getting up and going over to her.

"Josh is there," she said.

"And Josh is a grown man. He can take care of himself, but tonight, you need someone to take care of you. Let me take care of you tonight." He lifted his hands and gripped her shoulders.

"Are you sure about this?"

"Absolutely. I want you to stay."

She allowed her head to drop against his chest and asked, "Why are you so good to me?"

"Oh, I don't know. Maybe 'cause I sorta like ya," he said.

"You do?"

"Yeah."

"Just sorta?"

"Maybe a little more than sorta."

"How much more?" she teased, weary with fatigue.

"A lot more." He put his arms around her. She looked up into his eyes and thanked him. He walked with her to the bedroom.

She climbed onto his bed. "Stay here with me a little while," she said and he obeyed. She awoke sometime during the night and turned over in bed to find Scott still there. She reached over and touched his face with her hands and he opened his eyes. Then she put her arms around his neck and she pressed her lips to his, forcing her tongue into his mouth. Scott held her and kissed her back. "Make love to me, Scott," she whispered. "Please make love to me now." She began unbuttoning his shirt, placing little kisses on his chest. Scott didn't encourage her in her love making attempt. He just continued to hold her. She began tearing at his clothes and he only held her tighter, restricting her movement and when she realized she couldn't break free, she began to cry. He was confused and he felt helpless. He could only lay there and listen to her sobs. It wasn't that he didn't want to make love to her. Scott wanted to take her in his arms and make wonderful, passionate love to her, but not like this. He wanted her when she could come to him with the offer of her love. Then and only then would he engage in the act of lovemaking with someone he loved and respected as much as he did her. For a long time, they lay together, side by side, and although their bodies touched, a deep silence lie between them.

The following morning, Scott turned over in bed to find Rayanne putting on her shoes. "When I reached for you and you were gone, I was beginning to think that maybe I had dreamed last night," he said.

"Maybe you did," Rayanne said, none too friendly.

"If I did, it was some dream. I thought I'd died and gone to heaven." She didn't respond, she continued to tie her shoe laces. "About last night," Scott began, sitting up in bed, "you don't know how much I wanted you." Rayanne looked sideways at him. "Are you doubting that? Rayanne, I wanted you more than I've ever wanted anything before."

"You could've fooled me," she said.

"If I thought that was what you wanted, I mean really wanted...," he began but was interrupted.

"Look Scott, let's not analyze last night to death. I was tired, slightly emotional and at wits end. I needed someone and you were there," she paused, "or you weren't there, whatever the case, but I can assure you, it won't happen again." The words were like a slap in his face. Was she upset that he didn't take advantage of her vulnerabilities. Wouldn't she have been even more upset if he had. There was no way he would've taken advantage of her, no matter how much he'd wanted her or needed her.

"What are you saying?" he said. "Are you telling me you were just going to use me?"

"Isn't that what you guys do to us all the time?"

"No, not all of us and not all the time," he said.

"Well, we're not going to debate that point," she said finishing her laces.

Scott was upset and he didn't try to conceal it. "If that's how you feel about what didn't happened last night, then I agree. I'm glad things didn't go any further and it shouldn't happen again." Scott reclined in bed with his arms folded under his head.

Rayanne got up from the bed, lifted her arms into the air, saying, "I've gotta get going." She turned at the door and said, "thanks for last night. I don't know what I would've done without you."

"No problem," he said and without another word. she was gone. Scott sat up on the side of the bed and lit a cigarette.

Rayanne entered the house through the kitchen door. Josh was sitting at the table, smoking. "Morning Josh," she said, going to the phone and dialing a number.

"Good morning to you too," Josh said. "And where did you spend your night? It certainly wasn't here."

"You noticed," she replied, hanging up the phone after receiving a busy signal. She looked at him. Josh was an alcoholic and not only was he killing himself, he was worrying the rest of them to death. He'd been on the day to day program more times than she could count and it hadn't helped, not for any length of time, that is. Although he insisted he wasn't an alcoholic, that he could quit anytime he wanted, Rayanne knew he was deluding himself because alcoholism is an illness and it requires treatment. She redialed the number, this time, it rang. "Maxine, how is it going?" Rayanne said into the receiver.

"Everything's fine here. John told us what happened with Jeremy. I tried to call you last night, but I didn't get an answer. I figured you took a pill and crashed," Maxine said. Swan and Ruth were fine, Ruth had a restful night considering and Maxine was taking the day off so there was no need in Rayanne worrying about the baby or Ruth. Rayanne was meeting John downtown at 8:20, she told Maxine. "John just walked through the door," Maxine said, "he said he can pick you up."

"No, tell him I'll meet him there," Rayanne said. When she hung up, she made breakfast.

"I sure miss Mama this morning," Josh said, wanting to keep the conversation light.

Rayanne didn't respond, instead she asked, "did Mamie call."

"Not this morning. The phone did ring last night, but I didn't answer it," he said. When she arrived at Scott's, she decided not to call Mamie that night, but it'd nagged her so that she placed the call and left a message on her answering machine. Mamie had her own agenda and it was designed only to suit her needs.

"Let's just eat before the food gets cold," Rayanne said, extending her hands across the table to Josh, "Dear Lord, we thank Thee for this food that we're about to receive. Bless us Father and strengthen us here on earth each day in Your name and the name of Your Son, Jesus. Amen."

"Amen," Josh said.

Rayanne took one bite of eggs when the phone rang. "Hello," she answered. It was Mamie.

"What happened to Jeremy?" she demanded.

"He was arrested. Didn't you get my message?" Rayanne said.

"Yeah, that's why I'm calling. What's going on down there. You allowed my son to run the streets and now he's gotten himself arrested," Mamie said. Rayanne tried to interrupt, but Mamie continued, "Why didn't you call back this morning?"

"What good would that have done. Maybe if you started answering your phone at night, you'd know what's going on in other parts of the world along with everyone else," Rayanne charged.

"You know I don't answer my phone late at night," Mamie screamed.

"Bet this is one time when you wished you had." Rayanne knew that comment was mean, but she didn't care. She just couldn't resist. She was tired of Mamie always getting her way, it was time that she squirmed, if only for a short while. There was a silence, which was rare for Mamie. "Mamie, I know you're upset. We all are, but John and I are going back downtown this morning to see what we can do."

"My son is still in jail?" Mamie screeched. "Jeremy spent the night in jail?"

"There was nothing we could do, Mamie. John and I are going to do what we can this morning," Rayanne said, not wanting to get into an argument with Mamie this morning.

"Do you have an attorney?" Mamie asked.

"Of course."

"And he wasn't able to do any better than that"? Mamie asked and since Rayanne saw that as a rhetorical question, she didn't reply. "Rayanne, do I need to be there?"

"Mamie, it is 7:20 now. John and I plan to be downtown within the hour. There's nothing you can do between now and then. I'll call you as soon as I know more."

"If you're sure you can handle this mess without me."

"We'll do our best, okay?"

"What's wrong with you," Mamie snapped.

"Look Mamie, I've got a lot to do, so I'll call you later," Rayanne said.

"What's happening to my son?" Mamie asked.

"Mamie, we've been through this already," Rayanne said, tired, aggravated and she didn't want to talk with Mamie anymore.

"And we're going to go over it again. I want to know what my son is getting himself into down there?"

"You're asking me?" Rayanne said, intending sarcasm.

"Yes, I'm asking you."

"Well don't, because I don't have the answer," Rayanne said. "I've tried talking with you about Jeremy's conduct and you didn't do one thing about it, so don't start pretending you care now."

"I do care, but you're suppose to be looking after him."

"By your choosing."

"Only because I didn't want him living in the city getting in and out of trouble. Doesn't look like he's doing any better down there," Mamie complained. Rayanne didn't respond. "You can say what you want about me, but Jeremy was never arrested while he was with me," Mamie drugged in. Rayanne felt guilty when she thought, Jeremy should be with Mamie, then she wouldn't have the aggravation. "If you were as responsible as you claim you are," Mamie began, but she was interrupted by a pissed off Rayanne.

"Mamie, I don't want to hear this shit this morning. Do you understand me. The best thing for you to do is let me go on and do what I can or you put that fat ass of yours on a plane, get down here and take care of this mess, as you put it, yourself," Rayanne came back.

"Don't think I won't come if I need to," Mamie said and Rayanne thought, and don't think I would try to stop you, either. "I can get a flight out of here and be there this afternoon," Mamie said.

"That's up to you, but damn it, you tell me exactly what you want me to do," Rayanne said and met silence from Mamie. "Well, what do you want?" Rayanne raised her voice. "Should someone meet you at the airport?"

"Don't bother," Mamie said. "Just let me know something, if you don't mind." With that Mamie hung up.

"Just as I thought," Rayanne said looking into the mouth piece of the phone, before she hung up. She sat back at the table to eat her breakfast. "Now my breakfast is cold," she said, dumping a fork of eggs back onto her plate.

"Is she coming?" Josh asked.

"Who, Mamie," Rayanne said, got up and scraped the cold food into the garbage, "What do you think."

Rayanne got dressed and drove to the Detention Center where John was waiting. After posting bond, Jeremy was released, and John went on to work. Rayanne and Jeremy were alone in her car, heading home when she asked, "you want to tell me what happened?"

"Aunt Rayanne, I think you know the deal."

"I'm asking you."

"Where's my daughter? Is she all right?"

"She's fine. She's with Maxine," Rayanne said. "What about you?"

"Me? I'm okay."

"Jeremy, what's going on with you? What are you doing to yourself. You are behaving as if you don't even like yourself. What is it?"

"I don't know," he said shaking his head.

"Well, how do you feel about yourself. Don't you want the absolute best in life?" He didn't respond. "Jeremy, I am literally in love with myself and I try to do what is best for me. I have to have a positive attitude to love myself. That empowers me to do all the things I want to do. You see, I learned early in life that I am aller-

283

gic to poverty. I mean I get a rash just thinking about poverty," she laughed a little looking over at Jeremy. "So, with that in mind, I have to always put my best foot forward." They were quiet a moment. "Do you think you need this kind of mess in your life?" Jeremy didn't answer. "You're an eighteen, soon to be nineteen year old, black male, and now with a record..." Rayanne started.

"Go on," Jeremy interrupted, "say it. Tell me you told me so."

"I'm not going to tell you that. Do you think I'm happy about this, that this is some sort of game we're playing, to see who wins, who losses or who would be able to say I told you so?" Rayanne asked. Jeremy was quiet. He looked thoughtful. "Jeremy, I don't want that. Can't you see, no one wins in a situation like this. We're family and when there's a breakdown in the family, everyone loses. You need to be thinking about the kind of future you want for yourself and your daughter. You don't want to start off your life by getting into this kind of trouble. You're bright and capable of doing so much more. The future is ahead of you and it's up to you to make the best of it." Rayanne looked at Jeremy, and he was staring at her. "Say it. Say what's on your mind. Talk to me. Tell me what you're thinking."

Jeremy hesitated but Rayanne waited. "I was just thinking that you're so different from my mother. You are sisters, but you're nothing alike. She's a good lady and I love her, but I've heard so much about how I'm nothing, and I'm never going to amount to anything, that I was beginning to believe it."

"Jeremy, you can't allow anyone else's opinion to guide your life, especially when it is negative. We all make mistakes, but mistakes force us to grow up, and if we're smart, we learn from our mistakes."

"Aunt Rayanne, I've never completed anything or made good on anything in my life," Jeremy said, "so don't expect any big miracles from me."

"Your life is really just beginning and you're about to graduate. I don't know about you, but I think that's a major accomplishment. Jeremy, honey, you have to remember not to set your reality by your failure, but rather, you build on it. This world is filled with opportunities, but we've got to prepare. You'll be taking a big step soon, so build on that. Anyone can turn his life around if he tries. I heard someone speak once who said opportunities will come our way that we wouldn't believe, but when they come, we have to be prepared to grab it, even if we don't know what to do with it at the time. Grab it then because it may never come again. Jeremy, a fascinating thing about life is that we don't have to live where we are right now. There's always tomorrow. This isn't going to be easy, and I realize that we're living in difficult times, but we have to wonder what we want for our future and the future of our children. Jeremy, you can do anything you want to do. You know why?" she asked. He looked questioningly at her. "Because you're special. You have God given talents and He intends for you to use them. You're here for a purpose, and you'll soon realize it," Rayanne said, and as they drove past Mrs. Abigail's house, there was a shiny black BMW parked in the driveway and the 'For Sale' sign was gone.

"Looks like we got some new neighbors," Jeremy said, looking over his shoulder at the car. "Grandma and Aunt Bessie miss Ms. Abigail a lot. I heard them talking about her yesterday."

"I know, I miss her also. I have known Ms. Abigail all my life and she's just always been a part of this community and our lives. I am so sorry about what happened to her." When they arrived home, they called Mamie and before the conversation was over, Mamie gave both, Rayanne and Jeremy, a piece of her mind. Afterwards, Rayanne placed some fresh flowers on her father's grave and when she returned home, she and Josh had a heart to heart.

CHAPTER 36

 The sun had long since closed its doors and the moon was high and serene. There appeared to be a million and one things going on in Rayanne's life at that time, and her head was equally filled with thoughts, especially of Jeremy. It seems he was always into something and so much was happening in such a short period of time. As she stood on the porch, the wind gently touched her face and lifted her long brown hair, which she still allowed to grow and it hung inches below her shoulders. The gusts became stronger, causing the cotton robe to swirl about her ankles. She pulled her robe close to her body and held it against her throat. He still has things he has to work through, Rayanne thought and remembered her mother saying, "you raise your child the best way you can, but they grow up to be who they are." Rayanne had always tried to be there for Jeremy. He'd made some mistakes, and hopefully, he'd learn from them, and would grow as a result of them. She wanted to say something to him that would affect his life, to put him back on the right track.

 Rayanne went over, in her mind, the conversations she and Jeremy had on their way from the Detention Center the last time he had been arrested. He'd said he was nothing, and would never amount to anything. He'd heard it so much in his young life that perhaps he'd begun to believe it himself. Rayanne and her mother tried to impress upon Jeremy that it didn't matter what anyone told him, it didn't matter what anyone believed about him, that it was how he felt about himself that was important. She'd told him many times that he was special, that he would face adversities in his life, but he had to believe in himself and move past those obstacles. Jeremy was a teenage boy and with that, there could be problems. Rayanne had already decided she would try to be supportive of him and his endeavors, without being judgmental. Her thoughts moved further to the little soft bundle of joy, who lay in the crib, in one of the spare bedrooms. Swan was special to Rayanne. She was such a gift, brought so much joy to Rayanne's life. Swan gave Rayanne's life a new direction, a new path.

***

She heard the side door open and close. Josh had arrived and in what was considered his usual state now, drunk. As Rayanne began to prepare to go to bed, suddenly, she missed Scott. It had been days since she'd heard from him. He was one of her closest friends, and when four days had passed and still no word from him, Rayanne put aside her pride and called him. She got his answering machine, but she didn't leave a message.

CHAPTER 37

The Prozac that Ruth was taking appeared to have altered her personality, her demeanor, almost everything about her. Rayanne just wished she had known that her mother was being put on that drug. She would not've recommended it. She would have looked for other alternatives. She read everything she could find on the drug when she'd discovered her mother taking it. Prozac was considered the wonder drug for some who were faced with bouts of depression, but on the other hand, like a lot of other medications, there were side effects.

Mrs. Marshall, a retired nurse in her late fifties, was hired not only to look after Swan, but her mother as well, despite Ruth's objections. The idea of another woman doing things in her house didn't set well with Ruth. She resented it, she resented Mrs. Marshall and that resentment covered her like a looming cloud. Rayanne had explained why she brought help into the house, and she thought her mother understood, apparently she didn't.

Rayanne made her usual call home from work and Maxine answered the phone, sounding alarmed. "I stopped by to see mama," Maxine began, "she isn't having a very good day. I think it's that medication. I don't know whether she forgets she's taken it and takes it again or whether she's trying to harm herself."

"You don't really think mama's trying to hurt herself?" Rayanne asked incredulously.

"I don't know, but you know how she's been since daddy died and the situation with Josh can't be good for her," Maxine said, and Rayanne silently agreed. "Well, let me tell you what happened today. Josh came in so drunk he could hardly stand up. He pissed all over the kitchen floor right in front of mama and the kids."

"What," Rayanne said not believing.

"That's right and that drunken ass couldn't even clean up after himself," Maxine said.

Rayanne rubbed her forehead with her finger tips. "Do you think mama needs to see a doctor?"

"I think she's probably all right, but a little down, you know," Maxine said. After checking the medication, Maxine called Rayanne, and was satisfied that Ruth hadn't taken more then the normal dosage, still the affect it had on Ruth wasn't good. She had terrible mood swings.

Rayanne arrived home and when she spoke with her mother, she appeared to be her usual self. Josh was sitting in a chair, clean, but asleep. She put her things down and picked up the baby, who reached her hands up to meet Rayanne's. Mrs. Marshall came out of the kitchen. "How is that handsome grand son of yours, Mrs. Marshall?" Rayanne asked, holding Swan in her lap.

"Oh, he's just fine. They tell me he's growing like a weed," Mrs. Marshall replied, her eyes beaming with pride. "They're coming in a couple of weeks."

"That'll be nice. I know how much you miss them," Rayanne said playing with Swan's fingers.

"I sure do, but we talk often so that helps."

Rayanne gave the baby a bath, fed her and after playing with her a while, she put Swan to bed. She woke Josh, set the table and they ate the meal that Mrs. Marshall prepared. It'd been days since Jeremy had eaten any meals, other than breakfast, with the family and it was nice having he and Josh join them for a change. The meal was enjoyable, the conversation that evening was more stimulating and meaningful than it'd been in months and as it turned out, Rayanne didn't say anything to Josh about his drinking or the mess he made earlier that day. She was tired and was happy to be able to go to bed without having an argument. Good luck has a way of not lasting and within a week, Josh had a repeat performance. It was inexcusable and this time, she wouldn't let it slide. When Ruth and the baby were in bed, Rayanne returned to the den and switched the TV set off. She looked at Josh. "What's on your mind, Rayanne?" he asked.

"I heard about what happened here today."

"What happened."

"Let's not start this conversation tonight by lying, Josh. I heard about you pissing all over the house last week and it happened again today. Now, enough is enough."

"You mean that little accident I had. I'm sorry but it was an accident," Josh said, more nonchalant than Rayanne had ever seen him and that was enough to motivate her to insist that he get some real help, and once again Josh signed up at the center. He continued the program daily, he was released, and just when it seemed he was getting his life back together for the one hundredth time, Rayanne came home one day to find him kneeling over the commode, puking his guts. Ruth was bending over him with a wet towel.

"What's wrong with Josh now?" Rayanne asked stupidly, because taking in the entire picture, gave her the answer. She took the towel from her mother's hand, "go back to the den, mama. You don't need to see Josh like this. Go on, I'll take care of him."

"All right, Rayanne, but if you need me, you call me now, you hear," Ruth said, walking slowly out of the room.

It was painful seeing Josh that way, but it broke her heart seeing the impact her father's death and Josh's alcoholism had on her mother. Raymond and the children were Ruth's entire life, and when Raymond died, it left a void in her life that made it difficult for her to go on. As a result, she'd become a different person, a person her family and friends hardly knew. Everyone had noticed the profound change that had taken over Ruth's existence.

Rayanne opened the bathroom window to allow the stench to dissipate. She sat on the side of the bathtub, holding the towel out to Josh. "What happened this time, Josh?"

"I fell off the wagon again, Sis," he answered.

"Did you even try this time?" Rayanne asked. She and Josh talked extensively about his drinking and he had promised this time that he would try harder.

"I did. Believe me, Rayanne, I did but it got the best of me," he said.

"Just look at yourself. Look at what you've become. You're so drunk, you can't even hold your head up. Don't you see what this is doing to mama? Don't you care?"

"Are you blaming mama's condition on me?" Josh asked, his words slurred.

"Mama's suffering, Josh. She's not the person she used to be.

Her will is gone. Her strength is gone. She is suffering and when someone you love is suffering, you don't ask who's to blame. You just try to help. Mama doesn't need this aggravation. She needs our support," Rayanne paused, then said, "before it's too late."

"Don't talk like that," Josh said, choking back his tears, "I lost my daddy, I'm not gonna lose my mama, too." He sounded pathetic, every bit like a child, but she didn't have the patience to pacify him.

"Listen to yourself. Do you know how doggone stupid and immature you sound. You'd better get a grip on yourself. Wake up, Josh, smell the coffee and cut this bullshit out." Josh was intelligent. Why couldn't he understand that alcohol twists everything around, plays tricks on the mind and at times, it magnifies some situations, while others appear softer around the edges. No matter, the problem would still be there. Rayanne and Josh went through a verbal exchange, she'd talked to him as she never had and had used words that she didn't remember were ever a part of her vocabulary. "Now, either you get it together or get the hell out of here and stay away. You can have it either way you want, but you won't have both," Rayanne said, walked out of the bathroom, slamming the door behind her. She was surprised to see her mother standing in the hallway, staring at her. She was embarrassed, knowing her mother had heard every word she'd said to Josh. She took her mother's hand and led her back to the den.

"Is Josh all right?" Ruth asked, her eyes nervously darting towards the bathroom door.

"He's fine, Mama, just drunk."

"He can't help it, you know, and he ain't hurting no body."

"Yes he is, mama. He's hurting us all, himself most of all. Mama," Rayanne said after a moment, "there's so much that is wrong here. Things are complicated when they shouldn't be, but there's a solution to this whole mess. Maybe not an easy one, but there is a solution. I'm not going to give up until I've done everything that I can, but I need help, I need cooperation. I need that from you, Mama, and I need it from Josh." Ruth didn't respond, Rayanne continued, "I was thinking that Josh should be put into that intensive program in Florence."

"You want to send my boy away. You can't send Josh away. We'll get help for him some other way, but we'll do it right here," Ruth said.

"Mama, how many times have we tried it that way. A half dozen or more and what good has it done. None," Rayanne answered her own questions.

"Then we have to do something else." If Ruth had a solution, Rayanne wanted to hear it because she was fresh out of ideas. "Just don't you send my boy away," Ruth said, tears in her eyes, and there was determination in her voice when she added, "I'll never forgive you if you send Josh away."

Rayanne kneeled on the floor in front of her mother. "Mama, please don't fight me on this," she said, seeing something in her mother's eyes that wasn't present before and hoping that her mother didn't resent what she was trying to do, or that her action would affect the way they had always bond as mother and daughter. "Just think about what is happening. There are five of us living here and that includes a baby. Josh is doing things that is a threat to all of us. I'm having a lot of mixed emotions right now where Josh is concerned. I'm angry at him, I'm concerned for Josh, but I'm angry at myself for letting this situation get so far out of hand. I'm frightened for the rest of us. Josh is a threat to himself and the rest of us and we've got to do something about it. A little while back, he came in drunk and left a cigarette burning in the ash try. Well, it fell onto the floor and burned the carpet. There are times at night when he gets up to get something to eat, he doesn't wash his hands, he leaves water running in the sink, letting it run over onto the floors. I just happen to wake up one night and heard the water running. Josh was back in bed. He's urinated in bed so often, that we've had to replace the mattress twice, not to mention the carpet in that room." Ruth knew the situation was bad, but she had no idea it had gotten that bad. "There were times when he's made it as far as the back yard. I can't tell you how many times Jeremy and I have had to pick him up, bring him inside and put him to bed. There are lots of things, mama, but that doesn't matter now. I just want it to stop. So, you tell me, what are we going to do. Josh isn't in no position to help himself. I don't think he wants to help himself."

"I know this is hard on you. You're too young to have all these burdens on your shoulders," Ruth said taking Rayanne's hands into her own, "we're gonna do something about it. And, please take that buckle out of your brow." Rayanne hadn't heard her mother use that expression in a very long time. "You're gonna be old before your time," Ruth finished, and Rayanne felt everything was going to be all right. Ruth had always said that family had to stick together, they had to do what was necessary for each other. Rayanne loved her mother's expression, 'you can't pick out relatives just like you can't clean germs."

Rayanne and Maxine signed Josh up and everything was fine until it was time to drive him to Florence. Ruth had completely turned around, she reacted violently and swore again that she'd never forgive Rayanne if she took Josh away. Rayanne knew her mother would change her mind if Josh entered the program and she saw the difference the intensive treatment made in his life, but as it turned out, Josh didn't keep the appointment for admission to the Florence center. He signed up for the daily program, once again.

That night Maggie called. She was always a breath of fresh air. Ivory called. She'd heard from Dorian. She was happy, everything was fine and she loved France. She was pregnant, she said and she'd send pictures as soon as she was showing. "Bet that'll put some meat on those bones," Rayanne said, laughing. She was really happy for Dorian. She'd had a deprived childhood and deserved some happiness in a secured surrounding. Rayanne realized at that moment that she still cared for Dorian and although she was doubtful that they'd ever get back to where they were, she knew she'd always be there for her.

CHAPTER 38

$\mathbf{M}$axine entered the church. It was filled to its capacity. The crystal chandelier sparkled, the pews were red plush cushions and the woodwork shine as though it had been polished with oil. Maxine and Joe had married right out of college, in that church. They had two sons, Bruce and Bobby and although they spent a few happy years together, two years after Bobby was born, Joe split, they later divorced, and Maxine hadn't laid eyes on him since that time, until he returned, sporting a new wife. Maxine was left to raise the children alone, with no child support from Joe and with the rising costs of dental care, medical bills, food and clothing, there was very little money left for anything else.

Maxine found a seat in the fifth row from the front. She sat down, and when she lifted her head, her eyes met Joe's and they held only a brief moment before he closed his eyes and lay his head back against the seat, where he sat in the pulpit, next to the minister. The years had been kind to Joe. His rich dark skin was clean shaven, except for a mustache, that added to his good looks, and although Joe was older, he was even more handsome than Maxine remembered. He stood almost six feet, he was 185 pounds, and he wore his short cut hair combed back.

Maxine had told Joe's mother that she was very happily married and her family was fine, but the boys questioned their father's absence and asked about him often. Mrs. Duncan assured Maxine that Joe would get the message, but she refrained from giving Maxine his address or telephone number. She'd also assured Maxine that Joe was happy in his new marriage, as well, and he was sorry for any grief he might've caused her and the boys.

All through service, Joe avoided any further eye contact with Maxine. He delivered a powerful inspirational message, and Maxine thought it was good that Joe had turned to the Lord and that perhaps he'd grown up after all. Irene, Joe's new bride, a pretty girl, tall and slender, and well groomed, was at least ten years younger than he, and as a part of the service, she played the piano and sang as sweetly as a song bird.

Marcus and the children didn't go to church that Sunday because that was the way Maxine wanted it. She wasn't sure how Joe would react to the boys, and she didn't want them to pick up any negative vibes from their father. When Maxine approached Joe, he acted as though he was meeting her for the first time. He didn't ask how she was doing, and he didn't mention the boys. "How are you, Joe?" Maxine said, extending her hand.

"I'm fine, thanks," he responded, shook her hand briefly and released it.

"That's good. You look well."

"Thank you," he said flatly.

"The boys have been asking for you," she informed.

"I'll call later today," he said, without emotion.

"That's fine," Maxine said and smiled. "I'll let them know." Joe quickly moved away from her and on to other members. Maxine stood for a moment, observing Joe and she wondered how could a man who was once so sweet and caring turn so cold. She turned to walk away, and she looked up in time to catch a glimpse of Irene leaving the sanctuary. She followed her. "I enjoyed listening to you play and sing in there. I'm Maxine Richards," she said, catching up with Irene and extending a hand to her.

"Thank you, and I'm Irene Duncan, Mrs. Joseph Duncan," she replied, extending a hand gracefully to accept Maxine's. "I'm very glad to meet you. This is a wonderful church, lots of warm, kind people." Irene looked around, then returned her eyes to Maxine.

"Yes, we're a pretty good group," Maxine said, smiling and as she looked around, she saw Joe coming out of the sanctuary. "So how long have you and Joe...I mean Rev. Duncan been married?"

"It's four months now, and this has been the happiest time of my life," Irene said and paused. "I take it you know my husband, Joseph?"

Maxine was surprised that Irene didn't know that she and Joe were married and since he didn't tell her, she didn't think it her place either. "Yes, he's a home boy. How long will you two be in town?"

"We'll be here a couple of days," Irene answered as they walked over and stood under a large oak tree to shield themselves from the midday sun. It was late May and the temperatures already ranged from high eighties to low nineties. Maxine learned that Joe and Irene met when he visited her church as a guest speaker eight months ago, her parents invited him to dinner, and she and Joe began seeing each other. "We really got to know each other, and the rest, as they say, is history. Joseph and I do everything together. It's been that way since we met. He's the kindest, most understanding and honest person that I've ever known."

The person Irene described didn't sound at all like the old Joe Maxine knew, but she said, "Certainly sounds like a whirlwind romance to me."

"Oh believe me, it was. Joseph is the best thing that's ever happened to me. He makes me so happy." Irene stopped herself suddenly and said, "I suppose you think that I'm a silly babbler, but I get so excited talking about Joseph. What about you?" Irene asked, "Are you married?"

"Yes, I've been married twice, as a matter of fact. It didn't work out the first time, but I'm very happy with my second husband. He's a wonderful man, and we have three beautiful children. Maybe I should clarify that. I had two children, both boys, by my first husband, and Marcus and I have a little girl. They are great kids."

"That's wonderful," Irene smiled. "I hope Joseph and I won't have to walk that road again. Hopefully, once will be enough for both of us."

Although it appeared Irene didn't know Maxine and Joe were married at one time, she had to asked, "neither of you have been married?"

"Oh no. Joseph said he's never been in love until he met me, and he's the only man that I've ever loved. I can only say that I'm very glad he waited for me." Irene was acting like a school girl.

"I see. Do you plan to have a family?" Maxine asked and immediately said, "I suppose that's a silly question. Of course you and Rev. Duncan want children."

"Yes, Joseph loves children. He wants to start a family right away. He tells me that that's the one thing that will make our family complete." Members from the congregation approached them and shook their hands, and when Maxine and Irene were alone again, Irene continued, "The past eight months have been the happiest in my life. Joseph and I share everything. He's a good, honest man."

Maxine wondered how many times was Irene going to say how good and honest Joe was. "That's wonderful. Nothing like having a good honest man around the house." Maxine wasn't sure how much longer she could listen to Irene babble about a man whom she obviously knew very little about.

"Let me tell you what Joe said to me when we were coming here yesterday," Irene said. Maxine smiled pleasantly with Irene, but she felt nervous, perhaps a little frightened about what might come next. "He said he feels unfortunate never having had children."

"Really," Maxine said, feeling pain somewhere deep inside.

"Yes. When we talk about children, he always looks so sad, but that changes when I remind him that we're still newly weds and that there's plenty of time for children."

"He's really anxious about having children?" Maxine said, struggling to keep her voice calm. It was one thing for Joe to deny her, she thought, but to deny the children was just too much.

"Tell me about your children," Irene said.

Maxine took a deep breath to steady her voice. "My son, Bruce, is sixteen, he'll graduate high school this year, very smart boy. He skipped a grade one year, you know," Maxine said, with pride that was obvious.

"He did," Irene exclaimed, "that's wonderful." And, Maxine could tell she meant it. She believed Irene Duncan was a good person, and Joe was lucky to have her, but Irene, maybe she wasn't so lucky.

"Bobby's fourteen and smart as well. I think the boys compete for the best grades. One semester Bobby gets better grades, then the next, it's Bruce." Maxine shook her head, smiling.

"I think it's wonderful," Irene said in the sweetest voice.

"Marcia Raylyn, my daughter, she's the apple of her daddy's eye." The women laughed, with Irene agreeing that most little girls took that position with their fathers. "My youngest son, Bobby, he's a rascal. He's something else."

"That's how boys are at that age, I suppose."

What would she know about boys any age, Maxine thought, because Irene appeared very naive. "Bobby is a lot like his father, devious and cunning, a regular little con artist, but a real charmer. " Maxine wondered what Irene will think of Joe when she learns that he wasn't a part of his boys' lives and that they had no contact with him. She was sure to wonder what kind of man would desert his own flesh and blood. "They don't know much about their father. They haven't seen him in twelve years," Maxine relayed thoughtfully.

"I'm sorry to hear that," Irene said, easily understanding why Maxine divorce that jerk, whomever he was, "but keep the faith. I'm sure it will all work out."

Maxine looked at her watch, "I'd better be on my way. My family will be wondering what happened to me." She extended a hand to Irene, again. "It was very nice talking with you. Hope you and the Reverend will come and visit with us again soon."

"Thank you, and you take care."

"You too." Maxine released Irene's hand and walked away. She'd never remembered being so angry. She was too upset to stay and continue her conversation with Irene, and too upset to go home, so she drove directly to her parent's home and recapped the events to Rayanne. Maxine had gone through a gamut of emotions that last half hour, but after talking the situation over with Rayanne, she felt better, but she intended to bring all of that to Joe's attention, when they saw him later. On her way home to her husband and children, there was no longer a trace of the anger that had overwhelmed her earlier. As she drove the distance, she was aware that a part of her anger was replaced by pity. Pity for the young woman who'd fallen in love with a man, who was less of a man than any other man that Maxine had known. That poor young girl was innocent and trusting and she was in for a rude awakening. She fluttered those eyelashes like a silly school girl, walking around with her head stuck in a cloud. Well, she had a lot to learn. She had yet to grow up and become a woman.

That afternoon, Bruce and Bobby dressed up real nice, and they sat and waited for their father. They weren't sure whether he'd call or come, but in any case, they'd be ready. Maxine watched the boys, as they took turns, looking out of the window or staring at the telephone, which as it turned out, didn't ring, and Joe didn't bother to come.

Maxine didn't go to work on Monday. She got up, made breakfast, and drove over to Joe mother's house. His new blue Buick, wasn't there. They must be at a local hotel, Maxine thought. She didn't get out of her car, she and Joe's mother had never gotten along. Maxine turned her car around, drove back to her house, and she dialed a number. "Mrs. Duncan?" Maxine said when she answered the phone.

"Yes," Mrs. Duncan said.

"This is Maxine. How are you?" she asked, and said before Mrs. Duncan could respond. "Where's Joe. Are they staying at a hotel?"

"Joe and Irene left for Florida this morning."

"They left? But the boys wanted to see him." Maxine was shocked that Joe had left without a word to his sons. She was disappointed for them.

"I know that, Maxine," Mrs. Duncan said, "I gave Joe your message. He told me that he didn't want to interfere in you and the kid's lives, didn't want to confuse them, you know." Confuse them, Maxine thought, not believing her ears. Bruce is half grown, and Bobby is a big boy. They know that Marcus isn't their real daddy, they just wanted to know who their real daddy was.

"The boys were disappointed. All they wanted was to see their father and talk to him," Maxine said.

"Maxine, Joe is married again, to a lovely girl, and I think he wants to move on with his life. There's no need in you and Joe going through all this now," Mrs. Duncan said. There was no question that she and Joe could forget each other, but the children. How could a man, who calls himself a preacher, just forgets about his children. "Maxine, if this is about support for the boys, I'll be glad to help out in any way that I can."

"It's not just about money, Mrs. Duncan," Maxine said and wondered why this woman didn't understand why she was so upset.

"Then what is it?" Mrs. Duncan asked.

Maxine thought about that question but decided not to say what was really on her mind, because she felt if she had to explain it, then maybe it wasn't worth it. "All I can say is if your son calls himself a man of God, a preacher, then he's kidding himself. He must be a preacher from hell."

"Let's not be that way, Maxine," Mrs. Duncan said. "Just let me know what I can do for the boys and I will. Just leave Joe alone. Let him be happy."

She knew that Mrs. Duncan was largely a part of why Joe was the way he was. "I'm sorry you feel that way, Mrs. Duncan, and don't you worry about the boys. They'll be just fine. These are Joe's kids, and if this is how he wants to treat them, then so be it.

The choice is his." With that Maxine hung up, and she began to cry. She didn't cry for herself, or the way Joe had deserted her. She didn't even cry because she was so pissed off. Her tears were for her sons. The boys, who didn't really know their father and after all this time, still loved him, wanted to get to know him on some level and had looked forward to spending a little time with him. And, that's exactly what he was, she thought, their father, he wasn't a daddy, because a daddy would not have treated his children the way Joe had. What would she tell them now. She couldn't say that their father had cut his trip short because he wanted nothing to do with his children.

CHAPTER 39

Jeremy and Bruce graduated high school that Spring. That was the first time Mamie returned since the death of their father, when she'd left Jeremy and the baby. She'd called and sent a little money and an occasional dress for Swan, but no visits. The night before graduation, everyone was at the family house preparing dinner in honor of the graduates. It was a festive time and it would've ended that way had Mamie not gotten into an altercation with Jeremy. The incident could've resulted in a funeral rather than the happy occasion it was meant to be.

Mamie had gone out the night before and didn't get home until midday the following day, most of which she slept away. She'd joined the others in the kitchen that night, she didn't volunteer to help, but Maxine filled a bowl with white potatoes and pushed the bowl and a knife into her hands and said, "here, make yourself useful." This was one of those times when the girls caught up on what was going on with each other. They talked about their children, how they were doing in school, their own careers, the books they'd read and vacations, while listening to the radio playing in the background.

"All these hands working in here, I wasn't sure I was needed," Mamie said, sitting at the table where Rayanne and Ruth were snapping beans.

"We need all the hands we can get," Maxine said.

"Well, this ain't too bad," Mamie said, rolling her eyes around, "I'm just glad you didn't save the collards for me to clean." She laughed. Eunice and Christen, her sisters in law were the ones fortunate enough to be assigned that task, and each of them shot Mamie a pretended hateful look.

"Mamie will do the collards by herself next year," Christen said and they all laughed.

"Why wait until next year. Let's make her do them Christmas, or better yet, Thanksgiving," Eunice, who was Samuel's wife, said and they laughed some more.

"You girls better not hold your breath for that," Ruth said, a twinkle in her eyes. Between Maxine and Rayanne, they'd weaned Ruth's dosage of Prozac to less than half of what she'd been taking, and she'd bounced back to her witty, wisecracking self. She'd always been a great conversationalist and everyone she came in contact with loved her and was affected by her wisdom.

"Maxine, is that a new kind of makeup you're wearing?" Eunice questioned. "Your skin looks great."

"Girl, I switched from that other mess to Mary Kay products, and I love it. I got the whole kit a few weeks ago; the cleanser, toner, moisturizer, lipstick, all that. I like the way it goes on my skin, the way it feels, and I don't break out," Maxine said.

"Darn, Maxine, you sound just like one of those commercials. I like the way it goes on my skin." Mamie mimicked Maxine. "Are you sure they aren't paying you to advertise their products."

Everyone laughed except Christen and since Mamie wasn't one of her favorite people, Christen interrupted, "Maxine, your skin has always been beautiful. I don't recall your breaking out that much."

"She doesn't anymore," Mamie smiled slyly.

"Mamie, honey, do you ever think about anything else?" Ruth gave her daughter an equally sly smile.

"Of course I do, Mama," Mamie answered.

"Can we believe that, Mama," Rayanne asked continuing the joke.

"I don't know. This is Mamie we're talking about," Ruth teased.

"Can I help it if I've got it going on?" Mamie said.

"I know that's right," Eunice said giving Mamie five. Eunice and Mamie were friends for years prior to her marriage to Samuel. As a matter of fact, Mamie had liked Eunice so well, that it was she who was instrumental in the break up of Samuel's relationship with another girl in order to get him to go out with Eunice. He later proposed and they got married.

Ruth and Christen took refreshments into the den for the others. "Sammie tells me that I act like some machine and that I expect him to act the same way," Eunice said when Ruth was out of earshot.

"I know you're not trying to say that my brother is falling down on the job. I knew I shouldn't have allowed my brother to marry a heffa like you any way," Mamie said, laughing.

"Now see where you're going. I'm not saying that at all. I'm just saying he'd better keep on eating his oysters," Eunice said and more laughter followed.

"Tell me something, because Sammie is a Wilson, and he'll be a man until the day he dies. Ask mama," Mamie said and at that moment, Ruth and Christen returned to the kitchen.

"Ask Mama what?" Ruth asked, going over to check the pies in the oven as the girls chuckled.

"Oh, nothing, Mama. Just a little girls' talk," Rayanne said still laughing.

"Maxine, you have to hook me up with that Mary Kay lady. I really like the way that makeup looks on you," Eunice said. "My skin is changing, it's getting a little course and I need something to revive it."

"Why don't you try mine. We're about the same complexion, it should work," Maxine offered.

"Do you have it with you?" Eunice asked.

"I don't lug that stuff around with me," Maxine replied, "come over to my house tomorrow and we can try it on you."

"Sounds good." Eunice poured several glasses of lemonade and placed them on the table.

"Those should be ready in just a few minutes," Maxine said, peaking over her mother's shoulder into the stove.

"Mama, do you think we're baking enough pies?" Rayanne asked, looking at her mother.

"I think so. We have four sweet potato pies, four apple, two pumpkin and two lemon meringue. That should be plenty, but if they run out, I got a couple more out there in the freezer," Ruth said.

"What's in the freezer, Mama?" Mamie asked, her eyes darting from Ruth to Rayanne suspiciously.

"There's a couple of pies out there in the freezer," Ruth answered, tilting her head towards the back porch where she kept the large chest freezer.

"What kind of pies you got out there?" Mamie asked.

"Sweet potato," Ruth said, smiling wickedly, and sipped from the glass of lemonade that Eunice placed on the table in front of her.

"As much as I love your sweet potato pies, you have some already out there baked and you didn't say a word until now?" Mamie asked. Rayanne and Maxine looked at one another and shared a secret snicker.

Ruth wanted to know what that look was about, looking from one daughter to the other. "Maybe there ain't no more pies out in the freezer. Your sisters love my pies, too," Ruth said to Mamie and it was true, because Rayanne and Maxine, sometimes Jeremy, would sneak into the freezer and nuked a slice of pie whenever they felt like it.

"I think you may be right, Mama," Mamie said, looking from Rayanne to Maxine, "from the looks of things around here, I hope we don't run out of pies tomorrow." They all laughed. Maxine plugged in the mixer and began blending batter for a chocolate cake. It was Jeremy's favorite. They'd asked the boys what they wanted for their graduation dinner, and although the list went on and on, the women in the family made sure to prepare everything that was on their list. Rayanne checked the oven and removed the potato pies and placed the apple pies on the rack.

"Who moved into Ms. Abigail's house," Eunice asked.

"I don't know. I've never seen anyone there, just the car in the driveway and on occasions, the lights will be on. That's about it," Rayanne said, tossing a dish towel on the table.

"I hope it's somebody nice," Ruth said. "Me and some of the church members want to go and welcome them to the neighborhood, but we ain't never seen no body."

"Mama misses Ms. Abigail. She wants another friend," Maxine said.

"Yeah, I sure do miss Abigail," Ruth said.

The kids were in the den with the men, watching television. Bruce and Bobby had gone to see that Arnold Schwarzenegger movie. They saw all of Arnold's movies. They loved hearing him say, 'I'll be back,' and always when he came back, he was holy hell.

A record began playing on the radio that got everyone's attention. 'Been around the world and I, I, I, can't find my baby,' the singer belted. Eunice got up from the table and danced around the room as the conversation took on a debate as to the race of the singer, the opinion was split. Mamie said, "When have you ever heard a white woman sing like that." Just then, Jeremy came into the kitchen wearing patchwork jeans that hung low on his hips and a matching vest and his sneakers were strung only half way up. "Who is singing that song, Jeremy," Mamie asked, snapping her fingers and bobbing her head to the music. "She's black isn't she?"

"No, Mama, that's Lisa Stanfield and she's white. Got some pipes on her, huh?" he said and the ones who thought the singer was white gave each other five. Rayanne looked at Jeremy and thought how times and trends had changed. The kids wore jumpers with one suspender fastened, while the other hung down their backs, their pants hung so low on their hips that you wondered how was it that they didn't fall completely off, and some of their clothes were just oversized, but that was the style and who was it that brought about change. The young people and the times.

"Where are you going dressed like that?" Mamie asked him, a frown creasing her pretty face.

"I'm just going to hang out for a while," Jeremy said, looked down at himself and asked, eyeing his mother quizzically, "what's wrong with the way I'm dressed?"

"Nothing, if you want to look like you're wearing clothes that belongs to the Jolly Green Giant. Jeremy, your clothes are two sizes too large. You look like you don't have any behind," Mamie said, walking over to him and pulling his pants tightly to show the overflow of fabric. "Look at this. It doesn't make any sense to buy clothes this big."

"This is what guys my age are wearing, Ma, besides, the girls love the way I look," he said pouring a glass of lemonade from the refrigerator.

"He looks nice, Mamie," Eunice said, sipping her drink.

"Jeremy, you want a slice of that potato pie." Ruth knew how much her grandson loved her sweet potato pies also.

"Yeah, grandma," he said, smiling at her. Ruth got up to cut the pie.

"Listen how he talks to people. No respect at all," Mamie said.

"Chill out, Ma. Grandma and I are cool, right grandma?"

"Right, Jeremy?" Ruth placed a slice of pie on a saucer and handed it to him.

"Mama, you shouldn't have cut that pie tonight. There won't be a piece left for tomorrow, if he's going to start eating it tonight." Jeremy took the saucer, grabbed a hand towel, slid the pie onto the towel, and he was about to leave. "And, I want you back here before midnight, too. Graduation is tomorrow, and I don't want to be up half the night worrying about you," Mamie said, staring unblinkingly at her son.

"Why doesn't she leave him alone?" Maxine whispered to Rayanne.

Rayanne lifted her shoulders and said, "who knows."

"Did you hear me," Mamie said to Jeremy as he goes towards the sink.

"Yeah, I heard ya," Jeremy replied, looking defiantly at Mamie.

"Just as long as you did," Mamie said to Jeremy and Rayanne wondered why was she badgering him and hoping she stopped before the situation escalated into something they all may regret. Rayanne had gotten to know Jeremy better in the past nine months, she believed than his own mother had and he'd changed. His temper was quick, he was unpredictable and although she didn't think that Mamie should be afraid of her own son, why provoke him unnecessarily. "Just go on and get back before so late. I wanna get some sleep."

"Since when have you been up at night worrying about me?" Jeremy asked, becoming indignant.

"And you think I don't?" Mamie asked and everyone could tell her temper was about to flare.

"No, I don't, Ma, and if you really want to know the truth, I don't think you ever did," Jeremy came back, "so, I don't see why you wanna try and play mama to me now."

"See how fresh his mouth is?" Mamie said, showing anger.

"Jeremy, why don't you go on and try to get back early. And be careful, son," Ruth said, going over to him and patting him on the shoulder.

"I will, Grandma" Jeremy said, sticking the last piece of pie into his mouth and draining his glass.

"He's going to find what he's looking for out there in them streets before long," Mamie said.

"Leave the boy alone, Mamie," Ruth said.

"I'll see you later, Grandma," Jeremy said, putting his empty glass into the sink and kissing his grandmother on the cheek. He walked toward the door.

"If you're not back here by midnight, young man, you shouldn't bother coming back at all," Mamie said, slamming the bowl of potatoes and the knife on the table.

"Why doesn't she leave him alone," Maxine whispered to Rayanne again.

Rayanne whispered back to her, "I don't know. She's your sister."

"You go on Jeremy, and we'll see you later," Ruth said wanting to cool the brewing situation that was heading towards a fever pitch.

"He makes me sick. He'll just try to spoil the day for me tomorrow. He's no good, just like that old daddy of his. Ain't going to amount to nothing any way," Mamie said.

"Mamie, for Pete's sake, "Rayanne said, "give it a rest and leave him alone."

"I will not leave him alone. I'm sick and tired of him walking around here with that arrogant attitude of his," Mamie hurled the words at Rayanne, then she turned her attention back to her son. "Who do you think you are? You are nobody. You hear that? Nobody. You got nothing. You don't want nothing? You are nothing,"

Jeremy turned at the door. "So what's up, Ma? You can't get a date with nobody's husband tonight? Is that why you're coming down on me?"

"Don't you talk to me like that, you hear me," Mamie said, charging up to Jeremy and slapping him hard across the face. What happened next gave Mamie a wake up call. Jeremy grabbed the knife from the table and if Samuel hadn't come into the kitchen to see what the commotion was about and reacted with lightening swiftness, catching his hand, Jeremy would've put the blade into Mamie's chest. Needless to say, that scene stirred the house up and although after everyone calmed down and no one wanted Jeremy to go out in the state he was in, he went anyway.

Later that evening, after everyone had left and the house was quiet, the three sisters talked. "You see how he is, what he's become? Jeremy's got a violent streak in him that going to get him into trouble. That boy would've killed me tonight if Sam hadn't stopped him," Mamie said, shock still lined her face.

"No doubt about that. My God what is happening to our children. It makes you wonder what kind of future some of them have to look forward to," Rayanne said across the table from Mamie and Maxine.

"I have no idea. I don't even know what's going on with my own son," Mamie rubber her hands together and shook her head. "I don't even know what he intends to do with his life. He doesn't talk to me. I don't have a clue what's on his mind," Mamie said sadly.

"You give him such a hard time, you push too hard, Mamie," Maxine said, but Mamie ignored her.

"I'd hoped that Jeremy would go to school and become a doctor or lawyer or something. You know, make something of himself," Mamie said, still rubbing her hands together.

Most parents have those kinds of dreams for their children, Rayanne thought, and she understood why Mamie felt as she did, but she said, "May be the kind of life you want for Jeremy isn't as important to him as it is to you."

"That's just it. I don't know what's important to him. I don't know what he wants out of life. To tell you the truth, I don't even know him anymore," Mamie said, and asked, "why doesn't he talk to me?"

"Perhaps because you don't listen to him," Rayanne said and waved to Maxine, who left the room silently.

"Good night, Maxine," Mamie said nonchalant, then to Rayanne, "do you have any idea what his plans are?"

"He's going into the Air Force," Rayanne answered.

"The Air Force?" Rayanne heard Mamie exploded as she got up to checked on the baby who was still asleep. Rayanne closed the door and returned to the kitchen. "Jeremy's going into the Air Force?" Mamie almost whispered when Rayanne sat back at the table.

"Yes, I think that's his plan," Rayanne said.

"And, he's not going to college?" Mamie was beside herself.

"Mamie, we all would've preferred that he went straight to college, and perhaps he will one day, but it's his choice and the Air Force isn't a bad choice for now. He can get a handle on his life and an education at the same time." Rayanne hesitated a moment. "Jeremy is very confused right now, you have to know that. He's been dealing with a lot, but he's handling it."

"What about Little Charlotte? What is he going to do about her?" Mamie asked, searching Rayanne's face.

"Swan? We'll take care of her."

"You're going to take care of the baby yourself?" Mamie asked incredulously.

"Yes. Swan is no trouble at all, besides, Jeremy isn't going to be able to get his life in order while trying to take care of a baby. I'm not saying it can't be done, because single parents do it all the time, but it helps when you've got a support system working for you."

"That boy has disappointed me time and time again. I had

such dreams for him," Mamie said and Rayanne knew that was a big part of the problem. Those were her dreams.

"Jeremy's got dreams of his own, and we've got to support him in the choices he makes, if they are reasonable," Rayanne said.

"And you don't mind taking care of the baby? Won't that cramp your lifestyle?"

"My lifestyle changed when I returned to South Carolina," Rayanne said. She'd be lying if she said there aren't times when she could be doing something else, but she'd come to realize how precious children were. "I want to provide a safe and nurturing environment for Swan. She's so precious. Mamie, children are a gift to us, a wonderful, delightful gift, and I want Swan to have a chance, and Jeremy as well. My contribution may not do much good, may not do any good, but if there's any way that I can help, I sure want to. Jeremy is a man now, and we're going to have to give him some space."

"A man isn't a man if he can't take care of himself and his family," Mamie said a bit snooty.

"He will, but we will have to support him, be there for him," Rayanne said.

"But the Air Force?" Mamie's disappointment refreshed on her face.

"Yes, and the bottom line is that this is his life, his decision and we've got to back away and support his choice," Rayanne said. "So what do you say?"

"What if he gets into the service and finds that he doesn't like it? Those military facilities are so regimented."

"We can't deal with a lot of what ifs, but the reality of right now. So what do you say?"

After some thought, Mamie said, throwing her hands into the air, "Oh well, why not?"

"I don't hear a lot of conviction behind that statement."

"Okay, I see where you're coming from. If this is what Jeremy wants, if this is what makes him happy, then I am all for it. I may not be happy with his decision," Mamie said, "but I will support him in this. At least I won't bad mouth him anymore." Mamie laughed.

"I'll say that's a big step toward making things better between you and your son."

"I suppose I could come home a little more often, look in on the baby and give you a little help," Mamie said and Rayanne smiled. Mamie offering to help, she thought. That was a first, and with her own granddaughter. Will wonders never cease. Rayanne was glad that their discussion didn't also turn into a boxing match. She didn't know about a lot of the conflicts between Mamie and Jeremy and what he'd gone through after his father left home as Mamie nor Jeremy had ever said, but Mamie did admitted to not being as supportive of her son as she should've been. Each of them, strong stubborn individuals, each liked having his own way. They could never reach a compromise. Although, Rayanne wished that Mamie had handled things differently early on, now was a good time to start. She remembered with sadness, the look on Mamie's face when she and Jeremy had the altercation. It was an unfortunate situation that could've been avoided.

Rayanne grew up in a household where the Commandments, especially the one that says Honor Thy Mother and Thy Father, was honored, and although she believed God is not vengeful, she did believe that one reaps what he sows. She didn't condone all of the choices Jeremy had made, but they were his choices and he'd be accountable. It'd been a consensus of the family that Mamie blamed Jeremy for the breakup of her marriage to his father, the rocky romances she had with other men and even because she was pregnant before she and Hank were married. It seemed she'd always blamed him for something, blame that had hurt Jeremy terribly. Why did it seem like human nature for someone to inflict pain and suffering on anyone who would endure it?

Jeremy volunteered for the Air Force immediately after graduation and would enlist into the military in September, which was a step in the right direction.

CHAPTER 40

"Hello?" Rayanne called out as she entered the house through the side door. It was a quarter past ten on Saturday morning, and the house was quiet, too quiet, and for that hour, it was unusual. Rayanne was happy that she was able to complete her meeting in New York sooner than she expected. After having done so, she took the first available flight back home. She picked up her car that'd sat three days in the extended parking section at the airport, and she drove home. Rayanne had missed her family very much, and she couldn't wait to see Swan. But, where is everyone, she thought. John and Christen had offered to keep Swan until Rayanne returned, therefore, she didn't expect Swan to be there to greet her, but where was everyone else. Perhaps Mrs. Marshall and her mother went shopping or something, Jeremy was in New York visiting friends because soon he'd be leaving for the Air Force, and Josh, there was no telling where he was, given his past record. "Hello?" she called out again, walking down the hall and putting her suitcase in her bedroom. The door to her mother's bedroom was closed, and she gently knocked, before entering. "Hey Mama. How are you doing? Are you all right," Rayanne said. Ruth pulled the covers close to her throat and stared at Rayanne. Her eyes held a wild frightened look, and she behaved as though she were cornered by something she didn't recognize. Rayanne moved closer to Ruth, doing so with caution in order not to upset her mother

311

further. "Mama, where's Mrs. Marshall?" Rayanne sat on the side of the bed. Her mother shrunk away from her, not wanting her daughter to touch her. She was taken aback, but she calmly got up, went back to her room and looked on top of the chest of drawers where she kept her mother's medication. She checked the day of the week on the bottles that were left, and just as she thought, her mother hadn't taken any medication in the three days that she'd been gone. Mrs. Marshall always stayed at the house whenever Rayanne was out of town, but why hadn't she given Ruth her medication.

Rayanne went into the room where Mrs. Marshall usually sleeps, but she nor her suitcase was any where in sight. Rayanne went into the kitchen and called Mrs. Marshall at her home. That was the first time that she'd gone out of town without leaving a number where she could be reached, and wouldn't something happened just on one of those occasions. She learned that Josh came in three days ago with some woman, informing Mrs. Marshall that her services were no longer needed and he sent her on her way. Mrs. Marshall informed Rayanne that she returned each day to check on Ruth but was refused entry. "I'm sorry dear, but that brother of yours and that woman, they took over after you left," Mrs. Marshall said.

"I'll have to deal with that later, but right now Mrs. Marshall, it seems Mama hasn't had her medication for several days, well since Wednesday. I want to get her back on it. What should I do?" Rayanne asked Mrs. Marshall since she'd been a registered nurse for more than twenty years at the local hospital. After Rayanne hung up, she followed Mrs. Marshall's instructions and she pulled the covers back up over her mother and sat on the bed beside her and waited for Mrs. Marshall to arrive, which didn't take very long. "Please stay with mama," Rayanne said to Mrs. Marshall, then to her mother, "I'll be back in a little while, okay?" Her mother stared at her, but she didn't respond. Rayanne opened the door to Josh's room where the smell of stale alcohol greeted her and where she found him and a woman in bed asleep. "Josh," Rayanne called out. The drapes hadn't been drawn and the room was dark, but Rayanne hit the switch and flooded the room with light.

"What? Who is it," Josh asked, his mind still in a fog. He and the woman had drank a lot the night before and neither was able to think clearly at that hour of the morning. "Oh shit, where'd you come from?" he said when he focused enough to see that it was Rayanne. He scratched his head and shook the woman. "Louise, get up, baby," he said. The woman mumbled something, turned over in bed, pulling the covers over her head. "Louise, you gotta get up, baby," Josh said, looking sheepishly at Rayanne.

"I want you to get up," Rayanne said, "put your clothes on and come to the kitchen." She turned and before leaving, she said, "and you get that," she pointed a finger at the woman, "out of here." Rayanne went back to look in on her mother. When Ruth looked at her, she imagined her saying, take it easy on him, honey. He's sick. He needs help. Remember, he wasn't always this way. She'd said those words before, a thousand times or more. When Rayanne was going into the kitchen, the woman was leaving through the back door and Josh was sitting at the kitchen table with his hands up to his head. "Josh, do you know what you're doing?"

"Rayanne," he said, "Louise and I took care of mama. Things just kind of got out of hands."

"Josh, Mama hasn't had her medication in three days, but what I want to know is why would you send Mrs. Marshall away?" she awaiting an answer. When none came, she said, "Why, Josh."

"I thought I could take care of her," he said, his head drooping. "I was just trying to help."

Rayanne stared at her brother, then she began making breakfast, "I don't know why Mrs. Marshall didn't call Maxine or John when this happened." She'd left Mrs. Marshall to look after Ruth and Josh had no right sending her away. He had a problem, he needed help. For years, they knew Josh had a problem and every time they decide to get help for him, he'd straightened up to the point where you really thought he'd be all right, but then as always, he'd get into trouble again.

"Rayanne, I have a couple of drinks, but I don't have a problem. I'm not an alcoholic," Josh said. It was worse than that, she thought.

"Josh, you drink every day."

"That's a lie," Josh growled.

"Well, every other day, what's the difference."

"You don't know what you're talking about."

"We're not going to debate that issue. All I know is that something's got to be done." She was busy around the kitchen with breakfast foods.

"Don't tell me you're gonna threaten to put me out again?"

Rayanne didn't say anything, but her thoughts were if he pulled something like that again, her solemn promise to him was that he'd be out of there so fast that it would make his head spin. Josh had such plans for himself, such dreams and he could've made it all happen. "You are allowing this problem to be the death of your dream. You've always said that you wanted to started your own business. Don't let your dreams go unfulfilled. You can do all the things you've always wanted to do. You've got great ideas, you're smart, creative and you are great with your hands. You can fix anything that is broken. You have a God given talent and you should put that talent to use. Remember what daddy always said? If God gives us a talent and we don't use it, He'll take it away. I can't tell you what to do. You're a grown man, but I hope one day soon, you'll get it together," Rayanne said and after a brief silence, "Tell me something? What was that you brought in here?" She placed her hands on her hips. "When you two find it necessary to spend the night together, stay at her place all right."

"I don't think so. She asked me who the hell were you. You see, some where along the way, Louise thought I owned this place."

"And just how did she figure that?"

"I don't know but in any case, I don't expect that she'll be coming back here," he grinned.

"Oh, no."

"No, because before the lady left, she asked why were you ordering me around in my own house. I told her that I was being ordered around by the owner. That's when she looked at me, gave me that neck action and told me not to call her anymore and that I could just kiss her black ass on credit."

"What?" Rayanne laughed. "That person was no lady." She laughed some more.

"That's what she said," Josh said and he and Rayanne laughed. Soon afterwards, Ruth and Mrs. Marshall appeared in the doorway. Ruth had showered and was dressed.

"What's going on in here?" Ruth asked. "Looks like I'm in time for breakfast." She winked at Rayanne. Yes, Rayanne thought, a very late breakfast.

CHAPTER 41

More than a year had passed since Raymond died and less than a month since Josh had spent another six weeks on a day to day basis at the rehab center when he staggered in again, drunk, but unlike other times, he was affecting high indignation, his perspiration struck profusely, and he looked as though he'd fallen down and wallowed in dirt at least twice before he made it in. Josh had lost so much weight by that time that his pockets met and grazed behind. It seemed that every new season set the stage in her life for something that was totally absorbing. There was always someone who wanted more, expected more and depended more and more on her, and although she always thought of herself as having untiring patience, lately she began to feel that she'd exhausted her stock of patience and sympathy. Her home had become part of a machine that badly needed oil. "Rayanne, I just can't get over daddy's death," Josh said when Rayanne complained. "I've tried to deal with it, but it's hard," he said, and he was crying again. That was the only excuse he could come up with as the quicksand rose around him. He'd used every excuse in the book to explain his drinking, and he was approaching an end. He really was beginning to look like death warmed over, and he would walk that road to the end unless someone intervene and took a firm hand. Didn't he know that their father's death was hard on all of them, but they were moving on with their lives and she knew that if something didn't happen to change his course, they'd be facing another tragedy.

"Josh, we're putting you in The New Tomorrow," Rayanne said, and lifted a finger to his protest saying, "and this is not opened to discussion."

Rayanne had expected a smooth departure. She'd drive Josh to Florence, have him admitted to the detox center and hopefully, when he was released, he would remain clean and sober. As it turned out though, Josh refused to go to Florence. By this time, he was out of control, threatened her and after she called the police, Josh was removed in handcuffs, leaving an upset Ruth behind. When Maxine called later that night, Rayanne wished she'd called earlier, perhaps she could've helped diffuse the situation, especially with their mother.

"It was hard wasn't it," Maxine said.

"Mama's so angry. She said she'll never forgive me. Maxine, Mama looked at me like she hates me."

"I'm sorry, honey. I should have been there for you. Is there anything I can do?"

"I'm okay, just worried about mama."

"Don't worry about mama, she'll come around. You had a tough job and you handled it," Maxine said. "Are you all right?"

"Yeah, I am, but what about you all. I hear the boys wrote to Joe, but no answer Huh?"

"Yeah, I got his address from Althea. They wanted it, Rayanne. It really pisses me off when someone hurts my children. Do what you want to me, but don't hurt my children. They're innocent and they get put through this crap. That ass acts like he doesn't want anything to do with his own children. If that's how he feels and he doesn't contact them, so be it, but if they want to write to him, then they will," Maxine said and Rayanne thought Maxine could say whatever she wanted, but she knew there was more going on with Maxine than she was telling her.

The following day, Rayanne and her mother were sitting in the den watching Our Voices. Ruth was as quiet as a mouse. Mrs. Marshall said she hadn't said a word all day, and when she went to bed that evening, she didn't even say goodnight. When Scott came by that night, he and Rayanne discussed the situation, he supported her and he agreed with Maxine that her mother would come around. However, the weeks that pass brought no change in Ruth's attitude, it seemed she avoided Rayanne whenever she could, then, she became depressed again. When Rayanne tried to get her involved in senior citizens programs, Ruth refused, saying she didn't consider herself a senior citizen. Heck, Rayanne thought, she, herself, felt like a senior citizen and that she should become involved in some of those programs herself.

CHAPTER 42

Labor Day was approaching, the weather was hot and sticky and Jeremy would be leaving soon. He was packing a lot of living into the weeks before his departure and as a result, he wasn't home very much. Maxine took Ruth and Swan with her to Charleston, and Rayanne was home alone when she received a call from Brenda, asking her to meet her and some friends for lunch.

Rayanne entered the Olive Garden and searched until she saw Brenda and Hilary waving to her. She waved back and walked over to the table and joined them. She was introduced to Jackie, a woman who resembled a younger, slimmer version of Della Reese, and who was in a nurse's uniform. Each girl placed her order. Jackie ordered only a salad, a glass of water and lemon slices. She pulled out a few packages of crackers from her purse, which surprised and baffled both Rayanne and Hilary, but they were really taken aback when she returned with most of the items from the salad bar and the hot bar. "I wouldn't have to resort to these measures if they didn't put such a price on everything," Jackie said, noticing the expression on the faces of the others.

Hilary looked at Jackie, then Rayanne and gave a small grin. "Things are expensive," she said. As they ate, everyone noticed that Brenda was unusually quiet. She was wearing large sunglasses that redefined the lines of her face and when she removed them and put them into her purse, Rayanne saw that she had dark circles around her eyes. She looked as though she hadn't had a good night's sleep for some time.

"Burning the candle at both ends, are we?" Rayanne smiled.

"What?" Brenda asked and although she was trying to act her usual spunky self, she was different.

"Still selling them houses?" Rayanne asked.

"Yeah, got a prospective buyer for the house over on Forest Drive. You know the one I told you about," Brenda said, picking at her food.

"The house you were showing last week?" Hilary asked, observing Jackie as she squeezed the lemon slices into the water, added some Equal and stirred up a nice glass of lemonade.

"She sells houses like hotcakes," Jackie said, stuffing her mouth with food.

"Oh yeah, the job is going very well," Brenda said, but without enthusiasm.

"Then what's wrong? Are you on your period again or is it PMS?" Hilary asked.

"No, I'm fine," Brenda answered, but they all knew that wasn't true.

"You don't seem quite yourself, Brenda," Jackie said. "Are the children all right?" She stirred her drink to dissolve the equal that was settled in the bottom of her glass.

"Oh yeah, the kids are fine. Everything's fine," Brenda said, "I'm just a little tired."

Something is wrong, Hilary thought and she said, "That young man probably walked out on her." Hilary laughed. Then, totally and unexpectedly, Brenda burst into tears. "Oh my God," Hilary whispered.

"Brenda," Rayanne said, looking closely at her, "What's wrong?"

"Did I say something to upset you," Hilary asked. "I was only joking. I didn't mean any harm."

"I'm okay." Brenda pulled some tissues from her purse and dabbed at her eyes, then she laughed." But you hit the nail on the head," Brenda said. The girls looked at her expectantly and Brenda went on to explain that Jason had ended their relationship. She'd invested a lot of time with him. She'd given him money, brought him clothes, everything. Brenda wiped her nose and put the used tissues back into her purse. "He didn't love me. He played with my heart to get to my purse. I did everything for this man. Why does this shit always happens to me?" A waitress came and offered coffee. Jackie accepted, but Brenda said, "No. I'm wired

enough as it is. But, here's the clincher. I told him I wanted a commitment, well he told me I should be happy with what we have,
that he's brought more than enough to my life that was one dimensional before we met. Can you believe that shit?"

"You're kidding?" Jackie exclaimed in amazement.

"I wish," Brenda said and hesitated. "But, enough about Jason. It was good while it lasted, but now that I know what he's all
about, it's over, I've cried and now it's time to move on," Brenda
pulled off a piece of yeast roll, spread some butter on it and popped
it into her mouth. Rayanne looked at her and winced at the thought
of all that butter. Brenda made a face at her, knowing the look, and
smiled.

"So what are you going to do?" Hilary asked.

"I'm going to concentrate on me and go from there," Brenda
said.

"That's a good first step," Rayanne said, surprised that Brenda
felt that strongly about Jason, or did she.

"I'm putting that ass hole behind me. It's his loss. What can I
say? It's good bye, so long and good riddance to Jason and to tell
you the truth," Brenda said, "I feel better already. Besides, I'm not
going to waste any more time crying over something that I can't
do a damn thing about. Time is a precious commodity. I'll just
keep the good memories close to my heart and fuck the rest. So
what's up with you guys?" she asked, and if she were acting, she
was doing a good job because it appears she was back to her old
self.

Hilary said, "there isn't a lot going on with me except getting
the adult care facility off the ground."

"How's that going, by the way?" Brenda asked.

"Real good, but a lot of hard work," Hilary informed. "So much
red tape getting Social Services involved."

"Are you still putting in a lot of hours?" Rayanne asked.

"Twelve hours a day, except on weekends," Hilary responded.

"That's a long day," Jackie said. "What do you do twelve hours
a day?"

"I manage my own adult care facility. We provide a decent
place for our people, we dispense medication, take them to ap-
pointments, consult with their doctors, keep their clothing, them
and their rooms clean. We have 26 residents and it gets hectic, but
I enjoy it." Hilary and Ben wanted to open their own facility for
years and although it hadn't been easy what with finding the right
location, funding and getting everything settled, they knew the

end results would be rewarding. "Anyway," Hilary said, "it's challenging, but it's rewarding to be able to provide a warm, loving environment for people who are not coming from such a place."

"I'm sure that it is," Rayanne said, "Josh is still in the center, I drive over every week, but he still refuses to see me. But not only is he angry at me, but Mama is so pissed off that she can barely stand to look at me." Rayanne felt a pang of sadness when she thought how her relationship with her mother had deteriorated. Rayanne had always thought of her mother as strong, energetic and very caring, but all that had changed.

"We all have got our share of problems, but we don't wanna talk about that," Brenda said.

" Good idea," Rayanne agreed.

"Yeah," Hilary agreed, "Let's talk about cheerful things."

"Brenda tells me you're a writer," Jackie said to Rayanne, changing the subject. "I was visiting my sister in Jersey when one of your plays was running. We saw it, and it was fabulous."

"I'm glad you liked it. Which one did you see?" Rayanne asked.

"After the Darkness. Girl, I laughed, I cried, and I applauded," Jackie informed, and when she said they had a famous person in their midst, Rayanne assured her that she was an average country girl, who happened to have had a run of good luck. Some run of luck because she had written more than a half dozen plays that toured this country and abroad. "Did I also hear someone mention speaking engagements. What do you speak about?" Jackie asked.

"That's something new that I'm about to embark on. I want to talk to kids about violence. Violence is taking over the country, so I want to go into the high schools and see if we can't head some of this off. I think it's important to save our children, if at all possible," Rayanne said.

"I heard that," Jackie said and asked, "do you have children?"

Rayanne mentioned the situation involving Jeremy and Swan. "Jeremy is going into the Air Force and Swan, she's precious," Rayanne said, her face taking on the glow of motherhood without biologically having had a child.

"You don't have any children of your own? "Jackie asked.

"Little Swan is like her own," Brenda answered.

"Yes, she is, but no I don't have any children, unfortunately," Rayanne said.

"No, honey, be glad that you don't. Kids can be a big headache sometimes," Jackie said.

"Don't believe her," Brenda said, "Jackie wouldn't give up

those headaches for all the tea in China."

Jackie lifted her shoulders. "I reckon you are right about that," she smiled, looked at her watch and drained her glass of the sip of lemonade that was left. She got up. "Girls, I've got to be getting back to the hospital. It was nice meeting you ladies," she said to Hilary and Rayanne, "and we should do this again."

"Yes, we must," Rayanne said.

"Take care, Jackie," Hilary said.

"I'll call you later, Brenda," Jackie said.

"All right, you take care, now," Brenda replied and Jackie hurried out of the restaurant.

"I'm going to have to be getting back to the center soon, myself," Hilary said and checked her own watch. She watched Jackie as she paid her bill and left, before saying, "Brenda, where did you find her?" Hilary began to laugh. Rayanne and Brenda joined in.

"I know. Jackie seems like an all right person, but I nearly fell off of my chair when she took the crackers from her purse, and I really couldn't believe it when she came back with all that food she had piled on her plate," Rayanne said, laughing.

"Did you see her bill? It was less than $4.00, and the woman ate like a person rolling logs," Hilary said and they continued to laugh.

"Jackie always does that shit," Brenda said.

"Why? She's a registered nurse by day, and she said she does private duty nursing at nights and weekends, so she can't be that hard up," Rayanne said, remembering Jackie had revealed that information to she and Hilary earlier.

"Jackie makes good money, but she has four kids that she is raising all by herself, two of them are in college, and the other two are in high school," Brenda explained. "She's not on public assistance, she's doing it all on her own."

"Gosh, it seems she's quite a woman," Hilary commented.

"You can say that again. Gee, I am sorry I laughed at the woman. I should be applauding her," Rayanne said, feeling ashamed about the comments she'd made without knowing the circumstances.

"And did you see the energy she has. Lordy, where does she get it," Hilary said, adding, "you know, I don't know what I'd do if I had to raise Jessica alone."

"It's no picnic," Brenda said.

"Hey, you two, I've got to run. I'll call you." With that, Hilary took a sip from her coffee cup, dabbed her lips with her napkin, and she left.

"Do you have a few minutes?" Brenda asked when she and Rayanne were alone.

"Yeah sure. What's up?" Rayanne answered and asked, looking up at Brenda, who had a serious look on her face.

"I want to tell you something, but I don't want the others to know yet," Brenda began. "It may not be anything at all, I don't know, but I need to talk to someone."

"Brenda, you know I ain't going no where with anything that you tell me personally," Rayanne said.

Brenda thought for a moment and the hesitation wasn't because she had any doubt that Rayanne would share what she was about to say. She knew she could trust Rayanne with anything. "I found a lump in my breast last week."

"You did?" Rayanne was sympathetic, "Oh, Brenda."

"I was examining my breasts while in the shower and there it was." Brenda looked at Rayanne, then looked away.

"I'm so sorry. Have you seen a doctor?"

"No."

"What? Why not?" Rayanne said in a voice that was just above a whisper.

"I will, I just haven't gotten around to it yet."

"Brenda, this is nothing to play with. We'll get you examined, and we'll go from there."

"Yeah."

"Call your doctor today, Brenda."

"I will call him next week."

"I want you to call today. Will you?" Rayanne was becoming alarmed and the silence that greeted her words made her wonder whether Brenda heard her. "Brenda, if you don't, I will. I mean it."

"I know," Brenda said with a little laugh. Rayanne knew now why Brenda was so upset earlier.

Rayanne said looking at Brenda. "Sometimes there is nothing to these lumps, except they will frighten us to death until we know that there's nothing wrong."

Brenda's voice cracked when she said, "Rayanne, I didn't mention this before, but I lost a sister and a cousin to breast cancer."

"I am setting up the appointment, and I am going with you."

"Rayanne, that's not necessary."

"I know, but I want too, all right," Rayanne said, then in a much softer voice, "we'll lick this thing together." Brenda smiled and brushed a tear from her left cheek.

CHAPTER 43

It was ten to midnight and Rayanne observed the moon as it shone brightly from high in the sky. The temperatures were in the low sixties, and on that October night, the sky was clear and there was a sprinkling of stars that winked in the night. Rayanne breathed in the clean fresh air and observed her surroundings from where she stood on the front porch. For a brief moment, all seemed fair and right with the world. Reality, though, has a way of raising its ugly head, forcing us to face whatever it is that's going on in our lives, regardless of whether it is good or not. She thought of Josh. He had gotten to the point where he wouldn't even speak to her when she called. Rayanne thought of what was happening in her neighborhood, what with the crime that had invaded their once quiet, safe community. She also remembered on more than one occasion, her mother saying there was something awful going on in Abigail's old house, but she never said what she thought it was.

She thought of Brenda and although her test results were negative, she was cautioned to have regular checkups and Brenda returned to her old bubbly, fun loving self. And Ralph. Lately, her mind was in a buzz about Ralph. Why was she thinking about Ralph. She wasn't sure, but standing on the porch in the brisk breezes, memories of what they shared came back to greet her. Rayanne took a deep breath to steady her breathing. She wish the thought of him didn't still have that effect on her. Rayanne's mind went back to a time when she and Ralph were a part of each other's lives, when they held one another all night, while listening to tunes by Marvin Gaye and Teddy Pendergrass. Although Ralph was calling again and the cards he sent continued to stack up and remain unopened on the top drawer of her dresser, Rayanne had refused to renew the relationship. It was strange. Ralph's letters remained unopened on top of the dresser and Dorian's were stacking up in the dresser drawer. There were times when she found her mind filled with wonder. What would her life be like had she not returned to live in South Carolina. If Ralph hadn't slept with Dorian, would he have betrayed her with someone else, if they'd gotten married? Those thoughts visited Rayanne on occasions, but that was all academic now because she had moved back to South Carolina, Ralph had slept with Dorian, and he probably would've cheated on her had she married him. What Ralph did was unforgivable. He had not only scratched the surface of trust and loyalty of their relationship, he'd broken it.

Rayanne also thought of Billy Peterson and the direct contrast of the relationship she had with him, where they would make a quick stop at some out of the way motel, for a slam, bam, thank you ma'am session in bed that left her totally unfulfilled. Afterwards, they went their separate ways, and wouldn't see each other again until Rayanne could free up time, which wasn't often. She wanted more than what he could offer and the night Billy proposed, she turned him down and at the same time, terminated the relationship. There was no point in him putting his life on hold. He'd made it clear that he wanted an emotional investment with Rayanne, but since she was not in love with him as she wanted to be with the man she chose to marry, their relationship ended amicable and Rayanne was back to where she was when she ended her relationship with Ralph. She was alone again.

***

Jeremy was on standby to go to the Middle East to help liberate Kuwait from that lunatic, Saddam. The country was in a quandary wondering what that idiot would do next. Rayanne was getting some decorations for Swan's birthday party that would be on Saturday. Afterwards, she and her friends would have dinner and they'd watched several episodes of Def Comedy Jam with Martin Lawrence, that she recorded previously, before settling down to a good card game.

Sixteen little boys and girls were at the party along with their mothers. Ruth had done Swan's sandy hair up in pony tails that hung below her shoulders, and bright pink ribbons, that matched her dress and socks, were attached to each of them. Rayanne and the other mothers watched Swan, in admiration, as she spent time with all of her guests. She was incredible and Rayanne marveled at her. It was fun watching Swan open her presents and hear her squeals of delight at discovering the contents. She received gifts of all kinds; savings bonds, educational toys, dolls, clothes. Mamie sent two dresses, and Jeremy sent a giant teddy bear and a promise that he'd be with her on her next birthday. By that time, Swan had expressed an interest in dance. Rayanne learned that three was the age requirement for dance, and she assured Swan that she would be entering dance school that year. Swan's mother had called only a few times since Swan came to live in South Carolina, and since she'd met and married some guy from Chicago and moved there with him, she'd called Swan less frequent. However, she did call and wished her daughter a happy birthday the day of the party.

"Look at you," Rayanne said to Swan after the party was over. "You are a little princess. Got your little hair all done up real pretty."

"Am I as beautiful as a princess, Aunt Rayanne?" Swan asked.

"You're even more so to me, honey," Rayanne assured. She was always amazed and surprised by Swan, how intelligent she was to be as young as she was.

Swan walked over to Rayanne. "I love you, Aunt Rayanne." She hugged her aunt's neck. It wasn't long after Swan arrived that she'd won Rayanne's heart completely.

"I love you, Swan," Rayanne said and released her.

"Thank you for my birthday dress. It's pretty."

"You're welcome, sweetheart and I'm glad you like it. Come on," Rayanne said, removing Swan's dress and leading her to the bathroom to bathe her. "Did you enjoy your party?"

"Yes, I liked it a lot. We had a good time."

"I'm glad you all enjoyed it. Hey, guess what?" Rayanne said changing the subject.

"What?"

"We're going to have more fun tomorrow."

"We are," Swan squealed.

"Yes, we're going to trim the Christmas tree," Rayanne said. Swan always liked looking at the Christmas tree in the past. This year she would be helping to hang the lights, which she was sure to enjoy.

"Weee, that'll be fun. Can I help?"

"May I help," Rayanne corrected, "of course you may. You're going to be hanging bulbs on the tree, tossing icicles, hanging ornaments and all that kind of stuff. Then, next week, we're going to ride around and look at some of the other houses that have been decorated."

"I can't wait," Swan said excitedly. Rayanne lifted Swan out of the tub, toweled her dry and slipped her into a pair of pajamas. She held Swan on her lap and read one of the books she received as a birthday present. Rayanne valued the influence she had on Swan's life, teaching her and helping to mold her. Once in bed and after saying her prayers, it wasn't long before Swan was asleep. Ruth had turned in early that night as well, she was a little tired. Rayanne had noticed something different about her mother earlier that day that had troubled her, but Ruth assured Rayanne she was fine. Just the excitement of the party was all, she'd said and she hugged and kissed Rayanne and Swan before going to bed.

Ruth died at 6:15 Sunday morning. Some time that afternoon, Rayanne walked through the backyard down to the lake, and as if the day wasn't unbearable enough, it began to rain. She stood as the rain pounded against the dried leaves, making them crackle. She'd lost a large chunk out of her life when she lost her father. Now, she was devastated. Was she going to lose everything she held dear in her life, she wondered. She had lost too much and could never remember feeling so alone. She felt like an emotional cripple as she turned her eyes to the sky and asked, "why? Why?" As she wept, alone, clinging to a tree, she felt a pair of strong hands turning her around. She was surprised to see Ralph standing there. They stood facing each other for the first time in a very long time.

"I had to come," he said and Rayanne's body sagged against his as she cried in the cold, in the rain, but nestled in Ralph's arms. And, as she stood in the comfort of his arms, the past came back to her and for a little while, it was as though they'd never parted. He was holding her, comforting her and providing the strength she so desperately needed.

Rayanne was vaguely aware of the multitude of people who came to the house. Food was brought, so much so that there was literally no place to put it all. Rayanne learned later that most of it was given to people who would put it to good use, and as with her father, the day of the funeral, they faced the same heartbreaking ordeal. The church was unable to accommodate them all and, as usual, flowers were everywhere. Ralph returned to New York the day after the funeral and Rayanne promise she'd keep in touch.

Ivory and Dorian stayed on a few days. They talked a lot, cried a lot and they'd even managed to laugh some, too, and by the time they separated, Ivory and Dorian hoped that their personal healing had begun.

Rayanne and her mother were very close before the incident with Josh, and although she felt they were resolving one set of circumstances where Josh was concerned, she was devastated by the loss of her mother. It seemed she was plagued with bad luck. Swan was very young, but she missed Ruth and her confusion was obvious when she passed Ruth's bedroom door and not seeing her there or any where in the house. Rayanne felt she'd experienced it all as she watched her days slip into nights, cold, lonely, depressing nights. It was no wonder she'd ended up on a therapist's couch.

***

Rayanne sat with pen and pad in hand, listening while Swan practiced on the piano. Swan was making a lot of progress on the keyboard, but on the other hand, Rayanne hadn't written anything decent in months. After putting Swan to bed and reading her a story, she removed her computer from the bottom of her closet and set it up in the den. At that hour, the house was quiet. Josh had not returned home after being released from the center and from what she'd heard, he'd remained clean and sober. And, although Josh hadn't spoken to Rayanne since he was released, she was pleased that he was taking care of himself.

She sat at the computer, and suddenly words began to formed in her mind, which translated into interesting sentences and her fingers seemed to race on uncontrollably for a couple of hours until she was interrupted by the ringing of the telephone. It was Aunt Bessie. "Whatcha doing?" Aunt Bessie asked.

"Just putting a few lines on paper," Rayanne responded, "how are you?"

"I'm okay. Just calling to check on my two favorite girls," Aunt Bessie said.

"We're doing good," Rayanne assured her.

"That's good. I'm glad you done start writing again."

"You hear anything from Stevie lately?" Rayanne asked sensing something in her aunt's voice. Aunt Bessie became quiet. "Aunt Bessie, are you sure you're all right?"

"He called last night," she replied.

"How is he doing?" Rayanne asked and wondered whether Stevie was in trouble again, was he hurt, what.

329

"Said he's doing all right. Gon' get this job next week that he put in for, he said," Aunt Bessie informed. And, Rayanne thought, he needs a little money to tide him over. The usual story. Hadn't she heard Aunt Bessie tell her that story a dozen or more times. "I went on and sent him what he says he needs to keep him from coming back here. I know that's a bad thing to say 'bout your own child, but that's how I feel. That boy scares me sometimes," she said. Rayanne wished there was some way that she could assure Aunt Bessie that she didn't have to be afraid of Stevie anymore. She'd been through enough at his hands and she didn't have to put up with any more of his nonsense.

"What can I do to help?" Rayanne asked.

"Don't you worry 'bout me, child. I'm gon' be all right. I tell you something, I'm proud to have a niece like you. I appreciate you looking after me the way you do, you know."

"I'm glad to do whatever I can." She wished Aunt Bessie would take her up on her offer and move in with her and Swan. Since both her parents had died and Josh was no longer living at home, there was more room than she and Swan would ever need. Aunt Bessie didn't mind visiting and spending a couple of nights on occasions, but she had no intentions of giving up her own home and moving in with anyone else.

"You know how we are when we get old," Aunt Bessie said, "all set in our ways and hard to get along with."

"How would you know, you're not old. You're one of those people who'll always be young, you are as flexible as anyone that I know and you certainly are easy to get along with. So you see, I've invalidated your reasons for not wanting to come live with Swan and me.

Aunt Bessie chuckled, "I knew I called you for a reason. You always make me feel so good. And, I can tell you're working everything out since you're writing again. Josh and his stubbornness, your parents. You're bouncing back. You sure got your mama's knack for bouncing back you know. What they call it? What's that word? Resilience? Ain't that what they call it," Aunt Bessie said and they laughed and were still doing so when they hung up half an hour later. Five minutes later, the phone rang again. It was Ralph. He wanted to visit that weekend.

Rayanne said, "Yes," without thinking about it and it was settled. She called Scott and during the course of their conversation, she mentioned Ralph's perspective visit and for the first few seconds, she was met with silence. She knew Scott was thinking that she was setting herself up for more pain. He'd always thought that was what Ralph's visits would bring. Scott had met Ralph and not only did Scott not like him, he wasn't at all convinced that all of the play was out of the man.

CHAPTER 44

Rayanne met Ralph at the airport at 9:45 that Friday night. Swan was spending the night with Marcia Raylyn which was something she did regularly on Fridays, whereas they rented movies and watched them and ate popcorn up into the night. Swan had taken a late afternoon nap so when Rayanne dropped her off at Maxine's, she was bright eyed and bushy tailed and she'd certainly be up at least until midnight. Rayanne and Ralph would have the house to themselves and have plenty of time to talk.

After they picked up Ralph's luggage and were in the car headed home, Ralph looked at her. "You look great." Rayanne smiled a little but remained silent. "I've been thinking about you a lot, Rayanne." She still didn't say anything. She was thinking about her therapy session earlier that day, when she'd told her doctor of the situation with Ralph and his impending visit. He'd told her that in order to understand and deal with what happened between Ralph and Dorian, she and her mother and some of the other things she'd been having trouble with, that she would have to understand how the things she had questions about could happen.

"When you get past that, one day you will look back, the pain will not be so bad and you will remember good days," she remembered her therapist saying.

She stopped at a red light and waited for it to change. Ralph didn't speak again until they were flowing with the traffic. "I never stopped loving you, you know," he said, after what seemed like a long silence, but it was actually only a few minutes. Rayanne looked at Ralph, then she returned her attention to the highway, as she maneuvered the car through the Friday evening traffic. It wasn't long before they were out of the city and on the interstate. "What happened to us, Rayanne?" Ralph asked and she couldn't believe that he'd come out of his mouth with that question. He'd started it all and now he was asking her what happened. You must know the answer to that one, Rayanne thought. One thing was certain. She'd never forget. "What happened to us," he repeated.

"I'm sure you haven't forgotten," Rayanne said, lit a cigarette and blew out a cloud of smoke.

"When did you start smoking?" Ralph asked, disbelieving.

"I hate these things," she answered, taking another draw from the cigarette.

"Then, why do you do it?"

"Something to do I guess," she said, annoyed, "I don't know. Why do people do some of the thing they do."

"You've always been against smoking, always the health advocate." When Rayanne didn't answer, he said, "You're not doing this just to get at me, are you?"

"I don't play those kinds of games, Ralph." She wondered what he thought she'd gain by doing something that could be harmful to her in order to get at him. "Perhaps I smoke for lack of something better to do." She looked quickly at him, "just don't worry about it. I don't smoke that often." It was true, Rayanne had just started smoking after her mother's death, and she didn't know why, because she didn't even like it.

Ralph looked at her a long time. She put the cigarette out, picked up the almost full pack of Salems from the console and returned them to her purse. He thought long and hard before he approached the subject that they'd avoided for a long time. That was the only thing that stood between them. He wanted her in his life and if he hoped to have a chance of her loving him again, they had to talk, try to work through the one obstacle that separated them. He had seen her only once since she'd learned about what happened between he and Dorian. That was when he came to be with her when her mother died. He'd wanted to say something about that situation, but he knew that the timing was not right. But now, it was time. "Rayanne, you have to understand how this thing happened," Ralph began.

"Oh, do I."

"Don't make this any harder than it already is. I want you to understand," he said and she wondered whether he actually thought that people exhibited that degree of understanding. She knew that the more he talked about that situation, the angrier she became. "We were so much in love that I thought that love would weather any storm."

"Must we talk about this now?" Rayanne looked at him and quickly returned her eyes to the highway, feeling a gamut of emotions welling up inside of her. She didn't want to be having that conversation with Ralph, not now, especially while driving.

"I think we should deal with it, get pass it and get on with our lives," he said as carefully as he could.

"I'm afraid that's easier said then done."

"Are we going to waste an entire life time because of one stupid mistake?"

"I suspect you'd be better qualified to answer that question for yourself," Rayanne said and Ralph looked at her as if he couldn't understand why she couldn't put the past behind them and move forward. He admitted it was a mistake, but he didn't think he should have to pay for that mistake the rest of his life.

"We can't avoid this any longer. We need to talk about it."

Rayanne thought for a moment, then she said, "Ralph, I thought we, you and me," she pounded her chest with one hand, "would love each other forever. I never thought something like this could happen to us. I thought it would be you and me forever."

"So did I."

"You did?"

"Don't act so surprised. You know I did."

"Then can you explain to me why you thought you had to do what you did." There was complete silence. "At least, you're not denying it," she said.

"I'm not confirming anything, either," Ralph spat out.

"Then what're you telling me," she said raising her voice. "You're not trying to say that you didn't make love with Dorian." There, she had said it. They were having a conversation about a situation that occurred some time ago, but it had remained fresh in her mind.

"It's not what you think."

"Oh no? Enlighten me, please," she said and the more they talked, the faster she drove.

"Will you please slow this car down," Ralph said, his eyes darting from Rayanne to the speedometer. She reduced the speed from 75 miles per hour to 55 and set the cruise control. "Now, talk to me, will you, calmly and quietly, please."

Rayanne took a deep breath. "Ralph, when I left New York and your phone calls and visits became fewer, I knew something wasn't right, but because I loved you, I didn't want to believe anything negative. No woman wants to believe that her man is fooling around. I'm not stupid but what I didn't know was that you were fooling around with one of my best friends."

"You're projecting the worst case scenario. I know what you're capable of when you let your imagination run wild," he said.

"What was there to imagine? Let's try this little scenario. What if I went to New York and fuck one of your best friends? Do you think you'd ever forget it or forgive me? Hell no," she answered her own question.

"I never meant to hurt you," he said softly.

"You knew this would hurt me. How could you not? Unless of course, you thought I'd never find out. Dorian was going through a lot. She was off of her rockers so who was going to believe her? Is that how it was suppose to go?"

"No, it wasn't that way at all." He paused to look at her. "Good God, what's happened to you. You've changed."

"Yet you can't see the reason for the person I have become, can you? You've always wondered what would ruffle my feathers, you've always wanted to see me venerable, remember?" Ralph had always thought of her as the articulate, goal oriented gal, who was as tough as nails. Nothing ever shook her. Well, she thought, there was a difference in being venerable and devastated, and she was devastated. He meant everything to her and she never thought he'd ever do anything to hurt her. She couldn't tell him how she'd suffered, agonized over missing him, but it was to the point of despair. "I watched our dream become a nightmare. I gave you my heart and trust you and what do you do with it."

"I know what I did, and I know I hurt you, but it would make all the difference in the world if you forgave me. Rayanne, I admit, I've made some mistakes, I've done some wrong, but it was never intentional. I never meant to hurt you. I love you, and I know you still love me." How arrogant and confident he is, Rayanne thought. He'd done something that was unforgivable and yet he felt he could just move back into her life at will and go on as though nothing happened. "Can you honestly say you don't love me?" he asked.

That maybe true, she thought, but she was moving that process along. She said, "I did love you, Ralph, but that was then, and this is now, and we can't turn back the clock."

"Then why am I here?" he snapped. With that and to his surprise, Rayanne jammed on the brakes and the vehicle skidded on the highway, leaving black marks as she pulled off onto the shoulder.

"You can go back to New York and your life back there anytime you want. Just say the word, and we'll be on our way back to the airport." She was almost to the point of hysteria. Ralph was caught off guard. He'd never witnessed such an outburst from her. He propped one elbow on the window, took a deep breath and scratched the side of his head. "What is it going to be?" Rayanne asked, about to explode from the frustration that had built for what seemed like too long.

"Let's just go on, please."

Rayanne looked at him. When she stopped the car, her immediate impulse was to turn around, drive back to the airport as fast as she could and order Ralph out of the car. That would've been childish, but what the heck. That's what she had started to do. However, what she did was checked the traffic, pulled back onto the highway when traffic permitted, and they rode the reminder of the way to her house in silence.

It was late and the temperatures had dropped considerably since she left home at 8:30 that evening. As soon as Rayanne entered the house, she call Maxine to check on Swan. She was fine and had fallen asleep watching the second movie. Aunt Bessie called to informed Rayanne that Mrs. Bennett, another neighbor had been mugged on the street in front of her house, on her way from the grocery store, and for the first time, Rayanne checked all the windows and doors before she began putting dinner on the table.

After a light meal, they settled in the den in front of the TV set and for the first hour, it was talk of Ralph's being back at work, what was going on in the stock market, what he was doing for fun, and his involvement with Big Brothers. "I'm trying to do what's necessary to hold onto my job and put some purpose back into my life. It hasn't been the same without you," he said. They brought each other up on what was going on in their lives and as the hour grew older, Ralph said, "Rayanne, it wasn't easy your being here and me there. This distance put such a strain on our relationship, but I want you back."

She wasn't sure what she expected him to say. She wasn't even sure how she felt about what he'd said, but she knew she had to say something. "Ralph, we've been apart for so long, we have separate lives. This is not a fantasy. This is real and we can never get back what we had."

"If you continue to think like that, you're right, we won't." He paused, wrapped his fingers together and took a deep breath. "We've got to get pass this, and we can. I feel a little out of place here, talking to you like this under these circumstances."

"You created these circumstances," Rayanne reminded him.

"I know that," he said in a whisper.

Rayanne remembered her life when everything was good, her world was perfect, and she thought she had a perfect life to go along with it. Little did she know how such a world can come crumbling down around one's shoulders. She realized that Ralph still had the capacity to tear her life apart, if given the chance, and she didn't want to take that chance. She didn't want to be hurt anymore. She'd lost so many people she loved, her life had gone into a downward spiral, and she wanted it to stop. "I don't think I can stand to lose anything else. It hurts too much." She got up and went to the kitchen. She could feel Ralph's eyes on her and for some reason, she thought she felt goose bumps exploding over her. She returned shortly with two cups of steaming hot coffee. Ralph sat back and extended his arm behind Rayanne onto the back of the couch, and they watched Def Comedy Jam. When it was over, Rayanne said, "Martin is so funny."

"He is," Ralph said, picked up the remote from the table, looked at Rayanne and asked, "Do you mind?"

"No."

Ralph pressed the buttons, turning off the TV and VCR, and he turned and faced her. "The last thing I wanted to do was hurt you, baby. I made a mistake, a terrible mistake. I'd do anything not to have had this happened and have you back. Christ sakes, Rayanne," he scratched his head, "haven't you ever made a mistake."

"Of course, I have. I make them all the time."

"Don't be sarcastic." He got up and walked over to the mantle. He picked up a picture of Swan, studied it and returned it to its place. Then he looked at the other pictures of the Wilson grandchildren. "Don't you believe in second chances?" he asked, looking at her. "If you would just think of what we had, maybe we could get back on the right track." There isn't enough time for that, Rayanne thought sadly, because although Ralph had meant more to her than any man in her life, too much had happened. They'd

337

drifted so far apart. "Do you hate me that much?" he said and waited for an answer. When Rayanne merely looked at him, he continued. "This isn't easy for me, either. It's hell when we're together like this, yet we're so far apart, but it's even worse when we're not together." Ralph walked back over to the couch and sat beside Rayanne. After a moment, he reached for her, but she got up, walked over to her music collection and selected a cassette that she'd put together and she put it in the tape deck. It was a mix of old songs, some not so old and some new ones, but they were all soulful ballads; the cool sultry voice of Regina Belle's 'Baby Come To Me,' Marvin Gaye's 'Sexual healing,' the O'Jays', 'Listen To The Clock On The Wall,' Teddy Pendergrass' 'It Don't Hurt Now' and Patti Labelle. The music was soothing for listening or dancing. Rayanne was sitting on the floor near the stereo now. Ralph took a sip of coffee from his cup, which Rayanne was sure was cold by now. "I can heat that up for you," she said.

"No, it's fine this way."

"You still drink it after it's cold, huh?"

"Old habits are sometimes hard to break." He got up, walked over and sat on the floor beside Rayanne. He began looking through the collection. "You've got some monster jams here, baby." He smiled at Rayanne. "Let me see what else you've got. Looka here, looka here," Ralph said with a gleam in his eyes. "Jennifer Holliday's 'I'm In Love,' Philip Bailey's, 'Chinese Wall,' Whitney, Billy Ocean, Rene and Angela. What? 'How Do You Stop' by my man, James, ' Do Me,' Meli'sa Morgan, Miles Jaye, The Deele, Prince, LaVert," Ralph said and a puzzled look crossed his face. "Who is this Dan Hill and Vonda Shepard? I don't think I've ever heard of them."

"Let me play it for you. It's nice, I like it." Rayanne took the cassette and put it on the tape player.

She listened as he whispered the names; Keith Sweat, Luther, Atlantic Starr, Vesta, Karyn White, StarPoint." When 'Can We Try' was over, Ralph liked it. "Hey, play that one again." She did and before the night was over, he persuaded her to dance with him.

Rayanne was awakened in the morning by the telephone. Maxine was taking the kids to the carnival, they'd have lunch at McDonald's and she'd bring Swan home by 3. After talking about the crime that had viciously invaded their community, they said they'd get together with some of the others and form some sort of neighborhood watch group. When their conversation was over, Rayanne said, "Let me speak to my baby." When Swan got on the phone, Rayanne said, "Good morning, sweetheart. How are you?"

"I'm fine," Swan said brightly.

"I missed you."

"I missed you, too. Were you afraid at home last night without me?"

"No, I wasn't afraid, but I missed you a lot," Rayanne conveyed.

"I'll be home to see you soon, okay."

"Okay. Are you being a good girl?"

"Yes," Swan quickly answered and with excitement said, "and we're going to the carnival today."

"Aunt Maxine told me."

"If you're lonely, Aunt Rayanne, I'll come home and stay with you."

"I tell you what, why don't you go on and have a good time at the carnival, and I'll see you later today. Then, I'll read that new book I brought you last night."

"You bought me a new book?" Swan questioned excitedly.

"Yes, The Little Alligator."

"Weee! That's one of my favorites."

"I know, and if you continue to be as good a girl we'll get the Ninja Turtles' next week."

"Yippee. I'll be good, Aunt Rayanne."

"Okay, have fun now."

"I will, and I'll be home soon, okay. Aunt Maxine wants to talk to you. I love you, Aunt Rayanne."

"And, I love you, Charlotte."

"You can call me Swan. I like Swan and I like Charlotte," Swan said, "but I don't like Stinkie." Stinkie was a name that Jeremy had called Swan on occasions, she didn't like it and had told her father so.

"I know. I don't like Stinkie either. Now, be good."

"I will. Good-bye, Aunt Rayanne. I'll see you soon."

"Good-bye, honey."

"So, how did last night go?" Maxine asked after taking the phone from Swan's hand.

"You are one nosy broad. You know that, don't you?" Rayanne said and it was true. Maxine always wanted to know everything about everything.

"Yeah, I know, but you still didn't answer me," Maxine said.

"I know," was all Rayanne said.

"Oh, I get it. He's right there beside you."

"Not in the way you think," Rayanne said, and looked over to observe Ralph sleeping on the couch where he'd spent most of the night. After informing her sister that Ralph didn't make any head way with her, that they'd spent the evening listening to music and catching up, Maxine let out a groan. Rayanne said, "See, I tell you you're nosy. Just hurry up and bring my baby home." With that, Rayanne hung up. When she came out of the bedroom, she was wearing a blue silk blouse and a pair of blue jeans that did wonderful things for her figure. Although she'd started to get a little pudgy around the waist, in that outfit, she looked like a million dollars. She walked through the den and into the kitchen. "Ralph," she called out to him, but he was no where in sight. She checked throughout the house, and although he wasn't there, the hall bathroom held warm moist air, which was evident that Ralph had showered and changed out of the clothes he'd worn from New York the day before and had slept in that night. Rayanne looked around outside and unable to find him, she returned to the kitchen and made breakfast, which they ate leisurely when Ralph returned. "I wondered where you were," Rayanne said across the table from him.

"I was down by the lake. I saw it when I was here the last time, but I didn't get a really good look. It is fabulous out there," he said extending a hand in the direction of the lake.

"I spent a good part of my childhood there. I use to go out there a lot when I wanted to be alone with my thoughts. My friend, Scott, thinks I should have a developer dig it out and plant flowers around the lake and put fish and ducks into it."

"That's an idea," he said, lifting a hand. "You could have some of the trees removed to open up that path a little to allow easy access, while also making the lake visible from the house. It would be beautiful, and I can't tell you what that would do for you creatively." Rayanne was thoughtful and bowed her head in agreement. "Who is this Scott that I keep hearing so much about?" Ralph changed the subject. Rayanne explained he met Scott when he was there before, that he'd been a friend of hers since she rammed him from behind one rainy morning. Ralph remembered Scott and wanted to ask Rayanne who he was when they'd first met, but under the circumstances, he'd let it go. But now, he wanted to know who Scott was and what was he to her. "And, please don't tell me he's just a friend."

"Don't tell me you're jealous," Rayanne said incredulously. She got up and began clearing the dishes from the table.

"You didn't answer my question," he said, getting up and going over to assist Rayanne in loading the dishes into the dish washer.

"Scott is a very dear friend, that's all." She turned and looked at Ralph briefly before turning her attention back to what she was doing. "I don't know what I would've done without him. He's been there with me through all my adversities, when both Daddy and Mama died, Josh's alcoholism, the problems with Jeremy...." Rayanne wouldn't allow herself to go further. She looked out of the kitchen window.

"And what happened between you and me," Ralph finished for her, he walked over and stood behind her. He placed his hands on her shoulders. Rayanne turned to face him. They stood only inches apart, his lips moved close to hers, but she brushed passed him. Although a lot had happened to put distance between Rayanne and Ralph, she knew if she allowed him to kiss her, just once, she'd be in his arms and loving him again, just as before. Because one kiss would've been too many yet a thousand would not have been enough. "I just bet he took full advantage of those adversities, too, didn't he?" Ralph said to her back pulling her out of her thoughts, before he returned and sat back at the table.

"Where are you going with this?" Rayanne turned and asked, her eyes matching his hard stare.

"Rayanne, I'm just trying to make things right between us, and I wish you wouldn't fight me so. I'm struggling here. Damn it, woman, I love you. Do you hear me. I love you." With that, Ralph sprung up so suddenly that the chair slid back, crashing to the floor, his movement startling her. "What do you want me to do, tell me."

"I don't want you to do anything. Let's just take this time and try to enjoy each others company and let the rest of it go, please," she begged, her eyes becoming bright with irritation.

"How long has it been since this thing happened? Six months? A year? A year and a half? I don't even know anymore, but we've never talked about it, not once," Ralph stormed and it was true. They'd loved each other passionately, he'd slept with one of her best friends and they ended their relationship without bothering to talk about what went wrong, what caused such a breakdown in their relationship.

"There's nothing to talk about. I've moved passed that and if I were you, I'd do the same thing," Rayanne turned her eyes quickly to him then she turned them away again.

"If you don't want to talk, you don't have to, but why don't you sit down and shut up," Ralph said.

"Excuse me," Rayanne said blinking.

"You heard me," Ralph said, then he said, pointing to a chair. "Would you please come over here, sit down and listen to me." She looked at him and although she wasn't sure what it was in his voice that made her want to obey, she did. "You don't have to talk, but please listen. Would you please do that?" Rayanne stared at him a moment before sitting. Ralph picked up the chair that he'd knocked to the floor and he sat and faced Rayanne. "I know you're angry, you have every reason to be, but please let me say something in my own defense. It may have been easy for you to move on with your life without me, but it's not the same for me. I miss you like crazy." He paused, stretched his hands out onto the table. "Have you ever sat and thought back to what we've been through together, what we meant to each other?"

"You asked me to listen, remember?"

"Okay, okay." Ralph tried to steady his breathing. "This thing that happened between, Dorian and me."

"Why don't you call it what it is" Rayanne spat out, unable to maintain her silence.

"No. Was, Rayanne, was. That's the operative word here."

"The point is, you were carrying on a sexual relationship with my friend behind my back. How was I suppose to feel about that? Dorian had a problem, Ralph. She was my friend, I couldn't be with her when she needed someone who was strong and supportive to see her through the difficult times. Why couldn't you just be there for her as a friend. I trusted you and you betrayed both Dorian and me in the worst way, why?" she said a crease in her brow.

Ralph sighed, looking helpless. "I'm not sure where to begin." Why don't you just start at the beginning, when you stared sleeping with Dorian, Rayanne thought. That would be a good place, since he wanted to clear the air. "I don't know, call it crazy or stupid or whatever you want," Ralph started out, "but I thought I did what I did for good reasons." He lifted a hand in protest when Rayanne was about to comment. "Please, let me get through this. When I said I thought I did what I did for good reasons, I meant it. The first night Dorian came over, she was really messed up. She'd learned that Henry wasn't getting a divorce, he wasn't going to marry her or continue to take care of her."

Rayanne interrupted saying, "Dorian didn't need anyone taking care of her. She had more money than she could spend in two life times."

Ralph sat silently until he was sure Rayanne was going to allow him to continue. "When Dorian came to me, she felt that everyone had abandoned her. She was a basket case." Ralph wanted to make sure he choose his words correctly, "I talked with her", he paused. "I promised her I would stand by her, that I wouldn't abandon her."

"Well, something must have changed your mind," Rayanne sneered.

"That night," Ralph continued as though she hadn't spoken. "I held her in my arms until she fell asleep. Rayanne, I too was very vulnerable at that time. I was lonely, I missed you too. I had built my life around you and when you left, I had no idea I had depended on you as much as I obviously did, because I was lost and I, too, felt abandoned. You have to remember, when you came back here to live, your parents weren't in desperate need of you. Sure they wanted you with them, but it was your decision to come back here to live. I guess I saw that as abandonment too. You and I were always the loving couple, and when you left, it put me in a tail spin. There was no discussion between us. You didn't ask me how I felt about your decision. You just decided to move and bam, you told me," Ralph said. So, what Ralph was saying was that he and Dorian comforted each other, Rayanne thought. Ralph sat in silence.

When Rayanne spoke, she said, "Did you stop to think what this would do to all of us?" Although she'd already heard more than she wanted to, since they'd started to talk, they might as well not just scratch the surface. This time, they would break it. "Go on, tell me every gory detail. Let me hear it all."

"Well when it got to be too late for her to go home, I offered her my bed for the night. She asked me to just stay with her until she was asleep." He lifted his hands. "I did and I suppose I must have dozed off. Anyway Dorian woke up during the night, and she was crying again. I tried to comfort her, then all of a sudden she was kissing me. It wasn't as though I was in love with her, or she with me, for that matter. You know me, Rayanne, I'm not in to white chicks."

"And, I suppose that makes it okay," Rayanne said," as long as the woman happens to be white, you can screw as many of them as you want and that makes it okay, because you are not in to white chicks."

"No, it doesn't, but I'm hoping that once you see where I'm coming from and have had a chance to process it, maybe you'll understand how it all happened."

"I wish I could understand."

"Are you still that angry at me after all this time," Ralph asked, a crease now in his brow.

"I should be," Rayanne responded.

"But you're not?" he pressed.

"No, I'm not angry at you anymore, but I...," she began, but Ralph interrupted.

"No buts. If you're not mad at me anymore, that makes it easier."

"I don't know whether it is or not. A person can't go around being angry about anything forever. It takes too much energy." Besides, what good would it do to waste her time and energy being angry about something she couldn't do a damn thing about, she thought.

"You don't hate me, do you?"

"On the contrary, Ralph. I love you and perhaps, I always will, but..."

Ralph interrupted again. "What are you saying. You're in love with me, but you don't want me in your life?"

"No, I'm not in love with you Ralph."

"I thought you just said you loved me."

"I did and I do, but there's a difference in loving you and being in love with you, and we'll just have to live with that difference, but it really doesn't matter."

"You're holding this against me."

"No, not any more, but the situation did tell me something about you. So, if you're trying to bring back some yesteryear for us, you should make a conscious effort to forget it and get on with your life."

"Is there someone in your life. Is that why you're being so hard on me," he asked.

"What difference does that make?"

"It makes a lot of difference. I don't want to beat a dead horse. If you have someone, I don't want to intrude further," he paused, "if you don't want me to. I mainly wanted you to hear my side of the story and to see if there is anything left between us."

"For a time, my life was pointless and empty, with one thing happening right after the other. But," she smiled, "there has been the one constant in my life that's brought me nothing but joy, uncomplicated, unconditional joy." Ralph looked at Rayanne. "Swan," Rayanne answered the question that hung on his lips, but he didn't ask.

"She's a wonderful little girl, but you're a vital women, and you need more. Children play a big part in our lives, but a woman like you needs a man."

"What I'm saying is that my life has purpose, it is filled with purpose." Rayanne smiled. "Swan is quite special and a word of warning, to know her is to love her. She's destined to steal your heart, she'll capture it completely. She's just that sweet." Rayanne continued to smile.

But her smile soon faded when Ralph said, "She was going to commit suicide."

"What?" Rayanne stared at Ralph, grasping his meaning, "Suicide?"

"None of this would've happened had I not seen the state she was in. I saw it in her eyes. Dorian needed help, she was desperate, and I believe with everything in me, that she would've killed herself had I not been there. It was a delicate situation, and I dealt with it the only way I knew how at the time. Rayanne, I knew Dorian long before I met you and I was never interested in her, not that way. I don't feel good about what I did. Had the situation been different, if there were any other alternatives." Ralph appeared to be struggling with himself for the first time, and Rayanne felt a pang of sympathy for him. She knew Dorian had become over wrought, but she didn't realize Dorian was at the point of wanting to take her own life. It must've been awful for Ralph, being caught like that. And, Dorian, Rayanne wished she could've been there for her. Ralph looked at Rayanne and was surprised as she extended her hand across the table to him. He took it in his and looked at it, then he looked at her. "I'm sorry," he said.

"So am I."

"Please believe me, baby. She would have killed herself." Rayanne didn't answer, but her eyes appear to convey understanding. After a moment's silence, Ralph said, "I enjoyed being here with you last night."

"So did I," Rayanne admitted and she meant it. Although one incident ripped their relationship to threads, it looked as though they were mending fences.

"This is asking a lot," Ralph began, "but I'd like to hear you say you understand. I can promise you if you say you do, I'll never do anything to disappoint you again." Rayanne got up from the table and was about to go to him, but suddenly the door bust opened, and Swan rushed in carrying a candy apple in one hand

and a stuffed teddy bear in the other. She ran directly into Rayanne's arms.

"Hey, Aunt Rayanne."

"Hey yourself," Rayanne said scooping Swan up into her arms, "how is my little girl."

"I'm fine."

"So what have we got here?" Rayanne asked, observing the goodies Swan held in her arms.

"I won this teddy bear, it's for you."

"For me? Oh honey, he's fantastic. Thank you," Rayanne said smiling at Swan and taking the bear from her extended hands. "I will take this present under one condition"

"What condition?" Swan asked.

"You will have to take care of Mr. Bear for me. Deal?"

"Deal," Swan said with a twinkle in her eyes. Rayanne handed the teddy bear back to her.

"And the candy apple is for me," Swan said and looking at Ralph, she said, "but you can have it, Mr. Underwood, if you want it."

"That's very generous of you, but no, thanks," he said, smiling at her.

Maxine poked her head through the door. "Hi, you two." Rayanne and Ralph greeted her. "I've got Marcia Raylyn and her friend waiting in the car. We're picking up a few things for the slumber party tonight."

"Ahhh, a slumber party," Rayanne said.

"Yes, and I was invited," Swan put in.

"You were," Rayanne said, putting her down.

"Yes," Swan said, "Marcia Raylyn wants me to be there. Can I go?"

"May I go," Rayanne corrected and said, "Yes you may go, but first, we're going to give you a nice bath and put you down for a little nap." After Maxine stated she'd pick Swan up in a couple of hours, she left, calling over her shoulder, "nice seeing you again, Ralph. Have fun you two," she winked at Ralph and left.

Rayanne sent Swan off to the bathroom. "Get up on your little stool and brush your teeth. Get the ones in the back real good too, okay? I'll come in and checked them in a minute and give you that bath," Rayanne said, taking the teddy bear and candy from Swan's hands. "I'll put these away for you."

"Okay".

"Now, go brush them teeth good".

"I will brush them real good, because if I don't brush my teeth and get them nice and clean, I'll get cavities and my teeth will fall out, right?" Swan said, turning her face up questioningly to Rayanne.

"That's right, now scoot. I'll be there in a minute all right."

"Okay," Swan said running off to the bathroom. Then she dragged her little stool up to the front of the sink in the bathroom, put toothpaste on her toothbrush and began to brush.

"She's quite a little girl," Ralph said to Rayanne.

"Yes, she is the best."

CHAPTER 45

Rayanne was surprised, when after she'd avoided talking with Scott the past two days, that he was the first person she saw when she and Ralph entered the club. She could hear the words of an earlier conversation she'd had with him, echoing in her brain. "Rayanne, you need to make a clean break from that man. I'm telling you, he isn't what you think he is. Get rid of him and get on with your life," Scott had said. Rayanne had told him that she wanted to get on with her life, but with Ralph. "What kind of life do you expect to have with a man who has screwed your best friend?" Scott had asked.

"Not my best friends," Rayanne said, "a friend." She thought about it. "Well, one of my best friends," she finally said because from the time she'd known Dorian, she had considered her a friend and as time passed, Dorian had become one of her best friends, and there was no denying that now. However, Rayanne still had not read a single one of Dorian's letters nor had she tried contacting her.

"A small technicality," Scott muttered more to himself than to her.

"Scott, I know you mean well, you're only trying to help," Rayanne said, "but I think Ralph and I are going to be able to work through this and have a life together." Ralph had confessed that he'd made a mistake, but he explained how the situation occurred between he and Dorian, and she could understand how something

348

like that could happen. "He's promised never to be unfaithful again," she said.

"And you believe him?" Scott asked, disbelieving. "You can't be that naive."

"The man made a mistake," Rayanne had said. "After all, he is human. So if I can forgive him and move on with my life, you should be able to." Scott had been hurt when Rayanne told him that it was her life and if she was making a mistake, then she'd be the one who'd suffer, not he, that she'd only really been in love once and that was with Ralph. Love was important to her. It was essential, like air and water and, to her, Ralph was important, too. Scott wasn't happy, but he agreed to back off and trust her to make the right decision.

Rayanne and Ralph found a table near the center of the room. Ralph ordered a glass of tonic water for Rayanne, and he enjoyed a scotch on the rocks, while listening to a jazz set. They'd stay through one more set and go home early because they were taking Swan to the beach the following day. As they were getting up to dance, Scott approached the table. "How are you, Scott?" Rayanne said and looked from him to Ralph. "You remember Ralph, don't you?" The two men shook hands and exchanged greetings. Rayanne heard Ralph mentioned something to Scott about a basketball game before she excused herself to go powder her nose. She knew the Knicks weren't playing that night, therefore, she wasn't interested in what else might be going on in the NBA. There wasn't much going on in the club that night. The band, although mediocre at best, was on intermission and the room was quiet, almost still. Rayanne had only been gone a few minutes, but when she returned, she could hear Scott and Ralph talking in low voices. Scott's face held a half smile that was tight and strained. What is he up to now, she thought and couldn't help wondering what was going on between them. For grown men, at times, she thought, the two of them certainly did act like little boys. She walked away from the table and up to the bar to speak to someone she knew. When she looked in the direction of the two men, her attention was divided. As she observed Ralph and Scott, she was suddenly aware of her attraction by the strength and good looks of the one man, and the sophistication, maturity and sometimes devil may care attitude, of the other. Her stolen glances and secret thoughts were divided as well, but for reasons she didn't understand. She felt a growing tension across her shoulders. Ralph was a man whom she hadn't had an emotional commitment with for some time, and

Scott was just a friend. Why, then, was she feeling the urgency to get Ralph out of the club and away from Scott. Rayanne returned to the table, and after finishing their drinks, she and Ralph left, but not before he placed a big juicy kiss on her lips. When they were in the car, Rayanne asked, "what were you and Scott talking about?"

"Would you believe that son of a bitch threatened me?" Ralph said, yanking the car in gear and speeding off.

"Threatened you? Scott?" she asked disbelieving. She knew Scott didn't like Ralph, but threatened him?

"Don't give me that surprised look," Ralph spat out. "You know the guy is in love with you. I've known it all along. I don't know why you don't see it." She hadn't seen it because there wasn't anything to see.

"Scott is just a good friend. He cares about me," she sighed. "He thinks of me as a big sister, that's all."

"I gotcha big sister. I'd never think of doing with my sister what Scott thinks of doing with you," Ralph charged, while gripping the steering wheel with both hands.

"You don't have a sister," Rayanne said as her mind returned to Scott and she remembered with a touch of sadness, the look she caught on his face when she looked at him as they were leaving the club.

"Well, if I did," Ralph whined, interrupting Rayanne's thoughts, "I wouldn't."

"Ralph, what are you talking about?"

"I'm talking about that joker back there. The way he was staring at you, practically drooling all over himself."

"You're being silly."

"I don't trust him, I know that."

"What exactly did Scott say to you," she asked.

"Too much," Ralph hissed.

"Well, don't think about it. Let's just get home." Rayanne rested her head back against the seat and not wanting to get into an argument with Ralph. She looked sharply at him, when he ran a red light, but she didn't comment. They rode the rest of the way in silence, except on occasions, Ralph mumbled something under his breath. Rayanne knew that whatever Scott had said to him had really pissed him off, and he was still simmering as a result.

There was a message on her answering machine from Brenda. Rayanne tried to reach her but got her machine instead. She said goodnight to Ralph after letting him know that she'd made up the bedroom across the hall for him. She needed time to herself, she wanted solitude and as she lay there in the dark silence with only an occasional vehicle passing in the night, she began to process Ralph and her earl.ɔ̃ conversation. When she'd gotten the solitude she thought she wanted, she was vexed. She didn't like it, and she ground her teeth in annoyance. Rayanne wasn't sure how long she lay in bed alone before she heard the shower when it stopped in the hall bathroom. She was staring out of her bedroom window at the light on the pole. She pulled the covers up around her neck, closed her eyes and turned over in bed. Unable to sleep, she turned onto her back and opened her eyes. That was when she saw Ralph's silhouette on the threshold. He was just standing there, but she knew from past experience that he was completely naked. "What are you doing here?" She asked.

"I didn't like camping out over there by myself while you're here in that king size bed alone," he replied.

"I think it builds character in a man when he has to do something that his heart isn't in."

"That's not the point. The point is you're here, and we can't put this relationship back together with all this distance between us," Ralph said spreading his arms around the room. "If you're here, I should be, too." Rayanne didn't respond. "It's going to take both of us to rebuild this relationship. We have to work together." As he spoke, he moved closer to her bed. "Right here is the place called hope. We can take this time to reflect, think about what we had, the wonderful times we've shared and how happy we made each other. Rayanne, we've always been magic together. When we made love, we shared each other's heart, soul and mind. It's important for me to find out what we have left. I want to know what you're thinking, what you're feeling." Ralph paused. "I need to know where I stand with you, and I think we should look at this thing and decide what we're going to do about it tonight," he paused again, "or we should close the door on this forever." Rayanne still didn't respond. Ralph went on, "You mean everything to me. I know I'm the one who fucked up. I know that. It's all my fault, and I take full responsibility, but I can't go on like this. I can't pay forever, so tell me Rayanne, what is it going to be?" Ralph stood still. Rayanne continued to look at him, but she didn't speak. Ralph sat on the side of the bed, and stared down at her.

"Ralph," Rayanne began, slowly.

"Don't give me a lecture, baby," he said, "just kiss me and let's hold each other and remember the times when we meant everything to each other." He lay across the bed and at first, he just touched her hand. Then he caressed her arm. He raised up on his elbow and kissed her gently on the lips. She didn't move away nor did she push him away. The kiss grew passionate, and she could feel the warm moistness between her legs. After all he'd put her through, he still had a powerful effect on her. "It's been a long time," he whispered when the kiss ended. Too long, she thought. "Do you still love me?" he asked softly. "Do you, baby?"

"I don't want to talk anymore tonight," was all Rayanne could say.

Ralph kissed her mouth, her eyes, her throat and his lips moved to her breasts. When his kisses returned to her cheek, he tasted the moist saltiness. "Baby, you're crying. Why are you crying?"

"I don't know, confusion maybe". She paused a moment. Then she said, "Yes, I'm confused, very confused."

"But are you happy that we are at least here together?"

Rayanne thought for a moment as she stared up at the ceiling she said, "yes, I'm happy. I'm so happy." There wasn't much else that she had, but she knew that love and happiness were both fleeting. She also knew that sometimes people were happier when they had fewer choices. And, when they made love that night, she gave herself to him completely, and without reservation. She wanted to trust Ralph again. She wanted to believe in him and the promises he'd made to her. People did different things for different reasons and she hoped that when she decided never to see Ralph again but had since changed her mind, that she had not committed some act of injustice against herself. If she did, however, she'd suffer it later, much later, because at that moment, she had only one thought in mind, and that was to be happy, and happiness was a long time coming.

"I get crazy when I think what we nearly gave up, what we almost lost," Ralph said afterwards, holding Rayanne. When she'd agreed to let Ralph come visit that weekend, she thought they'd spend an evening together reminiscing, but instead, they'd done much more than that. They'd created another wonderful memory. One that would be with them forever.

The following day, Rayanne got up early, went to the cemetery where her parents were buried and she put flowers on both graves. She kneeled on the ground between the graves and she talked to both of her parents. She told them that everyone was well, including Josh, she mentioned Ralph's visit and at the end, she told her parents she loved them and missed them. Then she said, as tears rolled down her face, " Mama, please forgive me". She got up, brushed the tears from her face, and she drove home.

At 9:45, after Swan arrived, the three of them went to the beach, played in the water and walked along the beach hand in hand. Later, Ralph and Rayanne beamed into each other's eyes, as they sat across the table from each other, eating hot dogs. Rayanne smiled that angelic halting smile at him, and he smiled back, thinking how that smile still embraced him like the sun on a summer's day. They'd spent one of the most gloriously incredible days together and as they drove home, it was a consensus between Rayanne and Ralph that they were moving in the right direction, they were getting closer to each others heart which was their goal.

CHAPTER 46

Sometime in the early morning, just before the sun came up, Rayanne sat at the kitchen table, sipping from a cup of coffee. She rubbed her head to ease the headache that she felt coming on. She didn't get much sleep the night before after returning from the Neighborhood Watch meeting. There had been more robberies and drugs in the community than ever and they were going to put an end to it. They were moving the program along, a plan was underway, and wouldn't you believe Aunt Bessie was elected Vice President of the Neighborhood Watch Program.

In another five minutes, Rayanne would leave to pick up Brenda and they'd head to the hospital. When Brenda had a checkup three weeks ago, the results weren't as they'd been on previous visits. Her mammogram was normal, but during the examination, tumors were found in her uterus and she decided on surgery after having had a lot of female problems and had gotten a second opinion. Brenda's surgery was schedule for 8:30 that Friday morning, and Rayanne arrived at her home at 6:15. Brenda's mother was taking the boys to her home, while Brenda recuperated. After promising Brenda's mother that she'd look after her daughter, Rayanne drove Brenda to the hospital.

Rayanne laid down the newspaper that she'd tried, without success, to read and she looked around at the others who occupied the 3rd floor Waiting Room, awaiting word from a doctor on someone's condition. She got up, walked to the window and looked out. It had begun to rain. She watched for some time, the traffic, moving up and down the street. An hour later, she was thirsty, and she wandered out into the corridor where she saw a water fountain she walked over to it, and took a drink before returning to the Waiting Room. It wasn't long before someone asked, "Is there someone here regarding Brenda Robinson?" Rayanne looked up to see a doctor standing in the doorway.

"I'm here about Brenda Robinson," a man, who appeared to be in his late 30's, early 40's, 5 feet, 11 inches, declared. The medium brown skinned man with short black hair, was wearing jeans and a plaid shirt, shot up to the doctor. "I'm her husband, Cardell Robinson," he said, his hands at his side.

Rayanne approached the two men. "I'm Rayanne Wilson, a friend of Brenda Robinson." Cardell nodded at her, then they turned their attention to the doctor.

"Mrs. Robinson is resting comfortably. We removed three tumors from her uterus and a cyst from one of her ovaries. Her ovaries are intact," the doctor said and answered the question that appeared to form in the crease of Rayanne's forehead. "She came through surgery very well, and she'll be put in a room in an hour or so."

"Thank you, doctor," both, Cardell and Rayanne said.

"You're welcome," he said. "The two of you might want to grab a bite to eat since Mrs. Robinson won't be put into a room for a while yet. There's a cafeteria downstairs. The food is not the best, but it's edible." The doctor smiled. Rayanne and Cardell thanked him again, and they went to have something to eat in the hospital cafeteria and as far as she could tell, Cardell was a sensitive, caring guy. He'd learned about Brenda's surgery from his sons. When he talked with Brenda only two weeks before, she hadn't said a word about the surgery. Everything happened so quickly, Rayanne explained, adding that it was a struggle just getting Brenda to see a doctor.

"She spent days preparing herself and the boys. I think she wanted to spare you," Rayanne said.

"Brenda and I have had our differences, but I care about her. I don't know why she'd want to deal with this alone," Cardell said and Rayanne could tell that he'd be around for a while. After Brenda was in her room and Rayanne was satisfied that she was all right, she left Brenda and Cardell alone, and she drove back home, with the intention of returning later to spend the night.

Rayanne arrived as Mrs. Marshall was vacuuming and they

waved to each other through the window. Swan was sitting at the table coloring and when Rayanne enter the house, she climbed down from the chair and rushed to Rayanne. "Aunt Rayanne, you are home."

"Yes, I am. How are you." Rayanne threw her purse to a chair, picked Swan up and carried her to a chair. Rayanne sat with Swan in her lap. "Did you have a good day?"

"Yes. Becky and I were partners, and we drew a picture at school today," Swan shared.

"You did? What kind of picture?" Rayanne asked, looking into that precious little face.

"A tree and some birds."

"A tree and some birds, huh?"

"Yes, and they are very pretty."

"I bet they are. What colors did you and Becky use?"

"Well, the tree is brown with green leaves, and the birds are red."

"Oh, red birds," Rayanne said, "how nice."

"Becky wanted to make them blue, but I told her the blue birds are boring."

Rayanne laughed a little and said, "What makes you think blue birds are boring?"

"Because when we colored one bird blue, it looked awful in the green leaves, but when we colored one red, it looked great," Swan said, "so we made them all red." Rayanne laughed again. "What's wrong, Aunt Rayanne. Why are you laughing?"

"I was just thinking that your picture must look a little like a Christmas tree."

"No, Aunt Rayanne, it just looks like a tree with green leaves and red birds," Swan said, looking so serious that Rayanne had to apologize and assured her that she wasn't making fun of the picture. Swan smiled.

"Well, when will I get to see this picture?"

"We get to bring it home next week," Swan said and stuck her finger into her mouth. Rayanne pulled Swan's finger out of her mouth, sat back in the chair and wrapped her arms around her. She'd missed Swan and told her so. "I missed you, too," Swan said and hugged Rayanne's neck. When she pulled away, she asked, "were you at the hospital with Mrs. Robinson?"

"Yes," Rayanne answered and brushed back the unruly sandy curls that had pulled away and dangled about Swan's forehead, from ponytails that were neat prior to Swan having spent several hours at the daycare. "She asked me to say hello to you."

"Tell her I said hello too. Is Mrs. Robinson feeling better now?" Swan questioned.

"Yes, all the bad things that were making Mrs. Robinson sick are now gone, and she is going to be as good as new very soon."

"Are you going back to the hospital today?"

"Yes, I promised Mrs. Robinson that I would come back to see her tonight," Rayanne paused a moment before saying, "if that's okay with you."

Swan looked up into Rayanne's eyes. "It's okay." She said and hugged Rayanne's neck tightly again.

"Are you sure?"

"Yes," Swan replied still clinging to Rayanne's neck.

"Then what is it, baby? What's wrong?"

"Aunt Rayanne, I don't want you to ever get sick."

"Honey, honey, I won't. Look at me," Rayanne said loosing the grip the child had around her neck, "look at me, sweetheart. I'm fine. Your aunt Rayanne is as healthy as a horse." Swan looked up into Rayanne's eyes blinking as she explained that she wasn't going to get sick. "That's why it's important to go to the doctor and get checkups often to make sure that you don't get sick, or if you get sick and the doctor knows soon enough, then he can make you better. So you don't have to worry your pretty little head about that, okay?" With that, Swan appeared to be all right again. Then she informed Rayanne of some new games they'd played in school and the new words she'd learned.

"And, I write my name, this many times," Swan said, putting ten fingers up, then she stuck her two index fingers into her mouth.

"You wrote your name," Rayanne corrected, she removed Swan's fingers from her mouth and touched Swan on her nose with a finger.

"I wrote my name, and I learned how to spell wagon, that's, 'w-a-g-o- n,' wagon, and smile, that's, 's-m-i-l-e,' smile."

"That's very good," Rayanne complimented. "It sounds like you had a very productive day."

"Oh," Swan said sliding down from Rayanne's lap, "my daddy wrote," she tested the word, 'wrote' "to me today."

"He did. Well, go get it and let's see what he had to say," Rayanne said, and Swan dashed to the kitchen and returned with all of the mail. Rayanne read the letter to Swan, pointing to every word in the letter, especially where Jeremy told Swan he loved her.

Jeremy had been promoted. He liked it in the Air Force, and

although it was early in his career, he'd said he was going to make a career of it. Always when Rayanne finished reading one of Jeremy's letters to Swan, she'd fold it and give it to Swan. "Go put it with the others," Rayanne said and Swan dashed off with the letter in hand. Rayanne could see Swan's excitement to know that her father would be coming home soon to see her. It was obvious that she loved her daddy very much and for such a little girl, she certainly had a lot of love inside of her, and she spread it around generously. Swan was a busy little girl, taking dance lessons, and Rayanne smiled at the thought of how cute she looked in her little leotard. She was giving Swan piano lessons, and she almost had chopstick down. Swan was singing on the Sunbeam Choir at church and going to school at daycare. She was doing lots of things, growing and learning daily. The vacuum cleaner stopped. Mrs. Marshall entered the den. "Mrs. Marshall, how is it going?"

"Everything is fine. Your Aunt Bessie called. She wants to talk with you about something, she said," Mrs. Marshall informed.

"Okay, thanks. I'll give her a call," Rayanne said and Mrs. Marshall resumed her work. "So young lady, what would you like to do today?" Rayanne said to Swan.

"I want to play on the swing," Swan said. She had a full playground there in her own back yard, a combination swing and slide set, a trampoline, sandbox and other play things that completed the playground. It was a child's paradise.

"All right. Let me go get changed."

"May I call some of my friends?" Swan asked.

"Of course. "Do you remember their phone numbers?"

Swan made a face and said, "Some of them."

"Okay, we'll call them when I get back," Rayanne said and went of to her room, when suddenly, there was the sound of thunder. She slip into a pair of jeans and a blouse and returned to the kitchen to find Swan standing at the solid glass door, staring out. As Rayanne entered the room, Swan turned and said very sadly, "it's raining and none of my friends will come out to play."

"Oh, honey. I'm so sorry," Rayanne said, kneeling down beside Swan. "Would you like to do something inside. We could go out and get a couple of movies and pop some popcorn. It would be just like going to a real movie."

"But I want to go outside and play," Swan said, her eyes brimming with tears.

"I know, Sweetheart, but it's raining and if you go outside now, you'd get all wet and catch a cold," Rayanne soothed. "You don't want to get sick, do you?"

"I don't care if I get sick," Swan said, wiping her tears away with the back of her hand.

"Yes you do. Why don't I read you a story," Rayanne said. "Would you like that?"

"I want to go outside and play with my friends," Swan said, and Rayanne became perplexed. She couldn't think, she was tired, and her brain wasn't working very well. She wondered what could she do that would make Swan happy. Lately, and not because she'd neglected the child, but because of other commitments, she hadn't spent as much time with Swan as she'd wanted, and, she felt guilty. Swan deserved much more than she'd gotten lately and Rayanne wanted to make it up to her.

She got up from the floor, went into her bedroom and when she returned, Swan was still standing at the door, staring out, her tiny face pressed against the glass. Rayanne kneeled beside her again and ran her hand across Swan's back. Swan looked at her, eyes moistened with tears, and she looked outside again. After a short while, the doorbell rang. Mrs. Marshall answered it and instantly, there was the patter of little feet, racing across the kitchen floor. One of the neighbors had brought her twins and another little girl over to play with Swan. The girls squealed with delight at seeing each other. The twins brought with them, a couple of their favorite movies, and they rushed off to put a tape into the VCR. Soon, the girls were settled in front of the set, where they spent the next couple of hours watching Bugs Bunny, Barney and Friends, and Beauty and the Beast, eating popcorn and having soft drinks that Rayanne served them.

CHAPTER 47

Rayanne arrived at the hospital at 7:30 that evening, as Brenda's mother and her sons were preparing to leave. Afterwards, Brenda, drifting in and out of sleep, and she told Rayanne about Cardell's visit. She awoke later during the night, laughing. When Rayanne asked what was so funny, she explained that many years ago, one of her sisters had the same surgery and when they told the children the reason for the surgery, her youngest son said he hoped he'd never have to have any tumors removed from his uterus. Rayanne chuckled softly as Brenda drifted off to sleep again.

Cardell came in shortly after 9 O'clock that evening. A nurse was checking Brenda's temperature and afterwards, she changed the bag of liquid that was connected to Brenda's hand. Cardell asserted that he'd be spending the night with Brenda, Rayanne took the cue and left but agreed to spend the remainder of the night at Brenda's apartment, rather than drive back home. She felt a warm tingling feeling when she saw the look Brenda and Cardell shared as she left the room.

After another night with very little sleep, Rayanne was awaken at 6:35, to a morning that was gloomy. It would be one of those days, because as she remembered, her day got worst. The door-bell rang, she answered it, and the young man who stood there identified himself as Jason, which Rayanne didn't doubt for a second, since she'd seen pictures Brenda had of him. She was sur-prise to see him there and wondered at the reason for his visit, in view of what Brenda had told them. "I'd like to see Brenda," the young man said.

"I'm sorry, but she can't see you right now," Rayanne said.

"Why don't you let Brenda be the judge of that," Jason said, his chest standing out, looking cool and confident.

"I'm sorry, what did you say your name was?" she asked, pretending not to remember, just to bring him down a peg or two.

"Jason," he responded, and she could tell he was a little put out. He looked as though the audacity that any woman could forget his name once he said it, was more than he could fathom. He thought it would forever be implanted in her brain.

"Jason, why don't you call her in a few days," Rayanne said.

"Why don't you march your fine behind in there and tell her I'm here," Jason came back and Rayanne was wondering what was it going to take to get through to him.

"We're going around in circles here, so listen to me. Brenda is not available so why don't you give her a call in a couple of days."

"Who are you? Her maid?" Jason said, forcing his way into the apartment. "Brenda," he called out, heading toward her bedroom. Brenda had shared with Rayanne and Hilary the intimate early morning rendezvous that took place between her and Jason, but Rayanne thought that was over, but, if that was the case, why was Jason there, demanding to see her.

"Brenda is not here," Rayanne called after Jason.

When he returned, he asked, "Where is she?"

"She's away for a few days."

"Where is she?" he questioned, staring her in the eyes.

"If Brenda wanted you to know where she was, I believe she would've told you" Rayanne shot back.

"When will she be back?" he asked, looking confused.

"In a few days."

"Then I'll be back." Jason flashed her a smile.

"You do that," Rayanne mumbled, going toward the door, hoping he would follow.

He did, but he said, "You got a problem with that?"

"No I don't got a problem with that," Rayanne was sarcastic. She wondered why Jason wanted to see Brenda now, why the urgency? It'd been several weeks since Brenda had seen him, and her disappointment at not hearing from him before going into the hospital was evident. Rayanne eyed Jason suspiciously and he noticed it.

"Why are you looking at me that way?"

"Brenda is a sweet girl," Rayanne began after a moment, "she acts tough, but she's as nice as can be and she allows people she cares about to take advantage of her. Brenda doesn't like being alone. She's looking for an emotional investment and I believe once she thought she'd found that in you. Apparently you wanted no part of that." Rayanne knew Brenda liked having a man around, but it was clear when the going got tough, Jason got lost.

"And you," he asked.

"Huh?" Rayanne said with a frown on her face.

"What do you like?"

Rayanne became pissed with the man. He was the most insensitive, arrogant, idiot she'd had the misfortune of dealing with. "We're not talking about me," she said.

"I just bet you're not afraid of being alone, or anything else, are you?"

"No, I like to face my obstacles head on. It's better that way," Rayanne said, her annoyance showing.

"I like a woman who isn't afraid of anything. It's a real turn on, and you are a beauty to boot."

"And, you're disgusting."

"Aaah, and sometimes beauty is the beast," he said, giving Rayanne a sexy stare and thinking this gal has got spunk. "Look," he said jamming his hands into his pockets, "I've got to get going. Let Brenda know I stopped by." Jason stood face to face with Rayanne, looking down at her and she could see, physically, why Brenda might be attracted to him. He was handsome and he had a great body, but he was as selfish as hell. When they reached the door, Jason turned to Rayanne. "What is your name?"

"Rayanne Wilson," She answered and stared coldly at him.

"Look Rayanne Wilson, I don't know what you think I did that makes you despise me so, but you might be wrong about me. I'm an all right guy. Maybe you're not giving me enough credit."

"Maybe you're expecting too much credit." Brenda deserved so much better than what he was offering. Brenda was many things to many people, and she was really good to Jason because she cared a lot about him and Rayanne told him so. "Brenda cared a lot about you, and you abused it. When you abuse my friends, I take exception to it. Some of you men don't seem to realized that a woman's love is a privilege, and not your right," Rayanne scold.

"Brenda knows how I feel about her," he began. But did he ever tell her, Rayanne wondered.

"Women want to be told and shown how her man feels about

her. Women don't want to have to guess at it. I just know that when she needed you, you weren't there, and it hurt her a lot."

"Maybe I should've open up more to her."

"Perhaps you should have."

"I'm not good at this love thing. I care about her, she's good people, but beyond that, I don't know. I mean, she's got kids almost as old as I am."

"What difference does that make? I'm certain you knew all that before you got involved with her."

"Yes, I did and as I said, Brenda is good people." Jason considered a moment before asking, "Do you think she still cares for me?"

"I'm the wrong person to ask," she said and looked toward the door.

"I think I came here today for all the right reasons, you know," he said.

"Really," was all Rayanne said. Her immediate impulse was to tell him to shut up and get out. Jason talked a really good game, Rayanne remembered Brenda saying some months back. She'd said that Jason could be a real sweet talker, a conniving liar, and he ran games on women all the time.

"I think I can make it up to her," Jason was saying. "I know I can make her understand how I feel. I'm the best thing that she's ever had. She's told me as much." He certainly doesn't over sell himself, Rayanne thought sarcastically. "Look, Brenda and I have had our ups and downs, and I got tired of her demands," Jason said and Rayanne thought he had a real conclusive way of showing how tired he was. Jason explain that he and Brenda were strong willed, they liked having their own way and it was difficult reaching a compromise. "But we had a good thing going there for a while," he said with Rayanne thinking, right up until he thought she had some life threatening problem. "So, she'll be back in a couple of days?" Jason asked, and gone was that silly, but handsome smile. He was serious then, but maybe it was too late. More than anything Rayanne wanted to tell Jason that he shouldn't cause problems in Brenda's life if he couldn't be the cure. "Let Brenda know I was by," he said again.

"I'll do that," she said curtly. Jason stared at Rayanne, turned on his heels and left, slamming the door behind him. Rayanne thought all Jason really had to do was be there for Brenda and be supportive, but he hadn't, so it was a mute point, and the only thing that Rayanne could think about Jason as he left was what a balless wonder he was.

CHAPTER 48

At daybreak on a cool South Carolina morning, Rayanne got up and sat on the side of her bed. Sometimes, she thought, the world passed right by her window, leaving her behind, but from her front porch, she was always able to put things in its right perspective, and it was those times when she was truly at peace. She and Ralph were together again as a couple and they were spending a lot of time together. She was happier than she'd been in years. They talked often by telephone, went on a recent cruise to Mexico and they did countless other things together. On one of Ralph's visits to South Carolina, he brought with him a three karat diamond ring, they were officially engaged and although the wedding date hadn't been set, they knew that nothing would stop them from walking down the aisle together this time. Her life had almost turned to perfection once again. There was only one thing that haunted her daily and that was the fact that her mother had died and hadn't forgiven her nor said she understood why Rayanne had Josh put into the rehab center. Rayanne remembered being hurt and disappointed about the argument she and her mother had only a couple of days before she died. It was leading up to Swan's 3rd birthday party when Ruth had fussed until she'd fallen into an exhausted sleep, but not before she tried to persuade Rayanne to drive to Florence, pick Josh up and bring him home where he belong. Ruth was aware that although Rayanne tried to see Josh and he continued to refuse her visits, she kept in touch with the doctors and knew of his condition at all times. He was getting the help he needed, but he was no where near being well enough to come home at that time. After such nights, Ruth would wake up the morning afterwards as though nothing had happened.

As she sat and thought, Rayanne wished she could talk with her mother, beg her forgiveness. When common sense took over and she knew that would never happen again, she asked God's forgiveness.

Brenda had recovered from surgery and had returned to work. After graduation, they all were busy, but when time permitted, they got together for dinner, an evening out or enjoyed a card game in one of their homes. Brenda was still selling houses, dating every chance she got and still maxing out her credit cards like there was no tomorrow, but there wasn't any talk about Jason, or Cardell for that matter. Rayanne didn't know whether Jason had told Brenda of their conversation, she just knew she hadn't.

Swan was four years old on Friday, and on Saturday, Rayanne invited family and friends over for the celebration. The party was set up in the huge indoor play room that had been added for Swan and which extended off from the den. While the kids enjoyed the party, Rayanne tried her speech out on the adults present, and she received constructive criticism, but as a whole, they thought she'd done a good job.

After everyone had left and Rayanne had listened while Swan read one of the books she received, they climbed into bed and talked and just before being tucked in for the night, Rayanne listened as Swan said her prayers. "Now I lay me down to sleep, I pray to God my soul to keep, if I should die before I wake, I pray to God my soul to take. God bless my dad and my mom, Grandma Mamie, Great Grandma Ruth and Great Granddad Raymond, who are in heaven with You, and please bless the rest of my family and friends, especially my friend, Becky and my aunt, Rayanne, Amen."

"Amen" Rayanne said and kissed Swan. She called Ralph and filled him in on the events of the day; the party, the dinner afterwards, the reaction she'd gotten to her speech, and the fact that he was sorely missed.

"I'm sorry I couldn't be there. Give that little lady my love and let her know I'm bringing her present when I come," Ralph said. Rayanne assured him that she'd pass that message along. So," Ralph said, "you tried out your speech on some friends?"

"Yes, and as I said, I got pretty good reviews, if you can call it that. They were kind."

"I'm sure you did just fine. Honey, you've got a great mind and you're a wonderful writer, so I'm sure the speech is great." Rayanne told him her writing of late has been anything but great, but she was happy with the way the speech had progressed.

"Oh, by the way," she explained, "the lake is completed, but it was quite a trick keeping Swan away from the back of the house while the work was being done." She'd hired a land developer to come in and remove some of the trees so that the lake was in full view from the back of the house. She gave strict instructions that all the dogwood and magnolia trees and some of the pine trees remained on the property, and an assortment of flowers were installed. Rayanne also planted some flowers, as her mother had done, that would create burst of colors all year. She had a deck built off of the den and a concrete patio in the back yard, that connected to the play room. A grill was built and grass ran the length from the patio to the lake. She had the back of the yard fenced in as a safety precaution for Swan, because she love the lake and Rayanne didn't want her to wander off there alone. Rayanne had also had a window seat with compartments installed in Swan's room for her dolls, books and all of the other things that she could put away and have easy access to.

"I'll bet it was," Ralph had said. "The questions must have gone on forever."

"Yes," Rayanne chuckled softly, "Aunt Rayanne, what's that noise, Aunt Rayanne, what's this, Aunt Rayanne, what's that." Rayanne and Ralph laughed.

"So what is my baby up to tonight?" Ralph asked.

"Just missing my baby," she replied. They talked about their wedding and the only problem was that Ralph wanted to continue to live in New York for a while after the wedding and Rayanne didn't want to leave South Carolina again. This was home for her and she wanted to keep it that way, but they loved each other and knew that they'd work something out, that with love, everything else prevailed.

After talking a half hour and before they hung up, Ralph had said he was going to turn in early, he was tired and he'd call her in the morning. When she hung up, she was happy and Ralph was happy, all her friends were happy. She'd even received a card from Dorian two weeks ago, stating she was glad that Rayanne was able to forgive Ralph and forget and was going on with her life. She apologized again and thanked Rayanne for being her friend. Rayanne put the card in the drawer with the other unopened letters that she received from Dorian. Everyone was happy for Rayanne and Ralph. That is everyone, except Scott. Rayanne remembered Scott saying, when she told him of their impending marriage and what their living arrangements would be for a while, that a husband's place was with his family, and his asking whether she was sure that was what she wanted. She assured him that Ralph was exactly what she wanted, and she thought she'd seen, in Scott's eyes, something that was beyond pain, and although she didn't quite understand what it was, that look returned whenever they discussed Ralph.

***

The sound of the doorbell interrupted her thoughts. She opened the door and Scott was there looking more handsome than ever. "Where's the birthday girl?" he asked after Rayanne stood back and allowed him to enter.

"She was asleep by the time her head hit the pillow. She had a full day, she enjoyed her party, and she told me to thank you for the present. She saved some birthday cake and ice cream for you, too," Rayanne said over her shoulder as she and Scott went into the den. Their relationship had advanced enormously. She and Scott weren't just good friends, they'd become soul mates.

"She did," Scott said smiling. "She's a great kid. I hope she liked her present."

"She did," Rayanne said and offered Scott some punch which he accepted and went and poured himself. She lay on the floor with a pillow that she took from the couch. "How's Donnie?" she asked when Scott was settled.

"He's fine. It's his mother who I'm worried about," Scott remarked and took a drink from his glass.

"You want to talk about it?" she asked.

"It's just plain stupid some of the things that women do, and that's putting it mildly."

"What is it, Scott? What's going on?" Rayanne asked. Frannie was back to telling Scott that he wasn't Donnie's father, which was nothing new, but it still totally pissed him off. She'd asked him to come over tonight, she wanted to talk, but when he got there, some guy was there. She introduced Scott as a friend, and the other guy as Donnie's father. That was crazy, Rayanne thought, but she asked,

367

"What happened?"

"Nothing. I was so damn mad that the only thing I could do was get the hell out of there, which I did as fast as I could. Rayanne, so help me, if I had stayed, somebody would've gotten hurt really bad," Scott said, scowling.

"Well, I'm glad you left because that wouldn't have accomplished a thing," Rayanne said, then she smiled, "besides what would I do if you got yourself into trouble?" Scott looked into Rayanne's eyes, then he took another sip from his glass. She watched him and wondered whether Frannie was telling the truth.

"I've got to admit," Scott said shaking his head, "there is a resemblance." And, as though he couldn't believe it, he said, "Donnie looks a lot like the guy. They could very easily be father and son."

"Scott, why don't you have a paternity test done. This way you'll know."

"Who am I kidding. I believe I knew even before Frannie started telling me that Donnie isn't mine." It was true, he'd been a little suspicious.

"Really? Gosh, I didn't know that. I'm so sorry."

"Don't Be. As they say, shit happens," he said, got up and walked toward the door to the hall, "can we just not talk about this tonight." Rayanne nodded her head okay. "What about a game of Bad Gammon or Scrabble. You decide and we'll play when I get back?"

"Scrabble," Rayanne said quickly, "but first, we'll have some cake and ice cream."

"Sounds good to me and watch me beat the pants off of you," he said.

"Promises, promises," she said, flirting with him.

"What?" he turned after hearing that comment. Scott was a whiz at the game and had beaten her many times, but when he saw that devious look on her face, he smiled, shook his head and walked down the hall to Swan's bedroom. He looked in on her, something he'd done from the time he first met Swan. He walked over to the bed, lifted Swan's arm and put it under the covers and kissed her on her forehead. "Happy Birthday, sweetheart," he whispered. "I love you." He returned to the den where Rayanne had cake and ice cream sitting on the coffee table. He picked up his saucer and spooned some into his mouth. "She's a wonderful little girl," Scott said.

"You get no fight from me," Rayanne agreed pushing ice cream into her mouth also. When they finished, Rayanne returned the saucers to the kitchen. Scott set up the board and waited for Rayanne to return. "Ralph and I decided to get married this Spring," she announced just as Scott sat on the floor facing her. He was silent. "Did you hear me?" Rayanne said, looking at him.

"Yeah."

"Well, what do you say?"

"Sounds like you already done made your mind up. What do you want me to say?"

"I want you to say that you're happy for me, for us, and that you want the best for Ralph and me. Scott, you're one of my best friends, and I know you want me to be happy. Well, Ralph does that for me. I'm very happy with him, and he is with me, and I'd like to know that we have your blessings." After a slight pause, Rayanne asked, "Why can't you be happy for me?" Scott wanted Rayanne to be happy, she was his best friend, but how could he tell her that he could see it happening all over again. He remembered how Ralph hurt her before. He was a self centered bastard who Scott thought put his own interests and needs ahead of hers. That son of a bitch had left her devastated before and for the life of him, he couldn't imagine that any man would do something like that to a woman like Rayanne.

"Baby, I just don't want you to get hurt," Scott began carefully. "Everything you've said about that guy, good or bad, I committed to memory and every time you mention his name, I replay it in my mind. Rayanne, I just don't know if he's the man for you."

"I know what you're thinking but Ralph and I have moved on, we're going on with our lives. I love him, Scott. I hope you understand."

"I can if you can. The man slept with your friend, he wanted to satisfy his own needs and I think he's capable of doing something like that again," Scott said looking at her. After a moment, he shook his head and said, "if you're sure you can live with what he did, than there's nothing I can do."

"There is more going on here than Ralph and my engagement, Scott. I think you're hurting because of what happened between you and Frannie tonight. I understand how you feel, and I'm sorry, but don't punish me. I'm here for you, and I want you to be here for me." She took a deep breath. "I care for Ralph and when you care for someone, you have to take some things on trust. Scott, you're very important to me. I want you in my life but the two of you have got to find a way to co-exist."

Scott listened to Rayanne, but he knew that a man like Ralph only cared about himself and what he wanted. He wasn't the type to commit totally to any one woman, and he told Rayanne so. "He's just not built that way."

Rayanne interrupted, shaking her head violently saying, "stop it, stop it right now. How can you say that. You don't even know Ralph."

"It don't take much to see through him. You could if you opened your eyes," he said.

"You're just not being fair. You're upset, and you're taking it out on me. You want to hurt me. It's not fair," Rayanne said, her feelings hurt. Why wouldn't Scott give Ralph a chance, she thought, twisting the large diamond on her finger. Ralph deserved a second chance.

"Rayanne, I do want you to be happy," Scott said to her honestly.

"If that is true, I want to hear you say it, and say it like you mean it."

"Okay," he said, staring at her, "I don't mean to be giving you no hard time. If Ralph is the man you want and he makes you happy, then you have my blessing." Scott tilted his head to the side.

Rayanne looked searchingly into his eyes. "Do you really mean that?"

"All I have ever wanted was for you to be happy, so if he does that for you, then I wish you two the best," he said, and Rayanne smiled. She knew that although Scott was miserable with the idea, he meant what he said. She leaned across the board and kissed him on his cheek. They resumed their game and Scott said, "I won't ever do that again."

"Do what?" Rayanne looked up from the board with a puzzled expression, but returned her eyes to the board. She was on the verge of beating this game and she didn't want to lose her concentration.

"Hurt you," he said. Rayanne looked into his eyes and held them as he said, "That's a promise." As he observed her from across the board, his thoughts returned to the time when Raymond had died and Rayanne was going through a really bad time, that no matter what the circumstances were, Ralph should've been there for her. She'd needed him more at that time than she ever had, or perhaps, ever would. It was the lost of her first parent. What was it again, the reason he couldn't be there, Scott reflected. Some fishing trip that he'd planned some months before, and that wasn't the only time that he'd hurt or disappointed her. There were the canceled visits, he'd done the unthinkable by sleeping with her friend, he wasn't willing to give up New York, yet, to move here and be with Rayanne once they were married, and who knows what else. Yet, Rayanne had forgiven him for it all. How forgiving can she be, he wondered. What was it going to take for her to see the guy as he really was.

The score for each game was 500 points, and Rayanne was winning. Scott had been a bit preoccupied, and after her 4th straight win, Rayanne didn't want to play any more. She told Scott he was no longer a challenge. She laid on the floor with her head propped up on the pillow. Scott laid on the floor along side of her. He whispered, "It's going to be all right." Rayanne's next move was unexpected and took Scott completely by surprise. She turned over into his arms, kissed him full on his lips, then she fell asleep. Scott lay there for some time just looking at her. Although Rayanne always wore her hair in a French twist or up in a pony tail, Scott wondered how it would look loose and falling around her shoulders, or spread out on a pillow. He was definitely a hair man and she definitely had a beautiful head of it, but he didn't really care whether she had hair or not, because she was the woman he'd fallen in love with the day they met. The day when he'd caused the accident, the rainy day when she hit him in the rear. Even before that day actually, because he'd first seen her long before then and although he'd never believed in love at first sight before, it had definitely happened to him. He could easily have avoided the accident. He'd actually caused it. Had he pulled up a couple of yards, Rayanne would've been able to stop before hitting him. Yes, he'd caused the accident and yes, he'd fallen in love with her. At 2 o'clock that morning, Scott covered Rayanne with a blanket and let himself out.

Rayanne awoke before day break. She picked up the blanket and pillow, she put them away and went in to check on Swan. She went to her own room and climbed into bed, pulling the covers up around her neck. In another six days, Ralph would be there, she thought with excitement flowing through her. She sat up in bed, lifted the phone from its cradle and dialed Ralph's number. He'd wanted to get a good night's sleep, and she felt sure by that time, that he had. The sun was beginning to come up. The phone rang three times before the sultry voice answered, "Hello?"

Rayanne quickly hung up. She'd dialed a wrong number. After

dialing again, the same voice answered. "Is this Ralph Underwood's residence?" Rayanne asked, thinking she couldn't have dialed the wrong number twice.

"Yes it is," that voice responded.

"May I speak with Mr. Underwood, please?" Rayanne said, her palms becoming wet and clammy as she got out of bed, gripping the phone tightly to her ear.

"I'm sorry, but he's not available right now. May I leave him a message," the woman said.

"Who are you, and where is Ralph?" Rayanne asked struggling to keep her voice calm.

"I'm Mandy and Ralph went for a run," the voice answered.

"Mandy, Mandy who?"

"I'm a friend of Ralph's. May I take a message for him?"

Rayanne took a deep breath, struggling to control the hysteria that was quickly mounting inside her. "No, that won't be necessary," she said and hung up. She was shaking all over and all she wanted to do was scream, then run, but she felt frozen in time. When she was able to get her legs to move, she turned and sat on the side of the bed motionless, not knowing what to do next. She simply couldn't think. She didn't know how long she sat there, or when she began to move around, she did know that most of the day found her in a daze, numb and she couldn't help wondering what was it that she'd done that caused her to suffer as she had. Either she'd done something that was wrong or hadn't done something that was equally wrong. Whatever the case, she'd paid and was continuing to pay. She collected herself and called Ivory. At the sound of Ivory's voice, she burst into tears. She told Ivory what had happened and when she hung up, she didn't tell a single other person about her new disappointment. She didn't know what to do, how she was going to put her life back together this time. She did know though that there was no way that Ralph was going to be able to talk his way out of what he'd gotten himself into this time. She'd never be able to trust this man again, ever.

CHAPTER 49

At 6:30 on Wednesday afternoon, the door bell rang. Ralph had flown in, rented a car and drove to Rayanne's house. They had dinner and immediately afterwards, Swan announced she wanted to go to bed. Rayanne told Swan a story while giving her a bubble bath, and just before Swan drifted off to sleep, she drowsily asked that Rayanne say goodnight to Uncle Scott for her. "What about Mr. Underwood?" Rayanne asked.

"You can say goodnight to him, too," Swan had said but gone was the smile that had lit up her face when she'd left the same message for Scott. It was strange how even though children were innocent, their insight into humans and their behavior, was sometimes better than adults. Swan was friendly and pleasant enough with Ralph, but not in the way that she was with Scott. She had established her own little relationship with Scott. During the years, Rayanne and Scott spent a lot of time with Swan and Donnie, taking them to the park, the zoo, the county fair, the mall, fishing trips and other adventures that they enjoyed together. They were like a family.

Rayanne went back to the den to find Ralph standing in front of the fireplace with both hands buried in his pockets. He stared at the flames that licked out and ate the logs that sat on the hearth, while sparks shot up the chimney. "Why are you here, Ralph?" Rayanne asked, standing in the middle of the room, looking at him.

"Do you even have to ask?" Ralph turned to look at her.

Rayanne walked over to the couch and sat. She cupped her

hands together against her mouth, then placing them in her lap. "Maybe I'm just stupid," she began, "but you and I were planning a wedding, a wedding that was to take place a few months from now. We made a vow to each other that we wanted the same things, that we would be faithful to each other and live our lives as a unit, husband and wife. Well, forgive me if I'm wrong, but I thought when we made that commitment, that we meant it. I did. I didn't take it to mean that there would be any outsiders interfering with what we shared."

"Why are you using the past tense? If you've already decided that we have no future together, then I have to wonder what am I doing here, as well," Ralph said.

Is he crazy or does he think I am, Rayanne almost said out loud. Instead, she said, "Why don't you just say what you came here to say, and then, I want you gone."

"Just let me explain, please," he begged, "just hear me out."

She lifted her hands into the air and said, "Go on, say what's on your mind, but I think you should know that it will take nothing short of a miracle to save us this time."

Ralph didn't like the tone of finality in Rayanne's voice. His jawbone jutted up and down at the conclusiveness of her statement and he became outraged, but he said," I believe in miracles." They went through an intense relationship. An indiscretion on his part had ended the perfect romance before, but they'd managed to put it back together, as they'd both wanted, so it was natural that emotions ran high now that the relationship was threatened again, but Ralph was desperate. Each of them taking a moment to calm down, Ralph began. "Rayanne, I love you, you and I belong together. There's no one who knows you better than I. I know your passion and your pain." He lifted a hand to quiet Rayanne's intended protest. Then he began to pace the floor, he either stared at his feet or the ceiling, but at the time, he didn't look at her. "Rayanne, I love you second to none, and I know you know that." And, it was true. It was then that Ralph turned to face her. He did love her and wanted to spend the rest of his life with her. "You're the consummate romantic," he picked up again, "and you don't want anything less in a partner. You want everything in perfect order, no flexibility. I'm not saying there's anything wrong with that, but who wants to be set in the old ways like old concrete? The only thing I find wrong with that is sometimes that way of thinking is not realistic. Baby, what's happened in New York hasn't diminished the way I feel about you. If anything, I love you more.

Honey, we're good for each other, we're good together," Ralph said, now kneeling on the floor, near where Rayanne sat on the couch. "You're a creator. You get to make things the way you want them to be. You like being in control, but that doesn't always work. We have to live life as it comes to us. There are bumps in everyone's life, and we're no exception. That doesn't mean if I do something or say something that you wouldn't do or say, that I don't love you because if you believe that, you couldn't be further from the truth." Ralph got up, walked to the window, and stared out into the darkness. He turned, looked at Rayanne and continued. "The woman who answered the phone, she didn't mean anything to me, absolutely nothing. Every one who knows me knows my heart belongs to you." Rayanne didn't respond. "Honey, it took both of us to start this relationship, and it should take both of us to end it, and I know this isn't what either of us want. I love you, Rayanne," he said, again kneeling in front of her, searching her eyes. He was like an actor on a stage, she thought.

"Are you finished?" Rayanne asked.

"I've just got one more thing to say. I was never once unfaithful to you while you were living in New York. Never once. Doesn't that tell you something?" Ralph said and whispered, "I love you, baby, and I want you in my life. We belong together. Neither of us would be happy without the other, you know that. I'm sorry, I didn't mean to hurt you, but you are my woman, and I'm your man." Rayanne looked at him and studied his face. For the first time since she'd known Ralph, he looked old, tired, defeated. As she continued to look at him, he laid both hands on her thighs and awaited her reply. She lifted his hands and stood up. She walked over to the window and peered out, not looking at anything in particulars. She gave considerable thought to all that Ralph had said and even more to what she was about to say, because once said, she didn't want to have to take the words back or repeat them. Rayanne knew that Ralph loved her. There was never a question about that, but he loved her in his own way, and that was the problem. She wanted him to love her unconditionally, the way she loved him.

Rayanne turned to face Ralph. He was still kneeling on the floor in a half turned position. "I have just realized tonight that after all this time, you don't know me. You really don't know me at all, and we can argue about that until morning, but all we'd be doing is running into brick walls all over the place," she said and Ralph looked at her confused. "If you think I would be accepting of the kind of relationship that you just described, than you must think I'm a complete idiot. I'm through with being hurt in this relationship. It is obvious you and I don't want the same things, so if the kind of relationship you want is the kind that I find between your words, then by all means I want you to have it. You deserve to have what you want, but it's not for me. Ralph, I've done a lot of thinking about us, but it was our conversation tonight that has had the biggest effect on me. When I think about us, I don't think I know you as well as I thought. You've done things I never thought you'd do and what do I do. I let you right back into my life and the reason was because I loved you. And because I did, I put you up high on a pedestal," she said lifting her hands, "but the problem, Ralph, is that you couldn't handle it, you got dizzy from the height." Rayanne paused. Ralph got up, sat on the couch, and clasped his hands together. "You're right about some things though," she continued. "Yes, I love creating. I create characters, I breathe life into them, and yes, I do control them in that respect. I like having a little control, everyone does. I don't think there's anything wrong with that, but obviously you do. Those characters I create are for a purpose, but not to cause any harm. They live the lives that I give them. They don't have choices. They don't have the luxury of living their lives as regular people who have the option of making their own decisions. And yes, you and I were good together, darn good, but we weren't necessarily good for each other. You've hurt me and disappointed me too often." She paused again. "You said you never cheated on me when we were together in New York." Ralph blinked, looking at her. "So what you're telling me is that if we went ahead with our plans and got married, you'd be faithful to me as long as I'm there with you but the minute my back is turned, you'd have some woman keeping my place warm until I came back?"

"No, Rayanne, it's not like that," Ralph said, shifting nervously in the chair.

"That's how it seems to me."

Ralph breathed deeply, his head bending low now, almost between his legs. He looked up, studied her face a moment. "Rayanne," he said, "if you love me," he got up and went over to her, they stood facing each other, "you won't throw this away." Rayanne tried to move away, but Ralph put out both hands and stopped her, "know what I wish," he said.

"Yes," she said, "you wish I'd be stupid enough to let you back into my life again."

Ignoring her statement, he said, "I wish things between us could be as they were twenty years ago." He let his hands slide down to her slender waist.

Rayanne was a level headed, strong willed girl and although her body still tingled at his touch, she knew there was only one option left open to her. She had to stand her ground, she had to end this once and for all. She removed his hands from her waist, but she held his hands in her own. "Ralph, I'm not going to do this anymore. It's over." She took a deep breath and looked at Ralph sadly. "For what it's worth though, I didn't cheat on you either, not once. I didn't want to. I didn't even think about it. Another thing, you said it will take both of us to end this relationship. Well, I don't think so especially since it was you and only you who couldn't seem to keep your pants on."

Ralph heard the words, all of them, but he didn't give up. "You never forgave me for what happened between Dorian and me, did you?" he said and the question surprised her.

"I did and you know it. If I hadn't, you and I wouldn't be back at this cross road again."

"So, we're going to let it go just like that. Rayanne, what I did was no different from what men have been doing for centuries. It didn't mean a thing. It's just something men do. For God's sake, it's just a man's thing. It was just something to do. You're the woman that I want and need. Can we give it one more try."

Rayanne smiled sadly at him and before she spoke, he knew her answer. There was something different about her demeanor. He knew it was over. "Sometimes there's pain that we can work through, then there is the kind of pain that never goes away. Thanks to you, I've experienced both."

"I'm sorry," Ralph said, and she thought she heard his voice crack. "I'm truly sorry."

"I know," Rayanne said in a whisper.

"What are we going to do now?"

"We'll start over and go on with our lives."

"I don't know what I'm going to do without you, baby," Ralph said, shaking his head.

"I'm sure you'll do just fine," Rayanne said, nodding her head up and down.

"What about you?"

"Don't worry about me. I'll be okay."

"I'm really sorry that I caused you so much pain. Please believe that," he said sadly.

"I do," Rayanne smiled, "and I want to know that you're going to be okay." Ralph didn't answer. He picked up his coat from where he'd draped it across the back of the couch. Rayanne reached into her sweater pocket and removed the ring he'd given her only a short while ago, and she handed it to him. He was about to protest, but she forced it into his hand, and closed his fingers around it. When she released his hand, Ralph opened it and looked at the ring. He looked at her, then he put the ring into his pocket.

"I'm sorry," he whispered, and he left. When the door closed behind him, Rayanne cried. Her body shook, as deep raking sobs escaped, erupting like a volcano. She was sorry too. Sorry about everything. She'd loved Ralph almost two decades and she'd lost him, but she was thankful that she had a new insight into the man with whom she'd planned to spend the rest of her life. It was simply a coincidence of timing that brought their relationship to this point. If she had not had an overwhelming desire to talk with Ralph that Sunday morning, she might never have gotten to know the real Ralph and would've married him and shared him and his love. Circumstances and time bring on changes, changes that we don't always understand, but maybe we are not suppose to. She continued to cry, she was closing the door on a relationship and opening the door to her future. Her tears weren't because Ralph didn't love her the way she'd loved him, and they weren't because she'd lost him and would be forced to face the future without him. She cried because something in her felt sorry for Ralph. Sorry that he may never be able to commit to anyone or be happy and have the quality of life that everyone deserves. Rayanne stood at the door and watched as Ralph walked to where he'd parked his car. She wiped her eyes clear of the tears, while others replaced them. She watched him until he got into the car, drove off and disappeared into the darkness. She would go through the bumps and bruises of losing him again, but at least this time, she knew it would be the last time. When they were in love, it was like a fire burning out of control. Rayanne had done things with Ralph that she'd never done before and may never do again. He'd taught her many things. In essence, he'd educated her taste buds to the many spices of life. He'd taught her to laugh, to cry, to forgive and to forget, but he didn't teach her how to erase the pain of a broken heart. This she'd have to do on her own. That chapter of her life was over, it was gone forever. She would turn the page and close that book. Tomorrow she would begin a whole new chapter in a whole new book.

CHAPTER 50

Rayanne literally submerged herself in her work the weeks that followed. But, there had been such a void in her life after Ralph that she couldn't find any real satisfaction in many of the things that she did. She put some finishing touches on the speech that she was to give at another high school in the next couple of weeks, and she wrote several chapters for a new book. She'd written a number of plays with enormous success, she had written several that didn't go anywhere, but she now decided to write a book, which would be more truth than fiction as it would, indeed, chronicle stages of her own life. The time that Rayanne spent at the nursing home, was rewarding. Communicating with the elderly was something she enjoyed. She found satisfaction from reading to one of them, giving flowers or a card to another for no special reason or just sitting and listening to them. It was gratifying, witnessing their joy because someone had remembered them. She'd even increased the time she spent counseling teenage girls as well. She was busy, but her personal life was taking a serious beating. One night when Rayanne had lived with the pain alone long enough, she decided to share her feelings. She had mentioned the situation to others but she had not gone into any great detail. One of the calls she made was to Brenda, who in turn called Hilary, and they agreed to get together. Hilary and Brenda drove to Rayanne's house, and after she told her story, Hilary said, "I haven't had anything quite like that to happen to me, so I can't say I know how you feel, but I can certainly sympathize with you because I imagine it must hurt like crazy."

"Of course, it hurts," Brenda injected. "I know. I've been there, but I can't believe that son of a bitch has gotten caught with his pants down again. I sure hope you got up close and personal with his ass."

"He should be taken out and shot," Hilary scorned, her lips turned down at the corners.

When Rayanne didn't respond, Brenda said, "What did Scottie say? Bet he's glad you are on your own."

"I don't know. I haven't told him," Rayanne said.

"Why not?" Brenda stormed.

"I haven't told anyone else except Maxine and Ivory, and they had the same opinion, that all men are alike," Rayanne said, "and Aunt Bessie. She didn't seem all that surprised."

"Smart woman, that Aunt Bessie," Brenda said.

"I still say he should be taken out and shot," Hilary repeated.

"Some men are just no good, they just don't know any better, but I'm wondering why haven't you mentioned this to Scott and let him help you through this instead of handling it alone," Brenda said. Rayanne knew she didn't tell Scott about she and Ralph because she didn't want to hear him say I told you so. "Well," Brenda questioned.

"I don't know," Rayanne said, "I just didn't." Rayanne looked from one girl to the next. Then, she went into the kitchen and returned with three cups of steaming coffee.

"So what have you been doing for yourself?" Brenda asked as Rayanne set the tray on the coffee table.

"I've been keeping busy," she said.

"Is there anything we can do?" Brenda asked.

"Yes," Hilary said, getting up from her chair, going over to where Rayanne sat, and she perched on the arm of her chair, "want to do something. Go out and tie one on, shop, just tell us what can we do to help?"

Rayanne told them that most of the time, she was in a lot of pain, "but for some reason, I'm all right today. I just don't know how long it will last." She'd had many years of history with that man, but she realized too late that she never should've taken him back into her life. That was a big mistake. "Some days I think the pain is gone and something will happen or I'll hear a song that'll remind me of Ralph, and I swear the pain is as fresh as it ever was," Rayanne said, and blinked back the tears.

"You poor thing. I'm so sorry," Hilary said, gently patting Rayanne on her back.

"The thing to remember is that you can't afford to fall apart over that nigger. Don't roll over and play dead. He ain't worth it. He's a shit head. You're alive, you've got so much going for you, and I tell you, I pity him because he has no idea what he's lost," Brenda said.

"I agree, Rayanne," Hilary said. "You've got to go on with your life."

"Life is filled with hurt and disappointments, but you really do have to move on by them. Leave them behind, in the past." Rayanne didn't know what she would've done without the support of her friends. Not to mention their understanding and friendship. "I know you will," Brenda said and winked.

"We love you, Rayanne, and we just want you to feel better," Hilary said.

"I do, I really do, and I'm lucky to have friends like you guys," Rayanne said, looking from Hilary to Brenda, "now enough about me. Just talking with you guys has made me feel so much better and I want to thank you." She looked at Brenda. "Now, it's your turn. How are things with you and Cardell?" Brenda met the eyes of her friends, smiled and looked off into space.

CHAPTER 51

Rayanne pulled the sheets from the bed and was putting on a fresh set when the phone rang that Saturday morning. She picked it up, but before she could answer, Maxine said, "Rayanne."

"Yes Maxine, what's wrong?" Rayanne asked.

"Rayanne, I've got a problem," Maxine said and relayed to Rayanne that she'd found a condom in my car. Rayanne encouraged her not to panic. There could be any number of logical reasons for the condom being there.

"A used condom, Rayanne? It was a used condom," Maxine screeched and the minute she said it, Rayanne knew that someone had a lot of explaining to do.

"What do you make of that?" Rayanne said. It was a rhetorical question, she didn't expect an answer.

Maxine said, "someone was screwing in my car. That's what it means to me, and I'm gonna get to the bottom of this." Maxine was really pissed off, and Rayanne knew exactly how she was feeling. "Either my husband or my fourteen year old daughter has been fucking in my car, and right now, I don't know which is worse," Maxine said, but Rayanne was thinking that there should be no question as to which was worse. Since whomever it was that had left the condom had at least had the good sense to use one, Maxine had better hope that it was her fourteen year old daughter and not her husband. Although Rayanne didn't condone someone Marcia Raylyn's age having sex, the situation would be much worse if Marcus was the guilty party.

"What are you going to do?"

Maxine took a deep breath, and Rayanne could tell that she was angry, at first, but that emotion seemed overshadowed by hurt, perhaps fear. "Rayanne, I don't know. I simply do not know. I can't go through another divorce. I'm in love with Marcus, and I thought he loved me."

"Marcus does love you. I have absolutely no doubt about that." Rayanne was trying to console Maxine, but she couldn't help wondering what had gone wrong this time. "Maxine, don't jump to the wrong conclusions."

"Could it be that my baby is having sex?" Maxine asked, grabbing any straw she could, but the truth of the matter, Rayanne couldn't imagine that either of them used that condom and left it there, but when Maxine explained that for the past three weeks, Bobby had been riding with other members of his track team and hadn't driven the car, so it couldn't have been him, it gave Rayanne good reason to be concerned and if she had her way, it certainly would've been Bobby. "I could handle this a lot better if it had been Bobby," Maxine said, then after a shaky laugh, said, "God, did I say that?"

"I know you didn't mean that, Maxine. You are human and it's only natural that you'd look for the safest solution to this, but as I said, there's some logical explanation for this whole situation, I'm sure."

"I don't know anymore. I just want this whole nightmarish situation to go away."

"Do you want me to come over?"

"No, I'm all right. I just needed to talk about this. Look, I'm gonna have myself a beer and get myself together, them I'm gonna get some answers."

"Maxine, please try to get some answers before you go accusing anyone," Rayanne pleaded. When they hung up, Rayanne sat on the foot of the bed, scratching her head with both hands.

"Are you all right, Aunt Rayanne?" Swan asked from the bedroom door, her face flushed with puzzlement. As Rayanne's head snapped up, she thought whatever else that might've been wrong in her life, it certainly wasn't Swan. She was a dream, the brightest spot in Rayanne's life. She was sweet, uncomplicated, beautiful, Swan.

My little girl, Rayanne thought, but she said, "come here, you." Swan rushed over to Rayanne, who lifted her up onto her lap.

"You have a headache?" Swan asked, holding Rayanne's face between her tiny palms, looking into her eyes.

"No, I don't have a headache. I'm fine." Rayanne said.

"You were holding your head like this," Swan said, aping Rayanne, "so I thought you had a headache.

"No honey, I was just thinking about something, but I thank you for your concern."

"I'm glad you don't have a headache. Donnie's mommie gets headaches a lot," Swan informed and Rayanne looked at her. "Donnie told me his mommie yells at him, then her head hurts, and she makes him go to his room. I don't think Donnie's mom is very nice."

"I'm sorry to hear that." Rayanne ran her hand over Swan's head and listened as Swan told her about times when they picked up Donnie, how his mother never smiles, and that once, she even gave Donnie a whack on the bottom, telling him he'd better be good.

"What make people mean, Aunt Rayanne?" Swan asked looking up into her face.

"Well now, that's a tough question," Rayanne said, pondering how could she answer it so that a four year old would understand. "Well honey, there are lots of reasons why people sometimes act that way. Being unhappy. They could be unhappy about something unpleasant that has happened to them, or they could become angry at one person and get mad and yell at another, which is not fair to do. Some times some people just like to make a fuss, but I think that most people really don't want to be mean. It just happens that way sometimes," she said as Swan looked thoughtful. "Do you understand?" Rayanne asked and Swan nodded yes. "Okay then, now, is there anything else you want to talk about or any more questions?"

"No" Swan replied.

"All right. Are you hungry? I am hungry. What about you?"

"Yes."

"What would you like for breakfast?"

"Let me see," Swan pretended to think, when all along she knew right down to the kind of syrup she would smother her French toast with, exactly what she wanted. "I'd like some French toast, eggs and sausage." She paused, her eyes twinkling, "and chocolate milk." Swan smiled up at Rayanne.

"You've had this planned all along, haven't you?" That was her favorite breakfast food and when Rayanne smiled at Swan, she squealed with delight, putting her index fingers into her mouth and nodding her head up and down. Rayanne hugged Swan once more, kissed her on top of her head, and answered Swan's un-asked question. "And, yes, you may help make breakfast." Swan smiled and Rayanne lifted her from her lap to the floor. Rayanne got up from the bed and said, "now let's get ready for that special breakfast."

CHAPTER 52

"That son of a bitch did what?" Scott stormed when Rayanne finally told him why she ended her relationship with Ralph. "Why didn't you tell me about this?"

"Because it was embarrassing," she said, still humiliated with the way Ralph had behaved.

"You don't have to be embarrassed about anything with me. Haven't I told you that before? You should know that by now,"he said. Scott didn't ask whether Rayanne had any regrets, he didn't asked how she was handling the situation, but he also didn't say, I told you so. Rayanne knew that Scott was angry at Ralph, maybe even a little at her, but he exploded when she told him that Ralph had called earlier that day. "What does he want now? Hasn't he done enough?" Scott got up and stalked around the room, his adrenaline level, unparalleled to what it was at any other time that Rayanne had known him.

"Scott, calm down. Now do you see why I didn't want to tell you this?" she asked. "I'm dealing with it."

"This man is crazy as hell." He gave a short laugh and looked around the room. The two large pictures of Ralph that sat on the sofa table in the living room and the mantle in the den had not been taken down. Scott looked at the picture, and when he turned his eyes on Rayanne, she saw the question. She simply lifted her shoulders. She hadn't taken the pictures down because she'd wanted to avoid the questions she knew would come once she did.

She got up from the couch and silently gathered the pictures and put them into a drawer of a lamp table. "I'd like to take 'em and burn 'em, and put my foot in his," Scott's statement was interrupted.

"It doesn't matter anymore. Ralph is out of my life, so can we just forget him."

"He'd better not show his face around here any more. If he does, he's gonna have to deal with me," Scott said, and Rayanne knew he meant it. Scott returned to his seat beside her on the couch and he asked, "Where do things really stand with you and Romeo?"

"I told you it's over," she replied.

"Doesn't seem so. He's still calling you," Scott said and thought that Ralph needs to be told once and for all to leave Rayanne alone, that he'd done enough damage. He should butt out and be gone for good. "I think you need to set things straight with him. See him, call him, do whatever you need to do to put an end to this. You have told me time and time again that you don't want me involved in whatever this is you got going with Ralph, well then, you had better get him on his way, or I will. I'm not gonna stand by and watch him hurt you again. I care too damn much," Scott said and Rayanne knew he was right. Every time she thought she'd put Ralph behind, he'd call and open up the wounds all over. She had to put some closure on this situation. "That guy just doesn't get it. He had the best woman in the world and what does he do," Scott got up and walked over to the fireplace, "he acts like a damn fool." He turned and when he saw the look on Rayanne's face, he said, simmering down. "Okay, okay, what are we gonna do. How do we handle this?"

Rayanne couldn't have appreciate him any more than at that moment and she became weak with the realization, but she said, "Would you just hold me for a minute, please, because I am feeling really vulnerable right now." Scott complied and was glad to do so. When she felt she was whole again, she said against his chest, "Thanks Scott, but this is my problem. I'll handle it." She tried to move away, but he held her as they looked at each other. He put his arms around her tighter and drew her closer to him, and just as she knew her own name, she also knew that everything was going to be all right.

Rayanne invited Scott out to dinner one evening and when they returned, he told her that although he and Frannie weren't together, hadn't been for some time, and she was still as mean as a snake, he continued to see and support Donnie. Rayanne admired so many things about Scott and as she turned to tell him so, she found him staring at her. "What?" she said with raised eyebrows.

"Nothing," Scott lied, he looked away then he returned his gaze to her. Rayanne knew he had something on his mind and she knew if she waited long enough, he would come clean. "Loneliness is a two way street," he said after a while. "Neither of us has to be lonely, you know." Rayanne opened her mouth to speak, but he put a finger to her lips. "Rayanne, I think both of us have suffered enough. We need to put this thing together and get on with it." Rayanne stared at him. "I know how you feel. You don't want to take a chance, afraid you'll get hurt again. Well, I've been there. I'm scared too, but I'm willing to take a chance, with you. I'd like to make you and Swan my priority. I think we'd be good together. I can be whatever you want in a man. I care just that much," he said, he'd always had her best interest at heart. "What I'd really like to do is go to New York and thank that guy, then take his head off, but what I want most is to be here for you, however long it takes, a day, a week, a year or forever." Rayanne leaned away from him and looked at him for a long time. Then she got up from the couch, picked up a pillow, toss it to the floor and she lay on it. Scott rubbed his hands together. If only there was something he could do to make this woman know how he felt about her. He got up from the couch and slowly walked over to where Rayanne lay on the floor. He lay behind her, encircled her in his arms and held her. He whispered, "I'll always be here for you." That was the last thing he said to her that night.

Rayanne awoke the following morning to the aroma of coffee and bacon. She rubbed the sleep from her eyes with the back of her hand, threw back the blanket that Scott had covered her with and said, "Gosh, what time is it?" Scott informed her it was six-thirty and he was leaving to get to work. "Scott, about last night," she began, getting up from the floor and folding the blanket. She returned the pillow to the couch, but Scott interrupted.

"There's only one thing I want you and me to remember about last night. I meant everything that I said."

"How did I get so lucky to have someone like you in my life," she said.

"You musta just been born that way." Scott walked up to her, kissed her on her forehead and he left.

CHAPTER 53

The night Scott and Rayanne made love was one of the most spontaneous things that she'd ever done. It just happened. She arrived home that afternoon from work, she and Swan ate dinner that Mrs. Marshall prepared. Mrs. Marshall and Swan went through the flower seeds that evening because Swan and Rayanne would be planting them in Swan's little garden soon. Rayanne had just stepped out of the shower when the phone rang. It was Scott. "What's up," she said.

"Nothing much. What's going on with you?" Rayanne and Scott had seen each other on a regular basis after that night of his confession, but they never mentioned that conversation again. She'd liked Scott but it was a brotherly thing, a younger brotherly thing, if she'd had a younger brother.

"Not much. I'm going to see Malcolm X," she said. "Come and go with me."

Scott had wanted to see that movie himself. "Sounds like a winner. Want me to pick you up?".

"Why don't I meet you there." They decided to meet for the seven o'clock show, and Rayanne arrived at five to seven, where there were other late comers in line ahead of her. When she reached the window and was about to purchase the tickets, she saw Scott waving to her from just inside the theater, with a pair of tickets in his hand. She joined him, and they sat in the seats he'd held for them. The movie was filled to its capacity. While the coming attractions and the advertisements of what was available at the concession stand were previewing, Rayanne took the opportunity to look around in the theater and saw what appeared to be parents with their children. Now, she thought, this is what this country needs more of. It was wonderful seeing so many parents taking part in their kids development. The movie was packed with entertainment, humor, family life, what motivates some people, and, when it was over, Rayanne found that not only was she more in love with Denzil Washington and moved by his portrayal of Malcolm X, she'd changed her mind about the man and she promised she'd read every piece of information she could find. She wanted to learn more about who Malcolm X was. The movie was a must see, kind of movie. It wasn't a white movie. It wasn't a black movie. She wasn't even sure it was a racist kind of movie. It was certainly a people's movie. The entire movie had its purpose, but Rayanne loved the part when Malcolm discovered himself. For years she had this misconception about the man, had grown up in ignorance, listening to what she'd heard, rather than read and learn the truth, on her own. Although her initial impression wasn't completely wrong, it did appear that Malcolm taught racism at one time, but he had changed. She was glad that the movie had changed her mind to the point that she was eager to learn more about Malcolm, form her own opinion, rather than the one that had been formed for her.

Rayanne followed Scott to his house after the movie, he popped a CD in its player, she kicked off her shoes and curled up onto the couch. Scott returned with a Coke for Rayanne and something stronger, for himself. He sat on the other end of the couch from her. She'd noticed that Scott was a little distracted, and when exactly did he start drinking alcohol. Although she'd asked him several times whether everything was all right and he'd said that it was, she knew something was bothering him. "I'm here. Sure you don't want to talk about it?" she asked, extending an arm along the back of the couch.

"It's nothing. I'm just a little tired," he said and when he looked at her, she knew it was more than that. "I lost the bid for that apartment complex and I'm a little bombed out about it."

"Oh gosh, that's too bad," Rayanne said, sliding closer to him, "but there will be other contracts." She got up, "Why don't you let me give you a neck rub. That usually makes you feel better." She began to massage his shoulders. When his body began to relax, she said, "Now, tell Rayanne what's really bothering you." When he tried to come up with another excuse, she said, joining him on the couch again, "Talk to me. I'm here for you, and if you say so, I won't go anywhere until you're feeling better." She smiled in her usual teasing manner. Scott turned his head, glanced at her and smiled half heatedly. He got up and she watched as he went into the kitchen and returned with a fresh drink. He sat back on the couch. "Scott, what's wrong, and don't tell me it's nothing, because I know better."

"I don't want to get into that tonight," he said and stared at her a moment, got up from the couch and kneeled on the floor in front of her. He looked up into her eyes as though he wanted to say something, changed his mind, shaking his head and sat on the floor with his back against Rayanne's knees. Her fingers connected with his neck and she resumed the massage. She massaged his neck and shoulders for a time, then her fingers drifted to his face, and she massaged his temples, allowing her fingers to play along the side of his face. She ran her fingers through his beard and Scott moved his head from side to side, enjoying the massage and Silk, as they belted out "Girl You 4 Me." That was one of their favorites, along with other groups like Boyz II Men, Shai and Jodeci. She massaged his throat, then her fingers traced his mustache. She closed her eyes, engrossed in the music herself and as Scott turned his head slightly, her right thumb brushed against his lips. He caught her thumb in his mouth and Rayanne's eyes popped open as Scott began to sucked gently on it. It felt good, real good, so good, in fact that Rayanne closed her eyes again and when she realized what was happening, Scott had at least three of her fingers in his mouth. She tried gently to pull her fingers free, but Scott held her hand in place. Rayanne's pulse began to race as Scott sucked and nibbled on her fingers. In one swift movement, Scott got up from the floor, lifted Rayanne from the couch and began kissing her. He kissed her slowly and softly, at first, then the kisses became deeper. He kissed her over and over and what surprised her more than the kiss was that she responded. He didn't kiss her like she was a big sister, and he didn't kiss her like she was just a friend, he kissed her like the woman she was, and when their bodies drew apart, Rayanne thought how long it had been since she was kissed like that, had she ever been kissed like that. It felt so good. Scott kissed her forehead, her eyes, then her lips, again. When they withdrew, his eyes searched her face. Although, she wasn't sure what he was searching for, when he bent his head to kiss her again, her tongue darted into his mouth before their lips touched. "Rayanne, I love you," he whispered, when that kiss ended. "I've

391

always loved you." She looked into his eyes and for the first time, she didn't know what to say. Something was getting out of hand, and she had to put a stop to it. She backed away from him.

"Scott, I think I'd better go."

"Why?" Scott looked into Rayanne's eyes, then he repeated the question, "Why, Rayanne? Don't you know how I feel about you? I love you, and I think I have from the first time I laid eyes on you."

"Scott," Rayanne said, shaking her head, "I'm sorry. I'll call you tomorrow." With that, she left, with Scott staring after her. When she arrived home, Mrs. Marshall was returning to her room with a glass of milk. "Is everything all right?"

"Everything's fine. I just looked in on the baby and she's sound asleep," Mrs. Marshall reported.

"Okay, thanks Mrs. Marshall, I'm going to look in on her, then I'm going to bed myself. It's been a long day. Good night now."

"Good night, Rayanne," Mrs. Marshall said.

Rayanne called Ivory and shared some of what happened earlier that evening. When she was finished, Ivory asked, "Have you heard from Dorian?"

Rayanne didn't answer that question. Instead, she asked, "Is she all right?"

"Yeah, she's fine." When there was silence, Ivory said, "She misses you, Rayanne." Rayanne didn't respond. "I know, I know", Ivory continued, "This is between you and Dorian and I'm butting out".

"How is the family?"

"Just as fine as they can be?"

"And you?" Rayanne asked and Ivory knew something was troubling her.

"What is it, honey," Ivory asked. "What's bothering you."

"Nothing really, Ivory. I just wanted to hear your voice." When they hung up, Rayanne checked on Swan, then went to her room, took off her clothes and got into bed. After being there, she tossed and turned for a long time, trying to go to sleep, but sleep was the farthest thing from her mind. She played and replayed the evening in her mind. Why was she holding Scott at bay? She'd been with men her own age and some who were older but where did it get her. Who was she fooling. She didn't know how the situation with Scott would go or how long it would last, but she knew that no one in her past had ever made her feel the way Scott had. No one had ever touched her heart as he had. No one. And, although she didn't know where it would lead, she owed it to herself to give it a chance, because suddenly Rayanne was aware that she had fallen in love with Scott, too. With that realization, she got out of bed, got dressed and told Mrs. Marshall that she was going back out.

It had begun to rain and by the time she arrived at Scott's house, it had become a downpour. She ran to the porch, as the lightening sent zigzag streaks that lit up the sky, followed by giant claps of thunder. Rayanne was soaked by the time she reached the door and as she was about to press the doorbell, the door opened suddenly and Scott stood there looking down into her eyes. She rushed into his waiting arms and as they clung to each other in the doorway, kissing passionately, the rain slammed down from heaven. The kiss ended, they drew apart, and she asked, meeting his gaze, "Am I that predictable?"

"I wish," he said standing there, looking at her and not believing that she was in his arms. He stood back and allowed her to enter as she looked questioningly at him. "I called your house to see whether you made it home safely, and Mrs. Marshall told me you had, but that you were on your way back over here."

She wondered how Mrs. Marshall knew where she was going, then she remembered. Mrs. Marshall had said on a number of occasions, "that young man cares about you, young lady, and more than you think." Rayanne had told her they were just friends, but Mrs. Marshall's eyes always held a twinkle as if she knew something no one else did.

"Come, get outta them wet clothes," Scott said and after she'd changed into one of his shirts, she sat at the table across from him and sipped the hot tea that he made for her.

She looked at him for what seemed a long time. "What do you want?" she asked. Scott looked at her with a puzzled expression on his face. "What do you want, Scott," she repeated.

"I want you to be happy," he responded.

"My happiness is my responsibility. It's up to me to make me happy. I want to know what is it that you want. What do you want for yourself?"

"I want you in my life, I want that for the rest of my life. I want us," Scott said and he was certain that was exactly what he wanted. Anything less just wouldn't do. "Rayanne, you're on my mind all the time, I love you. What else can I say."

"What about Frannie?"

"I told you. I'll be there for the boy, but as far as me and Frannie, that's history," he replied and it was without emotion or regret.

393

Rayanne and Scott stared at each other for a long time. "Scott," she began slowly, "I'm carrying around a lot of emotional baggage. It goes with me daily. I don't want to mess up your life."

"Some wise man once said, whatever problems one might have, all one needs to do is meet them, greet them and defeat them," he said and smiled.

"Life really isn't quite that simple," Rayanne said, but she wasn't smiling.

"It can be," Scott replied and he knew that everyone had their own cross to bear, but he also knew that together they could find a solution to whatever problems they might be faced with. "Rayanne, I'm offering you a contract of love. All you gotta do is accept it." Rayanne looked at him and this time, she smiled.

"Quite the poet tonight, aren't you?" she said. Scott may have added a little humor to lighten the conversation, but he meant every word. He and Rayanne were so much a part of each other. He'd never felt for anyone the way he felt about her. He wanted to protect her, pulled her inside of himself and shield her from pain, if he could. He felt just that deeply for her, he said. "Oh Scott," was all she could say. It was becoming difficult to speak, difficult to breathe as her feeling for Scott took possession of her. He got up and walked around the table to where she sat. She lifted her glowing eyes to him and there was no mistake. Her love was there, shining for him to see. She wanted him to see, to know that she loved him as much as he'd said he loved her. Scott pulled Rayanne to her feet. He stood behind her, held her close to his chest and gently explored her neck with his lips. She turned to face him, she pushed his tee shirt up until it exposed his bare chest, and she kissed it. She opened the buttons on her shirt, revealing her breasts. A deep moan escaped Scott's lips when he caught sight of them. Rayanne moved closer to him, allowing her naked breasts to strike against his chest. This time, she initiated the kiss and when she did, the lights suddenly went out and although they knew it was because of the storm that was hammering outside as they withdrew, Scott said, "Hey, do that again." They laughed, and Rayanne placed a finger to his lips. She didn't want to make light of what was happening between them, because they really were experiencing a storm of their own.

"I want you to make love to me, Scott," she whispered, "make love to me now."

He looked searchingly into her eyes, then he kissed her. He swept her up into his arms and carried her to his bedroom. As he did, he whispered against her ear, "I want you to believe in me and my love for you." Scott laid Rayanne on the bed, she was too overwhelmed to say the words that she felt in her heart. She could only think how she felt. She did believed in him and his love, she knew he loved her. Making love with Scott was special, magical. It was like seeing her life pass right before her eyes. They really turned the century out, giving each other pleasure, deep satisfying pleasure. "Whose baby are you?" he whispered as their bodies moved together harmoniously. When she didn't answer, he repeated, "Whose baby are you?"

Rayanne opened her eyes slightly and spoke softly to him, "I'm your baby, Scott. I'm your baby."

"You are my baby, aren't you?" he asked plunging deeper and deeper into her.

"Yes," she whispered, dizzy with desire for him, "I'm your baby. You're my Scott, and I love you." Scott fulfilled every desire Rayanne had ever fantasy, and she was caught up in a web of passion that she welcomed as it possessed her mind, her body and caused her spirits to soar. Afterwards, they held each other, while only their hearts communicated. As she observed him later, Rayanne realized that Scott never did tell her what was bothering him earlier, but the look on his face, as he lay sleeping, told her that he was better able to handle whatever it was, because they'd handle it together. And, from that moment, Rayanne saw Scott differently. For the first time, she saw him, not as a younger man, but a man, and he was the man she loved.

CHAPTER 54

"**Y**ou look very thoughtful," Scott said, as he and Rayanne lay in bed together. "What's on your mind, pretty lady," he asked.

"I was thinking about you," she answered.

"Oh, really?" Scott said, a smile curling his lips. "What were you thinking about me?"

"I was thinking that with all that has happened in my life, the pain, not to mention the loneliness and all the time you were right here," she said as if she couldn't believe all that was happening between them.

"And just think what you've been missing all this time," he said looking at her body that was still lean, long and curvy. She was right out of a dream, he thought as he reached over and pulled her to him. "Know when I first knew I was really in love with you?"

"No, when?" Rayanne asked, an inquisitive smile on her face.

"Remember the night you called me, very upset I might add, telling me you'd killed a squirrel. Remember that?" He nearly snickered.

"Of course I remember and it's not funny," she said and gently nudged him in the ribs. "I can still hear the little creature hitting under my car. It did upset me, and another thing, I hit the brakes so hard that I almost had an accident."

"Poor baby," he said, hugging her closer to him. "All I knew was that if this woman got so worked up over hitting a squirrel, she must have a very tender heart, one that is filled with compassion." He looked at her and they laughed. After a moment, he said, "Do something for me".

"Sure, what?"

"Let your hair down," he said simply.

She looked at him and smiled. "Why don't you," she said, sitting up in bed. Scott sat up in bed beside her and slowly removed the hair pins from her hair. The thick locks fell to her shoulders and he ran his fingers through the mass of long brown hair.

"I really love this hair of yours, almost as much as I love you," he said. "I told you I'm a hair freak."

"I remember, " she replied.

Sometime later, Rayanne raised up in bed and Scott asked, "where are you going?"

"I need to be getting home," she answered.

"Why so soon? Tomorrow isn't a work day, and Swan is fine," Scott said sitting up in bed also. He was right, Rayanne thought. Swan was fine. Mrs. Marshall is a very capable person and it was a messy night, raining like cats and dogs and she'd already gotten soaked once and, aside from that, Scott didn't want her going back out that time of night, in that kind of weather. Rayanne lay back and they listened as the rain poured and slashed against the windows.

"I want to be home when she wakes up," Rayanne said.

"Who's gonna be here for me when I wake up," he teased.

"Scott," she said and sat up in bed again.

"I was only joking," he said, tilted his head to one side, "well, maybe I wasn't joking. I'd like nothing more than to wake up every morning with you, and knowing that Swan is in the room next to ours, would be the best thing I could ever ask God for." Rayanne didn't respond. "If you stay here with me tonight and let me take care of you, I'll make sure that you're safely at home when Swan wakes up in the morning." Rayanne settled back in bed beside Scott, she could never remember feeling more safe and loved, and Scott was true to his words. He got up early, made coffee and woke Rayanne.

The house was quiet when she arrived home, she slipped into her room and into her own bed. As she lay there, her mind was filled with thoughts. If only her mother had understood that she did what she did in order to try to save Josh. If only she'd understood. Well, she hadn't and because there was no way that she could now, Rayanne felt the guilt and would have to live with that guilt the rest of her life.

At some point, Rayanne must have dozed off to sleep. There was a soft knock at her door and when it was opened, there stood Swan. "Come here, you," Rayanne called out to her, throwing back the covers. Swan ran and jumped into bed with her. Rayanne asked, rubbing Swan's head, "what are you doing out of bed so early?"

"I wanted to see you and play with my toys," Swan said.

"Really," Rayanne said toying with Swan's hair. "What are we going to do today?"

Swan clasped her hands together, looking thoughtful. "Can we go to Burger King for breakfast?"

"Sure, but we'd better let Mrs. Marshall know before she makes breakfast or she'll be mad at us. We don't want to make Mrs. Marshall mad at us, do we?" Rayanne asked touching Swan on the nose.

"Oooh no," Swan said, excitedly pushing back the covers and jumping out of bed. "I'll tell her we're going to Burger King for breakfast."

"Mrs. Marshall may wants to come with us," Rayanne said.

"Okay," Swan said, rushing out of the room. Moments later, she returned and climbed back into bed. "Mrs. Marshall said she'll have breakfast with us."

"Okay. What else would you like to do?" Rayanne asked. She looked at Swan who was smiling. "What are you smiling about?"

"Why don't we invite Uncle Scott to have breakfast with us, too?"

"Sure, if you want to."

"Okay" Swan said, "I will call him. Swan called Scott and it was settled. He, too, would join them for breakfast. In fact, he would drive over and pick them up.

"You like Uncle Scott, don't you," Rayanne asked.

"Yes."

"I'm sure he'd love to know that you're so fond of him," Rayanne said.

"He already knows that," Swan said.

"He does?"

"Yes. You know why?" Swan questioned. Rayanne didn't answer, she lifted her eyebrows. "Because I told him so," Swan said, putting her fingers into her mouth and laughing.

"Oh, I see. I didn't know that. You two had a secret from me, huh?" Rayanne teased.

"Yes. Uncle Scott is my friend," Swan said and nestled close to Rayanne as they listened to the rain. "I love you, Aunt Rayanne."

"I know, baby. I love you, too," Rayanne said, holding Swan in her arms, and it wasn't long before Rayanne heard the soft, gentle sound of a child sleeping. As she looked down into the face of that sweet innocent child, Rayanne vowed that she'd do her best to keep Swan as safe and as happy as she was then. Another sound could be heard, the sound of a siren, wailing somewhere in the distance. What is it now, Rayanne thought? Who has gotten shot or stabbed or killed, now?

CHAPTER 55

"**A**untie Rayanne, are we still going to the super market?" Swan asked, interrupting Rayanne's thoughts as she sat at the kitchen table, reading a card from Mamie. She had already read the card twice, laid it on the table and stared off into space. She picked up the card again. Mamie hadn't been home since their mother died and now she was canceling this trip home and wanted to know what color dress and shoes Swan would like. She'd send them to her. She rarely offered the child money, and it wasn't as though Swan needed it, the thing was that Swan was her only grandchild and Mamie hardly ever offered.

"Yes, we are, but since when have you been so interested in going to the grocery store?" Rayanne answered and posed a question of her own.

"I'm interested now," Swan said, "so when are we going?"

"In just a short while. I was just reading this card from your grandmother, then I'll make my shopping list. After that, we can go."

"You read my grandmother's card already. Why are you reading it again?" Swan asked, the question creasing her forehead.

"Good question," Rayanne said, returning the card to the envelop and laid it on the table. She listed several items on a pad and looked up at the clock, 5:05. Then she looked at Swan, who was sitting at the table, watching her. "I'm almost finished," Rayanne said, noting the child's impatience. Swan sat with both hands on

400

the table, her fingers wrapped together, continuing to stare at Rayanne. She lifted her eyes and looked up at Swan questioningly.

"Nothing," Swan said to the unspoken question.

Rayanne returned her attention to her list and added other items. Swan sat and waited, she clasped her hands and unclasped them, until Rayanne said, "Okay, we can go now."

"Weeee," Swan responded.

"You really don't have to go if you don't want to," Rayanne teased, knowing that wild horses couldn't keep Swan from going with her to the grocery store. The question was why. She'd never had any interest in going to the grocery store before. Swan made a face when Rayanne insisted that she wear a sweater, but she obeyed after seeing Rayanne, with her hand on her hip, looking back at her. Rayanne gave a little laugh as Swan dashed off to her room for the sweater. When she returned, Rayanne was pulling her own sweater around her shoulders. They left the house through the back door. Rayanne opened the back door of her beige Volvo station wagon and lifted Swan into the car seat.

"Aunt Rayanne, do I have to ride in this seat?" Swan questioned.

"Yes you do," Rayanne said, strapped her in and closed the door. She got into the car and fastened her own seat belt and started the car.

"Why, Aunt Rayanne?"

"Why, what?" Rayanne asked, putting the car in reverse.

"Why do I have to ride in this seat? This is a baby seat," Swan said, making a face.

"Swan, you are a baby," Rayanne said, as she backed the car out of the driveway and after checking the traffic, they headed for the store.

"I thought I was a young lady."

"In a way you are" Rayanne said and looked in both direction before she crossed the intersection, merged and began to move with the traffic.

"Then, why do I have to ride in this baby seat?"

"Honey, because it's the law, like a rule. You know how we have rules at home. Well it's sort of the same thing. Laws and rules are to be followed, and when we don't follow them, we get into trouble, and if we get into trouble, we have to pay lots of money to get out and when we do that, we won't have any money left to buy toys or books or pretty dresses."

"Okay, so I have to ride in this seat because it's like the rules we have at home," Swan said, "like I shouldn't put anything in the VCR except a VCR tape, and if I do put something other than a VCR tape into it, the VCR will get broken and I can't watch my tapes, right?"

"That's right," Rayanne said and was amazed at how much children that age really understood.

"So, I have to ride in this baby seat until I'm 6, and if I don't, we will break the rule and," she said putting her fingers to her lips, "we'll get punished, right?"

"That's right. See how smart you are," Rayanne said, smiling and they rode along several minutes in silence. Then Rayanne suggested they play a game, which delighted Swan. "Let me see," Rayanne began, "what's red and hang on trees?"

"Apples," Swan said.

"Right. Okay, let's try another. How many letters are there in the Alphabets?"

"Twenty-six," Swan said and she began to say the alphabets. Other than calling a couple of letters out of sequence, she did good.

"Very good," Rayanne said. "Now, this is a tough one. What kind of fruit grows on trees in Florida and are the same color as the name of the fruit?"

"That's easy, Aunt Rayanne," Swan shouted, "that's an orange."

"Umm, you are good at this," Rayanne said. "Let's try a few more. What is the name of Dick and Jane's pet?"

"Which pet?" Swan asked.

"Dick and Jane's pet," Rayanne repeated.

"Which pet? Dick and Jane have two pets, a dog and a cat. Which do you mean?"

Rayanne suppressed a snicker. "Okay, then, their dog?"

"Their dog's name is Spot and their cat's name is Puff," Swan said matter of factly.

"That's wonderful. You're learning a lot," Rayanne said as they pulled into the parking lot, got out of the car and entered the store.

"Do you want to ride in the cart?" Rayanne asked, reaching for her. On the occasions when Swan did go to the store, she always rode in the cart.

"No, I want to help you do the shopping," she said, walking a little ahead of the cart.

"Oh, Okay. Anything in particular you want today?"

"Yes, but I'll let you know when we get to it," Swan said. They picked up items as they moved up and down the aisles. When they arrived at the shelf where the tuna, Treet, and sardines were shelved, Rayanne noticed Swan examining the selves, something she'd never done before, except for cereal and cookies. When Swan came upon the Vienna sausages, she became very excited. She picked up two cans and handed them to Rayanne, she picked up two more cans, then two additional cans and handed them to Rayanne. "Aunt Rayanne, will you make lunch for me tomorrow?" Swan asked, looking up into her aunt's face.

"You want to take lunch from home tomorrow?" Rayanne was puzzled because Swan had always like the lunches they served at the day care.

"Yes."

"Why? Don't you like the lunches at day care any more?" Rayanne asked. "I always thought you did."

"I do, but I'd like you to pack some of those little penises for me tomorrow."

"What?" Rayanne said, surprised at the name Swan had given the Vienna Sausages.

"My friend, Becky, brought some little penises for lunch yesterday, and I liked them. They were good." Swan looked up at her aunt and asked, "Aunt Rayanne, why are you laughing?"

"I was just thinking of something that happened today," Rayanne lied, picking up a can of the Vienna sausages. Now she understood why Swan had wanted to come to the store so badly and why she didn't want to ride in the cart as she'd always done. It all made sense now.

"Was it something really funny?" Swan asked, walking along beside Rayanne and looking up into her face.

"Yes it was," Rayanne responded as she tried to suppress a giggle. "Honey, these are Vienna Sausages," Rayanne said lifting a can of sausages from the cart and stifling a laugh that threatened to escape.

"Vienna sausages?" Swan said, "but Becky said they are little penises."

"Yes, I know, but they are Vienna Sausages, and I will pack some for you tomorrow." Rayanne returned the can to the cart.

"Ooooh, yummee," Swan replied.

"You like them that much, huh?" Rayanne asked.

"Yes." Afterwards, Swan walked down the aisles perfectly contented with her selected items and Rayanne continued laughing as she shopped. Little penises, she thought and laughed some more. Rayanne saw a friend, shared the story about the little penises, and they both laughed. As she drove home, she looked at Swan through the rearview mirror to see the pleased expression on her face. Rayanne began to laugh to the point that her eyes moistened with tears. Swan noticed Rayanne wiping at her eyes and cheeks. "Aunt Rayanne, are you crying?"

"No, sweetheart. I'm not crying."

"You have tears on your face."

"Something must've gotten into my eyes."

"Oh," Swan said and looked out of the window.

"We'll make one more stop, then we'll go home. I need to stop at the book store."

"You are going to buy a book?"

"Yes."

Swan, a thoughtful look on her face, asked if she could have a book as well. There were two books that Rayanne had heard her mention. "I don't know which book I want," Swan said.

"Decision, decision," Rayanne said, she and Swan had decided previously that she could have one book a week, "but you've got a little more time to think about which one you want before we get to the store. Which do you like best?"

"The Tree," Swan answered, without hesitation.

"Is that the one about the mother tree being upset over losing her leaves," Rayanne asked.

"Yes," Swan said, explaining that the leaves are the children the mother is losing.

"Then why don't you get that one this week and the other, next week."

"Okay," Swan said a little slow."

Seeing the look on Swan's face, Rayanne asked, "What was the other book you had in mind?"

"The Frog and The Shoe."

"Oh yes, I remember you and Becky talking about that one yesterday. Why don't we get both books this week, and we'll let next week take care of itself. How about that?"

"Oooh weee," Swan said, clasping her hands together, then she asked, "Which book are you getting?"

"I'm getting *Waiting to Exhale* by a woman named Terry McMillan."

"Waiting to Ex-hale?" Swan queried, separating the word. "What is Waiting To Ex-hale?"

"It's a book about four women who are friends."

"Do they have trees?"

"Yes, I imagine they do, but the story isn't about trees. It's more about friendship."

"Oh," Swan said.

"I'll keep the book for you, and when you're old enough to read and understand it, you'll have it. Deal?"

"Deal," Swan said happily, and looked out of the window. Little penises, Rayanne thought, laughing again.

"Do you have plans for this coming Friday?" Rayanne asked.

"No, Becky is going to visit her grandmother and Marcia Raylyn is spending the night with one of her friend."

"How would you like it if we picked up a couple of your favorite movies, pop some popcorn and spend an evening in front of the TV set?"

"That would be a lot of fun," Swan said beaming. "It'll be just like going to the movies."

"That's right," Rayanne replied.

Swan was a comical little girl, you wouldn't say she had a sense of humor, Rayanne thought, but she certainly was funny. She remembered once when Swan was about two and a half and was helping Rayanne wash her car after they had returned from a trip to North Carolina. Both doors to the car were open. Swan took the cloth from the bucket and as she turned to help wash the car, she hit her head. She screamed, dropping the cloth to the ground as Rayanne rush to her and took her into the house. As Rayanne tended to Swan, she assured Rayanne that she was okay, but that she wanted to go back outside to tell the car to shut up. Rayanne had laughed, but told Swan that it was perfectly all right to tell the car to shut up. There was another time when Rayanne was giving Swan a bath, and noticed Swan staring at herself in the full length mirror that hung behind the bathroom door. Rayanne had asked her what was she thinking about, and Swan told her that she wondered why she had a little butt up front and a large butt in back. There was yet another time when she and Swan were sitting out on the front porch and Swan was counting the stars. Swan in all her animation said, pointing a finger towards a star, "You'd better come on down now, before you fall." Swan had grown a lot since that time, but she still said some of the funniest things.

That night Rayanne entered Swan's bedroom to find her dressed in her pajamas, sitting on the window seat playing with her dolls. "Hey you. What are you still doing up?"

"I was waiting for you to read one of my books to me," Swan said, setting her dolls in their proper places, and she picked up a book before jumping up onto the bed.

"I thought you were going to read your own book tonight," Rayanne teased.

"Aunt Rayanne, you know I can't read real good," Swan said. Rayanne was teaching Swan to read and she was making progress, but there were still words she didn't understand or could pronounce. She'd begun memorizing some of the books Rayanne read to her and if you didn't know, you could be fooled by her calling out the words and turning the pages at the appropriate time. Swan had grown to the point where she colored pictures without going outside the lines, her enunciation and pronunciation were distinct and clear. She was quite a little person.

"Yes, I know, Rayanne said, "but you're getting there."

When Rayanne finished reading the book, Swan said her prayers and was tucked in for the night and as Rayanne left the room, the telephone rang. It was Maxine. Marcia Raylyn had told her that on the evening before Maxine found the condom, she'd gone to dance class and one of her friends had asked if she could put her books in the car. Sometime later her friend admitted that she and her friend had sex in the car and Marcia Raylyn was certain it was her friend who'd left the condom behind. Maxine had sound happy, and Rayanne understood. That evening, Rayanne showered and went to bed early with her book. She read nearly a third of the book that first night and couldn't put it down the following night until she'd finished it. She found as she read, that she inhaled so much of each woman's character, she could definitely identify with each of them and their situations, and when she exhaled, she drifted off to sleep.

CHAPTER 56

Rayanne awoke with a start in almost total darkness, and for a split second, she was unsure where she was. She'd gone into Swan's room the night before because Swan was having a nightmare and Rayanne wanted to be there with her until she felt safe and was asleep again. As it turned out, Rayanne fell asleep as well. At 7:30 that morning, the doorbell rang. It was Josh. Rayanne hadn't seen him in weeks and she'd missed him. She smiled and was about to embrace him, but he pushed past her and went towards his old room. Josh was gathering some more of his things. He'd found himself a place he told Rayanne. She knew he was still angry at her for having had him committed and she understood his anger, but she'd hoped that he would realize and understand also that she did what she had to do in order to save him. It mattered that he was angry at her, but she could live with that. The important thing was that he was alive and she hoped he'd stay that way for a long time to come. Before Josh left, he told Rayanne he'd get the rest of his things later, he turned away from her and left the house with the tails of his top coat flapping wildly.

***

Rayanne ran into Brenda at the fitness club that she'd recently joined. She hadn't worked out much after leaving New York. The only form of exercise she'd gotten lately was an occasional walk to the lake. After undressing and climbing into her leotard, she entered the exercise room and took a place on the floor next to Brenda. "Hey you," Rayanne called out to her, falling into the routine.

"I didn't know you come here. Why haven't I seen you here before?" Brenda asked, stretching and sweating.

"I just started a couple of weeks ago. It's time I took better care of myself," Rayanne said, beginning to work up a sweat herself from the vigorous routine.

"Well, you certainly are seriously about it," Brenda said and laughed, trying to keep up the pace, noticing that Rayanne, who merely smiled at her, hadn't missed a single beat since she fell into the routine.

"I'll tell you one thing," Brenda said between pants, "when we're through here, I'm gonna find an ice cream shop and I'm gonna get the biggest cone of ice cream that they have." With that, they both chuckled, as Rayanne fell backwards onto the floor, giggling. She recovered soon, however, and they continued the routine.

Outside, after the class was over and with towels draped around their necks, Rayanne talked Brenda into getting the largest cone of Yogurt, instead of ice cream. "I showed a house to some people today," Brenda said, taking a lick from the Yogurt cone.

"Oh yeah," Rayanne said looking at her with interest.

"A nice couple," Brenda informed, "he's an engineering instructor and she's a doctor in Pediatrics."

"Where is the house?" Rayanne asked as they walked toward their cars that were parked along the curb near the yogurt shop.

"Wildwood," Brenda said, looking up at the sky smiling and Rayanne knew it was at the thought of the commission she'd be getting on selling that house, or any house in that neighborhood. "There are some beautiful homes out there. Does it look promising?"

"Yeah, they told me they'll get back in a couple of days, but, I think it's gonna go through because Mrs. Redmond whispered to me that house is going to belong to her," Brenda said, her eyes twinkling.

"Sounds good to me, girlfriend, good luck," Rayanne said, licking her Yogurt. "How are things at home?" she asked changing the subject.

"Rayanne, they couldn't be better. Chris and Devin are bringing in good grades, they are keeping out of trouble. Even Cardell and I are relating as never before," Brenda said and Rayanne could see how happy she was. They stood on the sidewalk near Brenda's Jaguar and after a few more minutes of talk, they embraced each other, got into their cars and drove away.

CHAPTER 57

"You're screwing him, aren't you?" Brenda said one evening when the three girls met to see a play that was being held at the Township, which they'd purchased tickets for more than a month before.

"Ssssh," Rayanne said, looking around, hoping no one in the crowd heard Brenda.

"Shit, you're glowing. You have the look of absolute ecstasy," Brenda said.

"What is she talking about now?" Hilary asked. Rayanne lifted her shoulders and pretended not to know either what Brenda was talking about.

"What about this scenario," Brenda said to Hilary. "Rayanne is screwing that young buck's eye balls out of his head," then she said to Rayanne, "aren't you?" And, before Rayanne could answer, she added, "I can always tell."

"What are you talking about?" Rayanne asked, staring blankly at Brenda.

"What's this? Don't tell me you're holding out on us. You aren't going to share your little business with us." When neither girl responded, Brenda said, "Well, you don't have to admit it, but I'm telling you, Rayanne Wilson, it shows. You look like a peach. You are glowing," Brenda said and Rayanne wanted to say there goes that imagination running wild again, but she didn't because

Brenda was telling the truth. Only, Brenda had no idea how truly happy she was, Rayanne thought.

"Rayanne, something's going on with you? You do look great. A woman usually looks her absolute best when she's in love," Hilary said, interrupting Rayanne's thoughts, "or when she's pregnant."

"Or as I said, fucking," Brenda said. Then, as though a light bulb went on inside her head, she said, "Are you pregnant?"

"No, I'm not pregnant," Rayanne declared.

"But you are in love," Hilary said.

Rayanne paused a moment, then she admitted, "yes, I'm in love."

"What?" Brenda said smiling, looking from Rayanne to Hilary, then back to Rayanne.

"I'm in love. Didn't you hear me?" Rayanne said.

"I knew it. I knew it," Brenda said.

"Why haven't you told us. This should be the happiest time in your life," Hilary said, and it was true. Rayanne was happier than she'd been in a very long time.

"It is Scott, isn't it?" Brenda asked. Rayanne nodded affirmatively. "Well you go girl," she said.

"I'll say," Hilary agreed.

"Scott is exciting, spontaneous, caring, and listen to this. He plays with my hair. The man plays with my hair. God, I love a man who plays with my hair. To tell you the truth girls, Scott is everything Ralph wasn't."

"Ralph who," Hilary teased, and the girls laughed, because she was the serious one who rarely joked about anything.

"Hilary has taken that stick out of her butt since she started letting Ben eat that cat," Brenda said and it was followed by more laughter. Hilary's attitude had changed, along with her appearance. She'd cut her hair in that Halle Berry or Toni Braxton's style, which looked great on her, her clothes were more fashionable, and she'd began wearing contact lens, which allowed her eyes to show, adding a whole new dimension to her face that the unattractive horn rimmed glasses had concealed for years. It would've been difficult to know just how attractive Hilary was had she not made the change. The woman looked ten years younger, she was more hip, she looked great. "So tell us, Rayanne, how's it going?" Brenda asked.

"Great," Rayanne replied. "He really does it for me. Scott does everything that he can to make each day important for me. The man hasn't just taught me how to love freely, he's taught me how to trust again. To tell you the truth guys, Scott isn't just the kind of man I'd like to spend the rest of my life with, he is the man I want to spend the rest of my life with," Rayanne said with certainty.

Brenda reached out and gave Rayanne five, saying, "I heard that, girlfriend."

"When did all of this happen?" Hilary asked.

"Kind of recent, actually," Rayanne said, feeling warm inside at the thought of Scott.

"Tell us about it, every nasty, slutty detail," Brenda said, and Rayanne obliged, beginning with the night when they'd first made love. She knew in her heart that what she felt for Scott was real, very real, because what she'd felt for any one in her past was like a shadow on the wall in comparison to what she felt for Scott.

"You're really happy, aren't you," Brenda said when Rayanne finished her story.

"More than you can imagine," Rayanne said, and her friends were happy about her new found joy.

"I don't know why you didn't tell us. You're not ashamed of being in love with a younger man, are you?" Brenda asked.

"No, I'm not ashamed of the relationship with Scott, but I do value discretion," Rayanne responded.

"To hell with discretion, we're your friends. Besides, any man who makes you as happy as you obviously are, should be paraded around like a king," Brenda said.

"Sure 'nuff," Hilary said.

"Listen to Hilary," Rayanne said to Brenda, "She's become a totally different person, the way she looks, the way she dresses. The girl has got it going on."

"You got that right," Brenda said.

"Enough about me," Hilary said. "Tell us more about you and Scott."

"There isn't much more to tell. We're very much in love, and we're going to see where it takes us."

"I don't blame you. Scott's a great guy," Brenda said. Both, she and Hilary met Scott some time ago and they'd liked him. Brenda as much as said she thought Scott put the 'M' in Man. "He's fine."

"He's a hunk," Hilary put in. Brenda and Rayanne looked at each other and laughed. In the past, Hilary would not have voiced that kind of opinion but now, she openly agreed with Brenda's assessment of Scott.

"I'm certainly glad that the age thing doesn't bother you anymore," Brenda commented.

"I think it's great," Hilary agreed, as the line moved about a yard. Rayanne smiled at how happy she was that she'd had the good sense to realize that age was just a number, as Scott had said. It didn't spell man, and it didn't mean a thing as long as the people involved loved each other, took care of each other and made each other happy. There was so much violence and unhappiness going on in the world, Rayanne thought, that it simply didn't make any sense to make each other more miserable than they already were. She remembered saying to Scott not long ago, the myth about younger men and older women.

"What is that myth?" Scott had asked and answered, "you mean the one about easy sex, without commitment or the one about having an older woman take care of the guy?"

"It's not a myth, Scott. It's a fact. Besides, ten years from now, what will you want with a woman eight years older," Rayanne said, and she was never happier than when he replied, "the same thing I want with her now."

The line had move not more than a few yards the first 15 or 20 minutes, but then it began to crawl and it did so like a snake with a purpose. The patrons entered the Auditorium and found their seats. Brenda was seated between the girls, she made a face and said, "ain't nobody asked me what's going on in my life."

Rayanne and Hilary laughed, and Rayanne said, "feeling left out, are we?" They laughed.

"Damn right," Brenda pouted.

Rayanne said, still laughing, "What's going on with you, Brenda?"

"Oh, nothing much," Brenda replied. "Same ole, same ole."

"Oh heck no, now I know you've got something to say," Hilary said.

"That's right, so tell us. What are you up to?" Rayanne asked.

Brenda looked at each of them, paused, then said, "there's one little thing I could share with my best friends."

"You sold another house," Hilary said jubilantly. "This woman is going to be a millionaire, and soon."

"No it's a little better than that," Brenda said.

"What?' Rayanne asked.

"Better than selling an expensive house?" Hilary said, "and getting a huge commission."

"Well, more exciting, then," Brenda replied, then she said softly, "Cardell and I are back together."

"What?" Rayanne jumped from her seat, unable to contain her excitement for Brenda. "You lying."

"I don't believe it. Yeah she's lying," Hilary said.

"No I'm not. We've been together two months now, and girls, it's great. It's simply been wonderful. Cardell is more loving and considerate than he's ever been, and I don't need to tell you how happy the boys are."

"Darn it and you kept this from us all this time," Hilary screeched.

"Sure did. Are y'all mad?" Brenda asked, laughing that infectious laugh that was so like Ivory's, Rayanne thought.

"No, we're not mad," Hilary replied. "We're happy for you, but I don't know how you kept quiet. The excitement would've killed me. I would've been knocking on doors, telling everyone."

"I haven't seen you guys in a while, and I wanted us to be together when I told you. Y'all sure y'all ain't mad?"

"No," Rayanne and Hilary said in unison as Brenda continued to laugh.

"That's good, 'cause I wouldn't give a damn if you were. I figure the hell, you'll get over it," Brenda said, laughing some more.

"Girl, things are looking up," Rayanne said, and they embraced one another. There was a combination of laughter and crying, while the other patrons looked on. "Let's get out of here," Rayanne said, brushing the tears from her face. "This calls for a celebration."

"It certainly does, but what about the play?" Hilary asked.

"We can see the play another time. It'll be here for another week, besides it's not one of mine," Rayanne said jokingly but added on a more serious note, "we can come back next week."

"And we'll have to stand in that long ass line again," Brenda said, her face wrinkled up.

"So what?" Rayanne said.

"Right, so what," Brenda agreed, lifting her shoulders.

"Yeah, sooo whaaat," Hilary said. Laughter followed and they left the auditorium. When they were out on the street, they gave their tickets to the first three persons they met who didn't already have tickets for the play.

Brenda hailed a taxi, they climbed inside to ride several blocks to Main Street, to one of their favorite restaurants. While on the way, Brenda said, "Maya Angelou is coming to Benedict next month."

"I know, and I can hardly wait to see her. I saw her only once, and she was dynamite," Rayanne said.

"I've seen her several times, and she's something. She's in-spired me for years," Brenda commented.

"So, we're going?" Hilary asked.

"Of course, we are," Rayanne responded.

"Solid," Brenda said. "It'll be great." She paused a moment, eyeing the scenery as their taxi rolled down the street. "Girls, my priorities certainly have changed. I see thing differently now. Re-member when I use to charge everything?" she asked.

"Who could forget that," Rayanne laughed.

"Well, back then, there was a void in my life. I was searching for something. I just wanted everything and I didn't have a care about accepting responsibility. I use to charge things that I didn't even want. I ran those cards up to the hilt. I swear there was a time when I thought I'd owe Jesus Christ and God Almighty would hold a second mortgage. Well, I don't feel that way now. I shop, yes, but shopping and charging are not that important to me any-more. God has answered my prayers and given me insight into other things. I've got my husband back, my kids are good kids, they're happy, they're in school and doing really good, and I'm selling houses like a mad woman. My life is good and I'm very happy and thankful."

"You deserve all the happiness you can get, Brenda. I am happy for you," Rayanne said.

"That goes for me too," Hilary said and they smiled at Brenda. Then Hilary asked, "what about your upcoming speaking engage-ment, Rayanne."

"I'm speaking at another high school day after tomorrow," Rayanne replied. "I hope I can make some impression on them."

"You just lay it out to them, give it your best shot and I'm sure you'll reach some of them. If you reach 10 percent of them, heck," Brenda threw up her arms, "even 1 percent, for that matter, you would've done your part. But I know you. You'll get through to them. You've got that gift. You certainly reached Jason. Six months too late," she laughed, "but you reached him nonetheless." Rayanne gave a little laugh, herself. Brenda had seen Jason only once since he and Rayanne had that little discussion but she'd made it clear that she had no interest in him and that if he didn't want to tangle with her husband, that he'd stay away. Jason never returned after that.

"You'll be a smash," Hilary said.

Rayanne didn't say anything. When she wrote the speech, she'd put a lot of thought into it. The words had come straight from her heart. She didn't sugar coat it or polish it up. She was playing hard ball, she was being honest. "We shall see whether I'm a smash or whether I will crash and burn," Rayanne said, then in a voice that was almost a whisper, she said, "We shall see."

The taxi stopped, they got out and walked towards the restaurant with their arms around one another. "Yeah girlfriend, you're going to be a smash," Brenda said.

"And, you are the eternal optimist," Rayanne said.

"That's true, too," Brenda said. "If Cardell can change and Hilary let's her old man go to the Y, then anything is possible."

"Shut up," Hilary spat out and laughed.

"I will not," Brenda said.

"And just think, I thought she had confidence in my ability," Rayanne teased.

"I do and you know it. What I'm saying is that you don't have a thing to worry about. All you have to do is walk your ass up on that stage, make eye contact with them little bitches and drive by shooters, you know, get their attention, let your hair down, girlfriend, and rap on. You'll have them eating right out of your hands," Brenda said.

"Goodness gracious," was all Rayanne could say.

CHAPTER 58

Spring was a time for new hopes and new beginnings. The birds communicated with each other as they twittered in the trees and darted off in pairs. Rayanne stood on the front porch. She closed her eyes, she looked out of her window, and she thanked God for His many blessings. In less than two hours she'd stand before an audience of almost 2,000 students and faculty members combined, and speak to them on issues that would affect some of them for the rest of their lives. She'd be relating directly to individuals on topics that some of them may find offensive, perhaps condescending, while others might view as absurd and totally ridiculous, but hopefully some would identify with the message and find some answers.

Rayanne was dressed in a navy, linen suit, with lapels, one of which held a gold pin in the shape of a four leaf clover. It was a pin that her mother had given to her on her 21st birthday. She wore a white silk blouse, a single strand of white pearls with matching earrings and navy pumps and bag. She entered the auditorium. It was quite noisy. She brought with her, a large shopping bag that she placed on the floor by the chair where she sat. After a moment, the principal got up, walked up to the podium and said, " Good morning, may I have your attention, please?" The students immediately became quiet, and he prepared to introduce the speaker. He mentioned the fact that Rayanne was, at one time, one of the youngest and most successful playwrights in New York, that she'd acted in some of her own creations and he mentioned some of her other accomplishments. When he finally introduced Rayanne, she was met with a warm ovation, and she made her way, on shaky legs, to the podium. She'd only done this a couple of times and it still made her a little nervous. She looked out at her audience, took a deep breath and said, "Good morning, ladies and gentlemen." The crowd responded cordially. "How are you all this morning?" she asked and different responses came from the crowd. "First I'd like to invite each of you to take a ribbon from this bag." Rayanne passed the bag along to each person who sat on the stage beside her, and several students were invited to take the bag and assist in passing out the ribbons to the audience. "You will noticed that the ribbons are yellow. Yellow means friendship and in friendship, there is love, and if we can love one another, we can heal our state, our nation, our world. I want you to hold onto your ribbons and if or when you feel inspired, I'd like you to pin it on yourself. If there isn't anything that is said here today that moves you to want to bond with others and try to make your space a better place, then you may want to just discard your ribbon. However, if you feel a sense of unity and want to make a difference, please put them on and wear them proudly," she said. Even before she began her speech, some of the students began to pin on their ribbons.

"I'd like to speak with you this morning, ladies and gentlemen on issues that are of great concern to me. Issues that require solutions, answers. I don't proclaim to have the answers to the world's problems, problems that we are facing on a day to day basis, but together, we can talk about some of the things we can do to try to combat some of these problems and make the world a little better, and I think a little better, is something, don't you."

The audience responded, "Yes."

"Let's talk about violence, crime. I think a part of the crime wave that we are experiencing right now is directly related to drugs and the economy. One of the things I feel strongly about is education, because education does help equip us for better jobs and better jobs mean more income and more income can keep us from the path of doing something that is illegal. Therefore, education is important, very important. There aren't that many good jobs out there, but when employers look for new employees, you better believe that they are going to be looking at the persons best qualified," she paused, making eye contact with the crowd. "Some of the crime is because folks just can't find decent jobs, or jobs, period. So if you have got a man out there who is unemployed and he has a family, not in every case but in a lot of cases, that man is going to feel his world is coming apart, he has to take care of his family, he gets depressed, he takes his last couple of dollars and he gets that fix that will relieve his pain for a while, and I mean for a while because it is only going to be a temporary thing. It's going to make him feel good for a while, he is going to feel as free as a bird, but what he doesn't know is that with that first fix, he just compounded his problem. In addition to not having a job or money to support his family, he now has a habit to support, and, that habit becomes his mistress. You know what they say about mistresses. If you can't afford one, don't go out and get one," she paused. "Anyway, he now has this mistress, and he has to support it. He goes out and he robs someone, he gets caught and goes to jail or he hurts someone or someone hurts him in the process, and where is he? There is a number of reasons why an individual may turn to using or selling drugs. And on the other hand, there are as many reasons why that individual shouldn't. I am not going to give you the pros, let's try some of the cons. Well, maybe some of both. We look for this utopia, this ecstasy of passion, if you will, but what we really get is the agony of pain, defeat. Drugs give us some false sense of security. In other words, drugs destroys what would have been an otherwise good mind. Perhaps a brilliant mind. It distorts our thought processes. Drugs rip at the very fabric of our society. I tell you this, drugs are equal opportunity employers, if you get my drift. You may be riding around in a BMW, a new BMW at that, but do you have a house? Do you have any legitimate investments, a bank account in your own name with more than a hundred dollars in it? Probably not. We are sometimes caught up into selling drugs because it is perceived as being glamorous, exciting, attractive, and this is an area where I believe script writers, producers and directors should take some responsibility. For them it's the money. We sometimes get involved in that kind of activity to do so on a small scale, but let me tell you, ladies and gentlemen, what may begin as a minor situation can mushroom into something major, and get out of hand. Dealing or using drugs is trouble.

Another thing we have to remember about involvement in drugs is that we are the ones who take the risks. We take chances from the time we take possession of the stuff until we pay the man. We go out and take risks selling the drugs not knowing if we will have to kill someone to get the money for the man or be killed and the worse part, I think, is that we sell that stuff to each other, and for someone else. We don't even get the big share of the profit for all the chances that we take. We live our lives in fear from day to day wondering who is after us, who is going to take over for us if we are in jail or killed. Is it worth it? I ask you, is it worth it? We take all of the risks, we live like trapped animals, and we don't' even get the big pay off. We don't bring the stuff here. How are we going to get the drugs into this country. Do we have the planes to fly it in or boats to sail it in? No, but we are willing to risk everything to sell and make someone else rich and powerful, while we just go out and get taken out, killed, in some dark alley, alone, trying to make a score.

"I have visited schools and penal institutions where kids, such as yourselves, and adults, as well, who were arrested on drug charges. Some of them used very creative methods to conceal the drugs. Some used goodie powder packages, they stuffed it into ball point pens and ink pens, carved out pages in their books, etc., but that didn't keep them from getting caught. They get caught, my friends. What I am saying is some of those ideas could be used in more positive ways. To use those minds that way was a complete waste. Minds like that can inspire all kinds of wonderful ideas, and I don't have to tell you how angry it makes me to see those minds sitting idle in jail cells. Another thing that gets to me is that drugs are sold to kids, to pregnant women and anyone else who is willing to buy it. There is something about drugs that is so sinister, and when it is brought into the schools, we have to impress upon each other to just say no. There was a time when kids got into fights in school, there would be a little hair pulling and a little face scratching, but not now. Now we are getting security guards and metal detectors in our school, because along with the drugs, there are weapons, and kids are being shot, cut, maimed, and those are the lucky ones, because it gets worse. Many of them get killed. Those young lives are over. Don't destroy your sisters and brothers, your fellow man. If there ever comes a time when you have a gun and you want to take someone else's life, think. Take the time to think about what you are doing. Don't pull the trigger. Fifteen, twenty years from today, that person who has that knife or gun is trained on could be your son or your daughter. They could be the recipient of that knife blade or that bullet. The best thing to do young men and young ladies is to stay away from that kind of behavior, and start preparing yourselves now for a better way of life, where if there is a job out there, you be the best qualified and if there is no job, get the education to be able to help create jobs. All it takes to start is a little money and a good mind. Good business sense can make it happen. And, you can help the before yous and after yous, to make it. You have to think and prepare yourselves. I know peer pressure is hell, pardon me, please, but it makes me so angry when I see what is going on around me. I know peer pressure is tough, and I know the way sometimes looks dark and dreary, but we can make it, ladies and gentlemen. We can because we have to. If we become drug dealers or get involved in some other illegal trade, what are we going to tell our children, our families? We certainly can't tell them that. We want to be proud of our accomplishments. We want our families and our friends to be proud of our accomplishments. Who are we going to tell that we are a drug dealer, a pimp, a prostitute, a gambler, robber, a crook or the like. The thing we want to do is enhance our lives and those of others. God gave each and every one of us a life and a good head. He wants us to live that life, not gamble it away. Life is no game. It is real and it can be good, productive, worthwhile. If we choose to live our lives as one of those 'good,' Rayanne used her fingers to make quotations marks, "professions" that I have just named, there is no one who is going to be proud of us. It is important to look to the future and what lies ahead.

I have heard in my very few years on earth, that we didn't ask to come here, we didn't ask to be born, and we don't owe anyone anything. Well, of course we didn't ask to be born. How could we? But we do owe. We owe our parents for bringing us here, and we owe our foreparents. They brought us into a world that can be beautiful, if we help to make it so. Yes, we owe, ladies and gentlemen. We owe a lot. We owe our ancestors for the painstaking in which they helped in molding our lives. They taught us so much. Always to put our best foot forward. They taught us to not be afraid of failure because sometimes it is through failure that we learn and discover new ways of succeeding. They impressed upon us to look to each day for something good to build on, to find something special and different, as well as look to the future with promise and possibility. We owe them. They taught us first to believe in ourselves and to work through obstacles and not overlook them. We learned to believe that we can be whatever we want to be because we are filled with potential. They instilled in us the knowledge that it is all right to get discouraged, but never to give up. They taught us that the simplest pleasures are very often the most rewarding. Yes, we owe them. They nurtured us to always know that they love and understand us as well as let us know that they will always be there for us, even when sometimes we feel alone. They are with us even if in spirit only. Through their wisdom, we are at a point where we can respect our weaknesses and compliment our strengths. Their teachings have motivated us to not allow life to slip through our fingers, without affecting some change. They gave us examples to live by and dreams to realize for we know that without dreams, hope, goals and desires, is to be without purpose.

"Let's center our attention to some of the movies that we see. While I think everything has a purpose, I think that some of the movies we see influence us in such a negative way. We see the drugs, the guns, the killing, the tough guys. Everybody wants to be top man. That whole scene is glamorized to the point that we try to emulate the characters we see on the screen. We want to be the warrior, this is violence and that violence is being passed down to our children. Drugs and killings shouldn't be glamorized. We cannot glorify these acts of violence. Look at the suicide rate. It has increased due to mental stress. Then there is the fear that we have to deal with, and ladies and gentlemen, fear transforms into rage and aggression.

"Poverty areas are particularly vulnerable to television violence. Violence is disturbing and dangerous. There was a time when we could leave our homes without locking our doors. We didn't even have to lock them at night, but we can't do that anymore, can we? We sometimes get into trouble because we choose to see the glass as being half empty. Remember, that same glass is also half full.

"And to you, young ladies, remember to try to maintain your identities. Keep in control of your own minds and bodies. Don't let anyone dictate what you should do or where you should go. Let those decisions be made by you and only you. What I am getting at is teenage pregnancy. We can get pregnant when we have absolutely nothing else to do. Besides, why would you want to sit at home raising babies, when you are babies yourselves, and miss out on all that life has got to offer. You let these little boys know that you are smart and you have no intention of being taken in by anyone. There are some girls who are pregnant, some already have a baby or babies. There is no disgrace in that. I have always thought that if a girl gets pregnant, it is the good girl who follows through and has the baby, but if you are not pregnant and don't already have a baby, don't. At least don't do it right now. There is plenty of time for that. There are answers to some of today's problems, and we know what we have got to do. We have got to stay in school, get a good education, advance our learning, enlarge our educational level, build our positive attributes. Education broadens us as people, it opens our minds to new experiences and challenges, and it prepares us to face the future, and your future will look so bright, you will have to wear sunglasses." Rayanne looked around and she could see some of the students giving each other five. "We are living in times of such rapid change, and we sometime lose control. Remember, our past does not have to be our future. We can have wonderful, happy lives. Happiness is a choice, and it is life. Our lives depend on where we put our attention. Yes, I have been lucky. I am lucky. I have had some wonderful things to come into my life. I have been blessed, I have had some success, but it didn't come without a lot of hard work. I have had rejections, yes's and no's. I worked on changing the no's into yes's. There are tragedies out there, try to learn to turn them into miracles. As strange as it may seem, miracles do grow out of tragedies. We have got to find enough strength from within to determine our own worth, because, ladies and gentlemen, we owe. Take that little point of view and add it to your own repertoire, and you will make a quantum leap into whatever kind of future you choose for yourself.

"There is the topic of gangs. Gang banging is another area of disturbance. Don't you wonder why gangs even exist. That is so dumb. Why would an intelligent person want to belong to a gang. You don't need any one like that controlling your life, telling you what to do. There is no need for gangs. All that comes out of gangs is more violence, and cruel, horrible deaths. As gang members, we are killing each other. Don't you see that? To become a gang banger, you have to hate someone but the person a gang banger hates most is himself, and the question is why? Gangs are a dead end street. I see most gangs as kids who are confused. They don't know who to listen to anymore because the information given out is so contradictory. Don't destroy one another. Right now, please, would each of you turn to the person sitting next to you and tell that person you love him or her. Very good," she said when that was done, then she went on saying, "when you get up in the morning, tell your parents that you love them. I know what some of you are thinking, 'shucks, I'm a big boy. I ain't telling my mama and daddy I love them.' Why not?" Rayanne asked. "You tell the Lord

God Almighty that you love Him, don't you? I would imagine that God would say, 'how can you tell Me you love Me, someone whom you cannot see, yet you cannot tell man, whom you can see, that you love him.' Can't you imagine God saying that? You think about it. Think, my young sisters and brothers. Think about yourselves and your fellow man. Think about life and peace and joy and happiness and love, love for one another. We have to stop the violence and start to love. Those of you who have children, we have to tell them each and every day that we love them.

"Goals. Think about your goals, your dreams, think about your future. Always have a plan for yourself, because if you do not, then someone will have one for you. In each of us no matter how far down it is," Rayanne took a deep breath and exhaled loudly, "no matter how far down it is, we have love inside of us, and that's the key that brings all of the good things out of us, and brings us all together as one people. We have to love ourselves, love each other, and we have to teach that love to others."

Rayanne noticed more and more students pinning on their ribbons and she smiled. "We have got to have love in our own hearts," she said hitting her own chest, "before we can begin to have any hope. Remember we can accomplish anything in life that we want. You know why? Because we are all winners. There are no losers here. You hear me? There are no losers here. You are the best that this world is ever going to find. Be proud of your own self worth, because it is valuable. We are going to make our mark. We are going to affect change. We are going to be focused. We are going to be motivated and in the right direction. We are going to heal this country because this is our country and this space belongs to us. We are going to take care of each other. We are going to exercise our knowledge of the 3 R's which are?" she asked and the students responded, "Reading, Riting and Rithmetic." Then she said, "And we are going to add and practice an additional 3R's and they are Restraint, Responsibility and Respect. We are going to stay in school and not just to make something out of ourselves because we already are something pretty special, but we are going to improve on who we already are. We have an important legacy to pass on, a legacy to preserve our youth, and we," she paused again, "we are not through owing yet. We owe the children who have come into this world after us. We owe them. We owe them a future, ladies and gentlemen. They deserve it. They deserve a future...and so do we. We have got to stop the violence and start to love. Are there any questions?"

CHAPTER 59

"That jack ass is coming here again," Maxine said. "I'm sick of his shit. I don't care how he treats me or what he's done to me, but I will be damned if I'll have him hurting my children. I'm gonna put a stop to this crap. She was pacing back and forth in the den at Rayanne's house. Rayanne was quiet, sitting on the couch packing her suitcases. She and Swan were spending a few days in New York. She knew Maxine well enough to know that she needed to talk, to vent as much as possible. "And you know he's got that silly ass school girl who he calls his wife, hooked on all those lies. All I know is that she'd better wake up, take her head out of his ass and grow up." Maxine paused a moment, then she started up all over again, "I should've busted a cap in his ass when he was here before. He doesn't know who he's fooling with, does he?" Maxine asked. Huh uh, Rayanne thought, but she didn't answer. "But I'm gonna get his black ass this time," Maxine said and added, "I hope he isn't so naive as to think that he won't have the bitter with the sweet. You know what I'm saying." Un huh, Rayanne thought, but she still didn't comment. "You just wait. I'm gonna get him good."

This time Rayanne asked when she thought Maxine had wound down some. "What are you gonna do?"

"I haven't made up my mind yet, but he'll be sorry," she said, and Rayanne knew she meant it.

"When is he coming back here?" Rayanne asked.

"A week from Sunday," Maxine answered. Rayanne had heard that Joe was coming again and although she didn't know when, she was sure that Maxine would make him pay this time. After a while Rayanne decided to change the subject to get Maxine's mind off of Joe.

"Thank you for taking my place at the Neighborhood Watch meeting tomorrow night, Maxine."

"Oh, that's no problem besides, it's not even necessary with Aunt Bessie there. She's a one woman Army," Maxine said and Rayanne had to agree, because although she was old, Aunt Bessie was feisty and the only person who she would let get over on her was her son. "What time is your flight?"

"4:10" Rayanne said. She'd finished her new book and had decided that she'd fly it to New York. She wanted to see her friends and that was a perfect time to do it. Marcia Raylyn would have gone with them but since she'd just started in the challenge program at the University, she'd have to pass on this trip.

"Maybe next time," Maxine said. Rayanne was sure there'd be lots of trips, but she was still concerned about the situation between her sister and Joe. "I'm okay," Maxine said, looking serious, "just pissed off."

"I know, but don't let it get the best of you. The way I see it, Joe isn't worth it," Rayanne said, and got up after placing the last two items into the suitcase.

"You'll be seeing everyone?" Maxine asked.

"Yes," Rayanne said, knowing Maxine meant Dorian, since she'd told Maxine that Ivory mentioned that Dorian and her family would also be visiting New York at the same time.

Maxine really believed that was why Rayanne had picked the time she had to make the trip. "I'm glad," she said a little absent-mindedly. Rayanne was glad too that she and Dorian would be seeing each other again under different circumstances. Perhaps, in time, they will be able to work out their differences and become friends again.

"Did you get the travel toys for Swan?" Maxine asked, interrupting Rayanne's thoughts.

"Yes. I've packed them in the carry on bag."

"Do you plan to see Ralph?" Maxine asked looking at her sister. "I suppose not after what Scott told him he'd do to him if he didn't back out of Rayanne's life and leave her alone.

Rayanne looked up from the suitcase that she'd just closed. "No, I don't think so. I wish Ralph well, but I ain't got no business with that man."

Maxine shrugged her shoulders and asked, "where is Swan?"

"She's napping. I'm going to get her up in a few minutes and get her dressed."

"I'd better be getting home. You two have a good trip, and thanks for listening, Sis." With that, Maxine hurried out through the rear door.

***

Rayanne would never forget the way Swan's eyes lit up at seeing New York by night. Her eyes held a certain fascination by the lights, the people, traffic, everything. She was in complete awe, and although she whispered to Rayanne in the plane on their returned trip that she liked New York very much, she liked South Carolina better. After dinner the evening they returned from New York, Rayanne remembered how much she enjoyed seeing her old friends again. She and Dorian talked, but they didn't make much progress. But Scott, she truly missed Scott and her first telephone call, when she returned, was to him. He wasn't there, she left a message.

Rayanne hummed as she drove to the grocery store and just as she was pulling out of the parking lot, she saw Scott's Explorer parked on the street. She waited for the light to change, then she drove around, parked beside his truck and waited for him. She didn't have to wait long, because shortly after she parked, she saw Scott coming out of a building, only he wasn't alone. He was walking with Donnie and a tall attractive woman who had to be Donnie's mother. The threesome walked to the Explorer, got in, and Scott drove away, without even a glance in her direction. For years Rayanne had listened to him tell her how unhappy he'd been with Frannie, what a slut and vindictive person she was. Well, the cozy little scene she'd just witnessed was far from the picture he'd painted. They looked like a happy family, and the effect it had on her was like a knife turning its blade in her heart. What was it about her that made men lie to her, deceive her? Would she ever be happy? She wasn't sure what to expect from Scott, but she never thought he would've hurt her so. Rayanne wished Ralph hadn't called her earlier, they'd said things they shouldn't have, she was angrier than she'd been in a long time, and he would have to end the conversation by saying, "all men lie and cheat."

When Scott called that evening, Rayanne lost it to the point that she didn't ask any questions. She accused him of lying and cheating, she told him she knew now that he'd never ended his relationship with Frannie, and she told him she should never have gotten involved with him. Scott always had a hot temper, so when she attacked him, and he came back with, "you have to remember, Rayanne, I had a life before I met you," she was devastated and when she hung up the phone, she felt whipped. She'd lost all the energy she had when she returned from New York and she was dazed as she walked around the house. What is wrong with these men, she wondered. Are they all crazy, or is it me?

Aunt Bessie answered her phone on the first ring. Rayanne poured Swan a glass of milk, set it on the table and she told Aunt Bessie about her trip.

"Sounds like y'all had a good time." Aunt Bessie paused. "Rayanne, is everything all right?"

"Everything's fine," Rayanne said, "I'm a little tired. What about you. Are you all right?"

"Stevie's back," Aunt Bessie said.

"He is?" Rayanne questioned. Aunt Bessie told Rayanne that Stevie tried to attack her again but she'd managed to get into her room and locked the door."

Rayanne's voice was flooded with concern when she asked, "Where is Stevie?"

"He's in there somewhere, sleeping off that nasty old liquor and that other poison he's putting in his body," Aunt Bessie said.

"And you're sure you're okay?"

"I'm okay."

"You stay where you are, and I'll be there as quickly as I can." After Rayanne hung up the phone, she called the bus station and drove Swan over to John's house, she brought John to Aunt Bessie's and filled him in on what Aunt Bessie had told her. Rayanne used her key to get in, flipping on lights as they went along. A chair was turned over and lay on the kitchen floor. Rayanne was frightened for Aunt Bessie. What has he done to her, she wondered. "Aunt Bessie," she called out. No answer, "Aunt Bessie," she called again, but still no answer.

"Stevie," John called out. "Stevie, where are you?" There was no answer, and they proceeded towards Aunt Bessie's bedroom.

Rayanne tapped lightly on the door, "Aunt Bessie, it's me Rayanne." The door opened slowly, and Aunt Bessie stood there, shaken and distraught and with dried blood under her nose. Rayanne was shocked by her aunt's appearance. She took her by the hand and lead her to the bathroom, but not before she heard John swear under his breath.

"That son of mine. I don't know what I'm gonna do with him. He comes in here, tears the place up, takes what he wants and then he's gone again," Aunt Bessie said and when John asked where Stevie was, she said, "I reckon he's in here somewhere 'cause he had too much of that old poison in his body to go too far."

John walked away from them to search the house. "I don't know what this world is coming to," he said. Aunt Bessie was about to comment, but Rayanne quieted her.

"Ssssh," Rayanne said. "Let me take care of you." Rayanne dampened a towel and gently and silently she wiped the blood from her aunt's nose. She couldn't believe Stevie had done that to his own mother. Aunt Bessie explained that he didn't actually hit her, although he tried. She'd gotten the bruises on her face when she was running away from him and ran into a door. Rayanne led Aunt Bessie into the kitchen.

"There ain't no telling what he woulda done if he'd caught up with me," Aunt Bessie said, and she assured Rayanne that she didn't hurt anywhere else.

Rayanne told her she'd called the bus station and if she agreed, they'd have Stevie on a bus to New York that night. "You just tell me what you want," Rayanne said.

"I want him to go and I don't want him back until he knows how to act." At that moment, Aunt Bessie didn't care where Stevie went or what he did, she just didn't want him to do it in her house. Rayanne was infuriated about what her aunt was going through. She shouldn't have to give up on her only son, her only child.

"We'll get him out of here. Don't you worry," Rayanne assured her. Rayanne and Aunt Bessie were joined by John who led Stevie to a chair and stood over him with his fingers rolled into two huge fists and if she knew John, Rayanne was sure that he'd already punched Stevie once or twice. Rayanne and John took Stevie and his small suitcase, to the bus station. She left them in the car and knowing that Stevie didn't have any money, she went inside and purchased a ticket, using a credit card. Stevie was leaving South Carolina that night, no matter what it took.

"Your next bus departs at 11:30 for New York, right?" Rayanne asked the ticket agent.

"No ma'am. The next bus out of here for New York is 12:30,"

he responded.

"But when I called earlier, I thought you said a bus leaves at 11:30."

"I'm afraid you must've misunderstood me. We haven't had a bus to leave here for New York at 11:30 for some time now," he explained. Rayanne checked her watch. Goodness, she thought, does this mean I have to sit here for two hours?

"Ma'am, do you want the ticket?" the agent asked Rayanne as she looked at her watch, again. Only a minute had elapsed. It was just 10:15. "Are you making the trip, ma'am?" he asked looking a little annoyed, as there were several people in line behind her, waiting to purchase tickets.

"No Sir. My cousin is, but he doesn't want to," Rayanne said, and paused a moment, "let me ask you something please. Will he be able to cash in this ticket?" She was a little relieved when he told her the ticket could not be cashed in if a credit card was used to purchase it.

He explained, "if you charge the ticket on that credit card, he can't cash it in with me but he can sell it to the next passenger who walks through the door to buy a ticket, for the full price, half price or whatever. It just depends on how badly he wants the money or how badly he wants to stay here. Now if you wanted to cash it in, you would suffer a small penalty, but other than that, there would be no problem."

"I see," Rayanne said, she walked over to the bus schedule, studied it, then back to the line.

"Is there some reason why you think your cousin might not be on that bus?" the ticket agent asked when the line had advanced and she stood before the agent again.

"He's just that kind of person. He's my cousin, but he's not a very nice person. His mother wants him gone and so do I," Rayanne said as the agent handed her a one way ticket and returned her credit card and just as she was about to walk away from the counter, the agent said, "young lady," he looked thoughtful, "the next bus pulls out of here in an hour and twenty five minutes. You give me that ticket back," he said and although Rayanne obeyed, she was puzzled. "What is your name, Miss?" he asked.

Rayanne looked at him, still puzzled, but she said, "Rayanne Wilson."

"Your telephone number, Miss Wilson?" he asked and she gave it to him. "Where is the passenger?"

"He's outside in the car," she said, looking over her shoulders, nodding her head in the direction of her parked car where John and Stevie waited.

"You live here in town?"

"Yes I do."

"You leave him here and go on home," the ticket agent said, "I'll hold onto the ticket and put him on that bus, personally."

"Would you do that, sir?" Rayanne was joyful, relieved as she handed him the ticket. She couldn't believe her good luck.

"Yes, Miss. You go on, and I'll take care of this for you."

"You're a God send. Thank you very much, sir," Rayanne said and she returned to the car. She taped on the rear window where Stevie sat slumped in the back seat and motioned for him to let the window down. He obeyed and she placed her elbows in the window and looked at Stevie. "Stevie, the next bus for New York leaves here in a little more than an hour, and I want you on it. You have hurt your mother enough. I don't know what's gotten into you, but if you ever come back here and do something like this again, I'll have you arrested, cousin or not. And, you can believe it won't be before I personally see to it that you get your behind whipped, and we'll see how you like it. You got that?" Rayanne said. Stevie attempted to defend himself but she wasn't interested in his lies. She was more concerned with getting him out of South Carolina and his mother's life.

"Why don't you just get out of the car, Stevie and wait on the bus inside, okay?" John said. He had exercised an enormous amount of patience because he wasn't the type to be toyed with when he was pissed off.

"I just want to know what Rayanne is talking about," Stevie slurred.

"We are not going to get into it. Just get your things and get out," she said.

"What's wrong with everybody?" Stevie asked, looking from Rayanne to John.

"Stevie," John said getting out of the car and jerking the back door to the station wagon open, "if you don't get out of here, I'm going to break your damn neck. Do you understand that? Am I making myself clear? Now move," John ordered. Stevie dragged himself out of the car, and staggered towards the bus station. They drove off after he was inside and they went back to Aunt Bessie's. She was reading her bible when Rayanne entered. It took a little persuasion, but she was successful in talking Aunt Bessie into spending the remainder of the night with she and Swan.

Rayanne was pressing a dress that night for Swan for church when the phone rang. It might be Scott, Rayanne thought or she hoped. "Hello?"

"Miss Wilson? Miss Rayanne Wilson?" the voice asked. It wasn't Scott.

"This is she," Rayanne replied, trying to recognize the voice on the other end of the phone.

"Miss Wilson, this is Mr. Barkley down at the bus depot," he began, "I just wanted to let you know that the package is on its way."

"Thank you, Mr. Barkley. Thank you very much," Rayanne said. Aunt Bessie was sitting at the table having a cup of coffee and eyeing Rayanne nervously. "Stevie is on his way back where he came from," Rayanne said, "and I don't think you're going to be having any trouble out of him any time soon." Aunt Bessie didn't say anything at the time. She simply nodded her head back and forth and sighed and sometime later, she whispered a prayer.

CHAPTER 60

In Rayanne's memory, although less than one year had passed since she ended her relationship with Ralph, he seemed like such a long time ago, and she knew she owed the majority of this revelation to Scott. He'd been there for her all the time. She remembered the night she fell in love with Scott and all the wonderful times they spent together since that time. He'd shown nothing but love, compassion and understanding for her, until now, but why, Rayanne wondered. She thought, of all the men she'd become involved, she'd found that Scott was one of the few that she trusted completely. It'd been almost a week since she last spoke with him, their last conversation was fresh in her mind and after not hearing from him, her imagination had begun to run wild. Was Scott involved with someone else, had he re involved himself with Frannie, had his and Frannie's relationship never ended. After she'd seen Scott with Donnie and Frannie Rayanne had called him, not simply inquiring what that little episode was all about, but she'd been rude, her statements laced with accusations and demands, and she didn't give Scott an opportunity to explain. He'd been so put out by her tone and the fact that she didn't trust him, that he didn't bother to explain or offer an apology.

At 1:10 in the morning, the phone rang. "Hello?"

"Hey baby. How ya doing?" he said in a whisper as though he didn't want to disturb anyone.

"Just fine," Rayanne said stiffly, however, relief poured through her at the sound of his voice.

"Baby, I've missed you so much." There was a slight pause. "I know I broke a promise to you," Scott began. What is he talking about, she wondered, almost delirious, which at that time, she was unsure whether that state of mind was due to lack of sleep or sheer happiness at the sound of Scott's voice, more than likely, the latter.

"I told you sometime ago that I'd never hurt you or do anything to have to say I'm sorry. Well, I'm sorry. I know I didn't handle our conversation very well the last time we spoke, but you caught me at a bad time."

"I'll say," Rayanne said sarcastically.

"You got it all wrong," Scott said continuing to talk not much above a whisper.

"That's what they all say," she came back, than asked, "Where are you, Scott and why are you whispering?"

"I don't know why I'm whispering. All I know is that I miss you and I want to see you."

"Uh huh," Rayanne said, the sarcasm diminishing. "You never did say where you are."

"Baby, can I see you right now?"

"Now? Scott, it's late," Rayanne exclaimed, but she was happy at the prospect of seeing the man that she loved. She'd been waiting to see him and hear his voice for what seemed like such a long time.

"I know, but does that matter?"

"It's almost two in the morning and by the time you get here, it'll be 3 O'clock or later."

"Not true my beautiful lady."

"Where are you, Scott?"

"Look out your window." Rayanne had experienced a number of emotions since she last seen or spoken with Scott, but at that moment, all she felt was love and desperate longing, as she lifted a slat on the blind to look out. She felt her body shudder with anticipation, because sure enough, Scott was sitting in his Explorer parked in her driveway. Rayanne opened the side door and allowed him to enter. All the anger and disappointment and betrayal she was feeling had quickly disappeared, and were replaced by the happiness of seeing him. It'd been a long time since they'd seen each other, a whole week, and darn, she thought, he looked so good, a little tired, but good. Rayanne and Scott stood motionless, only inches apart, just looking at each other. Scott looked extremely exhausted, as though he were carrying the weight of the world around on his shoulders. Rayanne lifted her hand and pressed her palm against his cheek. Then, she moved closer to him and placed a kiss ever so gently on his lips. No explanation was necessary. There wasn't a need for words, the unspoken words they felt in their hearts were enough. Scott pulled Rayanne gently to him. She allowed her tongue to trace over his lips, then probed deeply into his mouth, searching out his own. The kiss lasted a long time and when it ended, they whispered how much they loved each other, missed each other, needed each other. Rayanne felt faint as her heart raced faster and faster, running out of control. "I love you, baby," Scott whispered and his voice was hoarse. She smiled up at him, dazed with the love that flowed through her. Scott withdrew and pulled her behind him, "Come," he said, "we need to talk."

"What do you want to talk about?" She followed him into the kitchen, where he pulled out a chair and sat.

"You and me, Frannie and Donnie," he answered. Rayanne made coffee. Scott explained that the day she saw Donnie and Frannie with him was the day they'd gotten the results of the test, disclosing that he wasn't Donnie's father, Donnie had overheard them arguing, and had tried to kill himself. He'd ingested some medication his mother had around the house, his condition was near fatal and he was transferred to a hospital in Georgia. It was touch and go for a while, Scott explained, but Donnie had pulled through, and Scott made him promise never to do anything like that again. He assured the boy of his love and that as far as he was concerned, he'd always be his father. After a few days, Donnie was released, but prior to that, Scott never left the boy's side.

"Scott, I'm so sorry," Rayanne began, "I should have known that something was wrong, and that I should have trusted you. Can you forgive me for acting so childishly."

"You had every reason to act the way you did. Who could blame you. I didn't talk to you, gave you no explanation, I just tripped," he said.

"I'm just glad that everything is all right now," Rayanne said. They were silent as they looked at each other from across the table. "You should get some rest, honey," Rayanne said and touched his hands.

"I'm good. I just needed to see you."

Rayanne allowed a deep sigh to escape before saying, "I'm glad you're here."

"That brings me to one of the main reasons why I came to-night," Scott said, but she didn't care what the reason was. She was just glad that he was there. "I love you, Rayanne, and I want us to get married." He waited, but when no response came, he looked deeply into her eyes. "Baby, will you? Will you marry me?" When she still didn't respond, he said, "Do you want me to get down on my knees." Of course she didn't want him to do that, she thought. She loved this man more than anything.

"Yes, Scott, yes, I will marry you," she said.

Scott got up from the table and walked around to where Rayanne was sitting. He reached for her hand, took it and pulled Rayanne to her feet. "You've made me a very happy man," he said and he kissed her, and Rayanne had such a feeling of belonging. Scott sat and pulled her into his lap and he ran his nose along the side of her face and neck. "I heard about your speech."

"You did?" she said, relaxing against his chest.

"Sure did. Some of the guys on the site have kids who go to that school and the way I heard it, my baby knocked the socks right off of their feet." Scott was beaming.

She hoped she was able to reach some of them. She informed Scott that since that time, she'd received invitations to speak at other schools, even on the elementary level, which she was most interested in because she felt that was where it would be more effective, "that is where the real education begins".

"You're taking the bull by its horns. One thing for sure, baby, you care, you are trying to make a difference, and I'm so proud of you. That was a mean challenge you laid on them. You're a gutsy lady."

"Honey, I was scared to death, walking into those auditoriums and looking at those faces. Gods knows I never know what to expect from them. I just feel I have to try. There's such a need in this country for us to save our children. They're our future. Without them, we have no future."

"You got a lotta guts." She snuggled up to him and thought of the yellow ribbons that she took with her when she made one of her speeches. As she left the building, she'd noticed some ribbons that'd been discarded to the floor in the auditorium, but it was nothing in comparison to the number of ribbons that the students wore proudly as they went on their daily activities. "I think it's great that there're people like you who're willing to dedicate the kind of time and as much of themselves, as you do to these kids. They don't know how lucky they are. When I was a kid and even a young adult, I did things that you wouldn't believe," Scott said reflecting. "If I did those things now, I'd be in jail or worse, dead." Rayanne was reminded that he certainly had turned his life around. He'd told her things about himself, good things and bad things, but she'd loved the man he'd become. Scott squeezed her hands. "You care and that's what we need more of." He was right, she thought, caring was what was needed, and in an abundance.

"Caring goes a long way. If the parents and the communities became involved in what is going on, if they took an active role, it would go a long way towards fixing this country and ultimately, healing it. If enough parents don't take part in their children's lives, the communities aren't going to either. Parents have to do their part and not depend so much on the teachers and the police. More often than not when the police become involved, it's almost too late. It's going to take a combined effort. We've all got to help if we want a world decent enough to bring up our children." She was silent for a moment. She looked at Scott's hands encircling her waist as she sat in his lap. "Mama and daddy raised us to believe that our world was all right, safe, and at that time, it was, but it's no longer that way," Rayanne said sadly.

"It can be again. It can be safe again, but it's like you said, people are gonna have to get involved."

"You'd think that the government would put its money to better use. They stick big bucks in the wrong places, like the prisons for instance. They are making the prisons larger and more livable, which only seemed to attract people and what sense does that make. If they used their heads, put the prisoners to work and took away some of their privileges, we could see a difference. Some of these criminals wouldn't be so eager to be criminals. Also, if they came up with programs for kids after school, something that would keep them off the streets, that would help. It would be a start. They should try some preventive measures for a change," she said. "If we can reach or prevent even rehabilitate as little as one at a time, that would go a long way."

"I hear ya," Scott said.

Rayanne stared off into space. "It's funny how things change. I suppose it has a lot to do with putting our priorities in order. I remember some time ago, someone asked me if I had two wishes, what would they be."

Scott looked at Rayanne, a little puzzled, "what did you say?"

"I said with good health and happiness of family and friends being first and foremost, that I wanted the love of my man and a hit play. Something like that. I got the hit play, a number of them, actually, but if I were asked that same question now, I would answer it differently."

"How would you answer?"

"Well," she said thoughtfully, "health and happiness are still at the top of my list, and," she hesitated, "a healing of the entire world. I just wish this could be a good place to live again."

"My baby, the world's advocate," Scott said affectionately, then they were quiet. He held her and rocked her back and forth. After some time, they heard a dog barking somewhere as a wake up call to a new day, he asked, "Are we going to make the announcement in church tomorrow?"

"Announcement," she asked, rubbing her nose against his check, dazed with excitement.

"How quickly they forget," he said, eyes closed as he buried his face in her neck.

"Are you talking about our engagement?"

"Yes, that little thing," Scott teased.

"That wonderful thing," Rayanne corrected.

"Are we going to make the announcement tomorrow?" he repeated. Later today, she thought, because it's already Sunday morning.

CHAPTER 61

After services, Maxine approached Rayanne and Scott, who were standing on the concrete steps of the church, greeting others and being congratulated on their engagement. "Congratulations you two," she said.

"Thanks, Sis," Rayanne said, and they embraced.

Maxine then hugged Scott. "You make my little sister happy, you hear."

"You can count on it," Scott said, releasing her, "I love Rayanne very much."

"I know you do, and I'm glad you guys found each other," Maxine said, "be happy you two." Then as an after thought, "Joe gave a good message again today. That hypocrite, but I've got something for him," Maxine gave one of those smiles that didn't come anywhere near her eyes before she walked away. She got into her car, where her family was awaiting her, she waved to Rayanne and Scott, and Marcus drove them away. Rayanne didn't know, at that time, just what that something was that Maxine mentioned she had for Joe, but she knew he'd get it and whenever he did, it wouldn't be good.

It didn't take long for her to find out what Maxine had for Joe, because the following day he was arrested for non support. The way Rayanne had heard it, Joe and Irene were putting their suit-cases into the car in preparation to return to Florida, when two police cars pulled up in front of his mother's house, they hand-cuffed Joe and took him away, leaving a bewildered and shocked Irene, staring at the car as it disappeared down the street. "Well Irene," Maxine said, after relaying the story to Rayanne, "welcome to the real world."

***

Maxine visited Joe at the jail. She approached the guard and told him she was there to see her husband, Joseph Duncan, and she was shown to the window partition where Joe was already in his seat, waiting. He looked up as Maxine approached him, his jaws dropped. She was the last person he expected to see, needed to see or wanted to see. Maxine sat in the chair across the partition from him and picked up the telephone and motioned for him to do likewise, since he appeared too stunned to do so on his own. It took him moments to collect his thoughts. He picked up the phone and placed it to his ear, but he didn't speak. Maxine said, "Hello, Joe," trying to sound casual.

"Maxine?" Joe's single word was a question.

"I suppose you were expecting Irene," Maxine said.

"She is my wife," he spat sarcastically.

"For now, she is."

"What is that suppose to mean?" he asked, scorn on his face.

"Just that I was your wife once also. Now, there is a new Mrs. Joseph Duncan. I wonder how long it will be before you get tired of her and run off like you did with me and your children."

Joe took a deep breath to calm himself, but it didn't help because as he spoke, his voice began to rise until it was like a gavel in a judge's chamber. He said, "do you have any idea what you've done? You've ruined me. Do you realize what the ramification of what you've done will have on my career, my marriage, my life?"

Maxine looked at Joe and she studied his face a moment, she weighed her words before she spoke. "What I've done," she hissed, "what I've done," her eyes squinted to just cracks in her face. "What about what you've done. Do you think I give a damn about you, your marriage or your career? No, hell no, that's no, damn it, no."

Joe interrupted, saying between clinched teeth, "I can't believe that you put the white man on me." Disbelief dripping in his voice. It was as though he thought no matter what he did, that Maxine or anyone else would have the audacity to take so drastic a step against him, was beyond him. "I can't believe you put the white man on

440

me," he repeated.

"Joe, putting the white man on you was the least of what I had planned for you. Bruce and Bobby are your children. You're their father. It was you and I who brought them into this world, and you and I are responsible for them. What if I walked away from them like you did? What then? You seem to think I was so wrong by putting the white man," she made a face, "on you. If I'm so wrong, then so be it, because I don't give a damn. I'd do it again. Yes, I put the man on your ass, and I'd do it again in a split second, just like that," Maxine said, snapping her fingers, "in one split second."

"Good-bye, Maxine," Joe said and was about to hang up the phone.

Maxine motioned for him to put the phone back to his ear. Joe looked at her and if looks could kill..., but he obeyed. "Don't you dare hang up on me. If you do, I will tear this freaking place apart. Let's see how the reporters will treat that bit of news," she said. He stared at her through the glass window and there was something about the cold stare in her eyes that made him put the phone back to his ear, and he listened. "It's a damn shame that I would have to go to anyone, let alone the white man, to get you to take care of your own black kids. Joe, I told you a long time ago that you can fuck me over all you want, but don't fuck with my children. I'd rather eat shit and die then see them hurt," Maxine paused and turned her eyes to the ceiling. "This wasn't necessary, Joe. I tried to arrange for you to see the children, just to let them spend a little time with you, make them happy. I didn't think that was asking too much but obviously you did. You didn't want anything to do with them. Your kids ask for you often, they love you for some reason, why, I don't know, but all the same, they do. You were so high and mighty and involved in your own life that you couldn't even give them the time of day. Well, you gave me no choice, now, you will give more than that to the state," Maxine smiled ruefully, and she looked away. When she looked at him again, she said quietly, "Joe, I'm married to a wonderful man and I can't tell you how happy he makes me, and I'm only saying that to say this is not a vendetta against you for what you did to me, because as it turned out, your leaving was the best thing you could've done for me. My husband does things for me that you just wouldn't begin to understand. I'm in love with him. What I'm trying to say is that I didn't want to hurt you. I wouldn't ever think of intruding in your life had it not been for the children, and

I think you know that, but I will not allow you to mistreat them. I will not," she said, looking him in the eyes and he knew her well enough to know that she meant what she said.

Then he spoke softly, "If it's a matter of money, Bruce is almost eighteen, and...," he began, but Maxine interrupted.

"I don't give a damn if he's one day away from his 18th birthday. I don't give a damn if he only collects from you for just one day, just as long as he does. You see, it's not so much the money here as it is the damn principle. You have to stop being so selfish, thinking only of yourself. There are others who are important too, you know." Maxine looked at Joe, but there was no further comment from him. "One other thing, Bruce will be going to Clemson when he graduates high school and that will be a four or five year period, so you might want to think about that. Now, you have a nice day, ya hear." Maxine hung up the phone, got up and walked away from him without as much as a backwards glance, while Joe was left rubbing his head and staring after her. Maxine exited the building and was walking down the sidewalk, feeling the warm sun on her face when she saw a familiar face approaching her.

"Good morning," Irene Duncan said to her.

"Morning, Mrs. Duncan," Maxine said, took the limped hand Irene extended, into both of her own. "I was just visiting the reverend. He's all yours, now." Maxine released Irene's hand and walked away with a look on her face that was something close to blissfulness. Her next stop would be at a record shop. She was going to pick up a CD for her sons by some new rap group called Wu Tang Clan, that the country was going crazy over. The song was entitled 'Protect Ya Neck,' which Bruce and Bobby were raving about. Too bad Joe didn't know how to protect his neck, Maxine thought as she got into her car and drove away.

CHAPTER 62

"Mama and I talked the night before she died," Josh began, and paused to look at Rayanne as she'd gotten up to refill his cup with steaming hot coffee. Josh had stopped by, although he'd said he was in the neighborhood and had just stopped by, Rayanne hoped it was more. She hoped he still cared about her that he'd missed her as much as she did him, and was ready to put the past behind them.

"What do you mean? You were in Florence when Mama died," Rayanne said, "so how was that possible? Unless you called her."

"I got out," Josh said in a hushed tone, looking down at his hands that toyed with the handle on his cup.

"You got out?" Rayanne asked, she was surprised and a little puzzled.

Josh explained he'd gotten to know one of the nurses at the Center pretty well, they'd talked a lot about his mother, he explained that his mother was ill and that he had a bad feeling about her all day. He needed to see her. He promised he wouldn't drink, the nurse believed him and helped him get out. He hitched a ride home. Josh looked up at Rayanne. When she didn't respond, he said, "I came here, and Mama and I had a long talk."

Rayanne whispered, "Mama never said a word."

"I know, and I wanted to make sure that you didn't know. It would've just given you something else to worry about," Josh said and sighed.

"So what did the two of you talk about?" Rayanne asked.

"We just talked. Like I said, Rayanne, I'd been having some

443

really strange vibes about Mama, and I just had to see her." He sipped from his cup. "You know, when John came to the center and told me Mama had died, I was hurt, I was miserable but I wasn't surprise because I felt something was going to happen."

"Lord Josh," Rayanne said as she sat back in her chair and it was her time to sigh, "when will the pain stop. When will the pain just go away?" For a while, they sat in complete silence. Then Rayanne looked at Josh, she studied his face. He looked better than when she'd last seen him. The tired lines were gone and so were the bloodshot eyes that had been so much a part of his life the last few years. Josh had turned into a submissive individual since he started drinking, and submissiveness had become a way of life for him, but there was something different now. The question was what was he doing with his life. The thought wasn't to be nosy or to pry, it was out of genuine concern.

"What am I doing with my life?" Josh said, reading her mind again. "That is what you were thinking, right?" That was exactly what she was thinking and it was a fair question given his past, but she wouldn't actually ask. Josh looked at his sister and smiled. "Rayanne, I know I've made a mess of my life, and I made mama and your life miserable, as well. I lied, broke promises, used Mama to be able to do the things I wanted, and I knew some of them weren't good, but I did them anyway. I've been whining, and pissing and moaning most of my adult life, and I had to put an end to that. I had to put all that silly ass shit behind me, so now I'm getting on with my life." Rayanne didn't say anything. She just listened. "I've gotten the treatment I needed, I go to my AA meetings, and I haven't touch a drink since I left the center," Josh said and stopped suddenly. "Rayanne, I'm gonna make it this time." Rayanne and Josh had always been close, so much so that each knew what the other was thinking without a word being spoken between them. They'd been more than siblings, they were friends, but along the way, their friendship had gone sour. As she looked at her brother now, it was with a new found respect. Respect for the man her brother once was and had become again. "I want to try my hand at something close to my heart," Josh was saying, "I want to build furniture. I've always wanted to do that, and who knows, if I work hard at it, I may even be able to sell a few pieces."

"I'm sure you're gonna do very well," Rayanne said, remembering the table and chairs he made for her dolls when they were kids and when Rayanne and Josh laughed, each knew that they were having the same thought.

"The furniture wasn't too bad either, was it?" Josh asked.

"No, not bad at all, but daddy had a time keeping his good lumber out of your way," Rayanne said, they laugh some more and it felt good. It was good.

"I talked with Mr. Dixon last week, and he and I are gonna put some pieces together and see what we can do with them. I'm not gonna push, I'm gonna take my time and I'm not gonna get discouraged if something doesn't work out. I don't expect miracles over night. This is gonna be a gradual process, but I know it's gonna work this time. I'm gonna give it my best shot."

"That's all you've got to do, Josh, and I'm sure, it'll work out," Rayanne said, beaming, as she looked down at her hands. She was so glad to have her brother back. "Josh, I'm so proud of you. I just wish Mama could be here to see you this way. She'd be so happy."

"Mama knew," Josh said after a moment. Rayanne's head snapped up. When Josh came home to visit their mother, they talked like they hadn't done in years, he had said, it was great. "Mothers are something else, you know. They know us better than we know ourselves, I think. She and I talked about my problem, and she told me she knew I was gonna kick this habit. She had so much faith in me, the power of faith is something else. Rayanne, Mama was no good after daddy died. She loved us, but after daddy, she was just wasting away. I honestly believe that Mama lived until she knew things were gonna be all right with her children, me in particular," he said, smiling weakly.

"You're probably right, Josh," Rayanne said, wistfully. She got up from the table, sat her coffee cup in the sink and looked out of the window. "There are so many things I wish I could change."

"Like what?"

"You know, the unpleasant things that happened between you and me. You're my brother, Josh, and I love you. I never wanted any hard feelings between us. Look at all that's happened. You and I were so close, but we got to the point where we barely spoke to each other. That's not right. We're family," she said and turned to face Josh. "You know what I wish more than anything?"

"What?"

"I wish Mama could've seen us together like this and that I'd been able to make things right between her and me. She was so angry at me when I took you to Florence, she hated it, and she never forgave me. I've regretted that more than I can say. I wish she could've understood my reasons."

445

Josh was quiet. Then breaking his silence, he said, "She did." Rayanne waved a hand at him letting him know he didn't need to say that for her benefit. She knew and would have to live with the fact that one of the people she loved most had gone to her grave, hating her. "Mama forgave you."

"I wish. You don't know how things were between us before she died. I'll never forget it as long as I live." She paused, "I just wish she could've understood but, then, what mother can forgive when someone she loves is taken away."

"Mama did understand," Josh said, and Rayanne felt good just knowing that he cared enough to try to make her feel better, and she appreciated it, a lot. "It's the truth," he said. "She told me."

"What are you talking about?" she asked, walking over to the table where Josh was sitting. "What did Mama tell you? Did she tell you she understood?" Rayanne asked incredulously. "What did Mama say?" The questions rushed out of her mouth.

"Mama became realistic there at the end. She told me she knew you had to do what you did, that you didn't have a choice. She said you did it out of love for me, that I would've died otherwise." Rayanne sat across the table from Josh and listened. "Mama understood, and she made me promise to forgive you, although I'm sure I would have anyway," he gave a little laugh, "after I blew off some steam." Josh told Rayanne it was the liquor that had him so out of control, that prevented him from understanding that everything that was happening to him was being caused by him. He couldn't understand that it was he who had to accept responsibility for his own action. Ruth had told Josh that she wanted to say to Rayanne so many times how sorry she was because of how she'd treated her, that she was too ashamed, but she had made up in her mind that she was going to ask Rayanne to forgive her. When Josh finished, he looked up, and Rayanne thought he was going to cry.

"Oh Josh," she said, reaching out and taking his hands into her own and when she blinked, tears ran down her face.

"Will you please forgive me, Sis? I'm so sorry about everything. It took losing both of our parents and a stay in a detox ward to make me see the light."

"It's gonna be all right. We're family, and we love each other, and I know it's gonna be all right."

When Maxine called that night, and Rayanne shared her revelations, Maxine was glad that maybe now, her sister could get on with her life. Maxine, also, had some news of her own to share. It seemed Irene learned the truth about Joe, but because she loved him and believed in his love for her, she'd stayed with him. She felt that with the kind of love the two of them shared, nothing could get in the way of their happiness. Irene believed she could help Joe become a better person, and who knows, Rayanne thought, perhaps she could. Rayanne had never put much stock in the old adage, a leopard never changes his spots. But the important thing was that Irene knew the truth about her husband, she loved him and wanted to save their marriage. She was equipped with the knowledge that Joe was no Saint, and if she could live with that knowledge, then she could deal with the situation as she saw fit.

***

Rayanne had just turned off the TV set. The UNCF Telethon had just ended, South Carolina had raised over $10,000, and the overall total for the United States was over $11 million. It was wonderful seeing people come together for such a worthy cause, in the name of love and commitment in insuring an education for our children. The performances were great, especially Patti and Gladys. Those women gave such outstanding performances that Rayanne almost gave each of them a standing ovation from where she sat in her den.

The hour was late, the house was quiet as a tomb, and Rayanne was experiencing some difficulty in concentrating on the exam papers that required grading for the following day. She picked up a copy of Essence Magazine, leafed through the book and read the article by Susan Taylor. The message Susan brought to her readers every month was invaluable. She always restored hope and peace and love to one's soul. Rayanne found enormous satisfaction from the articles in the entire book, but when the magazine arrived each month, 'In The Spirit,' was the first section she read and reread throughout the month. Susan Taylor was one of the people who inspired her most, along with Maya Angelou, Bev Smith, Maxine Waters and Oprah Winfrey.

Josh had left long ago, and of course, Rayanne would've forgiven him if there was something to forgive him for. There wasn't, but she did thank him over and over for what he'd given to her. It was like having freedom put back into her life. He'd given her peace of mind, and with that, she knew there wouldn't be a need to continue to see her therapist.

She looked at the letters she'd just finished reading. How many of them were there, twenty-five or thirty? They were the letters Dorian had written to her during the years, none of which she had

447

read previously. She picked up the test papers again, looked at them, then she laid them back on the couch and put her hands up to her face. "Mama forgave me?" she whispered, incredulously. "Mama forgave me," she said the words out loud this time. She wanted to hear the words, needed to hear the words. She'd felt guilty for so long because of not being able to reconcile her differences with her mother before she'd died. She'd felt guilty about having had Josh committed to the Rehab Center, guilty because of the way her father had died and that guilt had weighed heavily on her. She'd never be able to fill the void left in her by the loss of her parents. That kind of loss, one almost never completely recover. She'd suffered enormously, and she knew she'd never feel completely whole again, but at least now, she'd be able to put the guilt to rest, and, knowing her mother forgave her, made it a little easier, and she thanked God.

Rayanne walked over to the telephone, lifted it up and a smile touched the corners of her lips. She dialed 0 and when the operator answered, Rayanne said, "I'd like to place an overseas call to France."

CHAPTER 63

Harry's telephone call was both a surprise and welcomed. Rayanne had contacted everyone about her engagement to Scott. She hadn't talked with Harry, but she'd sent him a note and had followed it up with a message for him to call, and he did.

"How are you, Harry?" Rayanne said.

"Can't say I'm as good as you, my dear. So you're going to tie the knot, are you?" Harry said.

"Yeah Harry, I think I'm gonna do it this time. It feels right," Rayanne said, "it really feel right. I love Scott very much. He and I are looking at rings this week."

"I'm happy for you, doll," he took a deep breath and added, "I never thought he was good enough for you anyway."

"Really," Rayanne responded and laughed without humor, "is that true?" She knew Harry was referring to her relationship with Ralph.

"Yes it's true. There was just something about Ralph that didn't sit well with me. I couldn't put my finger on it, but I for one am glad that it's over between the two of you."

"You never said a word."

"I didn't have to. You're a smart girl, and I knew sooner or later you'd figure it out for yourself. Your mother, the sweet lady that she was, didn't raise no fools."

Yes, Mama was sweet, Rayanne thought, but she was more

449

than that. Much more. She was everything that was good, everything that a mother could be, and no one could ever replace her, but Rayanne said, "You're giving me too much credit, Harry, because I almost didn't."

"The important thing is that you did," he replied.

"Have I ever told you how important you are to me?" Rayanne asked.

"Only about a dozen times or so," Harry said and chuckled.

"Well, I'm telling you again. You're the absolute best." After a slight lull in their conversation, she changed the subject, "And, how is Cinnamon?"

"She's fine, sends her regards."

"You two are coming to my wedding," Rayanne said and it was more a statement than a question.

"Of course. My wife loves weddings. Weddings make her happy, and I love keeping her happy."

"Cinnamon is always happy and why wouldn't she be. She's got a man who simply adores her, worships the ground she walks on and has given her two wonderful kids."

"It's more than that," he teased, "Cinnamon is still spending my money by the truck loads and that is uppermost on the list of things that make her happy, but you know money in general makes you women happy."

"Among other things," Rayanne came back and laughed.

"When are the girls coming in?"

"Ivory is flying in next week, and she and Dorian will come again the second week in next month. We'll do the fittings for the gowns, take care of some other stuff, and we'll have a good visit. It'll be fun, like old times," Rayanne explained, then added, "I just hope Ivory fits into her dress. She's pregnant again, you know?"

"Get outta here," Harry said.

"Yeah. She's had the Ultra Sound and it's a boy. She and Desmond are really looking forward to the new addition."

"I bet so. That's great. You're happy, too, aren't you?" Harry said. "You sound wonderful."

"I'm feeling so much better these days, Harry" she replied.

"Let me know what I can do. Anything at all," Harry said and Rayanne knew he meant it and she thanked him. "This is some shindig you're having."

"It's only money," Rayanne said with a smile.

"Women," Harry said, "but speaking of money," he chuckled softly. "I tried to reach you yesterday. I was anxious to tell you that the fish are biting about your new book."

"You're lying," she said, she was surprised and elated at the same time.

"Serious business. 'My Little Girl' has got them jumping," Harry said. "My phone's ringing off the hook."

"Gosh, I can't believe it. That's great".

"Is that all you've got to say? I remember some years back when this was the kind of news you wanted to hear more than anything."

"I still do, and I hope I don't sound ungrateful, Harry, because I'm extremely happy, just surprise".

"I don't know why. You're a great writer."

"I just hadn't been able to put anything decent together in a long time. This seems so unreal."

"You've had a lot going on in your life. It's understandable that you've had a slow period, but it looks as though things are back on track and we're in business again."

"I love you, Harry," Rayanne said, affectionately.

"I know you do," he replied, "we'll be talking soon. See you at your wedding."

When Rayanne hung up the phone, she jumped up and squealed with delight, clasping her hands together. She turned to leave the kitchen, when she saw Swan standing in the doorway with a coloring book and crayon in her hands.

"Are you all right, Aunt Rayanne?" Swan asked.

Rayanne walked over and kneeled before her. "Yes darling, I'm fine. Finally, my little girl, everything is fine."

Swan wrapped her arms around Rayanne's neck and squeezed. "I love you, Aunt Rayanne," she said.

"And, I love you, Swan," Rayanne said, "I love you very much."

CHAPTER 64

That night, in Scott's bed, Rayanne snuggled up closely to him and she thought of the call she'd received from Harry several days ago. Scott had been working on a job out of town and she had been so involved with the Center that she hadn't had an opportunity to share the news about the book with him yet. They'd just watched Mariah Carey's video, and when she sung 'Hero,' Rayanne though of Josh and a smile lit up her face. He'd gotten his life back and was doing the things he'd wanted to do. Ruby had taken up with another man and although Josh didn't like it, he'd accepted it and was moving forward. He'd done well, so far, and to Rayanne, Josh was a hero, even if he was a hero only to her.

"Who are all those guys?" Scott asked, interrupting Rayanne's thoughts, pulling her out of her reverie. He folded his pillow so that it was doubled under his head and lay back down. "I've never seen that many rappers on stage at one time before."

Rayanne turned her attention to the TV set. "That's Wu Tang Clan," she said.

"Who, who Clan?" Scott asked, looking briefly at Rayanne, then back at the set.

"Wu Tang Clan," she repeated.

Scott said, "Oh, that's Wu Tang Clan. I hear they're blowing up all over the place. I've heard some of their stuff, but I ain't never seen 'em."

"Bobby and Bruce are always talking about them and Brenda tells me that her sons, Chris and Devin are in to them also. She says these kids are buying everything that has Wu Tang's name on it," Rayanne said.

When the video was over, Scott said, "Well all right. They seem to be pretty talented." He turned the TV off after that video, then he was thoughtful again. "It took Swan a while to get to sleep tonight. Is she all right?"

"Yes, she's fine, just excited about us getting married. Mrs. Marshall said she had a long nap this afternoon, so it took a little while for her to drift off tonight, but she's fine," Rayanne answered. "She asked me to say goodnight to you."

"How did she know you were coming to see me, tonight?"

"Because she's a smart little girl."

"She's a terrific kid. It's gonna be so nice when we can be together, without either of us having to get up and go home," Scott said.

"I know," Rayanne said, looking up at Scott. Then she turned over onto her back, lifted her left hand and smiled admiringly at the ring on her finger. Scott took Rayanne's hand, and he looked at the ring also.

"You like it?"

"I love it," Rayanne answered as her heart sung songs of happiness.

"So, how was your day," he asked after a moment, brushing her hair away from her face.

"I had a great day, a wonderful day. It could not have been better. Christen called earlier, she thinks she's pregnant. I hope she is. She and John have been trying so long."

"Ooooh, I see. That's why John has been walking around here with his chest sticking out," Scott chuckled softly.

"She's got an appointment next week and we'll know then."

"Children certainly do complete a family," Scott said and he turned Rayanne so that they faced each other. "How do you feel about children?"

"I love children ".

"I'd like us to have another little girl just like Swan and maybe a boy or two."

"Another little girl and a boy or two. My goodness. You must think you've got a young woman here beside you," Rayanne teased.

"Baby, you're as young as you feel, so tell me, how young do

453

you feel," Scott teased back.

"Oh, about sixteen."

Scott sighed, looking down at Rayanne's pretty, shiny face. "We're gonna be together for a very long time. Can you think on those terms?"

"I can think as far as," she paused and looked adoringly at him, "forever. Is that long enough?"

"Sounds perfect to me." He held her closely a moment before releasing her to say, "Honey, I know planning a wedding is women's doing, but I'd like to make one suggestion."

"Sure," Rayanne said softly, "what is it?"

"I'd like Swan to be a part of our wedding. I don't care which part she plays, well except the bride, 'cause I already got the perfect person for that part, but I'd like her to be in our wedding and be a part of our lives in every way," he said. Rayanne blinked and felt so much happiness at that moment that she could hardly stand it. "Well, what do you think?"

"Sweetheart, that's wonderful. You're wonderful," she said and when they kissed, she wanted to swallow his lips.

"Happy?" he asked when the kiss ended.

"What do you think?" she replied and after a moment, she told him they had a lot to talk about, that there was so much that she hadn't shared with him.

He'd simply said, "we've got all the time in the world, so whenever you want to talk, I'll be here."

CHAPTER 65

That summer proved to be one of the happiest in Rayanne's life. She and Scott had been married nearly two months, and she was still sending out thank you cards for the wedding gifts that they received. Ivory and Dorian had met Hilary and Brenda when they came for the wedding, they all had some of the same interests, and they agreed to keep in touch. It wouldn't be surprising if they got together again either in South Carolina, New York or perhaps in France where Dorian and her husband lived. These were friendships that they wanted to keep alive.

That Saturday morning, Scott had gone out with his softball team, Rayanne was sitting on the front porch and had just licked the last envelope to seal it when Swan stuck her head out of the door. "Aunt Rayanne, are you busy?" she asked, squinting up her face against the brightness of the sun as she walked out onto the porch to join Rayanne.

"Not any more," Rayanne said stacking up the envelopes, "What's up?"

"I just want to talk to you," Swan said.

"Come over here and sit beside me," Rayanne said and waited until Swan walked over to her, climbed up into her lap and sat. "I said sit beside me, not in my lap," Rayanne teased. Swan crinkled her nose and laughed. "So, tell me, what's going on in that pretty little head of yours?" Rayanne asked. Swan poked a finger into her mouth.

"What did we say about putting dirty fingers into our mouths?" Swan didn't answer, but she immediately removed her finger from her mouth and clasped her hands together in her lap. "We'll get germs, right?" Rayanne said.

"Right," Swan replied and Rayanne questioned what Swan wanted to talk about. "A couple of things, actually."

"Actually, huh? oh, I see, and, they are?"

"When Auntie Christen has her baby, she's going to be my cousin?"

"Yes."

"Do you think she'll like me?"

"Of course the baby will like you," Rayanne answered, "but what makes you think the baby will be a girl? The baby could just as well be a little boy, you know."

"I suppose that's true," Swan said, a thoughtful expression on her little face, "but I hope the baby is a girl."

"Why? Wouldn't you like a little boy cousin just as much?" Rayanne asked. Swan smiled and clasped her tiny hands together, "Well, wouldn't you?"

Swan hesitated a moment before saying, "Yes."

"You don't sound like you do," Rayanne said, holding Swan closely, "tell Auntie Rayanne, what's going on with you. What's on your mind?"

"I've decided on a name for the cat that you and Uncle Scott bought me," Swan told her. Scott and Rayanne had bought Swan a cat for her 5th birthday, the child loved animals of all kinds and she treated that cat like a baby. The day the cat was delivered, Swan took over caring for it and she did everything for it except the litter pan. That, she wouldn't touch.

"You have? That's great. What is it?"

"Actually, I liked the name you mentioned more than any of the ones that Becky or I though of," Swan said.

"Really? Well, don't keep me in suspense." Rayanne gently tapped Swan on her nose with the tip of her finger. "What is it? What have you decided to call her."

"Sapphire," Swan revealed, "I've decided to call her Sapphire. I think it's cool." Rayanne looked out across the front yard. It was a beautiful day, a perfect day from were she sat on her front porch, and she thanked God for his many blessings. She thought of John and Christen and how happy they were about having an addition to their family. They'd wanted a baby for so long and just when it seemed they'd given up or at least had stopped talking about it, Christen became pregnant and the thought of it made a little smile touched the corners of Rayanne's lips. She almost laughed out loud, thinking of the morning sickness that plagued John daily. Maxine and Marcus were as happy as they could be, Bruce was doing well at Clemson, Bobby at USC and Marcia Raylyn had graduated high school that Spring.

Rayanne remembered the phone call she got from Mamie that morning. She'd gotten the job that she wanted and had talked so much about, in that advertising agency. She was their new Vice President and she was thrilled. It took different things to make people happy, and Rayanne was happy for her and only hoped that Mamie would always be as happy as she was then. She still hadn't found the man of her dream, but she was happy, and when you think about it, that was the important thing. Ivory and Desmond had toyed with the idea of moving South, nothing definite, but they were thinking about it. Dorian and her family were doing well. She was operating a model agency in France. Rayanne often saw her name in the fashion magazines, and they wrote to each other or spoke by telephone at least once a month now.

Rayanne thought of her conversation with Scott that morning before he left for softball practice. Some of the proceeds from her book would go towards funding a center for disadvantaged people. She had a meeting scheduled with a group of people from the City and County Council offices and others who were concerned about what was going on in their town as well as across the country and they wanted to make a difference. The Service Center would assist teenagers in earning money to further their education, kids who didn't have any other legitimate resources to do so. They would perform community services, assist in day care centers, and do other odd jobs as a way of helping themselves to better themselves.

Rayanne also thought of how much safer her own neighborhood had become. After they formed that neighborhood watch, things were better, they had gotten rid of the drug dealer who had moved into Abigail's house. Amazingly enough, it was a group of women who'd gotten rid of him. They'd gotten together, and caught the drug dealer going into his house one night. They tied his hands together, ripped his pants from his body and it was Aunt Bessie who pointed the barrel of a shotgun into the crack of his behind and told him if he wasn't out of that house and the neighborhood within twenty-four hours, that the next time they caught him, she'd pull the trigger. Needless to say, the house was vacated immediately and a new For Sale sign was posted in the yard the following month. A number of women participated, and as the saying goes, there is power in numbers, especially if it's a number of fed up women. Those women had taken back their neighborhood and they intended to keep it and keep it safe for their children and themselves. Scott had laughed at Aunt Bessie's feistiness when Rayanne revealed to him that Aunt Bessie was a regular Calamity Jane, with that shotgun in her hands.

Rayanne and Scott's conversation that night was the one that prompted her to stop taking her birth control pills. It seems everyone was having a baby. Who knows, perhaps they'd be announcing an addition to their own little family soon. Scott had said to Rayanne that he knew that when she became pregnant, that her parents, especially her mother, would be smiling down from heaven at her.

Rayanne looked at Swan sitting in her lap, so peaceful, so happy, and she smiled and breathed in the sweet fresh air. She gave off a little sigh, a happy sigh, as slight breezes drifted across the porch, hinting the air of jasmine and magnolias. She hugged Swan close to her, and thought how fortunate she was to be surrounded by such wonderful people. Family and friends were important to Rayanne, they always were, and they always would be. She felt like a whole person again. All of the guilt and uncertainty had faded away from her life, leaving her happy and free. She'd suffered enough, and it was God's will that her suffering stop. She turned her eyes to the sky and silently thanked God for everything He'd put into her life, her past, her present and her future. Rayanne thought how frantic Ivory had been at the thought of becoming involved with a younger man. She, too, had that same concern, but things were working out very well and she knew that was only because in each situation, there was a lot of love and respect, and as Scott had always said, "age ain't nothing but a number," and Rayanne still believed it.

She and Swan walked across the yard and Rayanne stood barefoot in the flower bed. She felt the soil between her toes as they walked through Swan's little garden. "What do you think, Aunt Rayanne?" Swan asked, looking up into Rayanne face and interrupting her thoughts. "What do you think of calling our kitty Sapphire?"

Rayanne looked down into Swan's face and said, "I think it's cool, too, Swan. I think Sapphire is a real cool name."

458